# Carol Kirkwood

# Secrets
## *of the*
# Villa Amore

HarperCollins *Publishers*

HarperCollins*Publishers* Ltd
1 London Bridge Street,
London SE1 9GF

www.harpercollins.co.uk

HarperCollins*Publishers*
Macken House, 39/40 Mayor Street Upper
Dublin 1, D01 C9W8

First published by HarperCollins*Publishers* 2023
This edition published 2024
1

A catalogue record for this book is available from the British Library

ISBN: 978-0-00-855096-7 (PB)

This novel is entirely a work of fiction.
The names, characters and incidents portrayed in it are
the work of the author's imagination. Any resemblance to
actual persons, living or dead, events or localities is
entirely coincidental.

Typeset in Meridien by Palimpsest Book Production Limited,
Falkirk, Stirlingshire

Printed and bound in the UK using
100% Renewable Electricity at CPI Group (UK) Ltd

MIX
Paper | Supporting
responsible forestry
FSC™ C007454

This book is produced from independently certified FSC paper
to ensure responsible forest management.

For more information visit: www.harpercollins.co.uk/green

I would like to dedicate this book to everyone
that has read my first two books *Under a Greek Moon*
and *The Hotel on the Riviera* – and come back for
more! And if this is your first foray into my books
then a big fat HELLO to you, welcome! I hope you
all enjoy *Secrets of the Villa Amore* and thank you for
your unending support xxx

# Prologue

## Salerno, October 1943

'To Italy!'

'To freedom.'

'And to victory!'

The two young soldiers joined in heartily with each toast, raising their glasses high in the air before crashing them together with cries of '*Salute!*' They shouted and cheered with the rest of the patrons, hammering noisily on the wooden tabletop. It was the safest thing to do right now; impossible to know from appearances who was friend and who was foe.

The evening was growing late, the atmosphere increasingly raucous in the backstreet bar. Its windows were blacked out, its interior lit by a dozen strategically placed candles. The men looked at one another nervously.

'Shall we leave?' the older of the two suggested quietly.

The younger nodded and they drained their *amaro*, a locally produced, bitter-tasting herbal liqueur. They swayed unsteadily as they stood up from their wooden stools – this was far from their first drink of the evening – pushing their way through the throng of uniformed men, all yelling and singing and carousing.

They emerged onto the deserted street. The breeze was warm but carried the acrid smell of smoke and the stench of diesel from the ships in the harbour. There was a palpable sense of tension in the air. They'd already lived through three years of war, and it seemed it was far from over yet.

The soldiers – both dark-haired and handsome, with the muscular build of labourers turned military men – made their way up the hill towards their quarters. All lights were extinguished for the night-time black out, the vista an oppressing blanket of darkness. When the sun rose, it would reveal cerulean skies and a shimmering sea, soaring mountains and the traditional picture-post-card buildings spilling down to the wide bay, but these days no one was interested in the view.

Salerno had been heavily bombed in recent weeks, the scene of fierce fighting. Italy had withdrawn its support for Germany, and the Allies had landed in Sicily before making their way to the mainland. Now the country had been split in two, with Mussolini's supporters in the north and those loyal to King Victor Emmanuel in the south, effectively a state of civil war.

The younger man jumped as a bicycle appeared out of the blackness, the rider almost crashing into them before swerving at the last moment. The man was already skittish and on edge; the mood in the city was one of constant threat, and soldiers had been advised to always travel in pairs.

Moments later, a group of men emerged through the gloom, wearing the field-grey uniforms of the Italian army. There were five of them, all drunk and full of aggression, blocking the way in the narrow street. One carried an open bottle of what smelled like home-brewed alcohol.

'We're going north, to fight with Mussolini,' he declared belligerently. 'Come with us, if you love your country.'

The younger man's eyes widened in alarm, anxiety coiling in his stomach. He tried to get past, but they jostled him and jeered. 'What? Are you cowards? You want your women stolen by the British and the Americans?'

The younger man had no one special waiting for him back home, but he knew his friend had a sweetheart he planned to marry, *she has fire in her eyes and her lips are a gift from Cupid* . . . he was terrified that she'd been caught up in the recent fighting.

'We fight for our king,' he shot back, a spike of adrenaline making him brave. *'You're* the traitor.'

There was a tussle in the darkness and blows were exchanged, fists flying as pent-up fear and anger found a release. The mood changed rapidly when one of the soldiers drew his weapon.

'Traitors should be shot,' he spat, his eyes glittering dangerously in the moonlight. He raised the gun and took aim.

There was a yell, a scuffle, and then a shot rang out across the silent city. A man slumped to the ground, clutching his heart, life seeping from him. Nothing could be done to save him; he was dead within seconds, the soldiers scattering, all suddenly sober as the blood seeped into the cobbles and trickled towards the gutter.

The two soldiers had fled along with the others, peeling off down an alleyway, their hearts heaving in their chests as they concealed themselves in a doorway, the whistles of the carabinieri could be heard close by.

They stared at each other in horror and disbelief at what had just happened. One of them had killed a man, a fellow soldier and compatriot. This crazy war had turned everything on its head, and now they were fugitives.

The younger man grabbed his friend's arm, shaking him out of his stupor.

'Run,' he hissed. 'We must run!'

His friend looked at him, terror in his eyes, but resolution too. 'Yes. We must run. But not together . . . alone.'

With that he darted out into the alleyway. Turning only once, he said, 'Remember, my girl, the promise?'

*Wait!* the young man wanted to shout, but knowing it was futile the word died on his lips. He nodded as their eyes met for a split second.

Then he ran too, and kept on running, and didn't stop until he was far away from that dreadful moment.

He couldn't know then that he would still be running fifty years later.

# Part One

# Chapter 1

**Campania, August 2005**

'Do you have to go?' Carina murmured, wrapping her arms around her fiancé as she gazed up at his handsome face.

'Yes,' Giorgio said firmly, disentangling himself.

'But it's less than two weeks until the wedding.'

'I have important business in the US, Carina. It can't wait.'

'You promise you'll be back in time? We have guests arriving the week before, and my parents have planned a family dinner, a party, a boat trip . . .'

'I'll be back,' Giorgio assured her, though Carina sensed his irritation at her questions.

She leaned in to kiss him goodbye, pressing her body enticingly against his as their embrace grew more passionate, her hands roaming over his chest and rumpling his freshly ironed shirt.

'I have to go,' he said, stepping backwards and smoothing down his suit.

'Giorgio, we're almost married. Surely it doesn't matter if we . . .' She let the question hang, an unspoken invitation.

'What difference does two more weeks make? We've waited all this time, we can wait a little longer,' he insisted. 'I'll see you in a few days.'

'I love you,' Carina called after him, as he walked towards the door.

'I love you too,' Giorgio replied, not stopping to turn around.

Then he was gone, and Carina was left fighting a whirl of emotions: frustration, confusion, disappointment.

The balcony doors were open and she moved across her bedroom to step outside, the welcome breeze lifting tendrils of her thick, honey-blonde hair, which had escaped the long plait in which they were tethered. The trace of a frown crossed her youthful face, the exchange with Giorgio having left spots of colour high on her cheeks. Her skin was lightly tanned, her almond eyes a rare shade of violet.

Carina exhaled as she gazed at the view, feeling any tension melt away. The land as far as she could see belonged to her father, Salvatore Russo; the undulating hills in shades of sage and sun-scorched ochre stretching away to the distant horizon. Beyond the manicured gardens that bordered the magnificent house, lush with greenery and leading to a secluded Romanesque swimming pool, lay row after row of sprawling vines, the dark grapes hanging like priceless jewels in the vineyard that had made the Russos' fortune.

Their land bordered that of her fiancé's family, the Bianchis, and the two estates were separated by a wide, shallow stream that began in the Avella mountains. It was this natural spring, with its mineral-rich water, that gave the grapes such a unique flavour, and made the Casa di Russo wine so special.

Carina had lived here all her life – except for her university days studying business in London – and her existence had been a charmed one. She and Giorgio had grown up together and it seemed natural that their friendship would blossom into something more as they matured into adolescence, with the accompanying rush of hormones. It was a union strongly encouraged by their parents, and Carina felt the weight of expectation – that it was their destiny to unite the two wine dynasties. They would marry at her family's palatial hillside property in Amalfi: the Villa Amore.

'Carina! Carina?' came a shout from her mother.

'*Sì, Mamma*?' Carina strolled back into her bedroom as Philippa Russo walked in, talking on her mobile phone.

'It's Bianca,' she explained, naming Carina's wedding planner. 'You need to decide about the stemware for the champagne reception. Flutes or coupes?'

It was all Carina could do not to roll her eyes. 'Whatever you think is best, Mamma. Your taste is always impeccable.'

'But it's *your* wedding.'

Carina thought for a moment. 'Flutes,' she said decisively. 'More practical.'

Philippa smiled as she replied to Bianca and ended the call. 'Of course, every girl dreams of practicality on her wedding day,' she teased, as Carina laughed.

Carina's mother, Philippa, was Scottish. At first glance, people often thought Carina was too, with her light skin and fair colouring, but those close to her knew that she was Italian through and through – fiercely loyal, quietly determined, with a stubborn streak that meant she wasn't afraid to fight her corner and stand her ground.

Philippa was the epitome of British elegance combined with Italian style. She was in her early fifties, her long blonde bob expertly cut and styled, the perfectly blended highlights given that little something extra from exposure to the Italian sun. She wore a shift dress in cream linen with a tan belt that emphasized her hourglass figure – less slender than it had been in her youth, but still adored by her husband. A simple gold wedding band encircled her ring finger, with classic pearls at her ears and throat.

'There's still so much to do,' Philippa continued. 'We have the family dinner tomorrow, with the Bianchis.'

'Yes,' Carina winced. 'Giorgio won't be able to make it, unfortunately.'

Philippa's brow furrowed, a flash of steel in her eyes. 'What do you mean, darling?'

'He's had to fly to the US on business.'

'But you're getting married in two weeks.'

Carina stiffened, knowing her mother would react like this. 'Yes, and I've just had the same conversation with him, but there's nothing he can do.'

'Carina, are you sure—'

Carina was saved from her mother's questions as she heard footsteps outside in the tiled hallway. Her father, Salvatore, knocked once then walked in without waiting for an answer. He strode over to Philippa and kissed her distractedly before turning to Carina, taking hold of her hands.

'*Cara mia*, you grow more beautiful every day.'

'I think you are biased, Papà,' she laughed.

'No, it's true – your mother will agree with me,' Salvatore said, grinning broadly. Carina thought that he was in his prime, undoubtedly still a handsome man. His thick black hair was flecked with grey, giving him a distinguished air, and his rich brown eyes sparkled with life. He was even more physically active now than he had been as a young man – playing tennis, or heading out on the boat they kept in Amalfi, when his hectic work schedule allowed – and his solid, muscular body was testament to that.

'I came to tell you both the news,' Salvatore announced. 'I've signed a deal with Heritage Estates. They've agreed to be the exclusive distributor for Casa di Russo across the whole of North America, with an agreement to increase the supply year on year over the next decade. We'll have to expand the vineyard and increase production, but this is what we've been working for, yes? It secures our future – for the whole family, but especially for you, number one daughter,' he told Carina.

'Oh, Papà, that's incredible,' she exclaimed, as she threw her arms around him.

In recent years, Carina had taken on a more active role in the family business. She'd expected that responsibility to go to her twin brother, Lorenzo, but he had shown little interest in the family business and now lived in Milan, where he worked as an architect. Carina, however, was an expert in viticulture, instinctively understanding how the frost, or the storms, or a fierce sun would affect this year's grape harvest. She could tell with the merest glance which ones were ready to be picked, and which should be left on the vine to ripen. Her nose was refined and her palate sophisticated, able to detect the full depth and range of flavours. In short, winemaking was in her blood, in a way it had never been in Lorenzo's.

Carina had a sharp business brain too, and her father had rewarded her devotion to the company by making her brand director of Casa di Russo. She'd more than risen to the challenge, recently overseeing an international campaign with Brad Pitt to raise the company's profile in the US. It had been a huge investment, but Carina had convinced her father it would pay off in terms of brand awareness and sales. Now it seemed she'd been proved right, and she was thrilled.

'Darling, I'm so happy for you.' Philippa kissed her husband in congratulations.

'Come, Carina, there is much to discuss.' Salvatore strode towards the door.

'Can't it wait until later?' Philippa interjected, her voice taking on a firmer edge. 'We were discussing the wedding.'

Carina looked from one parent to the other. She could sense her mother's frustration, and felt torn between the two of them.

'Nonsense, that can wait.' Salvatore waved away his wife's words. 'The wedding will take care of itself, everything is in hand.'

Swept away by his enthusiasm, the wedding preparations temporarily abandoned, Carina hurriedly followed her father out of the room while her mother mused that this wasn't the first time her husband had brushed his daughter's wedding aside recently.

Almost as if he believed it wasn't going to happen.

Pulling herself from her thoughts, Philippa made her way through the enormous house and downstairs to the kitchen to make herself a cup of tea. It was one habit from back home that she still hadn't lost after more than twenty-five years in Italy. She smiled as she saw her mother-in-law, Rafaella, kneading dough at the kitchen table.

'You don't have to do that,' Philippa said in Italian, shaking her head affectionately.

'I know, but I like to. It keeps me out of trouble,' Rafaella laughed.

'Would you like a cup of tea? I'm about to make a pot.'

'All right, thank you,' Rafaella replied, covering the dough and setting it aside to prove. Rafaella had been a beauty in her youth, and her sharp cheekbones and twinkling dark eyes meant she was still a striking woman. Wearing cropped navy trousers with a pale blue blouse, her grey hair cut into a flattering bob and a string of pearls at her neck, she was far more stylish than most Italian nonnas. Philippa felt lucky that she adored her mother-in-law; Rafaella had opened her arms to her from the very beginning, treating her like one of the family.

Philippa bustled around the huge kitchen, homely and cosy despite its size, her eye always drawn to the large window which looked out across the Russo vineyards to the mountains beyond. Today the sun split the blue sky, and there was already a sizzle in the air as the earth warmed under the heat of the Italian sun. The perfect weather for ripening the grapes. This morning, however, she was distracted. What on earth was Giorgio doing, leaving so abruptly less than a fortnight before they were due to be married? Even Carina seemed remote on the subject, if the call from Bianca this morning was anything to go by. Philippa thought back to her own wedding day and how excited she'd been to marry Salvatore, how she'd wanted every detail to be perfect. Everyone seemed so sure that Carina would marry Giorgio, it was almost as if the ceremony was a formality.

'How is your day going?' Rafaella asked as she began wiping down the table where she'd just been working.

'Busy, with the wedding plans. Although I just found out that Giorgio is leaving for a few days. He has business in the US.' Philippa's tone made it clear what she thought of that.

'The timing isn't the best, but he's an ambitious young man. He wants to provide for his family,' Rafaella said neutrally.

Philippa nodded, but she couldn't shake the feeling that something was amiss. 'I'd have been so angry if Salvatore had done that to me.'

'*Sono sorpresa!* You were always supportive of him, and you knew he had to build up his business. I think you would have understood, as Carina does.'

Philippa considered Rafaella's words. 'You think they're well suited?' she asked directly, though she had asked this question many times before, and always received the same answer.

Rafaella kept her gaze on the table as she cleaned, taking a moment to reply. 'All relationships are different. You and Salvatore were *un vortice*, a whirlwind, it's harder for you to understand that, for some couples, it plays out differently. This marriage will be advantageous for everyone. Stop fretting.'

Philippa frowned. 'But you were in love with Antonio, weren't you?' she pondered, naming Salvatore's father who'd died a decade earlier. Concerned that the question was too personal, she added, 'I'd never seen a more devoted couple.'

'Of course I loved him! How can you doubt that? But the situation . . . it was complicated.'

'In what way?' Philippa loved her mother-in-law but she could be frustratingly cryptic.

Rafaella shook her head. 'It was a long time ago, it doesn't matter now . . . after the war—' She clamped her lips tightly shut. 'No, this is not the time.' And went about her kneading with renewed gusto.

*When then?* Philippa knew that once she'd made up her mind, Rafaella wouldn't be swayed, and she'd get no more from her today. But the conversation had left her unsatisfied, and she found herself wondering what Rafaella was alluding to.

'Everything will be well with Carina and Giorgio,' Rafaella continued, changing the subject. 'The two of them are alike, they share the same background and understand one another. And after the death of his mother, Giorgio needs stability, and a strong woman to guide him.'

Philippa nodded. Once again, it seemed that Rafaella had given her pronouncement on the subject and expected no further discussion. Philippa longed to talk to Salvatore about her concerns, but lately – and for the first time in their long relationship – there seemed to be a distance between them.

Philippa had always counted herself lucky. The two of them had enjoyed an idyllic marriage, perfectly complementing one another on both a personal and professional level. Philippa had been instrumental in building up the business; when she'd first come to work for the Russos, they were exporting small amounts of wine and drowning in paperwork. Philippa had worked day and night beside Salvatore, and they'd shared and discussed everything in their lives. Recently, she sensed Salvatore keeping her at arm's length, as though he was hiding something. He seemed worried too, the furrows on his brow etched deeper than ever.

Whenever Philippa tried to talk to him about Carina and Giorgio, Salvatore shut her down immediately. He seemed determined that this wedding should go ahead, as did Rafaella, and Philippa couldn't understand why it was so important to them or why she felt that everyone was in on something apart from her. In all the years she'd lived with the Russo family, she had never felt excluded once. Now, for the first time, she was starting to feel like an outsider.

Glancing out of the kitchen window, she saw Salvatore and Carina stroll across the terrace, passing the fountain with its statue of Bacchus, the Roman god of wine and festivity, on their way to the vineyards beyond. Sometimes, Philippa felt that she loved and hated those grapes in equal measure. Yes, they had given her a wonderful life, with two beautiful houses, holidays to the South of France and the Seychelles, as well as the opportunity to mingle with interesting and cultured people, but it felt as though she was forever coming second to a pile of fruit – at least in her husband's eyes. It seemed to be a theme with the men in her life, she thought wryly.

Lately, that sensation was stronger than ever. Salvatore seemed distant, his kisses perfunctory. She told herself that after the wedding it would be different – they would be less busy, and she'd be able to devote herself to him once again – but deep down she knew it was more than that. They'd been married for twenty-five years, having celebrated their silver wedding anniversary in the spring, but their relationship had never felt the way it did right now.

Her eyes were drawn across the vineyard to the Avella mountains beyond; seeing their majesty and beauty never failed to lift her spirits.

Hopefully this wedding would sprinkle its romance on Philippa and Salvatore too, she thought, they certainly needed it.

# Chapter 2

Isabella De Luca was furious. She stood with one hand on her hip, trying to control her breathing, her full lips drawn together in an angry pout as she stared at the invitation in her hand.

It was heavyweight and elegant, embossed gold letter-press on stiff cream card, with the initials C and G intertwined in a heraldic coat of arms.

*Signor and Signora Russo*

*request the pleasure of your company*

*at the wedding of their daughter,*

*Carina Rafaella Russo to Giorgio Bianchi.*

'Why didn't you tell me?' Isabella demanded.

'Because I knew you'd react like this,' her father, Vito, retorted, plucking the invitation from between her fingers and throwing it carelessly onto his desk.

'I'm not going,' Isabella declared petulantly. 'I refuse.' Her midnight-black hair whipped around her face as she shook her head.

'Isabella . . .' She recognized the warning in her father's voice. It was a tone that could make grown men tremble in fear – she'd witnessed it. 'We will go, and we will celebrate with smiles on our faces. Salvatore Russo is a good man – I've known him for many years. Besides, it will be one of the social events of the year in Campania. A family as important as ours should be present.'

'But . . .' Isabella longed to stamp her foot in protest, but she knew that would only make her look childish. She stared up at her father, her eyes ablaze. She'd inherited her looks – and her temper – from him, both sharing the same olive skin, deep brown eyes and aquiline nose. But where Vito's dark hair was flecked with grey, Isabella's was thick and lustrous, cut to her jawline in a sleek, glossy bob.

Isabella had also inherited her father's unstoppable ambition. Vito De Luca's ruthlessness was the reason they owned their sumptuous thirty-room palazzo in the heart of the Campania countryside. Grand and ornate, built in the Renaissance style, it was lavishly decorated and filled with antiques, with painted frescoes on the soaring ceilings. Its terraced gardens boasted an enormous swimming pool, and there was even a private chapel on the property's grounds, which Isabella visited as infrequently as possible, her definition of sin at odds with that of the Church.

The De Luca family were at the head of a thriving business empire that included property, casinos, nightclubs and security. Their interests ran from the nearby town of Avellino, right across the province to the port city of Salerno and along the Amalfi Coast. Isabella assisted in the running of her father's empire and burned to take over one day. She wanted what her father had – money, power, control – and would go to any lengths to get them.

'Look,' Vito began, his tone softening. 'I know that you and Giorgio were an item once, but this is for the best. Giorgio Bianchi comes from a long line of vineyard workers, men who toil on the land. That is not what I want for my daughter.'

'That's not what *he* wants for his future,' Isabella protested, her manner proud and haughty, her dark eyes glittering. She was wearing a close-fitting dress in dazzling scarlet, embellished with crystals and a plunging neckline. She liked to show off her body, and her clothes were always expensive and chosen to show off her hourglass figure to eye-popping effect. Why shouldn't she have the best? Her father could afford it. 'Giorgio wants to move into business and start his own company, develop property – all the areas we could help him with,' she continued.

Vito shook his head, shutting down the conversation. 'No, I'm not letting Giorgio Bianchi anywhere near any of our assets.'

'Why not?'

'*Cara mia*, I've worked hard over the years. *Very* hard. I've made sacrifices, given blood, sweat and tears – quite literally – to get to where I am now. And if you think I'm just handing all of that to some upstart *peasant* then you're sadly mistaken.'

'Papà!'

'Besides, I think you'll find what Giorgio Bianchi wants for his future is Carina Russo,' Vito finished cruelly, waving the invitation in her face.

Fury burned through Isabella. She hated Carina with a passion – the stupid bitch was always running around town with her blonde hair and scrawny figure, playing at being a businesswoman. Apparently she'd just shot a campaign with Brad Pitt, and the profile of Casa di Russo wine was soaring. Now she was about to marry Giorgio Bianchi too. But Isabella De Luca didn't give up that easily, especially when she wanted something — or someone — as badly as she wanted Giorgio.

'Perhaps,' Isabella said, a smug expression crossing her face. Her father didn't know that she and Giorgio were still involved, even if their trysts were less frequent than they had been. There was no way he could be content to settle for Carina Russo: nice, conservative, *dull*. Isabella knew for a fact that they weren't even sleeping together. Giorgio had told her so himself.

Her father might have been dismissive of her past with Giorgio, thinking it was just a fling, but Isabella knew it went deeper than that. She'd been in love with Giorgio Bianchi. Dammit, she was still in love with him. What was more, she was sure that he loved her too – he just needed to be reminded.

'*Allora, principessa,*' Vito began, crossing the room towards his daughter, his tone conciliatory as he reached into his jacket pocket. 'Here's my credit card. Go and buy yourself a new dress. Something for the wedding, hmm? Cheer yourself up.'

In spite of herself, Isabella's eyes lit up. She had a walk-in wardrobe full of designer clothes, but she was always happy to add more. She would take the Ferrari for a spin to Ravello, see what she could find.

'*Grazie, Papà*,' she smiled sweetly, taking the card from him. She would find the perfect dress to show Giorgio exactly what he was missing out on. Yes, that was exactly what she needed to do.

Isabella De Luca had revenge on her mind.

Carina was walking in the vineyards with her father, her arm linked through his. The sweet, fruity scent of the grapes perfumed the air, the feel of the soil familiar beneath her leather shoes. She wore sharply tailored tan-coloured trousers, and a fitted white shirt, her diamond engagement ring sparkling in the sunshine.

'. . . And I've been speaking to some investors,' Salvatore was explaining. 'I don't want to give away more than ten per cent, but we'll need to upgrade the fermentation tanks and buy additional barrels, not to mention expanding the winery itself, hiring extra staff . . .'

'That's wonderful, Papà. You've worked so hard all these years, you truly deserve it.'

'Thank you, Carina. I know you love this business as I do.'

They made their way between the rows of vines and Carina plucked a grape from the bunches nestled amongst the sun-dappled leaves, popping it in her mouth. It was sharp and tart, but she could still taste the underlying sweetness. In a couple of weeks they would be ready for the harvest – a process which was still done by hand at the Russos' winery – but Carina wouldn't be here to see it. She'd be a married woman, off on her honeymoon, beginning her new life with Giorgio.

'*Presto*,' she proclaimed. 'In a fortnight, they'll be perfect.'

'You're right of course,' Salvatore said admiringly. Then, almost as though he'd read her mind, he added, 'I don't know how we'll cope without you.'

'Papà, I'm hardly moving to the other side of the world,' she reassured him. 'After the honeymoon, we'll be living on the Bianchi estate for a while. I'll be next door.'

She waved her hand across the fields, indicating the Bianchis' land on the other side of the stream. There was a small villa on the estate that was to be given to Carina and Giorgio as a wedding present; they would base themselves there until they decided where to settle permanently – an issue that was still a cause of disagreement between the two of them. And it wasn't the only subject they'd quarrelled about. In the lead-up to the wedding, with all its stresses and pressures, she and Giorgio had been arguing more than ever before.

'Is everything all right, Papà?' Carina asked, noticing how Salvatore was lost in his own thoughts.

'Of course. Why wouldn't it be?'

'You should be on top of the world after signing this deal, but you're worried. I can tell. Is there something you're not telling me?'

Salvatore hesitated, and Carina knew that her instincts had been correct. She couldn't tell if his concerns related to the business, or to her, but the mention of her living on the Bianchi estate seemed to have affected him. Would he miss her, was that it? The two of them shared a special bond; he'd been reluctant to let her go to London to study, and perhaps he was upset at the thought of her leaving permanently. Or did he have some concern about the family she was marrying into?

But no, that was absurd. Carina knew how badly Salvatore wanted this union to happen. Sometimes she wondered if this marriage was more about the two families than about her and Giorgio.

'There's something I need to talk to you about.'

Salvatore's tone made Carina nervous, but she showed none of her anxieties as she replied lightly, 'Yes?'

'We're going to have an unexpected guest staying with us in the run-up to the wedding.'

'Who?' Carina frowned.

'I'm hiring someone to look after you. I'm finalizing the details, but they'll act as your driver and bodyguard.'

'Papà, I—'

'I'm not taking any chances.'

'You're being ridiculous,' Carina burst out angrily. She hated the thought of this special time being overshadowed by anyone or anything. She certainly didn't want to be followed round by some oaf when she was having her final dress fittings, or visiting the beautician. Was he going to come with her when she went to the spa, or the masseuse? 'You're being paranoid. It was an accident.'

Carina thought back to that terrifying incident, almost a month ago now. She'd tried to banish it from her mind, but sometimes when she closed her eyes at night, it all came flooding back . . .

*'I can't believe how pretty it is here,' sighed Edie Stone as she stared round at the picture-perfect streets of Positano from behind her enormous Audrey Hepburn-style sunglasses. The enchanting, pastel-coloured buildings were nestled at the foot of the verdant mountains, the idyllic terraced gardens sweeping down to a turquoise sea that was almost too beautiful to be real.*

'I know,' Carina sighed happily. 'I feel like the luckiest girl in the world right now.'

It was just six weeks until Carina's wedding, and her best friend, Edie, had taken advantage of a break in her filming schedule and flown over from Los Angeles for a girly weekend. They'd been browsing in the stylish boutiques, picking out dresses for Carina's honeymoon and lingerie for her wedding night, and their arms were laden with stiff paper shopping bags tied up with ribbons. Now they were heading to a café for a refreshing drink and a proper catch-up.

The two women made a striking pair. Carina was undoubtedly beautiful, in a pale blue chiffon maxi-dress by ROX that draped perfectly around her slender body, her long, blonde hair swept up in a top knot with tendrils falling loose to frame her face. Edie's style was more edgy, her hair cropped short in a pixie cut and dyed white-blonde, her long legs encased in denim shorts teamed with a cropped shirt that showed off her tanned midriff. They turned heads even in a town known for attracting the cream of the glitterati.

'You don't get views like this in London,' Edie laughed, waving her arm to indicate the cobbled piazza leading to Spiaggia Grande beach, sleek white yachts bobbing on the Tyrrhenian Sea beyond.

'Oh, we had so much fun back then, didn't we?' Carina reminisced as she linked her arm through Edie's and they turned into a quiet backstreet where the stone walls were draped with bright pink bursts of bougainvillea, the subtle scent suffusing the air as the sun blazed overhead.

Carina and Edie had met during Carina's time in England, when she was studying at the London Business School. Against her father's wishes, she'd taken a part-time job working in the box office of the Wardour Theatre, which was where she'd met *aspiring actress, Edie Stone. Where Carina was cool and composed, Edie was loud and gregarious, and the two complemented one another perfectly, quickly becoming fast friends and renting a tiny, basement flat together in fashionable Notting Hill. Now Edie was on the verge of superstardom, her career going stratospheric, and they rarely found the time to see one another.*

*'I'm so glad you're here,' Carina told her. She had to raise her voice as she spoke, the noise of a car engine getting louder behind them. 'We hardly ever get chance to talk—'*

*'Look out!' Edie screamed.*

*Everything happened so quickly. Edie grabbed hold of Carina so hard it hurt, yanking her out of the path of the oncoming vehicle. Carina turned, her eyes widening in fear, as the black Maserati swerved across the narrow street, appearing to drive straight at her. The windows were blacked out, and she couldn't see the driver.*

*Carina screamed, and it took a moment for her to realize she was safe as the car sped off, tyres screeching. Edie had pulled her into the recessed doorway of a chapel; if she'd remained in the narrow street, the car would have hit her.*

*The two women stood for a moment, hearts pounding, adrenaline rushing through their bodies. In all the commotion, Carina had dropped her shopping bags. The contents had spilled out, strewn across the road, the delicate white lace underwear now spoiled and dirty. She stared at it, dumbly, as Edie went across to pick it up, her hands shaking. Carina knew that she would never wear it now – it felt tainted, unlucky.*

*'What the hell just happened?' Edie said, her voice shaking.*

*'I . . . I don't know,' Carina stammered, shocked to find that her voice was trembling too.*

*'Probably just a paparazzo,' Edie said, attempting to shrug it off. 'I've had a few following me in LA recently.'*

*'Yeah,' Carina paused before nodding numbly. 'You're probably right, why would anyone do that on purpose, who else could it be?'*

*But she couldn't shake the chill that had crept over her and that stayed with her for days afterwards . . .*

'Please, Carina.' Salvatore turned to her, and Carina saw the concern etched on his face. 'Let me do this. I'm worried, I . . . If anything happened to you. I would never forgive myself.'

Carina shivered, despite the warm, Italian sun blazing high overhead. Did her father really think it was necessary? He was probably being overprotective, she assured herself, just like all Italian papas. But if hiring a bodyguard would make her parents feel better, who was she to argue?

'Of course, Papà,' she relented. 'As you wish.'

He put his arms around her and kissed her on the forehead. Momentarily, Carina felt like a little girl again, safe and protected in his arms. Her father was clearly overreacting, but it was easiest to appease him. After all, Carina felt sure that she had no enemies. Who could possibly want to hurt her?

# Chapter 3

The entrance to the Russos' villa was undeniably impressive, Tom Ryan thought as he drove between two towering stone gate pillars with carved golden eagles perched on top. The wheels of his hired Mercedes crunched along the driveway as, about a mile in the distance, he saw the house come into view. It looked spectacular against the setting sun, the enormous palazzo ablaze with lights, the sky behind it a riot of pink and purple and orange.

Tom was still wondering whether he'd done the right thing by deciding to come here. He'd allowed himself to be pushed into it by his father, telling himself it would all be over in two weeks, and the money would cover his bills for the next six months.

Since leaving the army Tom had gone freelance, working in personal security. He'd looked after Hollywood stars, billionaire businessmen, politicians, diplomats and minor royalty. He took short-term contracts with no personal ties, preferring to do the job and move on to the next. The thought of spending two weeks at the beck and call of some Italian bridezilla, however, didn't appeal in the slightest. It was the sort of job he hated; reduced to a glorified shopping companion, waiting outside over-priced restaurants while spoilt rich kids ate into their parents' bank balances. It was mind-numbing.

But Salvatore Russo was an old friend of Tom's father, Peter, a wine importer with a fondness for Casa di Russo. Peter had asked his son to take on the job, arguing that Tom needed a change of scenery after everything that had happened. Tom had initially declined, but eventually relented, and now here he was.

He pulled up in the courtyard, stepping out of the air-conditioned vehicle into the warmth of an Italian evening. Tom was twenty-eight years old, blonde and blue-eyed, and prided himself on being in great physical shape. Exercise was a way of life for him, a habit he couldn't break since leaving the army, even though he was no longer contractually obliged to maintain his fitness levels. He still ran 10k every morning, worked out daily in the gym, and could bench-press 250lbs with ease. His clients expected it of him, and it kept him sane.

Skimming over the house with a well-trained eye, Tom felt the familiar prickle of curiosity and uncertainty that he always did at the start of a new job. The villa was spectacular: built in traditional stone, two storeys high but sprawling in its breadth, flanked by cypress trees which stood guard like sentries. A stone staircase ran down the left side of the house, reaching to the upper floor, wreathed in jasmine which gave off a delicate, fragrant scent. Pale-blue shutters bordered the high, wood-framed windows, below a gently sloping roof of weathered terracotta tiles.

Tom couldn't see a bell or knocker as he approached the imposing wooden door beneath a decorative stone archway. He imagined they'd have a security system, and wondered if he was being watched on camera right now. Experimentally, he tried the door; to his surprise, it opened. Tom paused for a split second, then entered.

He found himself in a spacious double-height entrance hall, with doors and corridors leading off in all directions. An elaborate chandelier hung from the ceiling, with baroque-style chairs on either side of the space, while in the centre was a circular, polished walnut table that held a stunning display of fresh flowers in an enormous Lalique vase. Bearing left, Tom came across an open-plan living area, with inviting-looking sofas arranged around an exquisitely patterned Florentine rug. Against the far wall, a half-moon table was clustered with framed photographs; curiously, Tom moved closer to examine them.

A handsome, smiling man appeared in almost all of the pictures, accompanied by an elegant woman, both of them raising a glass of wine to the camera. Tom recognized the couple as Salvatore Russo, his father's friend and business associate, and his wife, Philippa. There were pictures of them with various celebrities and well-known faces – Sophia Loren, George Clooney, Andrea Bocelli, Richard Branson – all drinking Casa di Russo wine.

Then there were the more intimate, relaxed family photos: a happy group of four posing in skiwear outside a chalet in the mountains; relaxed in swimwear around a kidney-shaped pool; laughing at the camera, their faces partially hidden, in fancy dress for a masquerade ball. Tom found that his gaze kept being drawn to one figure in particular – a young woman with long blonde hair and striking violet eyes, lightly tanned skin and a million-watt smile. He realized that this was Carina, though she was almost unrecognizable from the gawky teenager he remembered. His father had reminded him they'd met the Russo family once on holiday, when Tom was around fifteen, Carina and Lorenzo four years younger, but this couldn't be the same girl, could it?

'Whoa!' Tom let out a cry of alarm as he heard a furious yapping, and a ball of white fluff came hurtling out of nowhere towards him, jumping up excitedly. Conscious of the noise, and embarrassed to be caught snooping – he was aware he'd ventured further into the house than he should have done without making his presence known – he hastily began to retrace his steps while trying not to tread on the dog, an excitable Bichon Frisé.

Somehow, as the dog continued to bark, diving between his legs and nipping at his ankles, Tom lost his balance, crashing to the ground and finding himself sprawling clumsily on the Florentine rug.

'Bella! Bella, *che cosa c'è*? What's the matter?'

A young woman came running into the room, her emerald-green silk gown flowing out behind her, her long blonde hair tumbling down her back. As soon as the dog heard the woman's voice it ran straight over, scooped up happily in its mistress's arms.

Tom got to his feet unsteadily, brushing himself down, feeling like a clumsy fool and hideously embarrassed. He straightened up and looked properly at his rescuer, real-izing with horror that he was staring straight into the incredible violet eyes of the young woman in the photo-graph – only now those eyes were narrowed in suspicion.

'She's not much of a guard dog, so let's hope you're not here to steal something,' she said to him in flawless English with barely the trace of an Italian accent. Her eyebrows were raised questioningly, but her expression was mocking.

'I'm not, I assure you. Perhaps we should start over? My name's Tom Ryan,' he explained. 'I'm—'

'Ah! My bodyguard, sì?' she interrupted, a trace of a smile playing around her lips, as though she found the idea amusing.

'I've been engaged by Salvatore Russo. If you could let him know I'm here, I'd like to speak with him.'

Carina looked him up and down with an assessing gaze, and Tom wondered whether she remembered him from that meeting over a decade ago. Whether she had her own preconceptions of him, and if he'd shattered them or lived up to them. A small voice at the back of his head wondered why it mattered to him what she thought.

'Of course,' she said finally. 'Perhaps you'd like to freshen up first? I'll ask the housekeeper to show you to your room, then you can join us for dinner. My father will be there.'

'I don't want to intrude . . .' The last thing Tom wanted after the long journey was to feel like a spare part at a family dinner, forced to make small talk with a group of strangers.

'It's no intrusion,' Carina said, a flicker of amusement crossing her expression. 'I suppose I'll have to get used to having you around.'

Tom showered quickly and changed into black trousers and a black shirt, the long sleeves rolled up in a concession to the heat. He preferred to keep things simple; plain clothing felt more like a uniform, the dark colour enabling him to blend into the background.

His room was grand and ornate, with a four-poster bed and gold-framed Renaissance paintings on the walls, but he understood that he'd only be there for one night; the plan was for Carina to travel to Amalfi tomorrow, where she'd stay until the wedding, and Tom was to accompany her.

His hair was still damp as he jogged down the staircase, but the air was deliciously warm, the perfect temperature now that the sun had gone down. He hadn't been over-seas since he'd left the army, and the fragrant air and balmy heat brought back memories of another time . . . *Stop that* . . .Those memories seemed like a lifetime ago, Tom thought, shaking his head to clear it.

Tom strode through the house, easily able to remember the way he'd come. It was part of his training; to mentally map a new location, to remember every small detail. He kept a cautious eye out for Bella the dog, not wanting a repeat of his earlier humiliation.

As he passed the sitting room, he recalled the photo-graphs on the side table. He couldn't help stopping, glancing once again at the display. There was one picture in particular of Carina, a black-and-white headshot, professionally taken, that had captured her beautifully – the vivacity in her eyes . . .

A peal of laughter reached his ears and Tom quickly moved away, feeling like a guilty child caught with his hand in the biscuit tin. As he strode back out into the corridor, he almost collided with Carina.

'Signor Ryan,' she exclaimed, her eyes dancing. 'I was wondering where you'd got to. Come, we're through here.

Let me introduce – or should I say, *re*-introduce – you to my father.'

Tom followed Carina towards the back of the house, through concertina doors and out onto a flagstone terrace. A long table had been set up, beautifully dressed with a white linen tablecloth, posies of wildflowers, and citronella candles in hurricane lamps. Overhead was a trellised area, with over-hanging trees and twisted vines, fairy lights woven through the greenery and lanterns strung from the oleander trees.

Around the table sat half a dozen glamorous people, their conversation loud and convivial, gesticulating with their hands in the typical Italian style. The delicious smell of Mediterranean food drifted over to Tom, with hints of oregano, thyme and lemon, while the glasses of wine were rich and gleaming in the candlelight. Salvatore was in the middle of recounting a story, and Carina discreetly got his attention.

'Papà, you remember Tom Ryan – Peter's son.'

'Yes, of course. Of course!' Salvatore exclaimed, switch-ing to heavily accented English and shaking Tom's hand enthusiastically. 'How is your father? I hope he's well. *Dio mio*, but that man drives a hard bargain,' he chuckled. 'Here, I'll pour you a glass of wine. You must be tired after your journey.'

'Not at all,' Tom insisted.

'Nonsense.' Salvatore waved away his words, and Tom got the sense he was used to having his instructions obeyed. 'Tomorrow you start work, but tonight you are off duty. Come, join us. This is my wife, Philippa,' he said, indicating the graceful blonde Tom recognized from the photographs. 'And this is my neighbour and friend – soon to be family. Costa Bianchi.'

Tom smiled and greeted everyone, assessing each person. Even though he was sitting down, Costa Bianchi was clearly short in stature, with a florid complexion and dark hair that had almost fully retreated from the top of his head. There was something tense about him, a sense that he was not entirely comfortable in this situation.

'And this is my son, Lorenzo,' Salvatore grinned, with a theatrical sweep of his arm. 'We finally managed to drag him here from Milan.'

Tom leaned across to shake his hand, and Lorenzo responded warmly. He appeared polite yet self-assured, smiling as he looked Tom straight in the eye, his handshake firm.

'My beloved mother, Rafaella.'

'*Piacere di conoscerla.*' Tom shook hands with the family matriarch. Elegant and dignified, Rafaella appeared to be in her late seventies, but the sharpness in her eyes showed that she missed nothing.

'And, of course, this is my beloved daughter, Carina, who you will be looking after.'

'Yes, we've already met, Papà,' she laughed, as she sashayed past Tom and slid into her seat.

He caught the floral scent of her perfume as she passed, then Salvatore ushered Tom into the chair beside him. Philippa spoke to the housekeeper, Giulia, who returned with a bowl of spaghetti alle vongole which Tom gratefully accepted.

'This is delicious,' he remarked as he took a spoonful of the perfectly tender clams steeped in a garlicky tomato sauce.

'Thank you,' Philippa beamed. 'I love to cook, although I don't always have as much time as I'd like. Traditional

Italian recipes are wonderful, and of course I was fortunate to learn so many of them at the feet of my incomparable mother-in-law.' She turned to Rafaella with a grateful look. 'Now I'm passing them all down to Carina.'

'How wonderful to see the generations of the same family,' Tom commented. 'You all seem so close.'

'We're very lucky,' Philippa agreed.

The conversation flowed in a mixture of languages. Tom spoke a little Italian so could follow the discussions as he tried to get a sense of the relationships between everyone, watching the body language that said far more than words ever could.

'So, you're going to take care of Carina for me,' Salvatore stated, sitting back in his chair and regarding Tom.

'I can take care of myself, Papà,' Carina shot back.

'Yes, make sure you keep her safe for Giorgio,' Costa addressed Tom gravely.

'He could do the job himself if he was here,' Salvatore muttered, as Philippa jumped in smoothly, explaining, 'Giorgio had important business in the US.'

'He is very busy, very hardworking,' Costa added proudly. 'And soon he will have a family of his own to provide for.'

Tom smiled politely, sensing a rivalry between the two families. He wondered how serious it was – friendly competition, or something deeper? He glanced at Carina to see her reaction. She didn't appear to be paying attention, bending down to feed morsels of food to the dog which had come to sit by her feet. She looked up and saw him watching, raising one of her perfectly shaped eyebrows and he quickly glanced away, feeling that he'd been caught out.

'This wine is superb, by the way,' he said, changing the subject.

'I knew I picked this guy for a reason,' Salvatore chuckled.

'Yes, the Russos are very lucky to produce such a fine wine,' Costa chimed in. His words were slurred, and Tom wondered how much he'd had to drink. 'So lucky and so blessed. We Bianchis have not been so fortunate.'

His words caused a shift in the atmosphere, an awkwardness creeping in where the evening had been so relaxed and convivial. Tom was immediately alert, wondering what was behind Costa's cryptic statement.

'Let's toast,' Salvatore smiled, smoothing over Costa's comments. 'To wine. And to love. And to the joining of our two families.'

'To water under the bridge – literally,' Costa added, collapsing into drunken laughter as he raised his glass.

Tom stared at him for a moment, was that bitter laughter, he wondered, before joining in with the cries of *'Salute!'* as everyone clinked their glasses, the uncomfortable moment seeming to have passed. Giulia emerged to clear the dinner plates, replacing them with a luscious tiramisu. Tom devoured it, realizing just how hungry he was, then glanced across at Carina to see she'd only eaten a couple of bites.

'I'm going to bed,' she announced with a yawn, standing up and looking pointedly at Tom. 'We have an early start tomorrow.'

'We do?' he asked, feeling glad he'd switched to water. 'Then perhaps I'd better retire too. Goodnight, everyone. Thank you for your warm welcome.'

Tom followed Carina into the house, his eyes trained on her back, trying not to notice how the silk dress flowed around her body like water, sliding over her hips as she moved.

'Is this how it's going to be?' Carina mused, looking at him over her shoulder.

'I'm sorry?' Tom frowned, worried that she'd somehow read his mind.

'Are you going to be my shadow? Your job doesn't start until tomorrow, and I'm sure I can find my way back to my room safely.'

Tom raised his eyebrows, still trying to figure her out – couldn't work out if she was prickly, or teasing him. He heard Carina laugh softly and realized that's exactly what she was doing.

'*Buona notte, Signor Ryan.*' Her voice floated down to him as she ascended the stairs. '*A domani.*'

'Yes,' Tom murmured under his breath, wondering what on earth he'd got himself into. 'Until tomorrow.'

# Chapter 4

'The view's incredible,' murmured Giorgio Bianchi. He was lying, naked, on silk sheets, staring out of the penthouse windows of the Sunset Tower Hotel in West Hollywood, right the way along the Sunset Strip and across the city to downtown Los Angeles.

Lazily, he rolled over, an irrepressible grin stealing across his handsome features at the sight of supermodel Ashley Hall stretched out beside him wearing nothing but a black thong. 'The view's not bad here either,' he smirked, reaching for her, and kissing her hungrily.

She responded with equal lust, and Giorgio congratulated himself on being utterly irresistible to women. After all, he had Ashley here, and his adoring fiancée back home . . .

Almost as though she'd read his thoughts, Ashley pulled away from him and leapt out of bed. Giorgio experienced a fleeting moment of panic that he might have somehow

41

given himself away, but then she turned to look coquettishly over one toned, tanned shoulder.

'Drink?' she purred.

'Sure,' Giorgio grinned, back to his usual, confident self. 'I'll take a whisky over ice.'

He watched as Ashley bent over to grab two glasses from the mini bar, admiring the slender curves of her body, the way her long dark hair splayed across her naked shoulders. He must have been a saint in a previous life to get this lucky now, he mused.

Ashley fixed the drinks – a vodka, lime and soda for herself – and sashayed back over to the bed, switching on the television and flicking through the channels as she nestled in to Giorgio. It was a rare moment of calm in a relationship that was primarily based on carnal lust.

The two of them had met almost a year ago at Milan Fashion Week. Giorgio had been in the city visiting his friend, Lorenzo, and the attraction between Giorgio and Ashley had been instantaneous. It wasn't the first time Giorgio had cheated on his childhood sweetheart – regardless of what he'd said to Carina.

Ashley's star had been on the rise when they'd first met in the bar of the Hotel Principe di Savoia, but since then her fame had exploded. She was now a bona fide supermodel, known by her first name alone, and able to command tens of thousands of dollars before she'd deign to get out of bed in the morning.

Giorgio knew they weren't exclusive – Ashley was too wild, her lifestyle too unconventional to contemplate a steady relationship – but the chemistry between them was electric. They hooked up whenever they were in the same city, and they *always* had a blast. But even though their arrangement was a casual one, Giorgio doubted that Ashley would take kindly to discovering he had a fiancée back home in Italy, and he knew he was walking a fine line.

He reached for his phone, noticing that he had a message. It must have come in while he and Ashley were . . . occupied.

Hey babe, I miss you.
Are you thinking about me? Xxx

'*Cazzo*,' Giorgio swore under his breath. It was from Isabella De Luca. They'd had an on-off fling for a few months, but she didn't seem to be able to let it go. Normally, Giorgio would tell her to go to hell, but her father was one of the most important men in Campania, and he didn't want to piss her off.

'What's that?' Ashley strode back over, carrying the drinks.

'Nothing,' Giorgio said quickly as he deleted the message. 'Hey, isn't that your uncle's programme?'

The glossy opening sequence of a reality show was playing out on the television screen. Half a dozen women with big hair and surgically enhanced faces beamed at the camera, their yoga-honed bodies squeezed into revealing designer dresses, as the title scrolled in swirling gold letters: *Beverly Hills Dream*.

'Yup. And there he is! Hi, Uncle Sam,' Ashley giggled, raising her glass at the TV.

A rugged, sandy-haired man in his early forties was striding around a futuristic mansion in the Hills, a fawning woman in six-inch stilettos at his side. The two of them stepped out onto the terrace, champagne glasses in hand, stopping beside the enormous infinity pool with its sweeping views of Los Angeles. The woman's mascara ran down her cheeks as Sam Quinn delivered the immortal lines in his smooth Texan accent: 'I'm sorry, honey. It's not you, it's me. I'm just not ready to settle down.'

'You bastard!' She threw the contents of her drink at Sam, who still managed to look craggily handsome with bubbles dripping down his face.

'Don't forget to close the door on your way out,' he called, as she stormed past him. The camera lingered on him for a moment – he grinned to himself, then raised his glass in a silent toast to bachelorhood – before cutting to the next scene.

'That's classic Sam,' Ashley told Giorgio. 'He's such a heartbreaker, but there's always an endless line of potential new girlfriends queuing round the block.'

Giorgio felt a growing admiration for Sam Quinn. Ashley's uncle was good-looking, famous, with a multi-million-dollar property empire and a string of gorgeous women hanging off his every word. It was as though a genie had granted all of Giorgio's wishes, but given them to Sam instead.

'How are you related to him again?' Giorgio asked, trying to sound casual, though a plan was forming in his head.

'He's my mom's brother. The two of them were born and raised outside Dallas, but my mom went on vacation to Hawaii when she was twenty-one, met my dad and never came home.'

'That's so romantic,' Giorgio smiled, thinking it was the right thing to say.

'Yeah, it is,' Ashley agreed dreamily. 'Uncle Sam, on the other hand, fell in love with money. He moved to LA to try and make it as an actor, but studied for his real estate licence in between auditions and soon discovered he could make way more in commission than he could with walk-on roles in B-list movies. He's real smart. He didn't blow his money on clothes or cars, like I would,' she giggled. 'He invested it, bought properties of his own, flipped them and made a fortune. And *then* he got famous on TV, just like he'd always wanted.'

'Cool,' Giorgio said nonchalantly, swirling the ice in his glass. 'He sounds like a great guy.'

'Oh, he is. Like, my dad's not really ambitious – he's happy hanging out in Hawaii, working as a sports coach. Which is totally fine. But Uncle Sam gets me. He doesn't have any kids – well, that he knows about – but I'm like a daughter to him. I stayed with him when I first moved to LA, and he was so supportive. He understands that I want more out of life, that I was never gonna be satisfied working nine to five in a dead-end job.'

'I know, baby. You want the best. And you deserve it.'

'Cheers to that.' Ashley clinked her tumbler against his, leaning in to give him a long, lingering kiss.

'I've been thinking,' Giorgio said, when they came up for air. 'Maybe we need to take things to the next level. It's about time I met your family. Why don't we start with Uncle Sam?'

'You really want to?' Ashley breathed, her catlike green eyes widening.

'Sure.' Giorgio gave her his killer smile.

'I guess Uncle Sam could be a pretty good business contact for you too, huh?' she teased, and Giorgio had the good grace to look embarrassed. He realized he shouldn't underestimate Ashley – she might be a model, but she was more than just a pretty face.

'Sure, I can set something up,' she offered, putting him out of his misery. 'When are you free? I thought you were flying out tonight?'

'*Merda!*' Giorgio swore again, jumping up so fast that Ashley almost spilled her vodka. He grabbed his Rolex from the bedside table, checking the time. '*Merda!*'

'What the hell . . .?' Ashley exclaimed, an angry frown creeping across her perfect brow.

'I'm so sorry, *mi amore*,' Giorgio apologized, blowing her a kiss, realizing he had to keep her on side. 'But I have to go. I'm going to miss my plane.'

He ran to the bathroom and leapt into the rainfall shower, wincing as the hot water pummelled his skin, his back scratched and sore from Ashley's fingernails.

Giorgio had always seen himself as a property entrepreneur. He knew that his father expected him to take over the family wine business, but what about what *he* wanted, Giorgio thought angrily. Why did his life have to be about duty and honour? He just wanted to have fun – and make a ton of money. Ashley was the key to unlocking that world, the reason he put up with her diva outbursts and demands for expensive gifts. If she could get him a meeting with Sam Quinn, that would be the golden ticket.

Giorgio turned off the shower and grabbed a towel, drying himself quickly. He picked up his phone to find another message from Isabella:

Looking forward to your wedding, G. Are you sure
that's what you want? I could remind you what
you're missing . . . xxx

*Puttana!* Giorgio thought furiously. What was going on
with this girl? He'd told her it was over, yet she still –

'Baby,' Ashley called out in husky tones. 'I'm flying to
Europe in a couple of weeks. We could meet in Paris –
on September fourth.'

Giorgio swallowed. September the fourth was his
wedding day. 'I . . . I don't think I can do that, *mi amore*.'

He could almost hear Ashley's pout from the next room.

Christ, this was a mess, Giorgio sighed, wiping the
steam from the mirror, running his hands through his
wet hair. Carina, Ashley, Isabella . . . He'd thought about
breaking things off with Ashley, but really, he was doing
this for his and Carina's future, he told himself. If he
could pull off the property deal he'd been working on,
up in Orange County, he could make a fortune. *That* was
where the future lay, Giorgio believed – not back home
in the depths of the Italian countryside where nothing
ever happened, selling fusty old bottles of wine that no
one under the age of thirty was interested in drinking.

But Giorgio knew his marriage to Carina had to happen
– their lives were too interconnected, their families too
enmeshed. His father would disown him if he didn't marry
into the Russo empire and merge the two wine dynasties.
He knew his late mother, Vittoria, would have wanted it
too . . . Giorgio felt his heart contract, remembering his
beloved mamma, the one person who had always understood him . . . he brushed the thought away. Once Carina
had that ring on her finger, Giorgio would figure

everything else out afterwards. Sure, Carina might be a little difficult – she was certainly no pushover . . . her blazing violet eyes briefly flashed across his mind and he felt a rare stab of uncertainty but quickly brushed it away; he knew how to handle her.

Giorgio strode out of the bathroom to see Ashley sitting on the edge of the bed, sulking, an expression which only seemed to highlight those razor-sharp cheekbones and bee-stung lips.

'Baby, do you have to leave?' she protested.

'*Sì*, or else I'll miss my flight.' He tried to look contrite, knowing he was cutting it fine. He'd already missed the family meal that his future mother-in-law had been planning for weeks; Carina would kill him if he didn't make it back before the guests began to arrive. His father would string him up.

'If you stay, I'll make it worth your while,' Ashley promised. Her voice was low and full of desire as she stood up and strode over to him, wrapping her body around Giorgio's, her hand sliding down his chest. Giorgio groaned. Ashley was insatiable, and he was but a man, helpless and weak of flesh. What was he supposed to do when one of the world's most celebrated supermodels wanted him so badly?

He let Ashley reach for the towel wrapped around his waist, tugging at it so it came loose and fell to the floor, before she took his hand and led him back to the bed. Discreetly, Giorgio reached for his phone and switched it off, before turning his full attention to Ashley.

To hell with catching his flight. He would deal with the consequences later.

# Chapter 5

**Los Angeles, August 2005**

Edie Stone climbed out of her vintage Ford Mustang outside the famous Spago restaurant on North Canon Drive. She handed the keys to the parking valet and strutted along the sidewalk, where a handful of paparazzi gathered outside the restaurant took her picture. They all knew her name – a sure sign that she was on the rise – and she knew she looked good, channelling Bianca Jagger in a tailored white trouser suit with nothing underneath, only a couple of pieces of strategically placed body tape standing between Edie and a wardrobe malfunction. Dressing to get noticed was essential in Hollywood.

She posed happily for a couple of minutes, before heading inside where the hostess led her through the famous restaurant and out to the coveted tables on the patio. Nathan Jones – her boyfriend until very recently, and now her ex – was already waiting. He stood up to greet her, kissing her awkwardly on the cheek and she instantly regretted wearing something so 'LA' to their dinner. The familiar sight and scent of him made Edie's stomach flip, but she assured herself she'd made the right decision by breaking up with him.

'How are you?' she asked softly, as she sat down.

Nathan shrugged. 'I'm OK.' He looked tired, as though he hadn't been sleeping well. His chin was peppered with a light covering of stubble, but it suited him.

Nathan wasn't drop-dead gorgeous or movie-star handsome, in the way that every waiter or barista in Hollywood seemed to be, but he was undoubtedly attractive. Originally from Cornwall, he still exuded a casual, blonde surfer boy vibe, his rugged good looks a refreshing change from all the chiselled jawlines and fake white veneers seen on most of the LA wannabes. He was a cameraman by trade and had first met Edie working on a short film in London, before they moved to the US to conquer Hollywood together.

It had been Edie's decision that she and Nathan should split up. No one else was involved, and she simply felt that it was time to move on, to spread her wings and focus on her career. She hadn't been the best girlfriend in recent months – she'd barely been at home due to her hectic work schedule, and she was tired and irritable on the rare occasions they did manage to spend time together.

'You look good,' Edie said casually.

'Yeah, you too,' Nathan replied, his voice gravelly as his gaze ran over her body, taking in the sexy trousers slung low on her hips, the deep V of the jacket that skimmed her pert cleavage.

The restaurant was busy; it always was. This was a place to see and be seen, the atmosphere buzzing with conversation amongst Hollywood's movers and shakers. Across the room was Eva Longoria, on a date with a famous basketball player, while Keanu Reeves had just entered with his manager and agent. Edie felt a thrill of excitement that she was sitting amongst them.

'Thank you for bringing me here,' she smiled at Nathan, once the waiter had come and taken their order.

'No problem. Kind of ironic, isn't it?'

'What?'

'When we were together, you were so busy we hardly saw one another. It took us breaking up for me to finally be able to get a date with you.'

Edie squirmed uncomfortably, knowing it was true.

'How are the re-shoots going on *Dark Galaxy*?' Nathan asked, changing the subject.

*Dark Galaxy* was a big-budget sci-fi movie in which Edie had a supporting role. It was a real departure from the kind of parts she usually played, but she'd taken it for the experience of working on a blockbuster and it had been epic. Her next role, she hoped, would be the one to catapult her to superstardom.

Baz Luhrmann, in his usual offbeat, inimitable style, planned to re-work *Wuthering Heights* as a musical, called *The Heights*. Yorkshire girl Edie had been cast as Catherine Earnshaw – the famous Cathy, and the love of Heathcliff's life – a role she felt she was born to play.

'Great,' she replied. 'I finished my scenes today. Rehearsals for *The Heights* start soon, so I'm buried in the script for that.'

'If you need someone to run lines with, you know where I am.'

Edie laughed. They'd spent many hours together over the years with him acting – badly – opposite her, running scenes over and over until she was fully prepared. 'Thanks, Nate.'

'I'm proud of you,' he murmured. 'You're incredible. Achieving your dreams.'

'Thanks. So are you.'

Nathan frowned but the waiter arrived, breaking the moment, bringing roasted black sea bass for her, seared ribeye steak for him.

'Edie, I wanted to ask you about something,' Nathan began, slicing into his steak.

She raised her eyebrows questioningly.

'Carina's wedding. It's going to be difficult to get time off with this new job, so . . .' Nathan trailed off, the unspoken question hanging in the air.

Edie had met Carina while performing in *Les Misérables* in the West End; Carina was working evenings in the box office while she studied for her degree during the day. Despite being from very different backgrounds, the two women had hit it off immediately. Edie had been brought up by her mother after her father had left them; she had no contacts in the entertainment industry, and had to fight hard for every opportunity, clawing her way up from the bottom. She couldn't imagine what it must be like to grow up with money, to have a ready-made business role to step into, and have your passage through life smoothed and cushioned by wealth the way Carina had.

As Carina's best friend, Edie had been asked to be chief bridesmaid, and she knew that the wedding would be spectacular. Carina didn't need to worry about being outshone – Edie knew she'd look radiant as a bride –

and Carina had generously chosen a stunning couture bridesmaid dress in pale gold silk which flattered Edie's figure and looked fabulous on her. Yet every time Edie thought about the wedding, a ball of nausea settled like lead in the pit of her stomach. She should have been thrilled for her best friend – outwardly, she was – but deep down, after everything that had happened, Edie was dreading it . . .

'Perhaps it's best if you don't go,' Edie replied quickly, trying not to notice the look of hurt on Nathan's face. She knew it would feel like a kick in the teeth for him.

'OK,' he swallowed.

'I'm sorry, Nate, but we both need to move on and that's not going to happen if we keep getting together and hanging out. It's too painful.' Edie felt like a bitch.

But Nathan's face had changed, and he no longer seemed to be listening to her, staring over her shoulder into the distance. Had Tom Cruise just arrived or something? Edie wondered. It wasn't like Nathan to get starstruck.

She spun round in her seat, trying to see who he was looking at.

'Isn't that . . .?' Nathan began.

Edie's jaw dropped. '. . .Giorgio Bianchi,' she finished, her hazel eyes hardening. 'What the hell is he doing here?'

'Is that really him? Shouldn't he be in Italy, getting ready for his wedding?'

'Never mind that – look at who he's with! How on earth does he know *them*?'

Edie and Nathan watched in astonishment as Giorgio weaved his way through the tables, accompanied by model Ashley Hall and reality TV star Sam Quinn.

'I don't understand – what's he doing with those two?' Edie hissed. Giorgio looked as smug and arrogant as ever, she thought, with a stab of distaste. Ashley Hall looked incredible; diners were turning to stare and she revelled in every second, shaking out her silky corkscrew hair, swinging her hips in the skin-tight Hervé Leger bandage dress.

Giorgio was clearly basking in the reflected glory, enjoying being part of the circus that surrounded Ashley and Sam. He was still an arrogant prick, Edie thought angrily. Nothing had changed since the last time she'd seen him – and she didn't want to think about what had happened then.

'Should we go over and say hello?' Nathan asked. He'd met Giorgio on a handful of occasions and, although the two men were as different as chalk and cheese, Nathan was nothing if not well-mannered.

Edie looked at him as though he was insane. That was the very last thing she wanted to do. As she watched, Giorgio put his hand on the small of Ashley's back, guiding her through the restaurant, the gesture unmistakably intimate. Edie's eyes widened in shock.

'No way.' Edie downed her wine and stood up, ignoring her half-eaten food and turning to Nathan. 'Come on. Let's get out of here.'

She grabbed her clutch bag, threw Giorgio a murderous look, then stalked out of the restaurant.

# Chapter 6

Giorgio felt like the proverbial cat who'd got the cream as he strode through Spago – the hottest, most exclusive restaurant in LA – with Ashley and Sam. He knew heads were turning to look at them and the sensation was thrilling, even as he tried to keep his expression neutral, to keep the eager grin from his face. He found himself wondering whether, if he hit it off with Sam, he'd be invited to make a guest appearance on *Beverly Hills Dream*. Giorgio had always felt he'd be a natural on television.

He imagined his fellow diners speculating about who the handsome man was with Sam and Ashley – a Hollywood player no doubt, perhaps a movie mogul or filthy rich producer. Giorgio placed his hand on Ashley's lower back possessively, a gesture of ownership. That would really give the gawpers something to talk about.

He wasn't worried that Carina would find out about this little rendezvous; Italy felt like a world away right now, and he knew that however mad Carina got with him, he could always talk her round.

Giorgio enjoyed the fawning from the waiter as they were seated at their table on the patio, one of the best spots in the whole restaurant. As he sat down, he became aware of a commotion nearby, a couple standing quickly and pushing back their chairs, clearly in a hurry to leave. Some instinct compelled him to glance across and for a second he froze.

*Cazzo.*

Edie Stone, his fiancée's best friend, along with her penniless loser of a boyfriend – Nick or Neil or something. For a split second, he caught Edie's eye, but it was long enough to see the sheer hatred burning there. Giorgio swallowed, suddenly thrown off-kilter.

'Everything OK, baby?' Ashley purred, placing her hand on his. As though her touch had burned him, Giorgio whipped his arm away. Seeing the confused look on Ashley's face, he pretended to be smoothing down his hair, his fingers raking through his jet-black curls.

'Sure, *mi amore.*' Giorgio gave her a reassuring smile. When he looked back, Edie and her date had gone. Giorgio blew out the breath he didn't realize he'd been holding.

'So,' Sam grinned, his teeth exposed like a shark about to devour its prey. 'It's good to meet you, Giorgio.'

Giorgio forced himself to focus, returning Sam's smile as he remembered what was at stake – pretty much his entire future plans.

'It's wonderful to meet you too, sir,' Giorgio said smoothly, as he sat back and observed Sam. He was a giant of a man – at six feet four inches he towered over Giorgio – and he was made even taller by the trademark black Stetson he was sporting. He wore stonewashed denim jeans with a loose white shirt and

brown leather belt, and his skin was tanned and chiselled, like it had been carved out of rock. 'Thanks for
agreeing to meet me,' Giorgio continued. 'I'm a great
admirer of yours.'

'That's very kind of you to say,' Sam replied, apparently
enjoying the flattery. 'Say, why don't we kick this off
with a nice bottle of Saint-Émilion,' he suggested, clicking
his fingers in the air to summon a waiter.

It was the most expensive bottle on the menu. Giorgio
knew that Sam was making a statement: *I can afford the
best and I don't settle for anything less.* It was a power play.
Giorgio decided to take a risk.

'You could . . .' he began thoughtfully. 'Or you could
choose the Barolo 1997. Conditions were perfect in
northern Italy that year, but in France, a cold winter and
heavy summer rains spoiled the yield for the Saint-Émilion,
and the harvest was poor; almost a quarter of the grapes
were lost to botyrus – bunch rot, in layman's terms. The
Barolo therefore has a much smoother texture with big,
fruity flavours, and hints of chocolate and liquorice. That
would be *my* recommendation.'

Sam looked at him appraisingly and Giorgio held his
nerve, meeting Sam's gaze levelly.

'Well, you sure know your shit,' Sam laughed heartily
as the waiter appeared at his side. 'I'll take a bottle of
the Barolo. If it's bad, you owe me.'

'It won't be,' Giorgio said, increasingly confident.

'Giorgio's family own a vineyard in Italy,' Ashley
interjected.

'Is that so?' Sam raised his bushy eyebrows. 'Say, I'd
like to know more about the wine business, I been reading
about it. You know what produced the highest returns in

collectable investments last year? It wasn't gold. It wasn't jewellery. It wasn't even fine art.'

'Wine,' Giorgio nodded sagely.

'Almost twenty per cent return on a vintage bottle of Château Pétrus.' The waiter returned with the bottle of Barolo, pouring a small amount of the viscous, deep-red liquid into Sam's glass for him to taste. 'Ah, perfect timing.'

Sam took his time, bringing it to his nose and inhaling deeply. Then he took a sip, rolling the liquid around in his mouth, before finally swallowing.

'It's good, right?' Giorgio couldn't resist.

'It's superb. It seems I should trust your judgement.'

'Of course. He has great taste,' Ashley giggled, pointing at herself.

'So, tell me more about this little vineyard of yours,' Sam said, sitting forward with interest.

'It's in Avellino, in the Campania region. Inland from the Amalfi Coast. And it's over fifty hectares, so not so little either.'

'Nice. There's an excellent Taurasi produced down there. Casa di Russo. That's not yours, is it?'

Giorgio smiled tightly, trying to look unruffled at the unexpected mention of his fiancée's family business. 'No, it's not. Ours is Castello Bianchi.'

Sam screwed up his face. 'I haven't heard of that one.'

'Allow me to send you a couple of cases.'

'That'd be much appreciated. So, what's the land gonna be worth on a vineyard in Italy? Gotta be pretty good, right?'

'Not what you'd think. It's not the right place for a development if that's what you mean,' Giorgio frowned, trying to follow Sam's train of thought. 'Poor infrastructure, uneven terrain . . .'

'Anywhere can be a goldmine if you market it right, son. You say backwater, I say high-end, ultra-luxurious retreat for stressed-out city folk who want to get off the grid.' That shark-like glint of a smile once again. 'Could be a lot of untapped potential.'

'Uncle Sam, Giorgio doesn't want to talk about wine all night,' Ashley reprimanded him with a pout.

'I guess not. So, let's cut to the chase. Why did you want to meet me?'

'I'm not an idiot,' Ashley turned to Giorgio. 'I didn't think you wanted my uncle's blessing to propose or anything like that.'

Giorgio laughed lightly, trying to stay calm at the mention of marriage. 'Well, my family business is wine, but my passion is real estate,' he began, launching into the pitch he'd rehearsed in front of the mirror. 'My business partners and I have invested in a plot of land with great potential – Newport Beach, Orange County, the Balboa Peninsula. We've drawn up plans for ten luxury beach houses – they'll sell for at least ten million dollars each, a hundred million dollars total, of which a conservative estimate is twenty-five per cent profit. If you want in, we'd value your experience.'

The expression on Sam's face was inscrutable. He narrowed his eyes and looked at Giorgio. 'Not the land by the pier?'

Giorgio nodded, and Sam snorted and slapped his thigh.

'They've been trying to sell that swamp for years. They've taken you for saps. You do your homework, son?'

'Of course—' Giorgio began defensively, but stopped as Sam spoke over him.

'Or did you just see the dollar signs and sign any piece of paper they put in front of you?'

'It's prime real estate land,' Giorgio insisted. 'Ripe for development.'

'It's one of the worst places in the state for coastal erosion, prone to flooding, and mudslides from the Santa Ana mountains. If you even manage to get something built, you'd better hope you can sell them outright to cash buyers, because no bank in their right mind would lend on those properties. They'll be in the sea within a decade.'

Spots of colour had appeared high on Giorgio's cheeks, and there was a sick feeling in his stomach. He was saved from a further assault as the waiter brought the food, but suddenly Giorgio's rack of lamb looked completely unappetizing. Ashley was looking at him with anxious eyes, as she delicately nibbled a forkful of tuna tartare.

Sam rubbed his bristly chin, maintaining his poker face. 'You got all the building permits approved yet?' he asked finally.

'We've hit a few snags,' Giorgio admitted. 'But you have connections, could pull strings with the right committees. You said it yourself – marketed right, anywhere can be a goldmine.'

Sam grinned, hearing his own words parroted back to him.

'What do you need from me to come on board?' Giorgio pushed.

Sam deftly inserted his knife into the whole lobster he'd ordered, breaking the shell with both hands and pulling out the perfectly cooked pink meat. He had Giorgio dangling on a string like a puppet, and he knew it.

'You know what, son? I don't think all this business talk is suitable for the dinner table. Poor Ashley here is gonna expire with boredom. Now, why don't you tell me more about that family vineyard of yours. That sounds *real* interesting to me . . .'

# Chapter 7

## Campania, August 2005

The morning air was warm and sweet smelling, suffused with the delicate floral scent of sprawling azalea bushes and the earthy, fruity aroma from the vineyards. In the distance, a low mist hung over the gentle rise of the Italian hills, while the Russos' country villa was bathed in honey-coloured sunlight. Bella, the dog, was racing round everyone's ankles, letting out a volley of excited barks at the prospect of an adventure.

'I can't believe this is the last time you'll leave this house as a single woman,' Philippa hugged Carina tightly, holding onto her daughter as though they were to be parted for months instead of just twenty-four hours.

'Look after my *principessa*,' Salvatore told Tom gravely as he shook his hand then embraced Carina, planting a kiss on the top of her head.

'Yeah, bye, Sis. You'd better get going before Mamma starts getting your baby pictures out again,' Lorenzo said, which made everyone laugh. Carina's brother had been dragged from his bed to say goodbye, and he was standing bare-chested, wearing just his pyjama bottoms, blinking in the bright daylight.

Carina kissed Rafaella then scooped up Bella before climbing into the passenger seat of Tom's hired Mercedes. She was wearing loose trousers and a fitted vest that hugged her figure and revealed a glimpse of tanned cleavage, while her long hair was pulled back in a casual ponytail. She wore layered gold necklaces that glinted as the sun caught them, the precious metal complementing the diamond engagement ring on her left hand.

'I'll see you tomorrow,' Philippa promised, as she blew a kiss to Carina.

'Drive safely,' Salvatore instructed, as Rafaella and Lorenzo waved sleepily at the departing trio.

Tom turned the key in the ignition and the tyres crunched along the stony driveway, pebbles skittering in their wake. Carina spun round in her seat, waving at her family until they were nothing more than specks in the distance, turning back as they drove through the gate posts that marked the boundary of the Russos' land and began heading south on the narrow country road.

'The scenery here is so beautiful,' Tom said, taking in the view as he drove.

'The best in the world,' Carina agreed. She knew every inch of the countryside round here: the neighbouring farms in the foothills of the Picentini mountains, and the way the colours of the rolling fields changed with the seasons. Today, it was as though she were seeing everything through fresh eyes, imagining the way Tom was viewing the vista for the first time. Her gaze travelled over the wide sweep of the river, the clear water sparkling as it rippled over its rocky bed, and the orange-roofed villages dotted in the valley below them as church bells rang out from ancient stone towers. 'Can you stop the car?' Carina said suddenly.

'What? I—'

'Please, stop the car.'

'Why?' Tom was clearly wondering what on earth was happening, worried he might have a runaway bride on his hands.

'I want to drive.'

Tom shook his head. 'It's part of my job to drive you. Your father requested it.'

'Do you always do what my father says?' Carina asked, a teasing glint in her eye. 'I don't.'

'I do when I've signed a contract.'

'Come on, surely you don't want to spend the next few days being my chauffeur? Or are you scared that I'm a better driver than you?'

'I prefer to be in the driving seat.' Tom's focus remained on the road ahead, his palms resting lightly on the steering wheel. Carina found herself staring at his hands – they were large and strong, and her violet eyes drifted upwards to his muscular arms and his powerful shoulders. His chest was broad and well-built beneath his black T-shirt, and he exuded strength and authority.

His demeanour was a marked contrast to Giorgio, Carina thought as she pulled her gaze away. Her fiancé was full of excess energy, always on the go, always hustling, never centred in himself. Tom seemed like a man in complete control, who could take charge in any situation.

'Oh, I see, you're a good old-fashioned male chauvinist?' she challenged him. 'You think I can't drive as well as you?'

Tom's eyes flicked towards her, inscrutably, before looking back to the road but not before he caught the mischief in her eyes. 'Do you usually get what you want?'

Carina bristled. 'I'm not some spoiled princess,' she shot back, suddenly remembering how her father had waved them off, telling Tom to look after his *principessa*. She thought she detected a smile playing around Tom's lips and tried a different approach. 'Look, this is my final journey from my home to the place where I'm to be married. I'd like to drive it myself. Besides, you'll be right there beside me if anything happens. Which it won't,' she added hastily.

Tom raised an eyebrow. 'Well, I never like to disappoint a woman.'

'I'm glad to hear it.'

'Too fast or too reckless and the deal is off. OK?'

'I'll behave myself,' Carina promised, as Tom flicked the indicator and pulled in at the next rest stop. She gleefully slid out of the car, the two of them passing one another as they crossed in front of the bonnet, their eyes meeting in complicity.

'Now you'll see how Italians drive,' Carina grinned, gunning the engine and roaring into the road, so fast that the tyres squealed.

Tom's jaw tightened and he slammed his hand on the dashboard as he was thrown forward. 'Carina—'

'Can't you take a joke?' she teased, tapping the brakes and slowing down to a more sedate pace, merging smoothly with the traffic as they approached the *auto-strada*. 'Relax, Tom, sit back and enjoy the ride.'

\* \* \*

They wove through spectacular Italian terrain and Carina was pleased to see that Tom appeared relaxed as she drove, enjoying the stunning views, finally glimpsing the dazzling azure sea as they skirted the port city of Salerno with its sweeping bay and charming, pastel-coloured buildings, the dramatic ruins of Arechi Castle clinging to the mountainside above.

'*Stupendo*,' Tom murmured under his breath, and Carina smiled.

'This is why *I* should drive, then it leaves you free to – what's the word my mamma always uses? Gawp.'

'I wouldn't have thought of myself as a "gawper",' he replied good-naturedly. 'But I do appreciate beautiful things.' Their eyes met as he said this, Carina detected the compliment, and experienced a shot of pleasure.

They were at the beginning of the famous 'Amalfitana', the Amalfi Drive, which passed through some of the most naturally beautiful and glamorous locations in the world: Amalfi, Ravello, Positano. At times it was hair-raising, the narrow road hugging the rocky mountainside, twisting and turning round hairpin bends with only a low concrete barrier between the road and the sheer drop to the crashing waves below. But for sheer spectacle and breathtaking beauty, it couldn't be beaten.

'How's my driving?' Carina deliberately checked her mirrors, her hand sliding over to the gearstick. 'Do you feel in safe hands?'

'You handle it well,' Tom acknowledged, adding, tongue in cheek, 'though you go a little too fast at times. *You* should slow down and enjoy the journey. There's no need to try and impress me.'

Carina pretended to be outraged. 'How patronizing. I knew you were a chauvinist.'

'You've got me all wrong,' Tom protested, holding up his hands. 'I'm a feminist.'

'I'm glad to hear it,' Carina laughed. She was enjoying their playful conversation more than she'd enjoyed most conversations with Giorgio recently, where it was all tension.

'Tell me, have you spent a lot of time in Italy?'

'I've visited a few times. We bumped into you once, remember?'

'Oh yes, of course. I was only, what – twelve? Thirteen? I remember thinking you were very handsome.'

'You did?' Tom sounded pleased.

'Yes, although quite arrogant too. And your Italian was awful.'

'No change there then,' he laughed. 'Perhaps I'll get a chance to practise while I'm here.'

'You should. I'll teach you some phrases.'

'All right. Let's start with, "Tom is a much better driver than me."'

Carina narrowed her eyes. *'Il miglior pilota è Carina,'* she said, deliberately emphasizing her name as Tom grinned infuriatingly.

'So, you know many things about me, but I know very little about you,' Carina said, glancing over at him.

'There's nothing to tell.'

'Everyone has something to tell. We have to make the journey pass somehow. Or would you rather sit in silence?'

'I'm perfectly happy in silence.'

'Tom!' Carina laughed and quickly glanced at his hands, resting on his muscular thighs. 'Hmm, no wedding ring.

Although perhaps you don't wear one when you're on a job. Do you have a wife? A girlfriend?'

Tom remained tight-lipped. 'No,' he said eventually. 'It's not really compatible with this kind of lifestyle.'

'But you don't live like a monk, surely?'

Tom sighed, realizing Carina wouldn't give up. 'No. I don't live like a monk. There was someone once . . .' he began, then caught himself. 'And then there wasn't.'

Carina's eyes sparkled at the revelation.

Tom shook his head, clearly annoyed at himself for falling into her trap. 'Oh no, you won't get me that way. You want to talk? Let's talk about you. Tell me about your wedding. About Giorgio. About what colour the bridesmaids' dresses are, and what the canapés are going to be. Tell me everything.'

'You're teasing me, I know you don't care about the canapés. Ask my mother and Bianca, the wedding planner,' Carina laughed. 'I've left most of that to them.'

'But isn't that part of the whole business? Isn't that what all little girls dream about?' said Tom, and Carina wondered if she detected a note of bitterness in his voice.

'You're right. I certainly did. But when it finally came to it, I realized that's not what's important.'

Tom digested her words, looking out of the window and taking in the world-famous view of towering white cliffs covered with lush greenery, the expansive blue vista of sea merging with sky. The winding road ahead offered tantalizing glimpses of colourful fishing villages tucked into picturesque sandy coves, as noisy scooters wove daringly in and out of the traffic. The scent of lemon groves drifted on the sultry air, mixed with the briny tang of the sea. It was a feast for the senses. 'Tell me about him.'

'Giorgio?'

'Yeah. He's a winegrower too, isn't he? Part of the family business?'

'Yes. And he's an entrepreneur. That's why he's in the US right now – having meetings, raising funds, speaking to investors. But it'll be different when we're married.'

'In what way?'

Tom's question was innocent enough, but Carina felt inexplicably defensive. 'He'll stay in the valley most of the time, of course, and we'll run the business together. His father is getting older, he needs more help.'

'How long have you two been together?' Tom asked, steering them onto lighter territory. He pulled down his sun visor, glancing in the mirror at the traffic behind them.

'Forever,' Carina grinned. 'Honestly. He's always been part of my life. We were childhood playmates, then friends, then one day . . . we were something more. It was inevitable really. Everyone expected it.'

'Childhood sweethearts?'

'Yes. We didn't have that bolt-from-the-blue experience, where your heart starts racing as soon as you set eyes on someone . . .' Carina trailed off, her brow wrinkling briefly in thought. 'But Giorgio's very ambitious, full of energy, exciting to be around. He's changed since his mother died, though. Not everyone can see it, but I can. He's become . . .' A frown flitted across her face, which she quickly tried to banish, feeling disloyal. 'I think he wants to prove himself somehow, to make her proud. He feels that life is too short, and he's in a hurry to go everywhere. I know it's because he's still hurting.'

'What happened to her?'

'A car accident,' Carina said, her eyes never leaving the road. 'Not far from here. Vittoria had been in Ravello, having drinks with friends. Perhaps she had one too many. She misjudged a corner, took it too fast. Her car went off the cliff.'

Tom's face darkened. 'You mean . . .?' He let his gaze drift out towards the sheer drop on their left. The view might have been spectacular, but it could be deadly.

Carina nodded, a lump in her throat as she spoke. 'Costa and Giorgio were devastated. Their relationship hasn't been the same since. It should have brought them closer, but it didn't. They're so similar in so many ways – which is probably why they argue so much.'

'I'm sorry,' Tom said gently.

'I know Giorgio will really feel her loss at the wedding. To not have your mother there on your wedding day . . . Perhaps that's why he's been so—' Carina broke off, her features clouded. She frowned, noticing a black Maserati behind them, uncomfortably close.

'I lost my mother a few years ago,' Tom said quietly. 'The circumstances were different – we knew she was ill, so there was time to say goodbye, to make final memories. I can't imagine not having that opportunity.'

'I'm sorry. However it happens, it doesn't make it any easier.' Carina instinctively reached over and placed a hand on Tom's arm. She felt the warmth of his skin, and a crackle of electricity which surprised her and she pulled back quickly, suddenly feeling wrong-footed, like a teenager.

She glanced across at Tom but he twisted round in his seat, staring out of the back window, a frown on his face.

'Anyway, we're not far now,' Carina forced herself to sound breezy, to break the moment.

'Good,' Tom said, his tone serious, his face grave. 'Because I think we're being followed.'

# Chapter 8

**Campania, August 2005**

'I'm going back to bed,' Lorenzo yawned, after he'd waved goodbye to his sister.

'Anyone would think he was still a teenager,' Philippa observed, as Lorenzo sloped back inside, accompanied by Rafaella.

Philippa linked her arm through Salvatore's, resting her head on his shoulder. Seeing her daughter fly the nest had left Philippa feeling nostalgic and emotional, and she longed for comfort from her husband. It felt like the perfect time to speak to Salvatore about her concerns, and for the two of them to recapture some of the closeness they'd lost in recent months.

'Perhaps we should go back to bed too?' she murmured as she nuzzled against him.

Salvatore laughed, lifting her hand to his mouth and kissing it lightly as he disentangled himself. 'I need to start work, *cuore mio*, I have so much to do.'

Philippa's eyes widened in surprise. She tried to ignore the sense of rejection, telling herself that she should be understanding. The deal with Heritage Wines meant Salvatore was busier than ever, and she knew he was concerned about being away from the business for Carina's wedding celebrations in Amalfi. But there was something else too, Philippa was sure of it. Salvatore was eaten up with worry, and he wouldn't share what was troubling him.

'At least come and have breakfast with me before you start work,' Philippa tried again. 'Let's sit down together and talk, I feel as though I've hardly seen you recently. I asked Giulia to make fresh *cornetti* . . . Salvatore, you at least have time for a coffee,' she persevered, sensing that he was about to decline.

'Stop nagging, Philippa,' Salvatore snapped, wrenching his arm away. 'You should understand how much pressure I'm under. And you and Carina are spending money like it's going out of fashion – someone has to pay for this damn wedding.'

He stalked off in the direction of the vineyard leaving Philippa confounded. She turned towards the house, heading for the sanctuary of her private rooms which comprised a study, dressing room and bathroom across from their shared bedroom.

*What had happened?* Philippa thought as she climbed the sweeping staircase, her hand trailing over the smooth marble banister.

She knew Salvatore was feeling under stress with the ongoing demands of the new business, but they'd always worked through any challenges together. He'd never shut her out before. No, this was clearly something bigger, and she couldn't shake the feeling that it was related to Carina's wedding.

The unexpected change made Philippa wonder fleetingly whether he might be having an affair, but she quickly dismissed the possibility. Salvatore had always joked that he was married to the business and Philippa was his mistress. Now it seemed she was no longer enough to tempt him away from his obligations.

Philippa reached her rooms, closing and locking the door behind her. Peaceful and cool, decorated in neutral tones with mementos of her Scottish roots, the familiar surroundings immediately calmed her.

She paused for a moment to steady her breathing, catching sight of herself in the long mirror of her dressing room. She wasn't so different from the slender beauty she'd been when she and Salvatore had first met, was she? Inevitably time had taken gentle effect on both of them, but they'd aged *together*, understanding and appreciating the changes in one another.

Her gaze fell on the large white box that sat open in front of her wardrobe, the white silk garment inside escaping from its tissue paper and spilling out over the edges. Philippa stared at her wedding dress, assailed by memories.

She had taken it from its storage place in the attic to show Carina the previous day. The two of them had spent the afternoon laughing at Philippa's exquisite gown, with the puffed Eighties sleeves. Reminiscing about her wedding day had brought Philippa's current disquiet into sharp focus, and she couldn't help but remember her hopes and dreams for the future on that magical day over twenty-five years ago . . .

Philippa held the delicate fabric to her face, feeling the smooth sheen of the silk against her cheek, imagining that she could still detect the scent of the Miss Dior perfume she had worn on her wedding day.

*This won't do, Philippa.*

Salvatore had grown distant from her and she didn't know why. Her eyes drifted over to the window, gazing out at row upon row of grapevines that stretched as far as the eye could see. Finally, she spotted Salvatore, walking in the grounds with his second-in-command, Dario, gesticulating in his familiar, passionate manner. Philippa felt the undeniable pull deep in her belly as she watched him. She *did* still love him, she was certain of that, and she was prepared to fight for her marriage. But if Salvatore wouldn't fight for *her*, what then?

She was still young, and still full of curiosity and excitement about the world. Philippa didn't know what was happening to Salvatore, but she knew one thing. There was no way she was prepared to carry on being unhappy.

Something would have to change.

Carina's heart was racing; it was impossible to go anywhere on the narrow, single-lane road that wove around the vertiginous cliff-face, and all she could do was glance back at the black Maserati behind them. She couldn't see the driver's face.

'Keep your eyes on the road,' Tom instructed her. He remained looking straight ahead, using his visor mirror to watch the car that was tailing them.

As they turned off onto the private track that led to the Villa Amore, the Maserati continued on the main road, and Carina let out the shaky breath she'd been holding.

Moments later, they pulled up outside the majestic villa, which rose out of the cliff as though carved from the rock itself. It was painted pale pink, with white windows and white stone balustrade balconies from which it offered unsurpassed views over the Gulf of Salerno.

'Welcome to the Villa Amore,' Carina announced, almost laughing in relief. Her legs were shaking as she climbed out of the car, and she saw Tom looking at her in concern.

'It's OK,' he said quietly, as though talking to a skittish animal.

'But what about—' Carina broke off as Tom walked over, resting a hand reassuringly on her shoulder.

'I took their number plate. I'll make some calls. You're fine, I promise you. But from now on, I drive. OK?'

Carina nodded, bending down and scooping up Bella, burying her face in her soft fur for comfort.

'Signorina Russo, welcome!' came a shout as the front door opened and Paola Simoni, the housekeeper at Villa Amore who'd known Carina since she was a baby, burst into an effusive greeting. 'I'm so happy to see you, we're all so excited for your wedding!'

Paola was in her late sixties, round-cheeked and full-figured, her greying hair pulled back into a bun. She wore a traditional housekeeper's black dress with white collar and apron, and black lace-up pumps on her feet.

'Thank you, Paola,' Carina smiled, delighted to see her as she followed her into the house. She was eager to get inside, to safety. 'This is Tom, an old friend of the family, from England,' she continued, without elaborating further.

Paola stared at him – in curiosity, and appreciation – but knew it wasn't her place to ask questions. 'If you need anything,' she said to him, in halting English, 'Please ask.'

'*Grazie mille,*' Tom replied, and Carina was amused to see how Paola looked coy and smiled in return. Tom certainly had charisma.

They were standing in the opulent, double-height entrance hall, a mezzanine balcony overhead, the floor tiled in polished granite. Decorated in a neoclassical style, there were marble pillars and Roman statues atop heavy-looking plinths, sweeping archways and ornate mouldings.

'I didn't think anything could top the house in Campania, but this is impressive,' Tom said as he looked around.

'The villa was a gift from my papà to my mamma on the eve of their wedding,' Carina told him.

'Well, he set the bar pretty high for everyone else getting married,' Tom laughed.

Carina knew he wasn't referring to Giorgio, but she felt the sting all the same; would Giorgio have a grand gesture planned for her?

It seemed ironic, somehow, that her fiancé wasn't there with her in the run-up to the wedding, yet her father was paying for another man to follow her around. Carina had expected to find Tom's presence annoying and intrusive but, after everything that had happened today, she was grateful to have him with her. She turned to see him watching her and couldn't help but notice how he filled the space around him, his shoulders broad, his solid frame towering above her. Tom looked at her coolly; Carina realized she was staring at him.

'Paola, could you please arrange for Mr Ryan's bags to be taken to the blue bedroom,' she asked, confused at feeling a little flustered by his gaze. *That's why he's a bodyguard, he's good at throwing people off.*

'Of course, right away.' Paola bustled off, and Carina followed at a more sedate pace with Tom, showing him each room as they passed.

The house was a hive of activity; Carina could sense it already, hearing the shouts between the staff, the sounds of furniture being moved, and a gazebo being constructed. Over the next few days, her friends and family would begin arriving, and a spectacular party was being planned. Salvatore had even chartered a yacht to take everyone out to the Grotta dello Smeraldo, and the five days of festivities would culminate in the wedding itself. It was really happening, Carina realized; there was no turning back.

'This is the oldest part of the building,' she explained, as they reached a series of wood-panelled, low-ceilinged rooms. They were far smaller than those in their sprawling villa in the countryside, but each one was a tiny gem, lovingly restored and decorated immaculately. 'It dates back to the fourteenth century and has been in my family for generations. The building had been neglected almost to the point of ruin, but when my mother saw it she fell in love – almost as much as she did with my father – and it became her project. It took the best part of a decade to create the house you see now, but it was worth it.'

'It certainly was,' Tom agreed, and Carina felt a rush of pride. Once again, she saw the property anew, as though through Tom's eyes, taking in the grand fireplaces and tasteful frescoes, the way the distinctive Mediterranean light filtered through the picture windows, spilling onto the parquet floors. For some inexplicable reason she wanted him to love the place.

They climbed a spiral staircase, ascending two floors to the very top of the building.

'The family rooms are on this level,' Carina informed Tom. 'The floor below is used for guests.'

'Will you have people staying here for the party?'

'Yes. There are ten bedrooms downstairs, and they'll mostly be taken by family – people will be coming from all over Italy, from both our families. Everyone else will stay at the Hotel San Marco in town. I think we've taken over practically the whole place,' Carina laughed.

Tom nodded. 'I'll take a look around later. Security risks, access points and so on.'

'No problem.'

'Is there a basement?'

'There's a wine cellar.'

'Naturally,' Tom grinned. 'I'm looking forward to seeing that.'

'I'll show you later,' Carina promised. 'Now, your room is in here – ah, yes, your bags have been brought up already.' She pushed open the door to a room that was airy and bright, decorated in shades of blue as though mirroring the sea and sky beyond. Carina was anxious to see what Tom thought. She wanted him to like it too, though she wasn't sure why it mattered.

'There's the most wonderful view of the bay,' she chattered on. 'I know, because I have an almost identical view – I'm just next door,' she explained, her cheeks flushing as she realized how that might sound. 'My father suggested I give you this room, so you can be close by . . .'

'That makes sense.' Tom strolled over to the window, his hands in his pockets, languidly taking in the stunning views. The room looked out over the narrow terrace, dominated by an inviting swimming pool, and flanked by gardens on either side. Beyond lay the vista the region was renowned for – the sensational coastline in all its glory.

'Isn't it the most beautiful sight?' Carina said, joining him at the window. 'Once you've seen this view, it will stay in your heart forever.'

Tom fell silent, taking in her words. He turned to look at her, and Carina was suddenly aware of their proximity, his muscular body barely inches from hers.

'Signorina Russo?'

Carina jumped as Paola appeared in the doorway.

'This package just arrived for you.'

'Thank you.' Carina moved away, putting physical distance between her and Tom, grateful to Paola for breaking the moment.

Paola was holding a large cardboard carrier, the sort used to transport bouquets. Carina's heart leapt. Perhaps Giorgio had sent her flowers? She'd been struggling to get hold of him – he hadn't been picking up her calls, only responding to her messages with the briefest of replies. He rarely gave her flowers, but maybe this was his way of apologizing, of letting her know he was thinking about her.

'Let me,' Tom said anxiously, taking the box from Paola as she left the room.

'Oh Tom, it's only flowers,' Carina laughed as she opened it. 'It's too light to be a bomb . . .' She trailed off as she peered inside, her face crumpling in confusion.

'What is it?' Tom asked, moving her aside.

'I'm not sure exactly . . .' Carina took a step backwards as Tom reached inside and pulled out what had once been a bouquet of flowers. A dozen black roses, in fact. Only now they were dead and decaying, tied together with a red ribbon.

'I don't understand,' Carina murmured. The gesture felt somehow sinister, but she couldn't say why. She glanced up at Tom, and his face was deadly serious.

'Is there a note?' he wondered, looking inside once again.

'Yes,' Carina swallowed. 'Here.' She tore it off the front of the box, her stomach churning. Like witnessing a car crash, she found she couldn't look away from the horror unfolding in front of her. With shaking hands, she opened the envelope.

There was one word, written in stark black capital letters: BITCH.

Tom didn't even pause, sprinting out of the room and down two flights of stairs, back to the entrance hall and out of the front door.

Carina tried to follow but couldn't match his speed. She caught up with him as he came back inside. She was panting lightly, but Tom wasn't even out of breath.

'Anything?' she asked, half-hopeful, half-fearful.

'Whoever delivered it is long gone.'

Paola dashed into the entrance hall, looking flustered. 'What's the matter?' she asked. 'All this commotion!'

'Did you see who delivered the package you brought up to Carina?' Tom demanded.

'A moped courier. We had so many packages arriving this week, they're coming and going every few minutes.'

'Did you see their face?'

'No, they were wearing a helmet. Why, what's happened?'

Carina stared at Tom. She was still in shock and couldn't seem to think straight. Was the package really for her?

But who was it from? And what did they want? She realized Paola was waiting for an answer, and shook her head subtly at Tom. She adored Paola, but she was a terrible gossip, and Carina didn't want this getting back to her father.

'Nothing,' Tom replied shortly. He turned to Carina, his gaze intense. 'Can I speak with you, privately?'

'Of course.'

Tom gestured for her to go ahead, and Carina led the way to Salvatore's study, where she knew they wouldn't be interrupted. She felt sick, a cold sweat breaking out over her skin. Most of all, she was incredibly grateful to have Tom around. Without him, she daren't think about what might happen to her.

# Chapter 9

**Los Angeles, August 2005**

Giorgio Bianchi opened his eyes and glanced over at the sleeping form of Ashley Hall. There were no blinds or curtains at the floor-to-ceiling windows in the bedroom of her Bel Air mansion, and the moonlight flooded in, falling on the Egyptian cotton sheets draped across her naked body.

He wondered what had woken him, then heard his phone vibrating softly on the bedside table, the light glowing softly. He rolled over, reading the name on the screen: Isabella.

Then the ringing stopped and the notification popped up on screen: 11 missed calls. All from Isabella.

Christ, what was it with this girl, Giorgio thought in disbelief. It was as though she was stalking him.

He sat up and took a slug of water from the bottle by his bed. Tonight had been a great night. After Spago, he, Ashley and Sam had hit the bars in West Hollywood.

It was intoxicating to see how he was treated when he was with them, it was as though they were gods, rather than mere mortals. Both uncle and niece had fame, money, power, and Giorgio was dazzled by their lifestyle. He wanted it for himself.

He and Ashley had eventually bid goodnight to Sam, leaving him in the company of some very obliging ladies, before making their way back to Ashley's where things quickly got hot and heavy, Ashley's touch driving out all thoughts of Carina back home in Italy.

The phone began ringing once again, Isabella's name flashing angrily on the screen. Giorgio felt a deep stab of annoyance. He looked over at Ashley. Confident that she was sound asleep, her chest gently rising and falling, Giorgio rolled stealthily out of bed and pulled on his boxers, grabbing his phone and slipping noiselessly from the room.

'What do you want?' he hissed, as he hit the button to answer the call.

'Giorgio! How rude. Is that any way to greet an old friend?' Isabella purred.

'Isabella, it's the middle of the night here. You've been calling non-stop. What the hell do you want?'

'Middle of the night? Where are you?'

'LA. Not that it's any of your business.'

'Los Angeles? How glamorous. But why aren't you in Italy, with your *fiancée*?' She drew out the final word, making it sound sarcastic.

Giorgio sighed as he padded along the thickly carpeted corridors, past the giant nude black-and-white photograph of Ashley that dominated the landing, and down the wide, curving staircase where the walls were lined with framed prints of her most famous front covers: *Vogue*, *Sports Illustrated*, *W*.

'I'm working,' he retorted. 'Some of us have to make a legitimate income.'

Isabella laughed outrageously. 'Oh, Giorgio. You don't have to pull that bullshit with me. I know you too well.'

Giorgio bristled at the insult. 'What do you want, Isabella? Tell me before I hang up.'

'Well, I was just calling to RSVP.' Isabella's smirk was audible all the way from Europe. 'It's with great pleasure that I'll be attending your wedding.'

'Thank you for letting me know. Is that all?' Giorgio strode through the kitchen and opened a side door, stepping outside. The night air was cool and refreshing as he walked over to the pool, hidden from sight of the house by a perfectly manicured line of privet hedge. He could see the lights of the mega-mansions dotted across the Santa Monica mountains, and in the distance he heard the howl of a coyote.

'Why are you marrying *her*, Giorgio.' Isabella's tone was almost a whine. 'I know you don't love her. Not really. Remember when we drove to Sorrento and we checked into that little hotel and you wanted me to—'

'Yes, Isabella,' Giorgio interrupted. 'I remember.' He recalled every detail; Isabella was a wild cat, and she'd given him a night he'd never forget.

'We were so good together, you and I . . .' Isabella murmured, her voice low and seductive. 'Why would you walk away from that?'

'I'm marrying Carina,' Giorgio insisted through gritted teeth.

'You should be marrying me!'

'Goodbye, Isabella.' Giorgio went to ring off.

'Think about it, Giorgio. Think about everything I could offer you. Money . . . connections . . . power. Together we'd be unstoppable.'

'You know that can never happen.'

'My father is the most powerful man in Campania. You don't want to make an enemy of him.'

'Are you threatening me?' Giorgio laughed harshly. 'I don't need you. I've got money and connections of my own.'

'Have you, Giorgio?' Isabella's tone was one of disbelief. 'I think we both know you've benefited from my father in one way or another over the years.'

Giorgio had gone pale; suddenly he didn't feel quite so confident.

'When are you flying back?' Isabella continued, knowing she'd regained the upper hand. 'I could pick you up from the airport if you like, drive you back from Naples. We could have a little chat about what I could do for you, and what you could do for me . . .'

Giorgio hesitated, aware that he had to stay on her good side; Isabella could be dangerous and he knew it. What she'd said was true – her family were powerful, connected. He didn't want to piss her off.

'Look, it's late here and I can't talk right now. I'll call you, OK?'

'You promise?' He could feel her pout across the continents.

'Sure.'

'I knew you couldn't stay away from me,' she purred.

'Look, Isabella, don't do anything . . . Don't do anything crazy, you know?'

'I don't know what you mean,' she replied with faux innocence. *'Ciao, mio amato.'*

The line went dead, and Giorgio exhaled slowly. The moon was large and low in the dark sky and he stared at it, his mind ticking. He had a bad feeling in the pit of his stomach. Isabella De Luca was trouble with a capital T.

## Amalfi

*'Mamma mia*, it's been so busy today, I'm exhausted,' Paola exclaimed as she bustled into the kitchen, smoothing down her uniform. 'All the other staff have gone home and now it is just me. So, my little one, what can I get you and your guest to eat this evening?'

'Oh no, don't worry, you've done more than enough today and it's going to get even busier,' Carina insisted. In truth, she wanted to be alone with her thoughts, to finally stop pretending that everything was OK and try to process what had happened today; the Maserati following them, the bouquet of dead black roses arriving at the villa . . .

'But you must eat, Signorina Russo.'

'I'll make something. Honestly, I'm quite capable. You get off home – tomorrow there'll be even more to do, so you need to rest.'

Paola looked torn.

'Go,' Carina told her firmly. 'I'll be fine, I promise. I have Tom to keep me company.'

'All right,' Paola agreed finally. 'Thank you. I made chicken and rice for Bella – I'll give her a bowl before I leave – and I'll see you tomorrow, bright and early. Good night,' she addressed both of them.

'*Buona notte*,' Tom responded in Italian, making Carina smile.

Paola left, and Carina was suddenly aware that she was alone in the villa with Tom; it was one of the few times in her life that the place wasn't full of family chatter.

'Are you all right?' Tom asked softly.

'Fine. What shall we eat?' Carina said briskly, moving across to the deep stone sink and washing her hands.

'You don't have to make me anything.'

'I'd like to – it'll keep my mind occupied. Besides, I enjoy cooking. I don't get the chance to do it very often.'

'In that case I'll gratefully accept. Whatever you're making will be more than fine.'

Carina could feel Tom's eyes on her as she moved around the kitchen, setting a pan of water to boil on the range cooker, taking spaghetti and olive oil from the pantry, lemon and garlic from the storage cupboards.

'Would you like a glass of wine?' she asked, as she uncorked a bottle of Pinot Bianco.

'Thanks, but no. I don't drink on the job.'

'You're off duty now, surely?' But Tom just gave her another of his inscrutable half-smiles.

Carina hesitated, then poured a glass for herself and a water for Tom. He reached over and picked up the wine bottle, turning it over in his hands. 'Good choice. And it goes perfectly with lemon,' he added, as Carina began grating the zest.

She looked at him, impressed. 'You're quite the connoisseur,' she teased.

'My father's a wine importer. I couldn't help it.'

'My father speaks very highly of him,' Carina said, adding butter and cream to a pan. 'And you didn't want to follow in his footsteps?'

'No, I . . . decided to take a different path.'

'You were in the army, weren't you?'

Tom nodded.

'Do you miss it?' Carina saw his shoulders tense, and immediately regretted the question. 'You don't like to talk about it?'

'No,' Tom shook his head. 'It's all right . . . Your life is always planned for you in the army, and sometimes that can be a good thing. But I don't miss hearing that a mission has failed, or that someone didn't make it, or— Look let's not talk about this.' Tom looked up, forcing a smile onto his face. 'Nothing worse than listening to the grumblings of an old soldier. You don't want to know about me.'

*But I do . . .* Carina thought.

'How about you?' Tom asked. 'Do you want to be part of the family business, or are you desperate to escape as soon as you can?'

'Oh, I love it, I don't ever want to do anything else. My brother's the one who wanted to escape – he's studying to be an architect, in Milan – but I inherited the vintner gene.'

'Will you combine the two vineyards after the wedding?'

Carina frowned. 'I don't know. Giorgio and I haven't really spoken about it,' she said, knowing it was a lie. 'He seems to think that I won't want to work, that I'll become a mother as soon as possible and that will be my role.'

'Is that what you want?'

Carina hesitated '. . . I do want children eventually, but there's lots I want to accomplish first. Lots of Italian men are so traditional, and see a woman's place as being at home, becoming a mamma and then growing into a nonna. What about all the other parts of life?' Carina forced a smile, but deep down she was troubled. It was the first time she'd voiced her fears out loud – she hadn't even spoken to her mother or Edie about her concerns – and now she wondered whether she'd said too much or been disloyal by confiding in Tom.

'Let's eat on the terrace,' Carina suggested, as she dished up bowls of spaghetti al limone. Tom picked up their drinks and followed her outside, where they sat down at a wrought-iron table beside the balcony, Bella lying down at her mistress's feet.

'Do you ever get used to this view?' Tom asked, pulling his aviator sunglasses from his top pocket and slipping them on. The sun was beginning to set, pinks and oranges streaking the sky as the shadows lengthened across the pool. Two stone pine trees were silhouetted against the palatial house, while swallows swooped overhead in the twilight, darting in and out of a nest they'd built beneath the eaves. A sliver of crescent moon emerged, bright and white above them, and everything felt peaceful and calm. It was idyllic.

'I try not to get too blasé. I know I'm very lucky, and hope I don't take it for granted.'

'You love it here, don't you?' Tom said as he forked a mouthful of pasta. 'This is delicious, by the way.'

'Thank you,' Carina smiled, inexplicably pleased by his praise. It felt good to do something nice for someone and feel appreciated in return. 'Yes, I do love it. I spent time living in London, but my heart is always here. I don't think I'll ever want to leave.'

'You lived in London?'

'I went to university there, to study business.'

Tom said nothing, simply raising an eyebrow.

'You're surprised?'

'I'm slowly coming to realize that you're full of surprises,' he smiled. 'You're nothing like I expected you to be.'

'And what did you expect?'

'A diva,' he confessed. 'I almost didn't take the job.'

'I'm glad you did,' she replied, before she realized what she was saying.

It was growing dark and Carina stared out to sea at the pinpricks of light from the yachts bobbing on the waves. She wondered whether anyone out there was a threat; whether she was being watched right now by someone who wanted to hurt her. Since that day in Positano, the fear was always at the back of her mind, and today she'd been confronted with it – the implicit threat was impossible to ignore. She shivered, even though the night air was warm.

'Do you think someone wants to hurt me?' she asked Tom, studying his face intently to read his reaction. 'Seriously, I mean.'

Tom looked her straight in the eye. 'I don't know,' he said honestly. 'But you don't need to be afraid. Nothing will happen to you,' he insisted with certainty. 'I'll protect you with my life. I promise.'

# Chapter 10

**Los Angeles, August 2005**

'You can go right on through, ma'am.'

'Thank you.' Edie smiled generously at the attractive male attendant as he handed back her passport, then strolled through to the VIP lounge at LAX, Los Angeles International Airport. She helped herself to a selection of magazines and a glass of champagne, before finding a quiet spot by the window and sinking down onto one of the plush sofas.

Edie was dressed for travelling, in a casual tracksuit and an oversized cashmere scarf, a travel bag slung over her arm. From it, she pulled out the latest copy of the script for her upcoming movie, *The Heights*, and took a sip from her glass, as she tried to learn her lines for one of the pivotal scenes: where her character, Cathy, confides in the housekeeper, Nelly, of her love for Heathcliff.

Fifteen minutes later, her glass of champagne was empty, but she couldn't recall a single word that she'd read.

For some reason, Edie was finding it impossible to concentrate. She gazed out of the window, watching the planes take off into the smoggy LA sky, imagining all the exotic destinations they were heading to: Hawaii, Tahiti, Bermuda, Rio. Although Edie could hardly complain, she thought. She was flying first class overnight to Rome, before an internal flight to Naples. From there, a car would take her to the Villa Amore where, as chief bridesmaid, she was staying as a guest of the family. Edie had been to the magnificent house a number of times over the past few years, but this time, she would have given anything *not* to be going.

Her stomach twisted as she contemplated the next few days. After what she'd done, her friendship with Carina felt like a sham, but at least Carina was blissfully oblivious and for that Edie was grateful. She felt as though her terrible secret was waiting to be discovered, forever fearful that something would give her away. Edie was going to have to rely on all her acting skills to get her through this wedding.

Her phone beeped and she jumped. Nathan's name appeared on the screen:

**Have a safe flight. Give my love to Carina x**

Edie exhaled slowly, a whole host of emotions coursing through her, though guilt was the primary one. But she had to stay firm, Edie told herself. It was better for them both that they were no longer together. She didn't deserve a good guy like Nathan, and he'd be devastated if he knew what she'd done . . .

Edie picked up her script again, pushing the shame and anguish from her mind. She'd barely finished the page when a movement by the door caught her attention. A man – medium height, dark hair, expensive suit – had just walked in.

Her heart began to race, her gut clenching, but within seconds she realized with relief that he was a stranger. He glanced across at Edie and she smiled politely then cast her gaze back down, as her pulse returned to normal. She wasn't in the mood to make small talk.

For a horrible moment, she'd thought it was Giorgio. There'd been something in the set of the guy's shoulders, the tilt of his head, that had made her think of Carina's fiancé. Edie didn't know whether he was still in Los Angeles, but she'd considered the possibility that they might be on the same flight, and the thought made her shudder.

It had been a complete shock to see him in Spago with Ashley Hall and Sam Quinn. Edie wondered what on earth he'd been doing with them, but she felt certain it couldn't be anything good. She didn't trust Giorgio Bianchi one iota and knew from bitter experience what a snake he was. It was a mystery to her that Carina couldn't see it, that such an intelligent, astute woman could be so thoroughly taken in by him, but Carina was blinkered when it came to Giorgio. Their families were stuck together like glue.

Edie flashed back to her last encounter with Giorgio, at the Villa Amore. Carina had invited her to visit, and Edie had found it impossible to say no; she'd kept inventing work commitments, but Carina was persistent, and eventually Edie had given in, agreeing to a long weekend when Carina had mentioned that Giorgio would be away.

His plans had changed at the last minute, and the confrontation he and Edie had had was etched on her mind, playing on a permanent loop so that she was forced to relive it . . .

*'I didn't know you were going to be here,' Edie insisted, as she sat awkwardly in the opulent drawing room of Villa Amore while Giorgio paced menacingly before her. Carina had stepped outside to take a phone call from her mother. 'Carina said you'd be away.'*

*'If you've even so much as hinted—'*

*'Of course not.'*

*'Good. Keep your mouth shut.' His tone was cold. Edie wondered if Carina had ever seen this side of Giorgio. She hoped not.*

*'Look, there's something you need to know . . .' Edie began, her eyes darting nervously towards the door.*

*'Why should it interest me?'*

*Giorgio's dismissive retort fired Edie's anger. Until now she'd been scared and nervous. 'Oh, this will interest you all right,' she hissed.*

*She told him the basics – just the bare facts, without emotion. Nothing about how terrified she'd been, how heartbroken, how conflicted. Giorgio had regarded her coldly, not a speck of empathy or humanity crossing his features.*

*'How do I know you're telling the truth? Convenient that there's no proof any of this happened?'*

*Edie gasped as though he'd slapped her, his words crueller than any blow his hands could inflict.*

*'If you say anything to Carina, I'll tell her you're a lying, manipulative bitch. And who do you think she'll believe?' His eyes were cold slits. Like a lizard. Edie couldn't believe she'd ever thought he was handsome or charming.*

*She had a horrible feeling that Giorgio was right. Carina was her best friend, but her loyalty would always be to Giorgio and the Bianchis, and Edie would be out in the cold.*

*'But—' she began, stopping abruptly as Carina walked back into the room. Edie tried to compose herself, to force a smile, but Carina could sense immediately that something was wrong.*

*'Darling, we've missed you.' Giorgio held Carina by the waist and kissed her head.*

*Carina laughed. 'You're my two favourite people, I'm so glad we're all here together for once . . .'*

*Giorgio gave Edie a fake smile that didn't reach his eyes.*

*'Why don't we all go out for dinner?' Carina suggested.*

*Edie couldn't think of anything she wanted to do less. The idea of spending time with Giorgio made her feel sick.*

*'Edie's come all this way to see you,' Giorgio replied smoothly. 'You don't want me cramping your style. I'll leave you two to catch up.' He kissed Carina, shot a warning look at Edie, and strode out of the door.*

*Carina came to sit beside Edie, enfolding her in a warm hug. 'I'm so glad you're here.'*

*Edie stiffened in Carina's arms, and it took all of Edie's strength not to tell her the truth right there and then.*

'Ma'am? Ma'am . . .'

Edie glanced up. The handsome attendant was there once again, and the lounge was almost empty.

'They've just made the last call for your flight, ma'am.'

Edie started, jolted back to reality. 'Thank you,' she exclaimed, jumping up and grabbing her bag, ignoring the nerves jangling in her stomach as she rushed towards the departure gate.

**Amalfi**

Philippa had arrived at the Villa Amore that morning, and now she and Carina were strolling arm in arm through the quaint back streets of Amalfi. Tom followed behind at a discreet distance. He was wearing black trousers with a short-sleeved shirt and dark sunglasses; with his light tan and blonde hair, he could have passed for a monied, sophisticated tourist, one of the many who flocked to the Amalfi Coast in the summer months.

'I could get used to this,' Philippa whispered to Carina. 'Being followed round by a handsome young man.'

'Mamma!' Carina exclaimed in shock.

'What?' Philippa laughed. 'It's true. Just because you're married doesn't mean you stop noticing attractive members of the opposite sex. In all seriousness, I'm glad Tom's here, and so is your father. It sets our minds at rest, knowing he's with you.'

'How is Papà?' Carina asked, changing the subject. She absolutely didn't want Philippa to know about the car that had followed them yesterday, or the bizarre dead flower bouquet. 'I thought he might come with you.'

'Same old Papà,' Philippa said airily, not wanting her daughter to suspect that anything was amiss. 'Always working. He has some loose ends to tie up with the Heritage Estates contract, and I think he's worried about being away from the vineyard for too long. You know what he's like.'

'I know,' Carina nodded. She squeezed her mother's arm and added, 'I can only hope that in twenty-five years' time Giorgio and I are as happy as you and Papà. He loves you so much.'

Philippa fell silent, unsure how to respond. It would have been impossible to confide in her daughter that she and Salvatore weren't as blissfully happy as Carina thought they were. Nor could Philippa share her fears that Carina's marriage might encounter the same issues. Like Salvatore, Giorgio appeared to be a workaholic, and Philippa knew first-hand the problems that could bring; the feeling of playing second fiddle as your spouse worked round the clock, with birthdays and anniversaries no longer a priority, and your own aspirations never taken seriously. Philippa wasn't even sure that Giorgio realized Carina had ambitions of her own, and wasn't ready to simply stay at home and raise a future generation of Bianchis.

'You know, darling, love can change over time . . .' Philippa said tentatively, daring to broach the subject that had been on her mind for a while now.

'I know, Mamma, I'm a grown-up,' Carina answered firmly, putting an end to her probing, and Philippa understood. Today was a special day after all. It wasn't the right time to air her anxieties.

'Never mind. Come on, we're almost there.'

They were in a picturesque little passageway just north of the cathedral, in the warren of streets off the bustling Via Lorenzo, the main artery running through the heart of Amalfi. The houses were tall and narrow, painted in cream and terracotta and blush pink, so close together that it was almost possible to lean out of an upper window and shake the hand of your neighbour across the street. There were balconies on every level, with brightly coloured geraniums bursting from ceramic pots, and traditional wrought-iron lanterns hanging from the centuries-old buildings.

Moments later they reached the discreet shop front. It was tucked away between an antique book shop and a pasticceria whose window displayed delicious-looking cream puffs and delicate chocolate tartlets, strawberry-topped *millefoglie* and freshly baked *sfogliatelle* filled with lemon and ricotta. An ivory awning above the door read *D'Angelo* in gold writing, and a lone mannequin was displayed in the window, wearing an incredible gown made from vivid scarlet shantung silk.

The bell rang as they entered and Philippa waited expectantly. She never tired of coming here; it was a veritable Aladdin's Cave, with bolts of fabric stacked from floor to ceiling: finely woven taffeta that shone in the shafts of sunlight falling in through the courtyard door at the rear; gossamer light crêpe de Chine; brightly coloured taffetas; and even, Philippa noticed in surprise, a heavy roll of Royal Stewart tartan. Philippa knew that the first floor housed a workroom, where the walls were lined with apothecary cabinets, every drawer crammed to bursting with fabric-covered buttons and seed pearls and sequins, marabou feathers for trimming ball gowns and rolls of stiff grosgrain ribbon.

'Philippa!'

Lucrezia D'Angelo emerged from the back room through a white voile curtain and greeted her old friend. Lucrezia was an elegant Italian lady in her early seventies, perfectly poised and sharp as a tack. Her grey hair was swept up and she wore an elegant, beautifully cut navy-blue dress, gold-rimmed glasses on a chain around her neck.

Lucrezia had been a friend of the Russo family for many years. A renowned seamstress, she did all the tailoring for Philippa and Carina's clothes, nipping and tucking dresses and trousers so that the fit was impeccable. She also made incredible, unique, couture garments, and had dressed both women for prestigious events such as the Italian Wine Awards, the Venice Carnival, and the Amalfi Regatta. Lucrezia was a closely guarded secret among the well-heeled women of the region and, as soon as Giorgio had proposed, Carina had announced that she wanted Lucrezia to make her wedding dress – just as she'd made Philippa's twenty-five years earlier.

'Carina! Ah, but you look radiant my dear. You truly will be the most beautiful bride. And who is this?' Lucrezia asked, turning her penetrating gaze on Tom, who was standing rather awkwardly in the tiny shop. His bulk seemed magnified, his physical size dominating the small space.

'This is Tom. He's an old friend of the family,' Carina introduced him as she had to Paola. It seemed the easiest, most discreet way to explain his presence.

Tom stepped forward and shook Lucrezia's hand, addressing her politely in Italian.

Philippa was impressed. He had excellent manners, and from the little she'd seen already, he took his job of looking after Carina extremely seriously.

'*Va bene*,' Lucrezia nodded, with one final glance at Tom before turning back to Carina. 'You have lost a little more weight, I think?'

'Perhaps. It wasn't deliberate – I've been so busy with everything going on.'

'You must not lose any more. Today, we will make the final alterations and the dress will fit you perfectly.'

'I'll make sure,' Carina promised, adding laughingly, 'I'll have pasta and wine every night.'

'Your speciality,' Tom smiled, speaking without thinking. The three women turned to look at him.

'You must live a very sheltered life,' Carina laughed, coming to his rescue. 'I gave Paola the evening off and made dinner for Tom last night,' she explained, as Philippa raised her eyebrows in surprise.

'*Allora*,' Lucrezia exclaimed, clasping her hands together. 'Come with me, Carina. I have your dress ready.'

Carina took a deep breath and followed Lucrezia through the curtain to the back room, anticipation written all over her face. Despite her misgivings, Philippa couldn't help but feel flutters of excitement on behalf of her daughter. She remembered all too well the feeling of being fitted for her wedding gown – in this very same shop – and knew what a huge moment it was to finally see yourself in the dress that fulfilled all your hopes and dreams. It was a moment one could never forget . . .

'*Oh! Ma quanto sei bella!*'

Philippa was interrupted from her reminiscing as she heard Lucrezia's exclamations, followed by the clack of low heels on the stone floor. As Philippa looked up, Lucrezia pulled back the curtain and Carina glided through.

Philippa gasped, tears springing to her eyes as she took in the vision before her. Carina's dress was custom-made in white Italian silk, overlaid with exquisitely detailed, handmade Burano lace. Her arms and shoulders were covered, as befitted what would be a traditional, Roman Catholic ceremony, and the whole look was reminiscent of Grace Kelly's elegant style. The gown fitted Carina perfectly, emphasizing the curves of her body, her slim waist and perfectly proportioned figure. Philippa had been present at previous fittings but today, seeing the look of pride and happiness on Carina's face, she felt overwhelmed with emotion.

'You look incredible, my darling.'

'Thank you, Mamma,' Carina murmured. She turned slowly from side to side, staring at herself in the long mirrors either side of the door, then her gaze moved elsewhere, as though seeking someone else's approval.

Philippa turned her head to follow Carina's eyeline. She'd forgotten about Tom, standing silently at the back of the shop. He was silent, regarding her without speaking.

'You don't like my dress?' Carina asked him, feeling briefly anxious.

Tom hesitated before speaking, 'You'll make a beautiful bride. Giorgio is very lucky.' For a moment his gaze didn't break with Carina's.

'Poor Tom,' Philippa swept in. 'Wedding dress appraisal isn't in his job description, darling.'

They laughed, breaking the tension, and Philippa found herself wondering whether she'd imagined the expressions she'd seen on their faces.

'You *do* look beautiful, Carina,' Philippa said, embracing her daughter carefully so as not to damage the dress. 'Giorgio will be dumbstruck when he sees you walking down the aisle.'

Carina hugged her mother before returning to the changing room, but not before Philippa caught another look pass between Tom and Carina, one that only added to her worries.

# Chapter 11

**Amalfi, August 2005**

'Edie!' Carina bounced towards her best friend with a squeal of excitement, enveloping her in a warm hug. 'You look amazing – just like a superstar,' she grinned.

Edie was wearing a boho-style minidress with an oversized leather belt and gold gladiator sandals, the laces criss-crossing all the way up her slim, tanned calves. She looked perfectly at home in the glamorous surroundings of the Villa Amore. 'Hardly, after fifteen hours of travelling,' she demurred. 'I don't even know what time zone I'm in. But it's totally worth it to see you. I can't believe you're getting married!'

'I know. It's starting to feel very real now.' Carina squeezed Edie's hands and exhaled slowly. 'At least I have my chief bridesmaid here to support me.'

'Of course. I wouldn't have missed it for the world. Hello, Bella,' Edie exclaimed, bending down to fuss over the dog, who'd immediately come running up to her.

'Where's Nathan?' asked Carina, wondering if he was delayed getting all of Edie's luggage out of the car.

'He's . . . He's not coming. We broke up.'

'What? Why?' Carina looked shocked. 'When?'

'A couple of weeks ago. It's all cool, we're still friends. I just . . . There's a lot going on in my life right now. I was being pulled in too many different directions, and I was being a pretty crap girlfriend, to be honest. It's something I'd been thinking about for a while . . .'

'Oh,' Carina said, trying not to show how hurt she felt that Edie hadn't confided in her. Perhaps it was her own fault for being so wrapped up in the wedding that she hadn't noticed her best friend was struggling. Carina realized they hadn't talked properly for a while, and wondered what else Edie had been keeping from her.

'Let's not talk about that now,' Edie said, sensing Carina's unhappiness. 'It's almost your wedding day. We should be talking about your dress, and your make-up, and what you need me to do.'

'Mamma and the wedding planner have everything in hand,' Carina insisted as she linked her arm through Edie's and they strolled through the villa towards the terrace. 'Now, did you bring your bikini?'

'Of course,' Edie grinned.

'Perfect. Let's get changed and go catch up by the pool.'

'Oh, this is heavenly,' Edie groaned as she took a sip of her perfectly made Aperol spritz then sank back onto the pillow-soft cushions of her sunlounger.

Beside her, Carina stretched like a cat in the hot sunshine, the warmth delicious on her bare skin. She pulled her Jackie O sunglasses down as she stared out at the picture-perfect view, the jagged cliffs plunging dramatically into the bay where sleek white yachts sliced through the sparkling water. 'So, what happened with Nathan?' she asked softly, turning to look at Edie.

'It was . . . It didn't feel right anymore, you know? We were both so busy, like ships in the night, and it didn't feel fair – on either of us – to carry on going through the motions. We'd been together for so long – oh, I know three years is nothing compared to you and Giorgio, but it's like a lifetime for me. I'd never been with anyone longer than a few months before Nate. But it felt like it was time for both of us to spread our wings.'

'Do you still love him?'

Edie nodded, looking devastated. 'I can't just switch it off. But it was the right thing for both of us.'

'I'll miss having him at the wedding.'

'I know you liked him. And he's a great guy, I'm not denying that. I just needed space. A fresh start. He sends his love to you both. He wanted to come – we talked about attending as friends, but it wouldn't have felt right. I don't want him to get the wrong idea, or to give him false hope.'

'I guess it's a pretty brave decision,' Carina began slowly. 'To make the break if you feel it's not right. If you've grown apart.'

'Yeah . . .' Edie agreed, studying Carina as she spoke. 'And how's everything with you and Giorgio? Are you looking forward to being Mrs Bianchi?'

'Well, Italian women rarely take their husbands' names, so I'll still be a Russo . . .'

'Where is Giorgio? Is he in Amalfi yet, or is he at his father's place in the countryside?'

'He's actually still in Los Angeles. You could have brought him over with you,' Carina joked.

Edie smiled tightly. 'How come he's still in the US? There's only a few days until the wedding.'

'Work,' Carina sighed, taking a fortifying sip of her spritz. It was deliciously cold, with just the right amount of bitterness. 'He has some business deal going on – property, I think. I don't really know much about it, to be honest,' she admitted, relieved to finally be able to open up to someone. 'But he says he's doing it for me, and for our future.'

'I see.' Edie raised her eyebrows, unimpressed at the revelation.

'I know he's not your favourite person . . .'

Carina and Edie had never directly spoken about it, but Carina had always had the sense that her best friend and her fiancé didn't really like one another. Edie avoided the subject if Carina tried to raise it, whereas Giorgio was openly dismissive of Edie. He thought she was attention seeking, and implied that Edie had slept her way to the top, which Carina knew was untrue. Carina suspected that Giorgio didn't like Edie because he thought she was a bad influence. It was true that she brought out Carina's wilder side; the two of them had had so much fun together in London, and Giorgio had hated Carina living there, always suspicious of what she was doing without him.

'I just want to make sure you're happy,' Edie said forcefully.

'I am,' Carina insisted. 'Look, Giorgio's been through a lot these past few years. He was devastated by Vittoria's death, and he puts so much pressure on himself to be a success. But everything will be fine once we're married.'

There was a long pause. Both women sipped their drinks, luxuriating in the warmth of the sun beating down, the feeling of pure relaxation. Overhead, vapour trails criss-crossed the sky as planes flew into Naples airport. Fat bumblebees buzzed lazily around the oleander, and the scent of citrus carried on the breeze from the nearby orchards.

'Carina, there's something I need to speak to you about. I didn't know if I should say anything, but—'

'Edie!' a voice exclaimed.

Carina looked up to see her mother sashaying across the terrace towards them, with Tom following behind.

Edie got to her feet, smiling broadly. 'Mrs R,' she exclaimed, as the two women embraced one another warmly.

'I'm so glad you could make it. From what Carina's told me, it's a miracle you could fit the wedding into your packed schedule. I hear you're going to be the next Meryl Streep.'

'Oh, I wouldn't have missed it for the world,' Edie vowed.

'Carina, I was just going over the plans for the next few days with Tom in case there's anything that raises a red flag. I think we've covered everything, so I'll leave you all to it – poor Bianca looks like she could do with a hand. See you later, Edie, can't wait to hear all about Hollywood.'

'Bianca?' Edie turned quizzically to Carina as Philippa walked away.

'The wedding planner. Don't ask,' Carina said, shaking her head. But Edie's attention was already elsewhere.

'Who's this? We haven't been introduced,' Edie purred, looking at Tom with definite interest. Carina recognized the expression on her face; she'd seen it often enough on nights out in Soho, when Edie liked the look of someone and planned to go after them like a heat-seeking missile.

'I'm Tom. Good to meet you,' Tom said, stepping forward and offering his hand, which Edie eagerly took, her small palm swallowed up by his large one. Carina watched closely, wondering whether Tom seemed interested in Edie, or if his attentions were purely professional. Dressed in his trademark black t-shirt and chinos, it served to make him more striking than the unobtrusive presence he seemed to be aiming for.

'British too, by the sound of things,' Edie added flirtatiously. 'Are you a long-lost cousin that Carina's been hiding?'

'I'm . . .' Tom glanced at Carina, '. . . an old friend of the family,' he finished, using the same explanation they'd given Paola and Lucrezia.

'Right . . .' Edie said disbelievingly. 'How come I've never heard of you?'

Carina couldn't help but notice how good Edie looked in her neon pink bandeau bikini, her body Hollywood-toned from working out with a personal trainer, her skin flawless and glowing. Next to her, Carina felt self-conscious in her swimwear. She didn't have Edie's confidence and wondered if Tom was comparing the two of them, and whether she came off unfavourably. Was he starstruck? Was he attracted to Edie, or impressed by her fame?

'Actually, he's my bodyguard,' Carina confessed. 'You remember the incident in Positano, the last time you were here?'

'The Maserati that almost knocked you down?'

'Yes, exactly. I'm sure it was nothing, but my father got a little spooked, and . . . Well, you know how over-protective he is, so Tom's here to keep an eye on things. Just until the wedding.'

'Carina told me you were with her when it happened,' Tom addressed Edie. 'I'd like to ask you some questions whenever you're free. Anything you remember could help.'

'Of course,' Edie said, batting her eyelashes. 'You can talk to me whenever you like. In fact,' she added shamelessly, 'if you wouldn't mind applying sun cream to my back, we could start right now.'

'Edie.' There was a warning note in Carina's voice.

'What?' Edie replied innocently.

'That's not what he's here for.'

'Maybe not, but since he *is* here, he might as well make himself useful,' Edie giggled.

'I'm happy to oblige,' Tom shrugged coolly.

'I bet you are,' Carina muttered under her breath.

'See? He can protect you from bad guys *and* apply sunscreen at the same time,' Edie quipped, holding out the cream.

Carina intercepted the bottle before Tom could get to it. '*I'll* do it. It's not in his job description.'

'Spoilsport.' Edie stuck her tongue out playfully, spinning round so Carina could oil her back. 'I wonder what's got into you all of a sudden? She didn't always used to be this uptight,' Edie chattered on to Tom. 'When I first knew her, she was heaps of fun, but now she's about to settle down and become a wife, she has to be *sen-si-ble* . . .' Edie pulled a face, drawing out the final word.

Tom smiled. 'How long have you two known one another?'

'Ooh, about five or six years now, right?' Edie said to Carina.

'Yeah. I was working in a theatre box office – a part-time job around my studies,' Carina explained. 'Edie was the star.'

'Hardly,' Edie snorted. 'I was a chorus girl at the time.'

'But everyone could tell you were destined for bigger things.'

'So were you. Top of her course, this one,' Edie said to Tom. 'She got straight As in everything, graduated with a first. And now she's going to give all that up and let her brain turn to mush when she gets married.'

'Of course I'm not,' Carina objected, looking cross.

'But Giorgio won't want you working, will he? He'll want you at home, bringing up babies and keeping your mouth shut while he pursues his . . . business.'

There was something unexpected in Edie's voice, a darker undertone. Carina clicked the cap on the sun cream and handed it back. 'Finished,' she said quietly. 'You're all done.'

'Thanks, love,' Edie grinned, spinning around and flashing her biggest smile at Carina. The difficult moment seemed to have passed, and Carina was left wondering if she'd imagined it.

'Carina, your mother asked if I could take a look around the gardens, to get the lay of the land,' Tom said. 'Are you staying here? I'll be back shortly.'

Edie watched him go, her eyes raking over his tall, powerful frame.

'Stop it, Edie,' Carina laughed. 'Put your tongue back in.'

'Why?' Edie retorted. 'I'm single now. He'd be *perfect* for a fling, don't ya think?'

'No.' Carina lay back down on her sunlounger, feeling inexplicably irritated. She took a sip of her drink, trying to gather her thoughts. For some reason, she didn't like the thought of the two of them together, and hoped Edie would let the subject drop. Carina closed her eyes, resolving to put the subject out of her mind.

She didn't want to think about why the idea bothered her so much.

# Chapter 12

**Amalfi, August 2005**

The party was unbelievable, Tom thought, as he looked around the terrace at the swimming pool, which had been covered over and transformed into a black-and-white-tiled dance floor. A jazz quartet were currently performing on a raised stage at one end of the patio, and a photographer mingled amongst the crowd, discreetly snapping shots of the happy faces. Waiting staff in black tie circulated with glasses of champagne and sumptuous appetizers: crispy bruschetta topped with prosciutto and Grana Padano; white porcelain canapé spoons holding beef carpaccio seasoned with rock salt and pink peppercorns. It was like nothing Tom had ever seen before. And if this was only the prelude to the wedding, what would the main event be like? Extravagant, he had no doubt about that.

As he took in the lavish displays of flowers, and the giant wall-mounted projector screen showing photographs and home videos of Carina and Giorgio through the years, Tom found himself wondering whether this lavish display was really what Carina wanted. She'd struck him as easygoing and unshowy, and he wondered if this opulence was influenced by someone else – Philippa, perhaps? Salvatore? Giorgio?

He'd certainly misjudged her before he arrived, Tom thought with a pang of shame, having immediately stereotyped her as a demanding diva. That couldn't be further from the gracious, open-hearted young woman he'd met.

Tom watched unobtrusively as the guests arrived and waiters circulated. He was on edge today. If anything were to happen, this event would be the perfect opportunity, with everyone mingling and distracted, rife for a stranger to infiltrate unnoticed. Tom had run through the guest list with Philippa, and the external catering staff had all been background-checked, but nothing had given him cause for alarm. Still, he had to be on his guard. Carina was obviously more vulnerable in a crowd, and Salvatore had shared his fears that she might be harmed or kidnapped.

Even with his intelligence background, Tom had little to go on. He didn't know why, or even *if*, she was a target, which made it hard to assess where a potential threat might come from. But he would do his job to the absolute best of his ability, Tom thought fiercely. There was no way anything would happen to Carina on his watch.

He began to circle the terrace, his eyes never leaving Carina. She looked radiant in a simple white slip dress that highlighted her tanned skin and glorious figure, the minimal make-up letting her natural beauty shine through.

She seemed happy, practically glowing, as she chatted with family and friends, mingling amidst the clink of champagne glasses and the scent of expensive cologne, the swish of designer dresses and the dazzle of diamond jewellery.

Tom knew from the guest list that the cream of Italian society was in attendance, along with a handful of celebrities – including Edie. Carina's brother, Lorenzo, was here with his latest girlfriend, and so was Giorgio's father, Costa, who Tom had met on the first night. Salvatore's mother, Rafaella, looking exquisite in a chic, silver cocktail dress, mingled with the crowd, seeming to be acquainted with everyone and revelling in the grand social occasion.

Tom's eye fell on an eye-catching trio: an older gentleman, clearly the *papà*, with slick-backed hair and an expensive, hand-tailored suit. He carried himself with a certain presence, exuding wealth and power. He looked at the world as though he owned it. The woman on his arm was stylish in a classically Italian way, her clothes bearing unsubtle designer labels and dripping in gold accessories.

The third person appeared to be their daughter, and she was certainly dressing to attract attention. Her red dress showed off acres of bare flesh, her dark hair cut in a sleek glossy bob. She wore an enormous pair of sunglasses, and heavy make-up, her lips a brazen slash of scarlet. She was certainly striking, but clearly had more money than taste. Tom wondered who they were; he'd learned to trust his instincts in this line of work, and something about them had triggered his attention. He would ask Salvatore when he saw him and—

There was a sudden commotion by the door, with people turning to see what was happening. Tom moved quickly through the crowd, searching for Carina. He saw her face change – from uncertainty to an expression of delight as she flew over to the man who'd just entered and hurled herself into his arms.

There were cries of delight and even a smattering of applause from the onlookers as Carina threw her arms around the man and kissed him. Tom watched the scene, realizing what was happening and feeling like an idiot for his overreaction. So this was the famous Giorgio Bianchi. He was finally here – late to his own pre-wedding party.

Tom examined him critically; Giorgio was wearing a well-tailored light blue suit with a royal blue pocket square and a white shirt that was open a couple of buttons to reveal a smattering of chest hair. He dressed well, Tom had to give him that, even if the style was a little showy for his taste. He was handsome, granted – a head shorter than Tom, with black hair and thick dark eyebrows, a deep tan and a dazzling white smile.

Tom felt a prickle of dislike. He knew it was irrational – he'd never even met the guy – but from everything he had seen, Giorgio didn't treat Carina the way she deserved to be treated. There had been some reticence on Edie's part yesterday when the conversation turned to Giorgio, and he suspected she didn't like Carina's fiancé either.

Tom remembered how, on his first night with the family, Lorenzo had made a joke during dinner, implying that Giorgio was spoilt and selfish. Perhaps it hadn't been quite so light-hearted after all. Tom's earlier conversation with Salvatore had made him even more suspicious of Giorgio when he heard that—

'The happy couple, reunited,' murmured a voice beside him sarcastically.

Tom turned to see Edie standing there, looking at him with raised eyebrows. He had to admit that she looked great, albeit in a totally different way to Carina. Her halterneck dress was completely backless, exposing her toned shoulder muscles, the tanned flesh on display reaching right to the base of her spine. Her bleached-blonde pixie cut was styled in a fashionable quiff, and enormous gold statement earrings dangled from her ears. She grinned up at him impishly. Edie was clearly a lot of fun, and looked incredible. He might be on duty, but there was no harm in flirting, he told himself.

'Why do I get the sense you think the guy's a waste of space?' His comment was meant to be light-hearted, but Edie's face hardened.

'How very perceptive of you. It doesn't matter what I think, does it? I'm not the one marrying him. If Carina's happy, then I'm not going to spoil things for her.'

'*Is* she happy?'

'Is her happiness part of your job description?' Edie said mockingly, paraphrasing Carina's comment from the day before. She drained her glass of champagne and grabbed his hand, as the band struck up a jazz version of Beyoncé's 'Crazy in Love'. 'Shall we dance?'

'Now that's definitely outside my job description. *And* my capabilities,' Tom laughed. 'I'm a terrible dancer.'

'I don't believe you,' Edie pouted. 'Show me what you've got. Come on, don't be shy.' She began to dance in front of him, her body gyrating, her hips rolling hypnotically as she placed her hands on his chest, pressing her body against his.

'Edie, come on.' Tom took a step backwards. 'I'm working.'

'Later then,' she suggested, refusing to be put off as she wrapped her slender arms around his neck, reaching up on tiptoe to whisper in his ear. 'I'm staying upstairs. Third bedroom on the right. Come find me later – we'll keep the party going,' she added with a wink.

Tom took hold of her arms, untangling them from where her fingers were raking through his hair. He knew just how bad it would look if Carina – or, worse, Salvatore – saw them.

'Why don't you introduce me to Giorgio?' he suggested. 'Then I can see for myself what he's like.' In spite of himself, Tom was curious to meet Carina's fiancé. He told himself it was all part of his role; it would give him a better understanding of Carina's life.

'If you say so.' Edie raised an eyebrow. 'But don't say I didn't warn you.'

They weaved through the crowd, Edie greeting guests that she recognized. The attendees were a mixture of old and young, friends and family, but they all looked wealthy and well dressed, chattering in a mixture of English and Italian.

'Hello, Giorgio,' Edie said pointedly, as they approached.

Giorgio's brow tightened when he saw her, and Tom frowned, watching them with circumspection.

'You finally made it back from Los Angeles. You must have been very busy out there,' Edie said waspishly.

'Edie, how wonderful to see you again. It's been such a long time.' Giorgio leaned over to kiss her on both cheeks, and Tom noticed how Edie tensed when Giorgio touched her and how Giorgio's smile didn't reach his eyes. 'I've been working extremely hard out there. I have some very exciting projects in the pipeline.'

'You know, it's amazing we never run into one another. LA's such a small city. I even thought I saw you at Spago a few days ago.'

Giorgio's eyes narrowed. 'Oh, I think you must be mistaken. We move in very different circles, don't we? But who's this? What happened to Nathan?'

'This is Tom,' Edie replied, ignoring the question. 'He's not my boyfriend. He's Carina's bodyguard.'

Giorgio's dark eyes immediately flickered to Tom, taking in the man who'd been assigned to look after his fiancée. There was a moment's silence. Tom met his gaze, his expression neutral.

'Good to meet you,' Tom said, extending his hand.

'Likewise,' Giorgio said coolly, briefly shaking it. He let go and wrapped his arm around Carina's waist, pulling her close, and Tom couldn't help but notice what a glamorous couple they made. 'Well, you've done a great job,' Giorgio continued, 'But now I'm back so there's nothing to worry about.'

Tom looked from Giorgio to Carina. Giorgio held onto her possessively, and Carina seemed far from her relaxed self, as if Giorgio's presence had introduced tensions that weren't there before. There were undercurrents in the conversation that Tom didn't understand, and it appeared Carina didn't either.

'Well, I'm glad Carina's in good hands. If you'll excuse me . . .' Tom nodded at the three of them and melted away, resolving to keep an eye on events from a distance. But first, it was imperative that he speak to Salvatore. To tell him what he had discovered.

\* \* \*

Edie stood awkwardly between Carina and Giorgio. She was about to make her excuses when Carina suddenly waved across the crowd, her face lighting up with happiness. 'Flora,' she called excitedly. 'I must go and greet my godmother,' she explained to Edie and Giorgio before hurrying away.

Edie went to walk off, but Giorgio grabbed her wrist. She turned in shock. He was standing close to her, the gesture hidden by his proximity.

'Get off me,' she hissed under her breath, her eyes like fire.

'How dare you even show your face here, after everything you've done.'

'Everything *I've* done?' Edie burst out. 'I saw you the other night, with your hands all over Ashley Hall.'

Giorgio gripped Edie's wrist once again, pulling her through the crowd to a quieter spot in the garden, hidden from the main party by a cluster of oleander bushes.

Edie's heart was racing. She wondered if she should scream, but that seemed ridiculous. Of course Giorgio wouldn't do anything here, at his party, surrounded by all these people.

'I've told you before, and I won't tell you again – keep your mouth shut, Edie.' Giorgio's face was contorted in an angry snarl. Edie backed away from him, finding herself up against the balcony that ran the length of the terrace. She was uncomfortably aware of the vertiginous drop behind her.

'I won't say a word – but I'm not protecting you. I don't want Carina to get hurt.'

Giorgio laughed unpleasantly. 'It's a little late for that. I don't even know how you've got the gall to show up here today. Best friend? Chief bridesmaid? You're a joke.'

'One day she'll know the truth about you,' Edie shot back, her eyes blazing. 'You can't get away with it forever.'

Giorgio stepped towards her and Edie moved backwards, but there was nowhere to go, the stone balcony pressed against her spine.

'Careful there, Edie,' Giorgio warned. 'I wouldn't want you to have an accident. Then again, it might be better for everyone if you weren't around.'

Someone coughed behind him and Giorgio spun round. Tom was standing there, his arms folded across his chest.

'Everything all right, Edie?' he asked, staring coldly at Giorgio.

Giorgio shot him a filthy look. 'I thought you were Carina's bodyguard, not Edie's,' he spat sarcastically, before turning on his heel and stalking off.

Edie let out the breath she didn't realize she'd been holding. Her body was shaking and she choked back a sob, holding onto the balcony while she regained her composure.

'Thank you,' she said sincerely.

'What did you say to upset him?' Tom said wryly.

'He's an arsehole,' Edie burst out, in her strong, northern accent. 'I hate him.'

Right now, she was more certain than ever that she needed to tell Carina everything she knew, but Giorgio's threats had rattled her more than she wanted to admit. Everyone was keeping secrets, and it looked like Giorgio would go to any lengths to protect his.

# Chapter 13

**Los Angeles, August 2005**

Ashley Hall was apoplectic.

'Engaged?' she raged. 'He's *engaged*?'

They were in the Polo Lounge of the Beverly Hills Hotel, an iconic celebrity haunt that had seen deals brokered over brunch for the best part of a century. And right now, people were turning to stare.

Sam was beginning to think it had been a bad idea to tell Ashley in public.

'I'm sorry, darlin'. But you weren't serious about him, were you? I thought he was just another one of your toys.'

'It's not about that,' Ashley spat. Despite her fury, she still looked a million dollars in skin-tight leather trousers and a metallic silver corset, her dark hair pulled back in a sleek ponytail. 'It's about being made to look like a fool. *Nobody* crosses Ashley Hall and gets away with it. How the hell did you even find out?'

'Little rule for you, darlin'. When you're contemplating going into business with someone, you make it *your* business to find out everything about them. And I mean everything. What their favourite pizza topping is, how often they go to the bathroom – every damn thing.'

'I can't believe he did that to me. How dare he!' Ashley was swinging between outrage and tears. 'I'm no one's dirty secret.'

'I hear you, darlin'. No one makes a mockery of me, or my family.'

'Bastard,' Ashley raged, slamming her fist down on the table so hard it made her martini glass jump.

Sam sat back in his chair in the elegant surroundings, amidst the instantly recognizable candy-coloured decor, looking rather incongruous in his stonewashed jeans and cowboy hat. A thoughtful expression came over his face. 'Say, how about you and I take a little trip to Italy?'

Ashley looked momentarily confused, then she slowly smiled, her catlike green eyes hardening. 'Great idea, Uncle Sam. That slimeball won't know what's hit him.'

At the Villa Amore, Carina was deep in conversation with her godmother, Flora.

'*Ciao*, Carina.'

Carina turned to see who'd approached her. It took her a moment to place the young woman; her face was hidden behind large sunglasses and heavy make-up.

'Isabella,' Carina exclaimed after a moment, kissing her on both cheeks. Her tone was warm and friendly – Carina was all too aware that it was her party, and she had to be polite to everyone – but in truth she didn't know

Isabella very well. Lots of the guests here today were little more than acquaintances, but Carina understood it was also a social occasion for her parents and a great brand event for Casa di Russo wine at the same time. 'Thank you for coming.'

'Oh, I wouldn't have missed it for the world,' Isabella said, in a strange tone.

'That's so sweet,' Carina replied, unsure how to respond.

'You must be so happy to have Giorgio back,' Isabella went on. 'That wasn't a very nice thing to do, was it? Running off to Los Angeles right before your wedding. You must have been furious with him.'

Carina frowned, wondering how this woman knew all the details of Giorgio's whereabouts. She shrugged lightly, pasting a smile on her face. 'Not at all. He's building a business, and a future for us. I support him completely.'

'You're very understanding. Then again, they do say ignorance is bliss . . .'

Carina stared at Isabella, about to ask exactly what she meant, when the band suddenly stopped playing and there was a squeal of feedback through the speakers. Everyone turned to see Salvatore on stage, microphone in hand, and the crowd burst into expectant applause. When Carina looked back, Isabella had gone.

'First of all, I'd like to thank everyone for coming today and kicking off Carina and Giorgio's wedding celebrations in style,' Salvatore began, to whoops and cheers, as he stood on the makeshift stage, microphone in hand.

Philippa gazed up at him from the crowd. She looked glamorous and sophisticated in a black sequinned cocktail dress.

'This is just the beginning,' he was saying. 'We have some amazing surprises in store for you over the next few days, and my thanks, too, must go to the team who've helped organize everything so flawlessly.' There was further applause, as Salvatore beamed at the crowd.

'It's so wonderful to feel all the love around here today, for me and my family. My son, Lorenzo, is here for once – we tempted him away from the city,' Salvatore laughed. 'But most especially, of course, for my darling daughter, Carina. Very soon, she'll begin a new stage of her journey with Giorgio. Giorgio is like a second son to me. I've known him since he was born, and Carina has loved him for very many years. It's a joy to celebrate their union with you all today.

'This house – the Villa Amore,' Salvatore went on, 'has always been – as its name suggests – a house full of love. It was given to me by my parents – Carina's *nonno* and *nonna* – and I know my mother, Rafaella, is thrilled that she's starting her celebrations here. Sadly, my father, Antonio, is no longer with us, but I'm sure he'd be bursting with pride to see what a wonderful young woman you've become, my darling Carina. Everyone, if you could join me in a toast to my parents – Rafaella and Antonio.'

'Rafaella and Antonio,' everyone chorused, raising their glasses.

'And, of course, to Carina and Giorgio. May we all wish them a lifetime of happiness.'

Philippa echoed her husband's sentiments, but the words seemed to stick in her throat. She took a sip of champagne as Salvatore made his way down from the stage and the jazz quartet resumed playing. Perhaps she was expecting too much, or being unreasonable, but it felt odd that Salvatore hadn't mentioned her once. In a speech about love and family and weddings, wouldn't it be customary to catch her eye, maybe say something complimentary about his wife? Not to mention all the work she'd put into the party *and* the restoration of the house itself. Villa Amore would be little more than a pile of ruins if it weren't for her. She hated feeling resentful, it was so unlike her.

'Wait,' came a voice from the crowd, cutting into Philippa's thoughts. 'I'd like to say something.'

Costa Bianchi was pushing his way through the throng, awkwardly clambering up on stage, balancing what looked like a glass of Scotch in his hand. His words were slurred, and Philippa could see a look of alarm on Salvatore's face. Clearly this moment wasn't planned.

'I just wanted to say how much I'm looking forward to welcoming Carina into the Bianchi family. I wasn't blessed with a daughter, and now I'm going to have one,' Costa began, to 'aw's and murmurs of 'how sweet'.

'It's the light at the end of the tunnel . . . A union I've been waiting for, for many years now. We've had a tough time, us Bianchis. We haven't been as . . . *lucky* as the Russo family. Some people say you make your own luck, and the Russos certainly did that.'

His voice had taken on a harder edge. People were looking from one to the other, frowning uncertainly.

'A few years ago, we lost my darling wife, Vittoria. And now, I . . .' Costa's voice shook, and he took a swallow of whisky to steady himself. He seemed to realize what he was saying and stopped talking, raising his glass instead. 'To Carina and Giorgio. To a fertile and fruitful marriage. And to righting past wrongs.'

Rafaella gasped. Salvatore looked furious.

Costa raised his glass in the air, but no one said anything, the assembled guests confused and uncomfortable. There were a few echoes of 'Carina and Giorgio', but the party atmosphere had been punctured by Costa's awkward, impromptu speech.

Philippa looked to her husband in alarm; he signalled to the band to start playing, and they quickly burst into a tight rendition of Robert Palmer's 'Addicted to Love'. The crowd gradually dispersed, breaking up into groups and talking amongst themselves, the moment forgotten amongst plentiful Prosecco and delicious canapés.

Philippa pushed through the crowd to find Salvatore.

'Darling,' she said softly, placing a hand on his arm.

'Not now, Philippa.'

'Yes, now,' she said, determined not to be given the brush-off once again. 'What the hell was that all about?'

Salvatore shrugged unconvincingly. 'Who knows. The drunken ramblings of a bitter, lonely man.'

But Philippa wasn't taken in by Salvatore's excuses. 'I saw your face. I know you understood what he was talking about. I want to know what's going on, Salvatore.'

'Nothing's going on.'

His voice was growing louder, and people were turning to look at them.

'I'm not an idiot,' Philippa retorted. 'You're keeping something from me and I want to know what it is. Why won't you tell me?'

'This doesn't concern you,' Salvatore shot back. His voice was quiet and controlled, but he was clearly livid. 'Just stay out of it, Philippa. I have it under control. Now, where's Tom? I need to talk to him.'

He stalked off, leaving Philippa rooted to the spot, unable to comprehend that Salvatore had just spoken to her like that in front of people they knew. He'd been rude, dismissive, uncaring. And he was clearly hiding something that he refused to share with her.

Suddenly desperate to get away, Philippa turned to leave. She would lock herself in the bathroom and catch her breath for a moment, repair her make-up and calm down.

But as she began to make her way across the crowded terrace, Philippa felt a hand on her waist and spun round, shocked at the intimate gesture. When she saw who was standing behind her, she gasped, her hand flying to her mouth.

He was older, greyer, but still as handsome as ever. Even after all these years, she would have recognized him anywhere.

He smiled as their eyes met, laughter lines crinkling at the corners, his face lighting up. When he spoke, his voice was deep and mellow, smooth and well-spoken just like she remembered. She'd never forgotten him. Of course she hadn't – that would be impossible.

'Hello, Pippa, it's been a long time . . .'

Her first love.

'Harry Fanshaw, what are *you* doing here?'

# Part Two

# Chapter 14

**London, July 1978**

Pippa Campbell was late. She prided herself on being punctual and organized, but today the Underground strikes had got the better of her. As the red London bus crawled through Pimlico along Vauxhall Bridge Road, she jumped off and began to run, grateful for the fact she was wearing low-heeled Mary Jane shoes, not the towering platforms she'd worn to the Rolling Stones concert at the weekend.

It was almost half past nine when she finally arrived at the imposing terraced building on Stratton Street. There was no time to wait for the creaking old lift, and she ran up the three flights of stairs to Fanshaw Brothers' offices. She paused for a moment to draw breath and caught sight of her reflection in the age-spotted mirror on the wall; her cheeks were flushed, her blonde hair coming loose from the neat chignon she'd styled it in. She quickly retied it, adding a slick of Evette lip gloss and brushing away a dot of mascara that had landed on her cheek.

When her breathing had slowed down, Pippa opened the door and slunk across the room to her desk, trying not to draw attention. Thankfully, the smoke-filled office was quiet, the only sound Mrs Higson's typewriter clacking away along the corridor.

She hastily pulled a pile of files from her in-basket, opening the top one and picking up her pen. As she did so, a shadow fell across her desk and Pippa looked up to see Mrs Higson, Mr Fanshaw's secretary, looming over her.

'Mr Fanshaw would like to see you in his office.' Her expression was gleeful, and Pippa's heart sank. Mrs Higson was middle-aged, tall and brittle with badly dyed hair. She'd taken an instant dislike to Pippa, clearly resenting her appointment as the first female clerk in the company. The fact that at twenty-four Pippa was a decade younger than any of her male colleagues only made matters worse in Mrs Higson's eyes.

*Damn*, Pippa thought, as she stood up and smoothed down her dark blue A-line skirt, which she'd paired with a smart floral print blouse. Her appointment as junior clerk at Fanshaw Brothers Wine Merchants was the first step in achieving her ambition to become a career woman and travel the world. Growing up in the quiet, historic town of St Andrews, she'd dreamt of London with all its theatres and embassies, restaurants and galleries, its vast population drawn from all walks of life. Even now she had to pinch herself every time her daily commute took her past Buckingham Palace. Having spent her first month in her new job trying not to put a foot wrong, desperate not to give anyone cause to criticize her, it would be too awful if her late arrival were to result in dismissal.

'Of course. Right away,' she replied in her gentle Scots accent, not letting her inner turmoil show on her face as she followed Mrs Higson along the corridor.

'Ah, do come in, Miss Campbell.' Harold Fanshaw's door was open and he saw her approach. 'Take a seat.'

Nervously, Pippa did as she was told, glancing round at the wood-panelled walls, leather-bound books and framed certificates on the walls, trying not to feel intimidated. The main office was plain and functional, with cheaply painted walls and ugly metal filing cabinets, but Harold Fanshaw's office was decorated like one of the private members' clubs they did business with. They might have been almost on the cusp of a new decade, the 1980s, with rumours that a female prime minister could be victorious at the next general election, but the culture – and the decor – at Fanshaw Brothers harked back to the Edwardian era.

'Now, Miss Campbell, I wanted to speak to you,' Harold began. He was a small, slight man in his sixties, with receding grey hair and a grey moustache, but seated behind the enormous, polished walnut desk he looked extremely intimidating.

'Oh, please don't fire me, Mr Fanshaw,' Pippa burst out, before she could stop herself. 'I'm so sorry – I promise I won't be late again. It was the buses you see – the Tube wasn't running because of the strikes, and the traffic was so terrible . . . I had to sprint all the way across Green Park, and—'

'Calm down, Miss Campbell,' Harold said, closing his eyes and putting up a hand to stop her speaking. 'You think I called you in here to fire you?'

Pippa nodded, biting her lip. She had the terrible feeling she might cry.

'Why on earth would I fire one of my most promising employees?' Harold said, looking perplexed. As Pippa stared at him in shock, he broke into a smile – a rather unusual expression for Harold Fanshaw.

'I don't underst—'

'Do keep up, Miss Campbell. I thought you were on the ball, but perhaps I was mistaken.'

Philippa's relief was swiftly overtaken by alarm at the thought he might retract his words. 'Oh no, I am. Very on the ball.'

Harold raised his eyebrows, then continued: 'I've been hearing very good things about you. I know a hard worker when I see one, Miss Campbell, and I think you have great potential. I've had excellent reports from our clients – Alistair Rothwell of Broom and Travers mentioned you specifically, and he's notoriously hard to please.'

'Thank you, Mr Fanshaw,' Philippa said as calmly as she could muster. She didn't want to come across as ditzy and histrionic after her earlier outburst. 'I intend to continue working hard.'

'That's very good to hear. I'll be keeping my eye on you and your progress. Take you under my wing, so to speak. There'll be opportunities for you to get more involved in the company in the near future.'

'Thank you,' Pippa said again, worried that if she kept repeating herself Mr Fanshaw might not think she was quite as clever as he'd given her credit for. 'I won't let you down.'

'Excellent. Yes. Good.' Harold seemed distracted suddenly, and Pippa sensed that their meeting was over. 'Now, back to work for us both, eh?'

'Yes, sir.'

But Harold Fanshaw was already preoccupied by the letter he'd just opened, picking it up and beginning to read.

Pippa quietly stood up and let herself out, closing the door behind her. She was unable to stop herself flashing a triumphant smile in the direction of Mrs Higson, whose frosted features glared at her in frustrated annoyance over her NHS specs.

Well, that had been unexpected! Pippa was thrilled to discover that her efforts hadn't gone unnoticed. Perhaps she might even be promoted soon, she thought excitedly. Her parents, Jean and Gordon, would be so proud, and it would prove to them that this move south had been the right thing to—

'Oh, I'm so sorry,' Pippa exclaimed, as she collided with someone coming the other way.

'Not to worry, no harm done,' said a smooth voice. Pippa felt the heat rise to her cheeks as she disentangled herself and realized who it was: Harold Fanshaw Jnr. He had classic good looks, with wavy brown hair and a chiselled jawline, and he was dressed in a sharply tailored Savile Row suit. He carried himself with a confidence that presumably came naturally when you were the son of the owner and had grown up accustomed to considerable wealth. Harold Fanshaw Jnr was regularly away from the office, travelling for business, but whenever he was around there was an energetic buzz about the place. Once or twice he'd taken the time to speak to Pippa, and she'd found herself looking forward to his presence in the office more than she dared admit to herself. He was only a year or two older than her, but they were worlds apart.

'My head's all over the place this morning, Mr Fanshaw.'

'Please! Mr Fanshaw's my father. Call me Harry.'

His eyes raked over her, and Philippa knew what she must look like: her cheeks flushed and her eyes giddy and happy after her conversation with Fanshaw Senior.

'What's got you so hot and bothered?' Harry mused, looking at her with interest. 'Have you just come from my father's office?'

Pippa nodded, unable to keep the smile from her face. 'Yes, from a meeting with your . . . with Mr Fanshaw.' She was excited, longing to confide in someone and couldn't help the words from bubbling out of her mouth. 'He thinks I have great potential and a bright future ahead of me. I intend to repay his faith in me.'

Harry's lips twitched, and Pippa wondered whether she sounded hopelessly naïve.

'Well, naturally,' he replied. 'I'm glad my father finally spoke to you – I've been telling him he should for some time now.'

Pippa blinked. 'You have?'

'I like to think I have an eye for' – his gaze ran slowly over her in a way that made Pippa feel more flushed than she was already – 'spotting talent, and yours was quite obvious to me from the moment you walked into the office.'

'It was?'

'Absolutely. I mentioned to my father that you were clearly a sophisticated, intelligent woman who had a great deal more to offer. So I'd like to think that *I'm* the one who deserves the credit for setting you on the path to a brighter future.'

'I don't know what to say . . .' Pippa wasn't sure if she should be embarrassed but instead finding herself brimming with pleasure.

Harry stared at her for a moment, a thoughtful look on his face.

'Listen, I'm going away this afternoon for a few days, meeting suppliers up north. But when I'm back, why don't I take you for lunch? We can talk more about the company, and your future with us.'

'That would be . . .' Pippa struggled to find the words; it was all so overwhelming. 'That would be wonderful. I'd like that very much.'

'Excellent.' Harry beamed at her. 'Well, I'd better get on. Duty calls.' He gave her one final flash of that dazzling smile and strode off. She watched him go, and as if sensing she was still there, he turned around and winked at her.

For some reason this sent a thrill through Pippa and as she hurried back to her desk, she found that she couldn't stop smiling.

# Chapter 15

**London, summer 1978**

It was a week later when Pippa found herself getting to know Harry Fanshaw better than she'd dared hope, and she'd been delighted when he had appeared at her desk one day.

'Lunch?' he asked, his eyes twinkling, although it didn't seem like it was an option to refuse the offer.

She strolled with him along Piccadilly, passing the Ritz, and Fortnum and Mason, followed by the impressive façade of Burlington House. Pippa had yet another 'pinch me' moment as she noticed women stare at him with interest, throwing envious looks in her direction, and it put a little swagger in her stride, a secret smile playing around her lips that people imagined they could be a couple.

Arriving at the Café Royal, the legendary restaurant which had seen guests including Oscar Wilde, Winston Churchill, Brigitte Bardot and Elizabeth Taylor pass through its doors over the decades, they were shown to a table in the Grill Room and Philippa sat down in the chair the waiter had pulled out for her. He opened her napkin and spread it across her knee.

'I'll order for you?' Harry suggested, as Pippa glanced at the menu. 'I know what's good. We'll have the filet mignon,' Harry informed the waiter. 'And two glasses of the Bordeaux.'

'Wine?' Pippa said, looking shocked, after the waiter had left. 'At lunchtime?' She didn't think Harold Fanshaw Snr would approve, and neither would Mrs Higson.

'*Bien sûr*. It's what the French do, so it's very civilized,' Harry explained, leaning back in his chair and adopting an untroubled pose as he lit a cigarette. He offered one to Pippa but she shook her head. 'Besides, this *is* work. The Café Royal take our best wines. Maurice, their head sommelier, is a thoroughly good chap. I'll introduce you later. There's a lot you still have to learn.'

Their wine arrived and Harry raised his glass in a toast. 'To the delightful Pippa, and her bright future.'

'To success,' Pippa toasted in return.

'Now,' said Harry, settling back in his chair. 'Tell me everything about yourself.'

Pippa was enjoying drinking in her surroundings, she felt sure that Joan and Jackie Collins were dining a few tables away, and tried not to stare at the two glamorous women with big hair and expensive jewellery.

'It's clear you have a head for business and a formidable brain, so how did you find your way to London, and – fortuitously – to Fanshaw's?'

'Well, after I graduated from Edinburgh university I spent a couple of years working for an insurance—'

He interrupted her. 'That's not what I meant.'

'I'm sorry?'

'I could have got all of that from your CV. Tell me something I don't know. What are your ambitions in life? What's your favourite band? Your favourite food?' Harry paused, holding her gaze. 'Do you have a boyfriend?'

Pippa blushed but was saved from answering as the waiter arrived with their food. Her head was spinning. Harry Fanshaw was everything she'd hoped and more. It might have been the wine, but she was beginning to find him extremely attractive – however hard she tried to fight it. Having a crush on the boss's son felt like such a cliché, but Harry's charm was irresistible and the time flew by as they discussed music and films, art and wine, travel and politics. The filet mignon was followed by a sumptuous *mousse au chocolat*, and when Pippa looked at her watch it was half past three.

'Oh my goodness,' she exclaimed. 'I really must get back. I'll be in trouble. I have so much work to do. It'll be a late one for me tonight.'

Harry gave her a reassuring smile. 'Don't worry, you're out with me, and I'll let you into a secret . . .' Harry began, lowering his voice and leaning across the table.

'What?' Pippa was intrigued.

'I'm the boss's son. And one day I'll be running that place,' Harry whispered, his eyes dancing. 'A girl like you shouldn't be wasting her evenings stuck in the office,' he went on. 'You should be out having fun.'

Pippa smiled and excused herself to use the bathroom, which was just as spectacular as the rest of the building with flock wallpaper and wall-mounted candelabras. She felt rather tipsy, even though she'd switched to Perrier water, despite Harry trying to tempt her with another bottle. She examined her reflection in the enormous mirror, noting that her eyes were sparkling, her skin flushed. Damn, she was attracted to Harry Fanshaw. Perhaps she was being ridiculous, but she thought he might like her too. There was certainly a spark between them. But he was the boss's son, Pippa reminded herself. He was strictly off limits and she knew it.

She quickly retouched her make-up and headed back to their table, where she was surprised to find Harry chatting to a tall, well-heeled man, around Harry's age, with swept-back blonde hair and an aristocratic bearing.

Pippa looked at him uncertainly, but Harry didn't miss a beat.

'Pippa, let me introduce you to Charlie Beaufort. Would you believe we were at school together?' Harry laughed.

'Pleased to meet you,' Pippa said, extending her hand.

'Likewise,' Charlie nodded. He clearly possessed the same impeccable manners as Harry, but as his gaze ran over her, for a fleeting moment Pippa felt like a prize heifer at the Royal Highland Show.

'This is Pippa Campbell, one of Fanshaw's promising new additions.'

'I see,' Charlie smirked. 'And do you always take your *new additions* on boozy lunches at Café Royal?'

'Only the most promising,' Harry replied, and the other man gave him a knowing look.

'By the way, how's Venetia these days?'

'Oh, you know Venetia,' Harry said, his tone non-committal. 'It was good to see you, Charlie, but duty calls and we must return to the office.'

'Of course. Delightful to meet you, Pippa.' Charlie threw Pippa a look that made her feel uncomfortable again, before walking away.

Harry stood up, and Pippa followed him through the restaurant, dismissing her earlier discomfort, feeling as though she was walking on air. Her eyes raked over the back of his neck, the brown hair curling over his collar, and she felt a distinct pull in her belly, the sensation moving lower, as she desperately tried to ignore it. Having a crush on her boss's son could only lead to trouble.

As they strode through the door, back onto Regent Street, Pippa was assailed by the heat and the noise and people. She felt like Cinderella after the clock had struck midnight, thrust back into real life after a glimpse of another world. And Harry was the handsome prince, she thought dreamily.

'Thank you for today. I had a wonderful time,' she told him.

'Pippa,' Harry smiled, placing a hand on her lower back. 'I assure you, the pleasure was all mine . . .'

'You wanted to see me?' Philippa asked, as she knocked on the door of Mr Fanshaw Snr's office before pushing it open. Two months had passed since that fateful morning when Pippa had been terrified that she was about to be sacked. True to his word, he'd introduced her to some of their biggest clients, giving her larger accounts to manage and trusting her with more responsibility.

'Yes, do come in, Miss Campbell. Now,' Harold continued, as Pippa took a seat, 'what's your week looking like?'

Pippa frowned. 'I have the Portuguese shipment arriving this afternoon, and tomorrow I'm back-to-back with client meetings, so Wednesday will be catching up on paperwork.'

'Oh, Mr Rogers can deal with that for you,' Harold said dismissively, naming one of Pippa's colleagues. 'Can you brief him on what needs doing?'

'Of course.'

'Good, because Harry – that is, Mr Fanshaw Junior – has suggested that it would be beneficial for you to accompany him on a trip, and I have to say, I agree. Would you like that?'

'Yes, Mr Fanshaw, I certainly would.' Perhaps they'd be taking the train to Brighton – there was a new independent merchant there they'd just started dealing with – or even to Bath, where they dealt with a number of retailers and private clients.

'Excellent. Mr Fanshaw has a series of meetings with our producers in the Loire Valley. You'd leave on Wednesday and return Friday. Do you speak any French?'

'Yes, though I'm a bit rusty . . .' Pippa said, trying to recall her A-level studies; she'd always been good at languages. Her head was spinning. France? For three days? With Harry?

'Most importantly, do you have a passport?'

'Yes,' Pippa confirmed, feeling grateful that she and her best friend Flora had gone on a cheap ferry break to Holland after they'd finished university.

'Right, well, pass on all your details to Mrs Higson and she'll make the arrangements for you both. You'll fly to Paris, then drive to the vineyards. Anything else you need, liaise with Mr Fanshaw. He knows the ropes. Any questions?'

'No, I—'

'Excellent. Don't let me down. This could be the beginning of something big for you –. . .'

Pippa's stomach was doing somersaults. She closed her eyes and prayed she wouldn't be sick. She hadn't expected to be quite so nervous but, as she sat in her Air France plane seat waiting to take off, she was suddenly terrified.

'There's nothing to be scared about,' Harry said gently. He was looking dapper in a tan-coloured suit and Italian handmade leather shoes. 'It's perfectly safe.'

'I know, I'm being silly, but I haven't flown before,' Pippa admitted.

'I'll be with you, every step of the way,' Harry smiled, squeezing her hand, which sent a thrill through her, despite the nerves. 'Just hold on to me if you get scared.'

An hour later, they landed in Paris. She and Harry had chatted and laughed throughout the flight, she felt like she had known him forever. Perhaps one day, in the future, he might whisk her over to the City of Lights for a romantic weekend, she thought dreamily, before giving herself a mental pinch. She had to be professional, no matter how much the tingles running through her body urged her not to be.

London, and Fanshaw Brothers, felt a very long way away as Pippa and Harry sped through the French countryside south-west of Paris, with Harry behind the wheel of a hired Citroën DS convertible. They passed rustic farms and quaint villages, and as they motored further south, the enormous fields of corn and maize gradually gave way to gently rolling hills, with centuries-old churches and medieval towns sheltered by forests of ancient oak trees.

Pippa felt swept away by the magic and the glamour of it all, and she had to fight the feeling that she and Harry were almost on holiday together, she knew it was dangerous thinking, but couldn't entirely help herself. She reminded herself that however much she was enjoying being in France, she needed to stay focused.

She asked Harry endless questions, and he answered her queries patiently, but made it clear the preparation wasn't necessary. 'Remember, *they* want to impress *us*. They need us to sell their wine – and that means these trips are a lot of fun. They pull out all the stops and treat us extremely well, with lots of food, excellent wine, the best rooms in the château.'

Philippa was even more excited when, around two hours after they'd left Paris, they saw the signs for Château de Chenin and spotted an incredible building looming on the horizon.

'Is that it?' Pippa squeaked.

'*Bienvenue à Château de Chenin*,' Harry said with a flourish, as he turned onto the long, sweeping driveway lined by mature oak trees.

The château looked like something from a fairy tale. It was a white stone castle with turrets at either end, and a long, rectangular lake in front with water cascading over a marble fountain. It was set within formal gardens, with topiary hedges, blooming roses and grassy pathways.

Harry pulled up outside, onto the sweeping semi-circular gravel area outside the château. The front door opened and a tall, burly man dressed in corduroy trousers and a check shirt strode out. He and Harry greeted one another like old friends.

'Jacques Benoit, allow me to introduce Pippa Campbell.'

'Welcome, Mademoiselle Campbell, we are very pleased to have you here,' he said in heavily accented English.

'Thank you, I'm delighted to be here, and looking forward to sampling your wine.'

'But of course – shall we get started?'

As if on cue, a woman emerged from the château behind them carrying a silver tray holding three flute glasses, the liquid inside bubbling and sparkling.

'*Merci*, I adore Crémant de Loire.'

Jacques nodded. 'Better than champagne,' he added fiercely.

Harry looked impressed. Despite her excitement at being here, Pippa had done her research.

'It was given the AOC a few years ago, wasn't it? *L'appellation d'origine contrôlée*.' She added with confidence.

'*Très bien, mademoiselle*,' Harry grinned, tilting his glass in her direction.

'You see how it is smoother than champagne?' Jacques demanded. 'Crisp and refreshing.'

'It's superb,' Pippa agreed.

'*Bon*.' Jacques seemed satisfied. '*Alors*, how about a spot of lunch before we commence our tour? You must be hungry, *non*?'

Pippa nodded, realizing she was famished, as Harry replied to Jacques in a rapid stream of French, the two of them conversing easily as she struggled to keep up.

'I didn't know you spoke French so fluently,' Pippa said to him, as they followed Jacques around the outside of the enormous château.

'There's a lot you don't know about me. I'm hoping we'll discover rather more of one another before we leave.'

Harry held her gaze, and Pippa's stomach flipped. She had a feeling she was in for a whole lot of trouble over the next few days.

# Chapter 16

Jacques had laid on a simple but delicious lunch eaten al fresco in the shade of a sprawling oak tree. Afterwards it had been straight down to business with a tour of the sprawling vineyards, winery and the cellars. Then, of course, there'd been the sampling. While Pippa knew that you were supposed to swirl it around on the palate, some of the wines were so inviting that she'd taken an additional sip or two, and by now she was feeling rather tipsy.

'Dinner will be served at eight o'clock, in the west dining room,' Jacques told them at the end of the tour. 'Until then, you are at leisure to do as you wish.'

'*Merci beaucoup*, Jacques,' Pippa said in schoolgirl French, suppressing a hiccup. '*À toute à l'heure.*'

After Jacques had gone, Harry looked at her in amusement. 'Oh, Pippa, you're so sweet. "*À toute à l'heure, Jacques*",' he mimicked her with a smile.

Pippa knew him well enough to know there was nothing malicious in his teasing, and she was determined not to give him the satisfaction of seeing her blush.

'And you're so drunk,' she shot back, as Harry pretended to look scandalized.

'Perhaps,' he admitted. 'It's an occupational hazard, I'm afraid.'

'Terrible. Although I think I might be too.'

'Well, what do you say, my tipsy Pippa? Shall we take a walk through the vineyards? Sober up a little?'

At that moment Pippa would have followed him anywhere. The truth was that she loved being in his presence. Harry Fanshaw was funny, confident and intelligent, and he made *her* feel as though she could accomplish anything.

'That sounds exactly what I need right now,' she agreed, as they strolled across the yard,

The scenery was beautiful, a bucolic vista that looked as though it hadn't changed at all for hundreds of years. Beyond the verdant green fields to the west, the sun was beginning to dip over a patch of woodland, the rays catching the silvery sheen of a wide flowing river.

It was harvest season, and Pippa watched in fascination, marvelling at how quickly the men worked, deftly inspecting the grapes to see if they were the right size, before swiftly cutting the stalk and throwing them into their buckets.

'It's a real labour of love, isn't it?' she commented. 'So much hard work and effort going into one bottle.'

Harry nodded. 'In America, where the vineyards are often much bigger, they've attempted to automate the process, using enormous machines to shake down the grapes. But I don't think it tastes the same.'

'Have you ever been to America?'

'Of course, to New York, and I've been on a couple of

work trips to Napa Valley too. Perhaps that should be our next trip away together? Would you like to spend a fortnight in California with me, Pippa?'

'I . . .' Pippa found herself tongue-tied, unsure whether he was being serious.

'God, you're irresistible,' Harry looked at her intently. 'Can I tell you something?'

'Of course,' Pippa breathed, wondering what he was about to say.

'Things are changing at Fanshaw's. My father will retire soon, and I'm taking over.'

'So soon?' Pippa gasped. 'I can't imagine your father ever retiring.'

'It's my turn, to lead the company the way it should be led. He doesn't want to admit it to himself, but he knows it. We need to move with the times, embrace a new, younger customer, instead of the old dinosaurs he relies on now. When I take over, I want you by my side. Just picture it – the two of us, working together. A dream team.'

Pippa's heart was racing, intoxicated by the vision he was painting. It was everything she wanted: to be successful; to be with Harry.

'Yes,' she nodded. 'A dream come true.'

They stopped walking. They'd come a long way and the château was far in the distance, too far even to hear the shouts of the workers. They were all alone in the most beautiful, romantic setting.

'Pippa,' Harry murmured, softly stroking her cheek.

She closed her eyes and sighed with longing. She couldn't seem to hide her feelings anymore, and she didn't want to.

'I've tried so hard not to fall for you, but I can't help myself. You're making it impossible,' Harry told her. He cupped her face tenderly, his lips finding hers, gently at first but increasing in intensity.

Pippa felt helpless in his arms. There was no way she could have resisted; this was everything she wanted. Her body was on fire, every sense alight, desire racing through her.

'Harry,' she whispered, reaching for him, pulling him closer.

Harry's hands caressed her body, sliding down to her hips, driving her wild. She moaned, and the sound seemed to echo through the stillness of the landscape, bringing her back to reality. She pulled away, her breathing high and quick, her eyes wide.

'Pippa,' Harry said through passionate, urgent kisses. 'It's like you've cast a spell on me.'

Wordlessly, Harry took her hand, leading her over to where the long grasses swayed gently in the merest breeze. It was deserted, the only sound coming from the call of a bird high overhead.

Pippa's heart was beating fast, her mind swirling with excitement and nerves. Harry kissed her again, and they sat down on the soft grass which yielded beneath their bodies, tickling Pippa's legs. She lay back, gazing up at Harry's handsome face. She could hardly believe this was happening.

Harry languidly unbuttoned her white silk blouse, he brushed his thumbs over the soft lace of her bra, her breasts full beneath the fabric, and Philippa gasped. Then his hands moved lower, lifting her skirt, his fingertips dancing over her thighs.

Pippa wasn't a virgin; there'd been a couple of boyfriends at university. But she'd never experienced anything like this. No one had lit her body on fire the way Harry did, making her half-mad with longing.

She mirrored his touch, unbuttoning his shirt and running her hand over his trousers. He let out a groan, and Pippa revelled in the burst of power, that she could have this effect on a man like Harry Fanshaw.

'Pippa,' Harry breathed. 'I won't do anything you don't want me to . . .'

She placed a finger over his lips, stopping his words. 'I want you to do everything,' she confessed, almost shaking with need. Yes, she was nervous, but she wanted this more than anything. Harry bent his head to hers, their lips meeting again as their bodies melted together.

Afterwards, Philippa lay in his arms, their legs intertwined, basking in the warmth of one another's bodies. Her head was resting on his chest, and she could feel his heart beating, his breath gently ruffling her hair. She didn't want this moment to end, but she knew it had to.

Pippa rolled over to kiss him, sighing happily as Harry kissed her back with the lightest of touches, as though she were the most precious thing in the world to him. Then she sat up, pulling on her crumpled blouse and handing him his shirt.

'Darling Pippa,' Harry smiled at her, gazing at her in wonderment.

Pippa suddenly felt shy, with Harry's intense blue eyes on her. Everything had changed between them.

Harry stroked her cheek affectionately. 'You know,' he

began softly, 'we probably shouldn't tell anyone in the office about this.'

His words rendered her momentarily speechless, and Pippa shivered, quickly fastening her blouse and pulling on her skirt. The sun had disappeared behind a cloud, the two of them were momentarily bathed in shadow. Pippa looked at him, a question in her eyes, unable to hide the hurt she felt.

'It's for your sake, my darling. I don't want you to be the subject of malicious gossip. We don't want anyone starting nasty rumours, or questioning how you've progressed so quickly, do we?'

Philippa's heart sank as she realized Harry was right. 'What about your father?' she asked nervously.

Harry swallowed, suddenly serious. 'He likes you – I know he does – but in a professional sense. I don't know what he'd say about you and me . . . We need to introduce the idea slowly, give him time to get used to it. We'll have to be patient. Can you do that?'

Philippa nodded. She would have done anything for Harry Fanshaw. Today had changed everything.

'It won't be long until he steps back and hands over the reins to me, then we can be free. We won't have to hide anymore. God, I'm crazy about you.'

He pulled her to him, kissing her hard, and she surrendered to his embrace. He was right to be cautious, she told herself. Pippa didn't want anything to spoil this perfect moment, it was everything she'd ever dreamed of. She was blissfully happy, unable to keep the smile from her face.

And she was almost certain that she was falling in love with Harry Fanshaw.

# Chapter 17

Pippa pressed the code beside the imposing double-width door, eager to get inside and warm up. It was a cool spring day, and she was standing outside a traditional red-brick mansion block in Chelsea, its window frames painted white, with pretty Juliet balconies on each level. She knew Harry would be waiting inside, and the thought warmed her, despite the chilly weather.

Pippa had managed to get away from work a little early under the pretext of a client meeting. She would never have dreamed of doing something like that six months ago, but now she was smitten with Harry and couldn't get enough, taking any opportunity to see him.

Deep down, Philippa knew that she shouldn't be taking the risk. She was jeopardizing not only her job, but her whole future and professional reputation. Harry would be fine, she had no doubt about that; being the boss's son made you bulletproof. But though Pippa's head was saying no, the rest of her body was screaming yes.

The door clicked open and she stepped inside, barely noticing the wide curving staircase with the brown and orange swirly carpet or the letter boxes for each apartment on the wall beside the concierge desk.

'Good afternoon,' Pippa called out brightly, as the concierge nodded curtly. Pippa always felt he knew exactly what was going on, his glowering look conveying his disapproval.

Harry still lived with his parents in Belgravia, but Fanshaw Brothers owned this pied-à-terre just off the King's Road. It was occasionally used for visiting clients, but had now become Harry and Pippa's little love nest, and they met up here as often as they could.

Today, as she made her way up to the second floor, there was a woman coming down the stairs towards her. Pippa glanced at her briefly to see if it was anyone she recognized – a celebrity, perhaps, or another beautiful blonde going to visit Rod Stewart, who had a flat on the third floor. Her face wasn't familiar – she wasn't famous, and she wasn't blonde either – but she was certainly striking.

The woman was immaculately put together, her clothes unmistakably expensive, her brunette hair perfectly styled and a haughty expression on her aristocratic face. Pippa immediately felt intimidated, dressed in clothes she'd bought from the high street, her hair dishevelled and her make-up fading after a day in the office. This woman didn't look as though she'd ever had to work a day in her life. She was wearing a cashmere overcoat and a pillbox hat – not fashionable, but high-end designer – and she carried herself elegantly, clearly from a wealthy background.

As they passed one another on the first-floor landing, the scent of Arpège perfume filling the air, the woman didn't pay Pippa the slightest bit of attention, looking straight through her as though she didn't exist. She pulled a pair of gloves from her leather handbag, and a gold compact engraved with the initials VSS landed heavily at Pippa's feet, cushioned by the thick carpet.

'Excuse me,' Pippa called out. 'You've dropped this.'

The woman stopped, turning around. She reached to take it back and Pippa exclaimed, 'Oh, what a beautiful ring.' It was art-deco in style, with an enormous emerald glittering in the centre, surrounded by smaller diamonds.

The woman quickly whipped her hand back, as though she expected Pippa to try and steal it, depositing the compact in her bag and closing it swiftly. She didn't break a smile, or utter a word of thanks, but stared coldly at Pippa before turning round and continuing on her way.

Pippa was shocked. Some people had no manners, despite their good breeding; doubtless this young woman was rich enough to get through life without having to be nice to people. But Philippa was determined not to let the encounter ruin her good mood and she ran up the stairs excitedly, knocking on Harry's door.

He answered almost immediately, as though he'd been waiting for her.

'I knew you'd forget someth—' he began, breaking off as he saw her. 'Pippa! You're early.' He looked as handsome as ever, his brown hair ruffled untidily, his tie removed and his shirt untucked. He was clearly ready to relax; Pippa noticed two champagne glasses on the side and thought how sweet it was that Harry had prepared for her arrival.

'I couldn't wait to see you,' Pippa grinned as she stepped inside and Harry quickly closed the door behind her. 'I pretended I had a meeting with Driscoll and Sons – was that naughty of me?' she asked, her eyes dancing.

'Oh Pippa, you're always naughty – and I adore you for it,' Harry grinned, pulling her towards him. She could smell the coffee and cigarettes on his breath, inhaling the scent of aftershave on his skin.

'I've been dreaming about you all day,' he whispered, his hands running over the curves of her body.

'I was thinking . . .' Pippa began, as she undid the buttons of his shirt. 'Perhaps we should do something this evening. Go to a restaurant, or a club . . .'

'Sorry, darling,' Harry sighed, as he kissed her, sending a thrill through her. 'I can't. There's a gala dinner that I can't get out of. An opportunity to make some good contacts. Father will be furious if I don't show my face.'

'I could come with you,' Philippa suggested. Being in a secret relationship was starting to weigh heavily on her, especially when Harry seemed to spend all his evenings trying to cultivate a young and hip clientele for Fanshaw's, rather than the aristocrats and establishment figures his father favoured.

'Darling, tonight's going to be terribly dull, I'm afraid. I'll take you next time I get an invitation to Bryan Ferry's place, all right?'

'Really?' Pippa breathed, her head already filled with images of her mingling with Mick Jagger and Jerry Hall alongside David Bowie and Freddie Mercury.

'I promise,' he insisted, nuzzling her neck. 'God, Pippa I love you.'

She gasped in shock, as he said the words she'd been longing to hear, 'Harry, I love you too, more than anyone . . . or anything.'

They kissed passionately, and words were soon forgotten, conversation unnecessary, as they fell in a tangle of limbs and excitement onto the sofa in the lounge.

# Chapter 18

**Ascot, June 1979**

Pippa felt like the belle of the ball and knew that she was causing something of a stir in her Yves Saint Laurent gold brocade dress. She was at Royal Ascot, the horseracing meeting which was one of the social events of the season, alongside Harry in the Royal Enclosure. Pippa could never have imagined herself here, and she was dazzled by it all: the crowds, the glamour the spectacle. She felt like Audrey Hepburn in *My Fair Lady*.

She'd spent the best part of a month's pay on her outfit, and had even splashed out on a matching Frederick Fox hat, sitting atop her blonde hair which she'd styled in an elegant low chignon.

Harry himself looked dashing in his dark grey morning suit, with a sharply cut waistcoat and matching top hat. Butterflies were dancing in Pippa's stomach at the sight of him, her heart racing. Today was important. Not only was it an opportunity to impress Mr Fanshaw Snr, but his wife,

Harry's mother, Eleanor, would also be attending. If everything went well, perhaps Pippa could persuade Harry to tell his parents about their relationship.

'You look incredible,' Harry murmured as the two of them walked slightly away from the crowd, towards the parade ring.

'So do you,' Pippa sighed, gazing up at him. She longed to kiss him, to touch him, but she knew that she couldn't, and the restrictions made her want him more than ever. 'I can't believe I'm here,' she added, staring around at the racegoers in their finery, the famous racetrack lush and green in the summer sunshine.

'Well get used to it,' Harry smiled, accepting two glasses of champagne from a passing waiter and handing one to Pippa. 'This is your life now.'

They clinked glasses and Pippa felt a bolt of excitement shoot through her, sparks fizzing in her bloodstream. She was here today as a guest of Fanshaw Brothers; she'd been astonished to learn that the company supplied wine to Princess Margaret, hence they'd been allocated a limited number of the coveted tickets.

'Oh my goodness,' she exclaimed, as she noticed Roger Moore nearby, looking suave and sophisticated, just like his famous alter ego, James Bond.

Harry didn't notice; he was too busy saying hello to a trio of aristocratic young women, all tall and slender, with strawberry-blonde hair.

'Who are they?' Pippa wondered.

'The Spencer sisters – Sarah, Jane and Diana,' Harry explained. 'They're terribly good fun, and great friends with the royals. Sarah even had a fling with Prince Charles, apparently.'

Philippa's eyes widened, imagining what it would be like to date the eligible young prince. Rumour had it he was under great pressure to settle down and get married, and any attractive woman pictured in his vicinity ended up on the front page of the newspapers.

'Come on,' Harry grinned, jolting her from her daydreams. 'Let's go and place a bet.'

Pippa followed him across the enclosure as Harry explained how it all worked; what the odds meant and who the favourites were. Despite her doubts about their relationship, today she was reminded how wonderful he was. When Harry Fanshaw focused his full attention on her, Pippa felt like the only person in the world.

She placed five pounds on a horse called Diamond Jack, contrary to all Harry's advice, then returned to the enclosure, just in time to see the royal carriages making their way along the mile. An audible murmur ran through the crowd, a ripple of excitement, followed by applause as the majestic-looking Windsor Grey horses trotted past, pulling the open-top Landau carriages. The first contained the Queen, looking wonderful in a red-and-white patterned dress, accessorized with pearls and a large rose-shaped brooch. Prince Philip was seated beside her, while the Queen Mother and Princess Margaret followed behind in the next carriage.

Pippa clapped excitedly as the procession passed by, and the royals waved and smiled at the crowd.

'Oh, my mam will never believe it,' Pippa gasped.

The afternoon flew by, with the drinks and conversation flowing, the winners and losers cheered and cursed in equal measure. The more champagne they drank, the more Harry and Pippa let their guard down, with lingering looks and occasional touches, the chemistry between them threatening to boil over.

'Let's leave,' Harry suggested, leaning down to whisper in her ear, his breath hot against her neck. 'We could go back to the apartment and . . .' He didn't need to finish his sentence; Pippa knew exactly what he had in mind.

They were just turning to go when a red-headed man approached them, looking rather the worse for wear. His top hat was askew and there were sweat patches under his arms.

'Harry, my old fellow!' the man said, slurring his speech.

'Crispin, good to see you. This is my colleague, Pippa Campbell, but we were just leaving . . .'

'Of course, of course. Don't let me stop you. I just wanted to congratulate you on your engagement.'

Harry was pushing Pippa forward with one hand, speaking over Crispin as he tried to say goodbye to him, but the words rang out clearly to Philippa. She stopped in her tracks, a sick, cold feeling washing over her that had nothing to do with the alcohol she'd consumed.

She turned around to face Harry, her blue eyes glittering dangerously. 'Engagement?'

'Yes, I saw it in *The Times* yesterday,' Crispin waffled on, oblivious to the look of horror on Harry's face. 'The Honourable Venetia Stanhope-Smythe. You're going up in the world, aren't you? Bet your old man's bloody glad it'll be her father paying for the wedding, not him!' he brayed, but Pippa had stopped listening.

She was staring at Harry in disbelief; shock, and betrayal written across her face. She didn't even try to hide her feelings – she couldn't even if she tried.

'How could you?' she whispered, shaking her head. She could barely take it in. He'd told her he loved her, and she'd believed him. She envisioned spending the rest of her life with him . . . but it had all been a lie. He was engaged to someone else, and she was an utter fool for having believed anything that came out of his mouth.

'Pippa—' Harry began, his face ashen.

She turned on her heel and ran, too shocked to even cry. Behind her, she heard Harry shout, and realized he was following her. 'Pippa, wait, please, let me explain!'

Philippa didn't stop running until she was outside the main entrance, frantically searching the road for a taxi.

She set off to walk, but Harry grabbed her arm and she spun round to face him, shaking him off furiously.

'Explain? How *can* you explain? Are you engaged to someone else?'

The shame-faced look he gave her was all the answer she needed.

Overcome by anger, Pippa raised her hand and slapped him hard across the cheek. Harry barely flinched, as though he were taking the punishment he deserved.

Philippa pulled back her shoulders and stood up straight, tall and dignified, suddenly completely sober.

'You don't deserve me,' she told Harry coolly, as a taxi fortuitously pulled up and she climbed inside. Harry watched as the car drove off but didn't try to stop her.

Only when they turned off the high street far out of sight of Harry, did Philippa finally cry, the sobs wracking her body.

She'd adored Harry Fanshaw, trusted him, fallen in love with him, and he'd taken her for a fool. Well, she wouldn't make the same mistake twice. Harry Fanshaw was history.

# Chapter 19

**London, June 1979**

Harold Fanshaw opened the letter Pippa had just handed him with trepidation. His eyes skimmed over the words – it was brief and impersonal – and he sighed.

'Oh, Miss Campbell. I had hoped it wouldn't come to this. Are you sure I can't persuade you to stay?'

'Quite sure. It's for . . . personal reasons.'

'I see.' Harold steepled his fingers, staring into the middle distance as though wondering whether to say what was on his mind. Pippa stood in front of him, dignified and composed; she'd declined his invitation to take a seat.

'Look,' Harold began. 'I think I know what might have prompted this letter, if my suspicions are correct.' He took a long pause before speaking again, and Pippa could see he was picking his words carefully. 'My son has always been rather . . . headstrong and selfish. He pursues his own pleasure and often fails to consider the feelings of others. Does any of that description sound familiar to you, Miss Campbell?'

Pippa nodded almost imperceptibly as tears prickled behind her eyes. She didn't think she had any left to cry – she'd spent the whole weekend sobbing into her pillow – but Harold's unexpected kindness and understanding had caught her off guard. He opened his desk drawer, pulled out a clean handkerchief, and handed it to her.

'I hoped my suspicions about what Harry was doing were unfounded, and prayed it wouldn't come to this. Everything I said was true – you're a valuable asset to the company, and you should have played a key role in its future.'

'That won't be happening now,' Philippa said ruefully, seeing the life that she'd planned – in London, with Harry – disappear like a mirage. 'I trust you'll give me a good reference?'

'Yes, of course – never doubt that. I'm sorry to lose you, Miss Campbell.'

'Thank you. For everything,' Pippa added. She turned to go, but Harold stopped her.

'Wait a moment, would you? I came across an alternative opportunity and now . . . well, I'm wondering if it may be of interest to you . . .'

He rooted around on his desk, lifting piles of paper, as Philippa watched him sceptically. She certainly didn't want to take a job with one of their competitors; the idea of remaining in London, of bumping into Harry at events or even on the street made her feel sick to her stomach. But she would hear what Harold had to say; she owed him that much at least.

'Ah, yes, this is the one,' he said triumphantly. 'Casa di Russo.'

'The Italian red? The Taurasi?' Pippa responded immediately.

'The very same. Your knowledge and instincts are excellent; you're a natural in this profession.' He shook his head regretfully. 'They're based in Campania, outside the town of Avellino. The estate is about an hour from the Amalfi Coast.'

Pippa frowned in confusion. 'The position is in Italy?'

Harold nodded. 'Yes. They're looking for something of an all-rounder really, to manage the operations side of the business. Do you speak any Italian?'

'Not much,' Pippa admitted, wishing she could say she was fluent. She couldn't explain why but there was something about this opportunity that called to her, the idea that she could jump on a plane and just start again. She'd resigned herself to moving back to Scotland, living with her parents in St Andrews while she licked her wounds and decided what to do with the rest of her life, but she wasn't ready to give up on her dreams just yet. 'I'm a fast learner and a hard worker,' she said quickly.

'I know,' Harold smiled. 'I don't doubt you'd be more than capable. The language might not be an issue – they export a considerable quantity of their output to the UK, and a little to the US, so an English speaker would be extremely useful. Would you like me to give them a call and pass on your details? I'd be very happy to sing your praises.'

Pippa nodded. Her heart was racing. Five minutes ago there was an empty void in front of her, and now this chance seemed like the thing she wanted most in the world. She could just imagine it: Italian sun, beautiful scenery, food, wine, *la dolce vita*. And all of it more than a thousand miles away from Harry Fanshaw and his lies.

'Yes, please,' she said eagerly, her eyes shining. 'It sounds perfect.'

As Philippa boarded the plane to Italy, she felt no fear, only excitement. It was just two weeks since the conversation in Harold's office. It was three weeks since she'd found out that Harry had cheated on her, and she thought back to what a fool she'd been, certain now that his fiancée had been the woman she'd met on the stairs in his apartment block. Pippa remembered all the times she'd waited for a call from Harry that never came, believing his endless excuses about why he couldn't honour the plans they'd made. Even the presents he'd lavished her with seemed clichéd and impersonal; she cringed when she thought of the lingerie he'd given her, and wondered if he'd bought two sets at a time – one for her and one for Venetia. But there was no point raking over unhappy ground.

As the plane took off into the grey rain clouds that typified an English summer, Pippa allowed herself to dream about her new life. There would be glorious weather, beautiful scenery, delicious food and . . . what else? *Work*, she told herself, *the thing you love*. She'd sworn off men, she insisted.

Pippa accepted a glass of wine from the air hostess – a passable Pinot Noir – and flicked through the Italian language book she'd bought at the airport.

'*Sono molto lieta di incontrarvi,*' she murmured under her breath, enjoying the sound of the words, the way they felt in her mouth as they rolled around her tongue. *I'm very pleased to meet you*. It was a beautiful language.

She had learned that Casa di Russo was a family business – winemaking had been in the Russos' blood for generations – and now the father, Antonio, was stepping back as his son, Salvatore, took over. He had grand plans for the future but needed someone to assist with the day-to-day running, the finances and the paper-work, while he focused on the wine. To Pippa, it sounded like a dream.

In a little over two hours the plane began its descent. Pippa stared out of the window, her spirits feeling a prickle of excitement at the sight of the sparkling blue sea, smooth as glass when viewed from this height. The stunning Bay of Naples was dotted with brightly coloured fishing boats, and in the distance she could see the picturesque islands of Ischia and Procida, nestled beside the coastline, the rugged peninsula rising from the water like a dragon's tail.

As the plane came in to land at Capodichino airport in Naples, Pippa was treated to the most incredible view of Mount Vesuvius, which dominated the landscape around it, the deadly volcano now quiet and resting.

As Pippa exited the plane, she could almost have kissed the ground, she was so happy to be there; feeling like a weight had been lifted off her shoulders. She was imme-diately enveloped by a warm air that carried with it the salt of the sea and the faint tang of lemons, and for the first time in weeks she felt as though she could breathe.

Pippa had been told that someone would be at the airport to meet her and, as she left Arrivals and glanced around, she saw a card with her name written on it. She approached, smiling warmly at the man who held it.

'*Ciao, Signorina Campbell. Mi chiamo Salvatore,*' he said, extending his hand. He was tall – around a head taller than her – with tanned skin the colour of cappuccino and thick, unruly, dark hair that looked as though it was a long time since it had last seen a hairbrush. He was wearing shorts and a scruffy grey T-shirt, as though he'd just walked straight into the airport from the vineyard. Pippa was immediately struck by his presence; it was almost as if the air around him parted to allow him passage. His body was toned and muscular, his biceps and calves looked like granite and Pippa was struck by a sudden image of him bending down and touching the vines and fruit, testing their readiness for harvest. His stained T-shirt hovered above his waistband and Pippa couldn't help but catch a glimpse of his torso.

He followed her eyes and looked down at himself. '*Mi dispiace*. I have not dressed for the occasion, you can see.'

Pippa felt the heat rise to her cheeks at being caught out and shook her head to dispel the sensation.

'No, you look like you are dressed for the fields, which is probably where you have been. I'm sorry, I didn't mean to be rude.'

Salvatore waved his hand dismissively and shrugged casually. 'I *could* agree with you, but I aways look like this.' His eyes twinkled and Pippa couldn't help smiling back.

He thrust his hand towards her, and as she looked down at it, she could see the hardened skin on his finger-tips and the dirt under the nails. It was as if he was hewn from the earth itself and Pippa took it with her own. His grip was firm, his skin warm and rough.

'*Sono molto lieta di incontrarvi,*' she said carefully, and Salvatore looked impressed.

'Ah, you do speak Italian!'

'Well, no,' Pippa shook her head bashfully. 'Not really. But I'm a fast learner!'

'OK, I do speak a little English – *un po*,' he said with a shrug. 'But I am very good at making myself understood. Are you, Philippa Campbell?'

Pippa liked the way her full name sounded from his lips. It sounded far away from Fanshaw's. That's how she would think of herself now. Philippa.

Philippa couldn't imagine Salvatore ever being misunderstood. 'I've managed OK so far . . .' she searched in her head for the right word in Italian. '*Provami.*' *Try me.*

Salvatore regarded her with amusement. 'Challenge accepted.'

Her bright blue eyes sparkled as they met his rich brown ones, as he bent to pick up her suitcase. 'We will go well together, you and I,' he said before turning towards the terminal exit.

'Yes,' Philippa said, picking up her pace to keep up with this force of nature. 'I think we will.'

# Chapter 20

**Campania, June 1979**

'*Buongiorno*, Philippa! How are you? Did you sleep well?'

'Very well,' Philippa smiled at Salvatore's mother, Rafaella.

It was barely 7 a.m., but it couldn't have been more different from waking up in her attic room in Pimlico where the traffic streamed past on the busy road below: the rumble of buses; the honk of taxis; the clamour of pedestrians hurrying for the Tube beneath leaden skies that threatened rain.

Here, when she woke, it was almost silent. There was no traffic, just birdsong, and the occasional shout from one of the first vineyard workers arriving. Philippa fancied, if she listened hard enough, she could hear the distant babble of the stream that marked the border of the Russos' land, the one that Salvatore had explained gave the grapes their unique flavour and bouquet.

Her reception a few days previously couldn't have been warmer. Rafaella was a glamorous woman, with long, dark hair coiled and pinned on top of her head, and she had enveloped Philippa in a warm embrace as she entered the kitchen where Rafaella was presiding over a range cooker where various pots and pans were bubbling away. The smell of tomato, oregano and garlic made Philippa's stomach rumble.

Rafaella had held Philippa by the shoulders and taken a step back to appraise her, before pulling her in for a hug.

'*Mamma mia!* Harold did not tell me he was sending an English rose to our quiet valley.'

'I'm Scottish, actually,' Philippa told her, immediately caught up in the woman's embrace.

'A Celtic flower then! Either way I hope you will bloom here in our happy vineyard amongst the grapes.'

Rafaella hailed her son. 'Salvatore, Philippa is *bellissima*, no?'

Salvatore caught Philippa's eye and rolled his own. 'My mother likes to state the obvious.' Philippa felt an unexpected rush of pleasure at his understated compliment.

Rafaella tutted in an exaggerated fashion. 'You will find my son only thinks about wine and *the vine*!'

'Mamma, what else do you want me to think about?'

Rafaella raised her eyebrows and said, 'Philippa, happy grapes only grow where there is love and laughter. I can see from your eyes that you will bring much of that to the Russo family.'

Rafaella took her upstairs and showed her to her room, which was furnished simply yet beautifully and overlooked the vineyard in the Avellino valley and the rolling hills and mountains beyond.

When Philippa came down to dinner after freshening up and putting on a simple white shift dress and gold leather sandals, she was surprised to find the veranda which led out from the kitchen was filled with people seated at a large wooden table, which had been laid out for dining. Philippa felt herself swept up in helping to serve the steaming bowls of rich, red meaty sauce, vegetables and pasta, while the diners chatted loudly wishing her '*ciao!*' and '*benvenuta!*' as they plated up and poured generous glasses of wine for each other.

Once that was done, she heard her name called and looked to see Salvatore beckoning to the empty seat next to him, which she took.

Salvatore stood up and rapped on the table, saying to her out of the side of his mouth, 'I have to get their attention before they start eating, or it will be too late.' Then he spoke more loudly to the table.

'Now you hungry vultures, before you scavenge every last scrap of this beautiful feast, I must introduce you to the newest member of the Russo famiglia. This is Philippa.'

There were loud cheers and more good-natured shouting before Salvatore raised his glass. 'Philippa, this rabble are the workers of the Russo vineyard and every evening during harvest we eat together, argue together and often get drunk together. I'm sure you will soon fit in!'

Philippa laughed and to more cheers she clinked glasses with those around her, but it was to Salvatore that she said, 'I think I'm going to like it here.'

To which he said, 'It's either that or we will drive you crazy.'

But to Philippa, it already seemed like the Russo vineyard was the best place on earth she could possibly have found herself in.

'Please, help yourself,' insisted Rafaella, indicating the bread and pastries on the kitchen table, before preparing an espresso for Philippa, rich and strong, just the way she liked it.

That morning Rafaella wore a light cotton dress in olive green that seemed to emphasize her voluptuous figure, and sandals bought from the market and made locally from the softest leather. Philippa realized that she'd barely given a thought to her own appearance since she'd arrived in Italy. After so many months of dressing smartly for the office, it was a relief to throw on only what was practical for the weather, her hair tied back and her face bare.

'Philippa, I want to hear all about you, you can tell me while you chop and I fry.'

As Philippa helped Rafaella prepare lunch for the workers, she told Rafaella all about her family and coming to London, but was careful to gloss over Harry Fanshaw and his place in her arrival in Italy. He already seemed like a bad dream she'd had, rather than a painful reality.

Salvatore came into the kitchen, and immediately made a beeline for the freshly baked bread that sat on the counter.

'I'm starving. And Mamma, promise me you're not giving Philippa the inquisition?'

'Of course not,' Rafaella tutted at her son and slapped his fingers as he reached for more bread. 'My son is permanently hungry.'

'What do you expect? It's eight o'clock and I've been in the vineyard for two hours already.'

Rafaella ruffled her son's hair, which made him scowl, like a boy. 'My son is a hard worker, Philippa, but he has something special that will make this business an even bigger success than we have.'

'What's that?'

'Charm!' Rafaella laughed. 'Though that scowl is not very charming this morning.'

Philippa had learned that Salvatore was always outside, constantly monitoring the grapes to check which ones were ready for harvest. 'There are good days and there are grape days,' he told her, explaining that grapes might be ripe in one part of the vineyard and not yet ready for harvesting in another.

Philippa had spent her first few days acclimatizing herself to the business, their strengths and their weaknesses, and was slowly formulating a plan for how she could support the expansion. However, that day Salvatore seemed to have something else in mind.

'Have you got a good pair of walking shoes?' he asked her.

Philippa looked down at her feet and pointed to her sturdy trainers. 'Will these do? Where are we going?'

He grinned. 'Ah, you'll have to wait and see . . .'

An hour later, Philippa found herself walking up the side of a mountain.

Salvatore had driven them in his pick-up truck to the bottom of what looked to Philippa like a mountain range.

'I hope you like walking?' he asked her.

'You're not making me walk all the way up there today. are you?' She frowned.

'Philippa,' he teased, 'surely a little energetic stroll won't trouble you?'

'Of course not!' Philippa hated to be thought of as a weakling. 'I've walked up more Scottish mountains than you've had hot dinners.' And with that she strode off up the path.

'Wait,' he laughed, 'you don't even know where you are going!'

The two of them teased each other and joked as they walked upwards for a mile. Philippa was starting to feel an ache in her joints and her cheeks were flushed with exertion, but the views down to the town of Avellino were breathtaking and the air was so clear. Philippa didn't want Salvatore to know it, but she hoped that they wouldn't be climbing for too much longer. Trying to sound nonchalant, she said, 'Is it much further?'

Salvatore, now in front, shook his head. 'We are almost there.'

Philippa followed as he led her away from the main path, down an overgrown track which led into a deep, narrow valley, reminding her of a glen back home in Scotland.

In front of them was a wall of rock from which a waterfall cascaded into a stream that flowed into the valley. Philippa thought it was a quiet, magical place.

'It's beautiful,' she said.

'We are now close to the source of the Avella spring. It's where the Russo wine gets its unique qualities. This spring water travels from the top of this mountain, all the way down the valley, through our land and eventually meets the Ufita River.'

'Can you drink it?' she asked.

'Of course, here –' He grabbed her hand and pulled her gently down to the water. He cupped his hand and took a drink, then did the same and offered her his two cupped hands filled with the clear water.

Philippa hesitated but, encouraged by his warm eyes, she held his hands with her own and took a sip, her lips briefly touching his palm. It was cold, and something else too.

'It's sweet?' she said. 'I've never tasted anything like it!'

'Grapes have been grown in this valley since Roman times. The soil is volcanic, and hundreds of years ago, the vineyards in the region were almost wiped out when Mount Vesuvius erupted; the whole ecosystem was affected.'

Philippa shook her head in astonishment.

'Now you understand?' he said, his eyes filled with the passion of his craft. 'By the time it gets to the Russo vineyards, it's altered very slightly, but that sweet purity? That doesn't change, and it's what gives the wine its vigour and its vitality.'

'I can see why the wine is so special now. Does it feed the Bianchi vineyards too?'

Salvatore frowned. 'Not in the same way. The spring runs directly through our land. It's the natural course of the water, but the Bianchis . . .. Well, in Britain you would say they have not behaved like gentlemen, no?'

'In what way?' Philippa was intrigued.

'My grandfather, he and Grandfather Bianchi were old friends, both happy in their own vineyards, then old man Bianchi accused my grandfather of deliberately altering the course of the water to benefit his own grapes.'

'And did he?'

Salvatore gave her a dark look.

'Sorry,' she said, 'I didn't mean . . .'

'There were October storms one year and the rains came; heavy, bringing mudslides and much destruction; the whole valley was disrupted, the course was altered, but it was a natural occurrence.'

'Why did they make the accusation?'

He shrugged. 'Who knows. The Bianchis have always played fast and loose. Always money problems, too many friends in the wrong places.'

Philippa raised her eyes in a question.

'Camorra,' Salvatore said darkly. 'They said their wine turned sour that year, but it wasn't the Russos who ruined their wine.'

'What about the families now?'

'My father still bears the family grudge, but those days are over; we must work together to make good wine for the valley. Costa, the son, he is my friend.'

Philippa smiled. 'I can see why your mother has so much faith in you. You're a good man, Salvatore.'

'I wanted you to know about this place, Philippa, it's important to me.'

'Then it's important to me, too,' she said, meaning it for a reason she couldn't understand.

He gave her a smile that seemed to contain all the sun in the Avellino valley and grabbed her hand. 'Come on, I'll race you to the bottom.' Then he was off.

'Wait for me!' she shouted, and then laughed as he disappeared down the mountain, leaving her with a girlish grin on her face before she set off at a sprint, trying desperately to catch up with this man who had come into her life like a tornado.

# Chapter 21

Over the following weeks, Philippa settled in quickly, and Rafaella made her feel like one of the family. Her days were spent wading through the paperwork in the vineyard office. This clearly wasn't the family's strong point and Philippa found piles of unpaid bills and unprocessed orders, but also lots of enquiries from wine merchants across Europe who wanted to stock the Russos' wine.

Salvatore worked incredibly hard, Philippa had observed, with an oversight and knowledge of every inch of the vineyard and the valley beyond. He seemed to know everyone, and everyone knew the Russos.

Even though his father, Antonio, was nominally the head of Casa di Russo, he was clearly stepping back as Salvatore prepared to take over the family business.

'We don't produce enough to supply all the dealers who want it, it's why we want to grow,' he told her in Italian.

Philippa found Antonio more reserved than his effusive wife, but that was understandable as he spoke little English. Overall, there was a warmth within the Russo villa, and

Philippa found herself feeling further and further away from Fanshaw's and the upsetting events of the last six months.

Her evenings were spent around the cooker with Rafaella, who was teaching her the basics of Italian family cuisine. 'I was sad never to have my own daughter, or any more after Salvatore. We weren't blessed,' she told Philippa, sadly. 'But you are a welcome surrogate.'

They had a housekeeper who came in daily, but Rafaella ruled the roost and Philippa found that spending so much time with her was helping her adjust to life in Italy.

'Do you have plans this weekend?' Rafaella asked her one day, as she prepared a hearty breakfast for the family. Philippa had noticed that at the Russo vineyard, roles were fluid: one day she might be designing sales brochures, and two hours later she could be helping Rafaella round up the hens from the garden.

'No, nothing as yet.' Her work at the vineyard was all-encompassing, but when she had time, Philippa spent her spare leisure hours exploring the countryside on an old bike she'd found in one of the outbuildings, or catching a lift to Avellino with whoever was heading in that direction.

'Perhaps you could come with me to visit the Bianchis – Maria has invited us. You could meet her daughter-in-law, Vittoria. She's a similar age to you, and it would be nice for you to make a friend here. Her baby, Giorgio, is adorable. I hope to be a *nonna* someday soon,' Rafaella sighed, with a pointed look at Salvatore, who was piling scrambled eggs and toast onto his plate.

Salvatore didn't rise to the bait, saying instead, 'Mamma is never happier than when she is marrying me off.'

'What else is there but family, Salvatore, huh? It's your turn to add to ours, and your soulmate is out there, waiting for you . . . maybe, she might even be very close?' At this, Rafaella gave Philippa a wink, which immediately made Philippa blush, but Salvatore was cool.

'Mamma, Philippa might want some time to herself, to relax. She might not want to spend her day off with the Bianchis, anyway.'

'No, I'd love to meet them,' Philippa replied. She felt very lucky to have found this family who treated her like one of their own.

'The Bianchis, it's all trouble with them,' Antonio muttered in Italian. He was a handsome man in his early fifties with a Roman nose and rugged features, his dark hair flecked with grey. Philippa could see that Salvatore had inherited the best features of both his parents.

She didn't entirely understand what Antonio had said, but she got the gist of the sentiment – and of Rafaella's sharp rebuke to her husband.

'Stop living in the past. I don't understand why you have such a problem with them. Roberto and Maria are good people, and so are Costa and Vittoria. I think you're being a snob, just because they're not doing as well as we are.'

'It's nothing to do with snobbery. They blame the Russos for all of their problems.' Philippa noticed that Antonio looked trouble, a tight look passing across his features before he said, more firmly, 'That family are trouble, always getting in a mess and turning to the wrong people to help them out of their own.'

'You don't know that, you just believe the worst of them.'

'I know more than you think. There are ways of dealing

with things in this valley, we all know what they should be; the Bianchi's are risk takers who don't care about dragging others down with them.'

'Nobody is perfect, Antonio, and every man has his own story, which you understand well enough.' Rafaella looked at her husband darkly. 'Their lives . . . took many turns, no? Some of which have benefited us.'

Antonio fell silent at this, and an unusually tense atmosphere settled over the table. Philippa glanced at Salvatore, remembering what he had told her about the Bianchis and the rumours about their business dealings, but he shook his head imperceptibly with a guarded roll of his eyes. It was the first time she'd felt awkward around the Russos since she arrived, the first time it felt as though she was intruding on a private family discussion. Philippa drained her coffee and stood up.

'Well, I have a busy day ahead of me, so I'll head off now.'

'I'll come with you,' Salvatore said, rising to his feet, grabbing a hunk of bread and local ham to take with him. Philippa couldn't help but notice again what a powerful presence he had, his body strong and muscular from the heavy physical work, his skin deeply tanned from a life spent beneath the Italian sun. His clothes were casual, his hair unbrushed, and a smattering of stubble covered his jawline.

'I felt like I was intruding back there,' she told him as they walked together across the yard.

Salvatore sighed. 'The Russos and the Bianchis . . . it's complicated, and I don't understand the half of it myself. The people of this valley, well let's say it can all get a bit Romeo and Juliet sometimes.'

'The Montagues and the Capulets. A family feud?'

'We are Italians, let's say it's a speciality.'

'Right, I'd better be careful then.'

'Yes, before you know it, I may challenge you to a duel over who sits next to the window in our office,' he teased playfully, and Philippa realized that Salvatore seemed to make everything seem better whenever he was around her.

It also surprised her how this life had become second nature to her, how she couldn't imagine being anywhere else but this villa in Campania. There was still so much to learn, but she was soaking it all up like a sponge.

Not for the first time, she found herself wondering whether Salvatore had a girlfriend; he didn't seem to have time for socializing.

'How are you finding life here?' Salvatore asked, interrupting her thoughts.

'I love it,' Philippa said happily. 'I always thought my future would be in the big city, amongst the hustle and bustle, but now I'm not so sure, I feel like this place has enchanted me in some way.'

'You're not . . . what's the English word? *Nostalgia di casa*?'

'Homesick? No, not really. I mean, I do miss my parents, and my friends back home. Scotland feels a very long way away. But I'd much rather be here.'

'I am glad to hear it. Now, I must check the vines – would you like to come with me, there's a moisture to the atmosphere today, can you see it in the air?'

As she walked alongside him across the courtyard to the vineyards, Philippa looked up above; there was a smattering of cloud, the blue of the sky was a vivid cobalt, which contrasted with the lush green of the valley and the red earth of the soil.

'Why do I suddenly feel like I'm in a Matisse painting?'

They reached a row of vines, and Salvatore pointed to one of the grapes. It was still early morning, and Philippa noticed the fruit was covered in a fine dew.

'It's the sun and the air interacting; the grapes feel it and some of them will know it's their time.'

Philippa watched Salvatore's face as he touched the fruit and gently pulled it away from the vine, barely giving it the lightest tug as it fell easily into his waiting palm.

'Salvatore,' she asked, unable to stop herself, 'why don't you have a girlfriend?'

He smiled wryly. 'Girls . . .' he paused. 'I like them very much – I'm not a monk – but, well, my life is here. Most girls don't understand why I can't put them first and it makes them unhappy . . .' He looked at Philippa, his face honest and open. 'And that makes me unhappy, so I go on alone.'

'You deserve to be with someone.'

'And one day I think that will be so, yes, but whoever she is' – and he looked at Philippa in a way that made her belly flip – 'I will share everything of mine with her, but a little bit of my heart . . .?' He shrugged. 'It will always be in this vineyard, she must be happy to share me with the vines.'

Philippa didn't look away, enjoying being so close to him and hearing his innermost heart. At that moment, she wondered what it would be like to be that someone.

# Chapter 22

Whenever they were in the old stable office together, which was rare, they sat at two desks side by side, both piled with papers and binders. Boxes of loose files and archived documents were stacked up behind them. Philippa had suggested to Salvatore that he invest in a word processor, so that they could save all their files on floppy disk and speed up the process of filling out the export forms, but Salvatore had looked at her as though she were crazy. 'If the grapes can be picked by hand, then the paperwork can be done by hand too,' he stated in a way that brooked no argument. Philippa knew she'd have to work on him if the vineyard was ever to join the twentieth century.

Salvatore sat down at his desk, the ancient leather creaking under his solid bulk, and he was unusually quiet. 'Is everything OK, Salvatore?' she asked.

'Philippa,' he said, looking at her seriously, 'are you happy here?'

'Yes, of course,' Philippa frowned, surprised to be asked,

as she selected a folder from the shelf behind her. 'Why wouldn't I be?'

Salvatore paused, looking uncomfortable. 'I hope you don't think that I'm prying, but I ask the same question you asked of me. There is a man in your life back home in London?'

When she'd first arrived in Italy, Philippa still had some crying to do over Harry Fanshaw. It wasn't just the shame and humiliation at having to leave Fanshaw's, but Harry had been her first real love affair.

She paused, wanting to pick her words carefully. 'Before I came here,' she began, aware of Salvatore's rich, brown eyes upon her, 'I'd had my heart broken. Someone hurt me very badly.'

'Were you in love with this man?'

Had she been in love with Harry? 'I don't know. I was certainly in love with the idea of it. He wasn't good to me, and betrayed me, but I was foolish too. I got carried away when I should have known it was all a fantasy.'

'He is the fool,' Salvatore responded fiercely. 'I hate the thought of you upset and hurting. But I am glad it brought you here.'

He looked at Philippa with such honesty in his face that she felt the hairs on the back of her neck tingle. 'Thank you.' This was a side to Salvatore that she'd never previously seen, and his kindness made her heart swell in a way that Harry Fanshaw had never done.

'If he made you cry then he was not the right man for you. You deserve only happiness and laughter.'

Philippa felt so moved by his words that she didn't know what to say and buried herself in her work. But Salvatore seemed strangely agitated that morning. He couldn't seem to settle, disturbing Philippa with his sighs and exclamations.

Eventually, Salvatore slammed his notebook shut, so loudly that Philippa jumped. She looked across at him in alarm to find him staring at her, a determined expression on his face.

'Right, that's it. No more work today.'

Philippa frowned, wondering if he'd gone mad.

'How long have you been here now?' he asked.

'Just over three months.'

'And in all that time, have you been further than Avellino?'

'No, but I've been very busy and—'

'Then that must change. It's a crime that you haven't seen more of this beautiful country. I will take you to Amalfi.'

'What? When?'

'Now,' Salvatore declared, standing up purposefully. '*No time like the present*, isn't that the expression?'

Philippa thought of everything she had to do – the shipping permits and the inventory and the latest set of accounts. Then, seeing the firm set of his jaw, she laughed. Conceding defeat, she put the papers down and smiled at Salvatore. 'All right,' she agreed. 'You're the boss.'

The day had been magical. Salvatore had driven them into Amalfi in the family car rather than the battered pick-up truck, and they'd spent the day exploring the warren of narrow, winding streets, stopping for an exquisite lunch of freshly caught *frutti di mare* down by the marina. They'd marvelled at the magnificent cathedral, its façade beautifully lit by the autumn sunshine. There was a bride waiting outside with her father, her billowing gown trailing over the wide, steep steps, and Philippa watched in awe, thinking how happy the woman looked, and what an incredible place it would be to get married.

Now it was early evening and the daytime crowds who'd thronged the town were departing. Philippa and Salvatore had come down to the pebbled beach at the foot of the towering mountains and were strolling barefoot through the shallows, the crystal-clear water lapping at their ankles. The sun was beginning to drop lower, pink and orange hues washing the sky, and the moment felt perfect.

'Thank you for bringing me here,' Philippa said. 'It was exactly what I needed.'

'Me too,' Salvatore admitted. 'Sometimes I get too involved in my work. It's good to be spontaneous.'

Salvatore had told her about the other beautiful towns along the coastline – the ones she'd heard of, like Positano and Sorrento, and the ones she hadn't, like Altrani and Praiano. He'd promised to take her to all of them and Philippa had replied, truthfully, that she couldn't think of anything she'd like more.

The fact was that, however hard she fought against it or tried to deny it, Salvatore was starting to exert a pull over her, almost like he was the sun and she was his moon, drawn into his orbit. It wasn't only that he was handsome and charismatic; he was also different from the other men she'd encountered. He wasn't pushy or inappropriate or overly flirtatious – unlike the men who followed her along the street in Avellino, trying to convince her to join them for an *aperitivo*. He made her believe in herself – not like Harry had done, with flattery and sweet-talk, but with his trust and his confidence in her.

Philippa had come to realize that she looked forward to seeing Salvatore every day. He made everything brighter just by being around. He seemed to realize that she needed to be treated gently, and she hoped she hadn't put him off by being distant or aloof.

'I can't believe how beautiful it is here.' Philippa stared round at the pastel-coloured town clinging to the craggy rocks, the fishing boats bobbing on the cerulean waters. A few sun worshippers lay on loungers beneath blue and orange-striped parasols, making the most of the final rays, while others had drifted away to the beachside bars to enjoy an Aperol before dinner.

'How do you put it? It gets under your skin,' Salvatore agreed. Then he turned to her, an earnestness to his face as he asked, 'Philippa, do you think you will stay here, or move on?'

'I haven't thought about it. There's still a lot of work for me to do, and . . . I can't think of anywhere else I'd rather be. Your family have been so kind to me . . . You've been so welcoming.'

Salvatore nodded, taking in her words. 'There's another reason I brought you here today. I'd like your advice on something. A sort of . . . project.'

Philippa was intrigued. 'What is it?'

'Let me show you.' He strode out of the water, shaking his feet and slipping on his shoes as Philippa did the same. They returned to the car and drove a short way, up into the mountains behind the town, turning down a bumpy dirt track that looked as though it led nowhere.

'Where are we going?'

'You'll see. We're almost there.'

They climbed out of the car beside an old, ruined building, its plaster peeling, its brickwork crumbling. Some of the rooms were open to the elements, and the inner staircase had collapsed, the courtyard taken over by weeds as ivy ran riot across the ancient stone walls. Philippa could see that it must once have been incredible – grand and imposing, occupying this majestic position with sublime views over Amalfi and the Tyrrhenian Sea beyond.

Philippa didn't think she had seen anything quite so beautiful since she'd arrived in Italy. 'It's wonderful,' she gasped.

'This is the Villa Amore,' Salvatore explained. 'It's been in my family for generations, but it's fallen almost to ruin . . . I've been thinking recently, wondering what to do with it. Perhaps I should sell the land for development and put the money into the winery? Or I could restore it. Perhaps it could be a hotel, but I don't know if I have the time to focus on another business.'

Philippa was staring up at the remarkable building, wide-eyed. Its dilapidated state almost made it more enchanting, with a faded grandeur that was breathtaking. 'The Villa Amore,' she murmured. 'It's so romantic.'

'Yes. In Roman mythology, Hercules, the son of Zeus, was involved in a passionate love affair with a nymph called Amalfi. When she died, Hercules wanted to bury her in the most perfect place on earth. He chose this location on the Italian coast and named it after her. Legend has it that the Villa Amore was founded on the very spot where Hercules would come every year on her birthday, to sit and watch over her grave.'

'Oh!' Philippa exclaimed, moved by Salvatore's tale and feeling touched by the romance of the story. 'You can't possibly sell it. Surely you can restore it and rebuild it? It's beautiful, and unique, I've never seen anything quite like it. I would never, ever get rid of it if it were mine,' she added fiercely.

Salvatore considered her words. 'Thank you. It would be a serious undertaking, though. I wouldn't be able to do it on my own . . .'

They walked slowly round the building, to the terrace where there had once been formal gardens, but it was now an overgrown jungle leading to the cliff edge. It was almost dark, only a segment of the fiery orange sun visible as it prepared to drop below the horizon, the sky ablaze with purples, violets and reds. Salvatore sat down on a large rock and Philippa joined him, the air between them charged and heavy with unspoken words and emotions. She glanced across at him but the shadows had fallen across his face and it was impossible to read his expression. Philippa knew they would have to leave soon, but she didn't want this day to end.

'I wish I could stay here forever.'

For a moment, Salvatore didn't respond, but then he turned to her. 'Philippa, it isn't possible for me to hold these feelings in any longer. I know you've had your heart broken, and I don't want to rush you, but if you think there could ever be anything between us then I'll wait for you. As long as it takes.'

Philippa's heart began to race at his words, overwhelmed with joy at knowing she hadn't imagined the chemistry between them. The mention of her broken heart had jolted her; she realized that she hadn't thought about Harry at all for some time, and she knew that Salvatore was the reason for that.

'You don't need to wait,' Philippa said instinctively, turning to Salvatore. 'I feel the same, I didn't truly know it until now, but you mean everything to me. The vineyard and the family too.' He understood immediately. Knowing that she understood what mattered, he gently cupped her chin in his hands and kissed her.

Philippa felt the air rush, a bolt of electricity shooting through her. Hungrily, she kissed him back, as if she'd been waiting her whole life for this moment. It was perhaps the most perfect location in the world, overlooking the twinkling lights of Amalfi, the sound of the sea crashing in the distance as the sky turned to black.

He pulled away and spoke, his voice thick with passion and emotion. 'I will give you everything, Philippa.'

As Salvatore kissed her again, his hands caressing her waist as he pulled her closer, Philippa didn't think anything had ever felt so right. Harry Fanshaw was insignificant. He was her past and Salvatore was her future. She knew it without a doubt.

# Chapter 23

**Amalfi, April 1980**

Philippa was alone in the bridal suite of the Hotel San Marco in Amalfi. It was late, and it was the night before her wedding to Salvatore. Vittoria, as chief bridesmaid, had offered to stay with her, but Philippa had declined her kind suggestion, and it had been a busy day, seeing her best friend Flora, and her family, who had all come to wish the happy couple well. She wanted to spend her last few hours as a single woman by herself, to relax and reflect.

She changed into a plain white nightgown, cool and soft against her skin. Then she opened the balcony doors to let the night air flood in, brushing her long blonde hair as she looked out at the night-time view. The lights of the villas illuminated the mountainside below, the shoreline picked out by a line of lanterns. Beyond lay the blackness of the sea, a stunning full moon hanging low in the sky above, reflected on the rippling water.

Philippa could hardly believe that it was just ten months since she'd first met Salvatore. Tomorrow, she would climb the steps of Amalfi Cathedral – the Duomo di Sant'Andrea – to become his wife.

She remembered when Salvatore had first taken her to Amalfi; she'd instantly fallen in love with it – and with him – and recalled the bride they'd seen outside the cathedral. When Salvatore had proposed, Philippa had known immediately where she wanted to get married. She suspected that her parents were secretly disappointed that she hadn't returned home and married a local boy, but she knew they were happy for her. She was an invaluable support to Salvatore, in work and life, and the two of them were deeply in love.

With a start, she remembered the letter Salvatore had given her earlier that day, with strict instructions not to open it until she was alone that evening. She raced back to her room and picked up the envelope that was lying on the counterpane where she'd left it. She looked fondly at his messy writing as she tore it open, noting that it was written on thick, quality paper, not the everyday sheets they used in the office. It was written in Italian, but by now Philippa was almost fluent, and she and Salvatore communicated in a blend of the two languages. Her heart pounding, she began to read:

*My darling Philippa,*

*I almost can't believe that this day has finally arrived, the day when I will become your husband and you my wife, the two of us pledged to one another forever.*

*I wanted to tell you how much I love you, to promise you that I will always love you, and to say that I cannot*

*wait for you to become my wife. You have made me the
happiest and the proudest man on God's earth. You have
changed my life from the moment you entered it. You are
beautiful, intelligent, strong – an incredible woman, and
I feel so honoured and blessed that you've chosen to spend
the rest of your life with me.*

*I want to give you a gift, one that is a symbol of everything
you mean to me. My darling, enclosed are the deeds for the
Villa Amore. You adored it from the very first moment you
set eyes on it – just as I adored you. Now it is yours to do
with as you wish, and I know you will breathe new life
into it, just as you have to me, and to the vineyard.*

*You have my heart, and together our love will rebuild
the Villa Amore so that it is worthy of its name.*

*I will love and worship you, now and forever.*

*Salvatore*

Philippa gasped as she finished reading the letter, her
eyes brimming with tears of happiness. She loved
Salvatore so much, and she always would, she was certain
of it. The gift of Villa Amore was completely unexpected,
and she felt stunned as she pulled the thin, yellowing
piece of paper from the envelope, staring in disbelief at
the faded Italian words on the official document.

She and Salvatore had talked of the ruined villa from
time to time, occasionally visiting on their trips to Amalfi.
Philippa had often spoken of her ideas for its restoration,
chattering excitedly about the infinite possibilities: a
soaring entrance hall; a marble staircase; classical stone
plinths housing Roman statues. She'd never imagined
that Salvatore would give her the property as a gift. She
would make it extraordinary, she vowed, the jewel of the

Amalfi Coast. She wanted Salvatore to be proud of her, to make sure he never had any cause to regret the choice he'd made.

Placing the letter on the bedside table, Philippa was shocked to realize that it was almost midnight. Tomorrow would be the biggest day of her life and she needed to ignore the excitement and nerves fizzing around her body and try to get some sleep.

As she climbed between the crisp, cotton sheets, she pictured Salvatore's handsome face: his soft, full lips; the ever-present stubble that peppered his jawline; the softness in his eyes when he gazed at her. She couldn't wait to spend the rest of her life with him, to bear his children and grow old together.

Philippa felt certain that they would always love one another, and that Salvatore would never hurt her, like Harry had, or take her for granted. The two of them were soulmates; fate had brought them into one another's lives and they were destined to be together. In less than twenty-four hours, she would be his wife, and the moment couldn't come fast enough.

# Part Three

# Chapter 24

**Amalfi, September 2005**

'Harry Fanshaw, what on earth are you doing here?'
Philippa gasped. She could barely believe it was him. He
was older, greyer, but just as handsome as ever; ageing
like a fine wine, she thought, noting the irony.

She flashed back to the last time she'd seen him: more
than twenty-five years ago, standing outside Royal Ascot
in his morning suit, shame and guilt written across his face.

And now he was here, at her daughter's pre-wedding
celebration, of all things. Philippa's head was spinning.

'But how . . .?' she began, trailing off as a stunning
woman sashayed up to Harry and wrapped her arm
possessively around his waist.

'Pippa, allow me to introduce Ginevra Ferrari,' Harry
said, his easy charm as irresistible as ever. 'Ginevra, this
is Pippa Camp— I mean, Pippa *Russo*,' he corrected
himself. 'An old friend of mine, and the mother of the
bride, I believe.'

'*Ciao, bella*,' Ginevra greeted her, leaning in to kiss her ostentatiously on both cheeks.

Ginevra had a mane of jet-black hair, blow-dried and backcombed voluminously. Her appearance was vampish, with her enhanced cleavage spilling out of a corseted dress, her lips painted pillar-box red, her dark eyes heavily lined with kohl.

Philippa recognized Ginevra's name – and her face – from the front pages of tabloid newspapers and Italian gossip magazines. Ostensibly a fashion designer, Ginevra was a fixture on the society circuit, always on the arm of some exiled European count, or multimillionaire entre-preneur. Philippa knew that she'd been friends with Giorgio's late mother, Vittoria, which explained her attendance at the party. Yet why was she here with Harry?

'Please, call me Philippa.'

'Ah,' Harry's eyes twinkled. 'Philippa is so much more grown up. I still think of you as my—' he checked himself, 'as the Pippa I remember.'

'You seem to know so much about me and yet, here I am, rather taken by surprise.' She tried to keep her voice bright, and hope the tremor in it wasn't noticeable.

'Yes, well when I realized that I was lucky enough to be invited as Ginevra's plus-one, I couldn't help but do a little digging about the Russos – and there you were.'

Harry's eyes met hers and for a moment Philippa felt a rush of sensation. A flash of the pain and humiliation, but a dart of memory of their passion too. It momentarily threatened to overwhelm her, before she willed her natural politeness to take charge and forced herself to smile broadly. 'It's lovely to meet you again after all this time, Harry, and thank you both *so* much for coming;

the celebrations are going to be wonderful. Ginevra, can I get you anything? Do you both have drinks? Wonderful. Do excuse me, I have a few matters to attend to.'

She exhaled slowly as she walked away, trying to hide how much Harry's unexpected appearance had unsettled her. She could feel Harry's eyes on her as she moved quickly through the guests, heading for the house, impatient for a few moments alone to compose herself.

She wondered if Harry had seen the cross words she'd exchanged with Salvatore as he arrived. But the worst part – the thing she hardly dared to admit to herself – was that on seeing Harry again she'd immediately felt the familiar pull in her stomach, the chemistry between them undeniable.

*It's just the surprise*, she told herself. Or perhaps her feelings for him hadn't died like she'd thought? Maybe they had simply lain dormant, waiting to ambush her at the first opportunity. Seeing Harry again had stirred up a potent mix of emotions.

Philippa reached the bedroom she shared with Salvatore and slammed the door shut, her heart thumping, her reflection in the mirror showing flushed cheeks and glittering eyes. Right now, Philippa was certain of one thing: for the next few days, she needed to stay as far away as possible from Harry Fanshaw.

Carina glanced up as she saw her mother dash past. Philippa seemed distracted – she didn't notice Carina – but right now, Carina had other things on her mind.

She was standing with Giorgio, the two of them ensconced in an alcove beside a statue of Venus, attempting to have a quiet moment of reconciliation amidst all the hubbub. Giorgio was leaning against the plinth, his elbow resting against Venus's toes, as he stared moodily straight ahead.

'Are you OK? You don't seem it,' Carina asked, a palpable tension in the air between them. Giorgio had been gone for almost two weeks, returning four days before their wedding, but he certainly hadn't greeted her with the passion and delight a bride-to-be would have expected. She was also struggling to get a handle on her own feelings at his return.

'Yes, of course. Why wouldn't I be?' Giorgio's words were reassuring, but his manner was anything but.

Carina hesitated. Things weren't right between them and they both knew it. She felt torn, wondering whether she should confront their issues head on, or paper over the cracks and hope it could all be fixed later.

'You seem . . .' Carina began, unsure how much to say. 'I don't know, you don't seem very happy to be here.'

'Christ, Carina, I've just got off a transatlantic flight, I've been travelling the entire day. I've been slogging my guts out for the past fortnight, and you wonder why I'm not jumping up and down like a jack-in-the-box?'

'I just—'

'Just what?' Giorgio turned to face her, his eyes hard. Carina knew him too well, reading the tell-tale signs that might have been invisible to anyone else: the tension in his jawline, the rigid set of his back. She'd told herself that all she'd wanted was for Giorgio to be here, and now he was, he seemed like a stranger. Now he was in front of her, she realized that they had been strangers to each other for a long time.

'Come on, we need to talk to each other. You may have chosen to ignore it, but we are getting married in four days . . .' Carina kept her tone light, trying to cut through his dark mood, but that only seemed to make him more annoyed. 'How was the trip?'

'Why are you prying? We're not even married yet and already you want me to account for every hour I'm not with you. A good wife minds her own business, perhaps you need to learn that.'

Carina was taken aback by his words, anger and humiliation surging through her. She didn't deserve to be spoken to like that. 'Why are you being so callous?'

'Why are you being so sensitive? I'm exhausted, trying to put on my best face for this circus,' he sneered, jerking his head in the direction of the party. 'All I want is five minutes' peace without you nagging me.'

Carina narrowed her eyes. 'What's happened to you? When did you become so selfish and sexist? "*A good wife*"?' she scoffed. 'You sound like your father.'

'And you sound like *your* father – haughty, arrogant, looking down your nose at us Bianchis, thinking you're better than us.'

'That's not true,' Carina insisted, although she felt her cheeks colour and knew that he'd hit a nerve; perhaps there was some truth in his statement.

'Isn't it?' Giorgio stared her down.

Carina was speechless. She had the unnerving feeling that everything was spinning away from her. Outside the jazz quartet was playing and the buzz of conversation and laughter floated through to them, but to Carina it sounded muffled, as though she were underwater. She and Giorgio were supposed to be getting married within days, but instead they were at one another's throats. They couldn't carry on like this.

'Look, don't over-react, Carina, I'm just tired, everything will be OK,' he told her, giving her a perfunctory kiss on the head as he slipped past her, his face changing instantly; full of bright smiles and warm greetings as he approached his father and a group of their friends.

'Giorgio . . .' Carina watched him leave, struggling to comprehend what was happening between them. Today should have been perfect – a party in the most magical location, beneath the dazzling Italian sunshine, all their loved ones gathered in one place to celebrate with them – yet to Carina it felt as though everything was falling apart.

Over by the French doors, which had been flung wide open to allow easy access to the terrace, Tom discreetly watched the argument play out from behind his aviator sunglasses. He wasn't close enough to hear what was being said, but he could read the body language between them, noticing how cold and closed Giorgio looked, Carina's body language, and the way he'd left her visibly upset.

As Giorgio stormed off, Tom's attention remained on Carina. She stared after her fiancé, and the expression on her beautiful face was a mix of fury and despair, sadness and vulnerability. Something about the whole situation seemed wrong to Tom. If his training had taught him anything, it was to trust his instincts, and Giorgio didn't seem like a man who was overjoyed to be reunited with his wife-to-be.

Despite the short amount of time he'd known her, they'd already formed a bond, and it angered Tom to see her treated like this. But he knew it wasn't his place to interfere.

Edie caught his attention, a flash of white-blonde hair and tanned skin, as she made a beeline through the crowd towards her friend, enfolding Carina in a hug. At least she was in good hands, Tom told himself, watching the two women as they began to talk. Carina needed someone on her side – especially in light of the new information Tom had discovered. Which reminded him . . .

He glanced round and saw Salvatore walking towards him.

'The very man I was looking for,' Tom said.

'What do you have for me?' Salvatore's manner was as direct as ever, anxiety etched across his face as he glanced around to ensure no one was listening. Tom hesitated, and Salvatore nodded in understanding. 'Follow me,' he said, leading him through the house and into his private study. It was cool after the heat of the outdoors, calm in contrast with the noise of the party. Decorated in the same classical style as the rest of the villa, it was unlike the office in Avellino, this felt more like the space a man would use to unwind, to indulge his personal passions. There was an old chesterfield sofa underneath the window, newspapers and books seemed to cover every surface. The cluttered desk was covered with pictures of Salvatore and his family; one with him and Carina, her sitting in the saddle of a white pony as a young girl, gaps in her milk teeth as she grinned cheesily at the camera; one of Philippa, taken somewhere green and lush – maybe Scotland, Tom thought – looking beautiful as her blonde hair whipped around her face, laughter in her eyes. Its walls were lined with leather-bound books, silk velvet curtains fluttering at the windows.

Focusing on his purpose, Tom reached into his jacket pocket and pulled out half a dozen photos, handing them to Salvatore. The older man's eyes narrowed as he took in what he was seeing. Wordlessly, he handed them back to Tom.

Salvatore nodded, his expression grim. 'You have done good work.'

'There's more. My contact got back to me about the car that followed us.'

'And?'

'Camorra,' Tom said gravely, as Salvatore swore.

'I don't understand. What could they possibly want with Carina?'

'That's what I'm trying to find out.'

Salvatore looked thoughtful. 'There is no corner they can't work their way into, like a poisonous vine. Even at this party.' He nodded his head towards the garden.

'That guy, the one with the black suit and slicked-back hair?'

'Vito De Luca,' Salvatore said. 'He's here today, with his wife and daughter . . . we go back a long way, but there are others . . .'

'I'll follow every lead,' Tom promised.

'Anything else?'

'Unfortunately, yes . . .'

Tom took a deep breath and proceeded to tell him everything his investigations had unearthed, Salvatore's face turning to a mask of anger as the discovery hit home.

'Ashley Hall, here to check in,' Ashley purred, as she swept into the lobby of the Hotel San Marco, one of the most prestigious on the Amalfi Coast. It occupied an elevated position, a short distance out of town, up on the hillside with incredible views of the surrounding mountains. Inside it was traditional with a modern twist, the walls painted white with accents of deep blue and gold.

Sam Quinn strolled in behind her. The two of them were a distinctive pair, and Ashley enjoyed the curious stares from the other guests in the lobby. It happened everywhere she went – the murmurings of recognition, the envious looks, a frisson rippling through the atmosphere. She *loved* being able to cause a sensation.

'Ah yes, Ms Hall,' the seasoned receptionist said knowingly as she tapped on the keyboard and glanced at her computer. 'We've allocated you our very best suite – the bridal suite.'

Ashley raised an eyebrow but said nothing. She couldn't help but note the irony, her lips pursing in displeasure.

'The views are magnificent,' the receptionist added hastily, seeming to pick up on Ashley's annoyance. 'And Mr Quinn, you're in the Salerno suite. We're very busy this week, but we'll ensure you're not disturbed. There's a wedding in town and many of the guests are staying here.'

'Is that so?' Ashley's eyebrows soared even higher, her pout deepening.

The receptionist couldn't work out how she had said the wrong thing, but decided it was a good idea to curtail the small talk. 'Alberto,' she called as the bellboy scurried over. 'Please show our guests to their rooms.'

'Thank you,' Ashley said with a sarcastic smile, as she and Sam followed the besuited bellboy across the expansive lobby to the lift.

'Have you contacted your Italian stallion? Does he know we're here?' Sam asked.

'Not yet. I thought it'd be a nice surprise for him.'

'Set up a meeting. Tell him to come here, tomorrow. I bet he'll crap himself.'

Ashley smiled with relish. She whipped out her phone and tapped out a message with perfectly manicured nails.

'All done, see you later,' she smirked as the lift reached the top floor and the bellboy opened the door to her suite. Every detail was perfect, with a romantic four-poster bed draped with white voile, and a luxurious sitting room, an enormous bowl of fruit and a bottle of champagne sitting in an ice bucket on the coffee table. Ashley strode out onto the balcony, absorbing the breathtaking scene: dramatic cliffs tumbling down to the sparkling aquamarine sea, brightly coloured scooters speeding along the narrow roads, as beautiful people sunbathed on the terrace below.

It was the first time Ashley had visited this part of Italy, and it was stunning. She had a feeling she was going to enjoy herself this weekend. It looked like the perfect place for revenge.

# Chapter 25

The 150-foot yacht sliced through the sapphire-blue waters of the Gulf of Salerno, white waves churning in its wake. It was a spectacular vessel, with three levels of decks and a small army of staff in neatly pressed uniforms, *La Dolce Vita* written in swirling gold letters on the side of the hull and the Italian flag fluttering from the stern.

More than a hundred guests were on board, enjoying a champagne brunch – although some had started even earlier with bellinis and mimosas, despite it being before midday. Carina's friends and family had once again put on a glamorous display, the women in elegant kaftans and high-end beachwear, the men in designer swim shorts and linen shirts.

While the Russo family owned a smaller yacht, Salvatore had chartered this luxury cruiser especially for the second day of the pre-wedding celebrations to accommodate the large number of guests. The itinerary was set for them to sail the bay for an hour or two, before stopping at the Grotta dello Smeraldo – the Emerald Grotto – to swim in the shimmering viridian water after which the cove was named. Then they would all head for a late-afternoon barbecue at a stunning stretch of secluded beach, further along the picturesque coastline.

'Such a shame Papà couldn't make it,' Carina said, turning to her mother, thinking how elegant she looked in her chiffon maxi-dress that fluttered gently in the warm breeze. Carina herself was wearing a white playsuit that showed off her slender body and lightly tanned limbs, a halterneck bikini underneath ready for swimming.

'Yes, but you know your father better than anyone. Business always comes first,' Philippa sighed, and Carina thought she detected a trace of frustration in her mother's tone that Salvatore had been called away at the last moment. 'I thought Giorgio was coming?'

'He's . . . unwell. Tired after the travelling. He wanted to ensure he was fully recovered for the wedding.' In truth, Carina didn't know exactly what was going on with Giorgio. He'd told her that he'd drunk too much at the party, that he was jet-lagged and had work to do anyway, before asking Carina to make his apologies to their guests. It seemed as though Giorgio was pulling out all the excuses he could think of and, when Carina had pressed the issue, he'd once again become snappy and irritable.

Philippa fell silent for a moment. Carina had done her best to sound breezy and upbeat, and hoped her mother would move on to another topic.

'Darling, is everything all right between the two of you?' Philippa asked gently.

Carina opened her mouth to insist that it was, but found she couldn't lie to her mother. 'I think the stress is getting to both of us.' She forced a laugh, downplaying her concerns.

'Are you sure that's all?' Philippa asked. 'You haven't been yourself recently, and I'd hate to think . . . I remember being so excited when I was marrying your father, and you seem . . . different.'

Carina bit her lip, debating whether to confide in her mother and let it all out, all her fears and doubts about her relationship with Giorgio.

'Carina.' Philippa spoke quietly. 'You don't have to do anything you don't want to. You can tell me anything, you know that.'

Carina looked at her mother, the words she wanted to say forming on her lips . . . Then the sound of laughter reached her ears and she looked around the yacht at her friends and family having a wonderful time in Amalfi. They'd spent time and money travelling to her wedding, and she felt she had no choice but to continue down this path.

Carina shook out her long, blonde hair, trying to shake away her worries at the same time. Giving her mother her most convincing smile, she insisted, 'Honestly, Mamma, I'm fine. Giorgio and I will be fine. Everything will be different once we're married.' Inwardly wishing she could force herself to believe it.

She would speak to Giorgio later, she determined, to sort this out once and for all. They needed to, to make sure that this wedding was what they both truly wanted.

All of that would have to wait, however, as right now Carina had guests to entertain.

She caught Edie's eye and grinned at her. Edie was flirting with Tom, who was standing close to her, looking amused by whatever story Edie was animatedly telling him. Carina watched them for a moment, wondering if they genuinely liked one another, or if Tom was merely another potential conquest for Edie, someone to distract from the painful break-up with Nathan.

'Carina!'

'Nanny Jean! Flora! Thank you so much for coming today.' Carina threw her arms around her grandmother and her godmother as they appeared in front of her, both of them carrying a limoncello spritzer garnished with thyme.

'Oh, I wouldn't have missed it for the world,' Flora insisted, kissing Carina on the cheek. Flora Robertson was her mother's best friend from childhood, and she was small and dark-haired and tremendous fun. Carina adored her.

'Although I heard a few people didn't make it this morning. Overindulged in your father's hospitality yesterday,' Jean said, with a faint air of disapproval, as she fanned herself with her sun hat. No matter how many times she visited, she still hadn't got used to the heat or the effusive locals.

'I think the early start put people off too,' Carina explained. Everyone had been instructed to meet on the quayside at 11 a.m., but that felt like the middle of the night for those who hadn't gone to bed until the small hours.

'I'm rediscovering my sea legs,' Flora giggled, pulling aside her sarong to give a flash of pale, Scottish skin. 'By the way, Carina, I didn't know you knew Ashley Hall.'

'Who?' asked Carina and Jean simultaneously.

'Ashley Hall, the supermodel. I was reading about her in *Hello!* magazine on the flight over here,' Flora confessed.

'Oh yes, I've heard of her. But I don't know her. Why did you think that?'

'Some of the guests in the hotel were talking this morning. Apparently she checked in yesterday with her uncle. He's on a reality television show – I read that in *Hello!* too. We thought she was here for the wedding.'

'No, but how exciting! Perhaps she's here on a fashion shoot.'

'What's going on, ladies?' Edie asked as she strolled across. She looked stunning in a leopard print bandeau bikini that left little to the imagination, her feet bare on the glossy teak deck, her toenails painted fluorescent orange.

'We were just talking about Ashley Hall? From Hollywood and *Hello!* magazine,' Flora cut in. 'She has an egg-white omelette for breakfast, and an avocado salad for lunch. I don't think I've ever had an avocado.'

Edie suddenly looked ashen.

'Ashley Hall? Why are you talking about her?'

Carina thought it sounded as if Edie's voice was shaking a little.

'Do *you* know her, Edie?' she asked.

'No,' Edie replied quickly. 'Our paths haven't crossed. Why would I know her?'

Carina frowned, wondering why her friend was behaving so strangely. 'I thought maybe you'd come across her in LA. You're always saying it's a small town. According to Flora, she's staying at the Hotel San Marco.'

'She's *what*?' Edie's face darkened. 'Why on earth would she be here? In Amalfi? This week?'

'I don't know. Maybe she's taking a holiday,' Carina shrugged. 'Does it matter?'

Edie opened her mouth then quickly closed it again. 'I guess not. By the way, where's Giorgio today?'

'He's . . . not well. He might meet us at the beach later, if he's feeling better.'

Edie frowned.

'Darling, there's Giovanni,' Philippa cut in, touching Carina on the arm. 'You remember your father's old friend? I didn't get a chance to speak to him at the party yesterday, so I'd better pop over and say hello. Why don't you come too? He'd love to see you.'

'Of course,' Carina agreed, determined to be a good host as she followed her mother over to the bar, Edie's reaction forgotten for the moment.

Giorgio dodged nervously through the pretty streets of Amalfi, glancing around from behind sleek sunglasses, continually looking over his shoulder. He was all too aware that the town was full of his and Carina's relatives, and he kept expecting to bump into someone who would ask what he was doing. Of course, most of them would be on the boat by now, which was where he was supposed to be, but that didn't stop the prickle of nerves that crept over him, perspiration beading on his forehead as he moved through the summer crowds, scanning every face.

What the hell was Ashley doing in Italy on the weekend of his wedding? She had told him she'd be in Paris, so Giorgio had been shocked to receive a message from her that she was here, in Amalfi, staying at the very hotel that was hosting most of his wedding guests. She'd instructed him to meet her at the Hotel San Marco, but Giorgio had persuaded her to come to a little bar in a much quieter part of town, which was tiny, but he hoped there was less chance of running into someone he knew.

He wondered if she'd found out about the wedding and wanted him to call it off. Giorgio wondered what he'd say if she asked him. A life in California with rich, beautiful Ashley was not an unappealing prospect, and Giorgio once again congratulated himself on managing to seduce a bona fide supermodel.

He passed a yellow-walled church and strolled across a small piazza to a bar with round wooden tables shaded by red-and-white striped umbrellas. He spotted Ashley almost immediately, wearing an enormous wide-brimmed straw hat and oversized sunglasses, presumably in an attempt to go incognito and avoid any lurking paparazzi. But he was shocked to see who was sitting beside her: her uncle, Sam Quinn.

'Beautiful mornin', ain't it?' Sam grinned, clearly enjoying Giorgio's discomfort. He cut an incongruous figure in his tan boots and Stetson, still looking like a Texan cowboy, even here on the Amalfi Coast.

'What's all this about?' Giorgio asked guardedly, as he sat down opposite them.

'See, Ashley here's a little upset, but maybe you can help us both feel better.'

'You're getting married, Giorgio?' Ashley burst out, and Giorgio's ego was gratified to note that she seemed genuinely upset. 'How could you? Don't I deserve better than that? Why couldn't you have just been honest with me?'

Giorgio's mouth flapped open and closed, as though the idea of being honest with anyone had never occurred to him.

'I wasn't looking to tie you down,' Ashley railed, 'I thought you knew that about me, but I won't be treated like an idiot either.'

Sam placed his hand over Ashley's, encouraging her to calm down. 'Now, now, you two can sort out your little lover's tiff later. Giorgio and I have more important matters to discuss.'

'We do?' Giorgio squeaked. His shirt was beginning to feel tight at the collar, dark sweat patches appearing under his armpits.

'That deal you tried to cut me in on, in Newport Beach.'

'You're still interested?' Giorgio asked optimistically.

Sam threw back his head and laughed loudly. Customers at the nearby tables turned to stare, and Giorgio realized what a distinctive trio they made, the three of them standing out even in a town well used to wealthy and flamboyant visitors.

'The hell I am,' Sam chuckled. 'But God loves a trier. Y'see, Giorgio, I did a little digging around – on that project, and on you. Turns out you've got your fingers in all sorts of unpleasant pies. In fact, you're up to your neck in it, aren't you, son? In deals, in debts, and with some bad guys on your tail. Ain't that about the size of it?'

Giorgio had gone white, alarmed by Sam's startlingly accurate summary. The truth was, Giorgio didn't know exactly what he owed, or who he owed it to. He was living from moment to moment, hustling his way from one deal to the next in the hope one of them would come good and he'd finally make enough to pay off his ever-spiralling debts. He knew he'd overcommitted himself – he'd forged documents and bank statements to take out loans he couldn't afford – and now he was getting by purely on bravado.

Giorgio had set his sights on America, and to make it big as a property mogul, and he had no intention of starting small by renovating a clapped-out, one-bedroom apartment in Avellino. Giorgio wanted to be a big shot, a player, and there was nothing wrong with ambition, he'd told himself. The build cost of a five-star hotel or luxury mansion was peanuts compared with the profit he could make on the sale, so once he'd clinched a deal he could easily pay back his investors.

Only it didn't work out that way; there were escalating building costs, shady construction firms, failed projects. And then people started to come asking for their money, and the only way Giorgio could see to get it was to move onto another project, bigger and better than the last. He'd borrowed money from some friendly guys who'd turned out not to be quite so friendly and, in desperation, he'd started doing other work for them too. They'd made it horribly clear he didn't have a choice, and now things had gone from bad to worse and it wasn't just money he owed.

'I . . .' Giorgio began to stammer and stutter. For a moment, he considered breaking down and confessing everything, but he quickly rallied. *Fake it 'til you make it* – wasn't that what the Americans said? 'Look, what do you want from me?' Giorgio asked, his dark eyes hardening as he realized Sam wasn't playing games. He hadn't flown halfway across the world for a polite chat over coffee.

Sam took his time, picking up his espresso and taking a sip. 'A little bitter,' he commented wryly. 'See, son, like I said before, I've always had a hankering to own a vineyard. And it seems to me you've got a pretty nice set-up out here. So if you could see your way to helping me get what I want, then maybe I could help you out of this mess you've created.'

Giorgio frowned. 'But the vineyard isn't mine. It's my father's . . .'

'Oh, come now. I'm sure a clever guy like you can think of some way round that. It'll be yours one day, won't it?'

Giorgio opened his mouth to speak but no sound came out.

Sam rose to his feet, his six-foot four-inch frame looming over Giorgio intimidatingly.

'You've got twenty-four hours,' he growled, the jovial manner gone, a clear threat behind his words. 'Come on, Ashley.' Sam strolled off across the cobbles as though he didn't have a care in the world.

Ashley scrambled to her feet, her expression apologetic. As she crossed behind Giorgio's chair, she let her hand trail across his shoulders, scratching him lightly with her nails through the thin fabric of his shirt. Giorgio shivered involuntarily, a primal urge rippling through his body at her touch. She bent down to whisper in his ear, her lips brushing his neck. It was all Giorgio could do not to throw her over the table and make love to her right there in the piazza.

'I miss you,' Ashley murmured. 'We always had a lot of fun together. When you've got all this marriage business out of the way, give me a call.'

She winked at him, then pulled down her sunglasses and hurried after her uncle.

Giorgio stared after her, feeling a peculiar combination of aroused and terrified. But he realized he'd made his decision. Now he just had to go through with it.

# Chapter 26

'One . . . two . . . THREE!'

Gleefully, Carina leapt from the aft deck of the yacht, plunging into the warm, crystalline sea below. For a few seconds everything went silent, submerged deep in the waters as though she were in another world, hundreds of tiny bubbles rising around her. Then she kicked out, drifting lazily upwards before breaking through the surface where everything was noise and sunlight once again. Droplets shimmered on Carina's tanned skin as she pushed her thick, blonde hair out of her eyes and lay back in the water, drifting blissfully on the gentle waves.

'I'd prefer to stay on dry land,' Philippa laughingly called after her, as Carina waved at her mother.

There was an enormous splash in the water beside her and Carina looked up in shock to see Tom surface barely a metre away, shaking water from his face. A chorus of whoops and cheers came from the boat, Edie whistling at the acrobatic display.

'Sorry about that,' Tom said, but Carina could see the grin he was trying to hide. She liked it when he let the mask slip, when he stopped being so serious and she saw his playful side.

The sun rendered his blonde hair golden, and his shoulders bobbing above the water were sculpted and muscular, like one of the statues carved from marble at the entrance of the Villa Amore. Back on the boat, Carina had tried to avert her eyes when he stripped down to his tight swimming shorts, but he'd caught her looking all the same and just gave her that same unreadable smile that he always did.

Deliberately, provocatively, Carina had jumped from the side of the yacht, daring him to follow. Her parents had always loved boats and the sea and Carina had been a natural in the water since she was a little girl and was a strong swimmer; she had no qualms about leaping from the boat into the deep blue. Inevitably, Tom had dived off the side right after her without hesitation. She wondered if he was ever scared of anything. It didn't seem like it. She wondered if he really would follow her anywhere, what lengths he'd go to get her back if something happened . . .

Carina shivered, despite the heat of the day, and pushed those thoughts from her mind. The sea around her was filling up with people, and a few daredevils like herself were jumping from the deck, but most were cautiously descending the ladder instead. A handful of guests had stayed on board, opting not to swim today though the sparkling Mediterranean seemed irresistible to her. The sea was so clear you could see the small fish darting in the water below. The sun warmed her shivers away and she revelled in it.

'Oh, this feels good,' Carina sighed. 'It's wonderful to do something fun for a change that doesn't have anything to do with the wedding . . .' An unspoken question hung in the air, and Carina was grateful that Tom didn't ask it.

'The view's even better from the water,' he observed.

It took Carina a moment to realize what he was referring to, smiling as she saw him staring up at the mountains, the clusters of brightly coloured houses clinging to the slopes, impossibly picturesque.

'Yes, it's beautiful. But I have something better to show you. Do you want to see?'

'I'll follow wherever you lead. It's in my contract,' Tom teased, as Carina laughed, racing ahead of him through the water. She was fast, but Tom soon caught up with her head start, the two of them gliding through the water like dolphins.

As they approached the shoreline, Carina stopped, treading water as she turned to Tom. 'The yacht is so big, we couldn't get too close but this is one of my favourite places in the world. La Grotta dello Smeraldo,' she announced, her Italian accent rolling and melodic as she pointed to an entrance in the cliff-face.

From a distance, it had looked like nothing more than a change in the shadows, perhaps a trick of the eye, but as they swam closer it was evident that it was more extraordinary and unexpected, a soaring cave hidden at the base of the cliff, serene and otherworldly.

As they swam towards the entrance, Tom seemed awed as he took in the stunning blue-green water, shimmering like an emerald, that gave rise to the grotto's name.

'All of the tourists go to the Blue Grotto in Capri, but I think this is much more special. It's smaller, more intimate, and the light reflecting off the walls is like nature's fireworks.'

'You'd make a great tour guide,' Tom commented wryly.

'Perhaps you're too easy to please,' Carina retorted, blushing as Tom laughed and she realized how it sounded.

The two of them swam inside the hidden sea cave, which was empty of tourist boats; the silence broken only by the echo of the lapping water as the sound reverberated around the cave. Carina never failed to be awestruck by the cavernous interior; magical and atmospheric, it was almost like entering a cathedral, and the two of them approached with reverence, naturally lowering their voices which echoed off the jagged stone walls. Stalactites and stalagmites jutted and twisted, sunlight filtering through the holes in the rock to create a veritable rainbow of colours sparkling through the water.

Carina swam slowly towards the back of the grotto, as far as it was possible to go, before climbing out of the water, sitting on a naturally formed flat ledge of rock. In one swift, smooth movement, Tom pulled up to sit beside her, rivulets of water streaming down his body, making their way through the smattering of blonde hair on his chest, over the tight, hard muscles of his six-pack. The ledge was small, and they were forced to sit close beside one another. Carina could feel the warmth of his body beside hers, telling herself that the cooler air inside the cave was the reason she had goosebumps up and down her arms.

She was aware that her body was on display in the skimpy bikini but she knew that, pre-wedding, she was in the best shape of her life, her limbs toned and slim, her waist narrow but her bottom still curvy and full.

Her eyes slid over to Tom; it was impossible not to notice his firm, strong thighs, the fine blonde hairs leading all the way up to—

'It's the most beautiful thing I've ever seen,' Tom whispered, his eyes never leaving her face.

For a second, Tom seemed to be talking about something other than the grotto, and Carina tore her gaze away from his body, glad of the distraction. 'I love it here. It's so peaceful and calm. It's my own special place,' she laughed. 'I come here when I need to think. Or when I need to escape. As you can see, it's not always full of tourists.'

There was a beat of silence, then Tom said evenly, 'You must be glad that Giorgio's back.'

Carina didn't respond straight away. She realized that she didn't want to lie to Tom; she had the feeling that he would see straight through any pretence. 'It hasn't been quite how I expected. Not all hearts and roses and romance. I guess that's reality though, right? Real life has ups and downs.'

'As long are there are still ups.'

She sighed. 'Not for a while, actually,' her voice barely more than a whisper. 'Maybe it's the pressure of the wedding, or . . . perhaps I've been lying to myself.' She trailed off, grateful to Tom for not interrupting, for giving her the time she needed to organize her thoughts. 'I don't know, maybe things have changed between us. I mean, we've known each other forever. I've changed, I've grown up. And Giorgio's definitely different . . .'

Carina tried to keep the note of acrimony from her voice, but she couldn't hide her inner turmoil. It was the first time she'd voiced her fears out loud, and now she'd opened up, she didn't want to stop. Here, in the quietness of the cave, the sea gently lapping at their ankles, it felt as though they were in their own little world, safe from the reality of the world outside. Carina felt as though she wanted to stay there forever.

'I never imagined myself marrying anyone except Giorgio, but lately . . . Perhaps it's because it's becoming more real, you know? It's making me think, is this really what I want for the rest of my life? I don't know if we make each other happy anymore, and then I get frightened that we're together out of habit or convenience. Or maybe this is just totally normal pre-wedding nerves. What do you think?'

Tom swallowed. 'Do you still love him?'

'I don't know,' Carina confessed. She looked across at Tom, her expression almost desperate, as though searching his face for answers. Then the intensity became too much and she looked away, her gaze landing on a ridge of pearlescent rock shot through with purple and silver.

'Have you ever been in love?' she asked, unable to stop herself. She knew that Tom didn't like talking about himself, but there was something about the moment that felt right.

There was a long pause. Carina could see his chest rise and fall, the quietness of the cave seeming to emphasize every sound around them. Golden light reflected off the water and danced across the craggy walls. Tom closed his eyes. 'Yes.'

'What happened?' Carina whispered, not wanting to break the spell.

'She broke my heart.'

'Oh, Tom. I'm sorry.'

Suddenly it all made sense: aloof and standoffish; never getting too close to anyone. Carina didn't know the details, but she felt sure Tom hadn't deserved what had happened to him. She could see the memory etched on his face, the tension held in his rigid body.

'We were childhood sweethearts, like you and Giorgio,' Tom explained, staring at the water, as if he could see the past in it. 'We'd known each other through school, but when we were teenagers the hormones kicked in. I joined the army when I left college. I'd always known that's what I wanted to do. Rebecca and I split up – it was hard for her with me being away, and she was young, she wanted to go out and have fun with her friends. We were on and off for a couple of years – I saw her whenever I came home on leave – but then things got serious. We both grew up, wanted to settle down. Or, at least, I thought she did. I proposed, our families were thrilled, the wedding was planned and then . . . marriage for life. Or so I thought.'

Imperceptibly, Carina had moved closer to him. She could smell the sea salt on his skin, along with lingering traces of aftershave that the sea hadn't washed away.

'I got special dispensation from the army to start my leave a day early before the wedding. I planned to come home early to surprise her. Only I was the one who got the surprise. I found them together – such a bloody cliché. Rebecca and Ben, my best mate. My best man, in fact. With my fiancée, in our bed.'

Carina gasped, her hand flying to her mouth. She couldn't imagine how that would feel – to find out that the one you loved above all others, the one you planned to spend the rest of your life with, was far from the person you thought they were.

'So that's my story,' Tom said, looking at her for the first time since he'd started speaking.

'Tom,' Carina sighed, her voice laden with sympathy. She longed to hold him, to take him in her arms, but she held back. The moment felt too intimate, and she was afraid of what might happen if she did. 'I'm so sorry that happened to you,' she began, hoping to comfort him with her words. 'But you can't close yourself off to the world.'

Tom nodded. 'I know. When it first happened, all I wanted to do was hide away. I find it hard to be vulnerable, to give away too much of myself. But that was a few years ago now. It's taken me a while, but I think I might be ready to try again . . .'

Carina's heart was thumping. There was a connection between them, the air between them charged with electricity, and she was sure Tom felt it too. The intensity made Carina want to bolt in fright; she sensed this man had the potential to uproot her world. Something was drawing her closer to him and she didn't want to let go.

'Carina, I need to tell you something . . .' Tom began.

'Yes?' she whispered. Her pulse was racing, as their eyes locked. She felt sure he was going to kiss her, and she knew at that moment that she desperately wanted him to.

'There you are!'

They pulled apart guiltily, turning to see Edie swimming through the entrance of the cave, moving towards them.

'What are you two doing in here?' she asked curiously. 'Everyone's wondering where you are, Carina.' She raised her eyebrows provocatively.

'Oh, we were . . . just taking a few moments. A little time alone – it's all been so hectic.'

Edie had reached them and was treading water, staring at them inquisitively. Carina wondered how long she'd been there; nothing had happened between herself and Tom, but she felt inexplicably guilty. Edie had made it clear that she was interested in Tom, and Carina was an engaged woman; she shouldn't be flirting with the man her best friend was hot for, even if the chemistry between herself and Tom was growing increasingly impossible to ignore.

'We'd better head back.' Carina lowered herself elegantly into the water, Tom close behind her. She liked having him there, she realized. Always with her, always by her side. But this childish flirtation had to stop, she was getting married in three days.

*I don't want it to stop.*

She pushed the thoughts from her mind and began to swim, gliding out of the shadowy cave and into the sunshine.

# Chapter 27

Aboard the yacht, Philippa leaned against the sleek, silver railing, looking out to sea, her turquoise and cobalt blue maxi-dress ruffled by the welcome breeze. All around her, on the boat and in the sea, everyone was having fun and she was glad. The day was exactly what it should be: a joyous celebration of her daughter and her fiancé.

It was rather concerning, Philippa reflected, that Giorgio wasn't attending his own party, his absence a glaring hole that had been remarked upon by a number of guests. At least everyone seemed to be enjoying themselves regardless. It was equally strange that Salvatore – father of the bride and host of the event – wasn't there either. Philippa didn't want to dwell on the matter today, but it seemed impossible not to. The continued disengagement, private phone conversations, the sense that something was being kept from her . . .

'A penny for them, Phil?'

Philippa looked over to see Flora and her mother waving to her from their loungers on the deck.

Flora waved her champagne flute at her friend. 'This is the stuff, slipping down very nicely, darling, I can tell you. Come and have some!'

Philippa laughed, and joined them on one of the loungers, taking a glass of the effervescent liquid from a passing waiter's serving tray.

She took a sip, 'You're right Flora, it's delicious.'

'Now tell your mother and me all about these interesting guests. Who's that silver fox over there, he looks awfully familiar.'

Philippa followed Flora's gaze and felt her heart lurch as she saw it was Harry. Even though she'd known there was a chance he would be here today, it still took her by surprise. It was a strange and familiar feeling all at once, like seeing someone you recognized from a dream. Looking relaxed in a white linen shirt and chino shorts, with a straw trilby perched jauntily on his head, he was laughing and chatting with a couple of the other guests, and Philippa wondered if she wasn't the only one who thought he was looking dangerously attractive.

'Believe it or not, that's Harry Fanshaw,' she said with a sigh.

'What! That rotter you had a tawdry affair with all those years ago?'

'Less of the tawdry, but yes, the very same.'

'How has he ended up here?'

'He's a plus-one of Ginevra's.'

'What's all this about an affair, why don't I know about it?' said her mother, with a harrumph.

'Mummy, you would have been very disappointed in me if you'd known at the time, he was the boss's son.'

Her mother tutted, 'Well, if he was as good looking then as he is now, I can see why you fell for him.'

'Didn't he break your heart?' asked Flora.

'Yes, he did . . . but I got over it, like most people do.'

'And you wouldn't have met Salvatore and had this wonderful life – and cheers to that.' Flora clinked their glasses with her own. 'I wonder what would have happened if you'd married him instead?'

'We'd probably be divorced,' Philippa observed wryly.

Flora nodded, 'Yes, he looks like he's got women throwing themselves at him all the time.'

'Oh yes,' said her mother, 'he looks like he's still a bit of a catch.'

'My first love, Roger, the boy from school who was in a rock band, ended up running off with that girl in your class who looked like Twiggy. I've never forgotten him.' Flora shook her head sadly.

'A woman never forgets her first love,' her mother said and looked wistful for a moment. *We all have our secrets* . . . thought Philippa.

'Anyway, enough of this reminiscing, I'm going for a dip,' Flora announced, sliding off her sundress. In a flash she had clambered down the yacht's ladder into the cool sea.

'Come on in, the water's lovely,' she shrieked, beaming in a floral swimming cap. She and Philippa had known one another since childhood and, despite living in different countries, they always managed to pick up where they'd left off whenever they saw one another. It was a friendship that transcended time and distance.

'Maybe later,' Philippa laughed, as she waved back. It had been a whirl of socializing these last few days, and she was craving a little quiet and relaxation while the majority of guests had left the yacht.

'Pippa.'

She recognized his voice the instant he spoke her name. It wasn't a question or command. Just her name on his lips. She took a moment to compose herself before she turned around.

'Harry.'

They stared at one another for a moment, a silent acknowledgement of all that had happened between them and the time that had elapsed. Her nerves had settled, and the questions Philippa had lived with for more than twenty years, the answers she'd never received, were waiting to be voiced. This moment felt inevitable and for some reason, Philippa didn't want to rush it.

'Can we talk?' Harry asked. He tilted his head to one side expectantly, his eyes twinkling. Philippa could see that as well as his looks he'd retained that boyish charm and confidence where he expected his every whim to be fulfilled. She reminded herself that they were equals now; she was no longer his secret lover, his father's junior employee. He was a guest of her and her husband, enjoying their hospitality.

'Of course,' Philippa replied, striving to keep her expression neutral though her mind was racing, wondering what he had to say.

'Is there somewhere . . . quieter?' Harry glanced around, noting a handful of guests milling about on deck.

Philippa paused for a moment, understanding that Harry wished to be alone with her, before leading him inside and down the stairs to a private lounge area below. It was decorated beautifully, with plush cream sofas and accents of royal blue and gold. Glossy wooden side tables held oversized vases of fresh flowers, the whole room bright and airy with sunlight streaming in through vast windows on either side.

As she sat down and crossed her legs elegantly, trying to appear composed, Philippa tried not to think about that night, over twenty years ago, when she'd slapped his face and left him standing outside Royal Ascot on a sultry summer's day.

'Is Ginevra swimming?' she asked, as Harry sat down beside her.

Harry laughed, his eyes crinkling at the corners. 'No. As far as I know, she's still in bed. She doesn't like to surface before midday, so I left her sleeping.'

Philippa tried to dispel the image of Harry and Ginevra sharing a bed. He was clearly no longer with his wife, but Philippa was determined not to ask any questions; today, Harry could do the talking.

'I didn't know, you understand,' Harry began.

Philippa looked at him questioningly.

'That this was your party. Your daughter's wedding,' Harry clarified. 'Not at first, anyway. Ginevra asked if I'd accompany her to an event, and I said yes. It was only when we were on our way here that I put two and two together: the Russo family, Casa di Russo wine . . .'

'And are you glad you came?' Philippa asked coolly, 'Amalfi is a wonderful place, it would have been a shame for you to miss everything the place has to offer.'

'Yes, I rather am,' he answered. 'All thanks to your and your husband's hospitality and generosity.'

For a moment, Philippa couldn't help but feel some self-satisfaction at what Harry was seeing here today, what it meant to be a Russo, all they had achieved . . . if only he could see inside her.

'Is he here today? I haven't seen him.'

'No, he had urgent business to attend to in Amalfi.'

'I see. What a shame. I had hoped to meet him properly. To know more about the lucky man who captured your heart. The chap who won the ultimate prize . . .'

'Harry . . . that was a long time ago,' Philippa said warningly. She couldn't let him carry on talking like this, it would dredge up too many old memories. 'Besides, I'm not a trophy to be fought over.'

'I'm sorry. I couldn't help myself.'

'Don't bring up the past, Harry. Let's leave it where it is.'

'You're probably right.' Harry looked crestfallen. 'But I could never forgive myself if I left here without letting you know that losing you was the worst mistake of my life.'

'Please don't—'

'And I'm sorry, Pippa. I'm truly sorry. I behaved abominably towards you. But I was a different person back then – spoiled, selfish. I've regretted it ever since.'

Philippa closed her eyes, trying to control her emotions. She'd waited so many years to hear him say those words.

'I should never have done what I did.'

'Then why did you?' Philippa turned to him accusingly, all of the memories resurfacing; the pain, the humiliation.

'Because I was an idiot. I was too dazzled by wealth and glamour and peerages. But I truly loved you, Pippa. I need you to know that. None of it was pretence or artifice. I fell for you, for real.'

Shakily, Philippa exhaled. She didn't know how to respond; all she could do was be honest. 'Once upon a time I'd have given anything to hear you say that. Now . . . well, we are both different people.'

'Perhaps. But I wanted to tell you anyway.'

Neither of them moved. It was clear the conversation was still far from over, the air still heavy with regret and recrimination.

'My marriage to Venetia broke down a few months after the wedding,' Harry explained without prompting. 'Unsurprising, really. It would never have worked. We were far too different. I don't even think we loved one another, not properly. We were simply swept up in the moment.'

'Did you have children?' Philippa asked, suddenly curious.

'No. Which was probably for the best. I don't think I'd have made a good father – certainly not at that age.' He fell into a reflective silence.

'Why are you telling me this, Harry?'

'I needed to explain.'

'If you've come looking for absolution then you're forgiven. There is no need for a post-mortem. It's ancient history.' Though right now, it felt like anything but.

'Christ, Pippa, you're still so beautiful. So poised and in control, but I remember the passion—'

'Don't you dare,' Philippa warned, but Harry wouldn't stop.

'You might not believe me, but I've never loved anyone the way I loved you. I spent the rest of my life looking for it, trying to recapture what we had.' His blue eyes sought hers intensely and it took all of Philippa's will to resist their lure.

'You threw it away,' she shot back. 'I adored you, I would have done anything for you, but that wasn't enough.'

'I was young. I was an idiot.'

'Yes, you were, but that doesn't excuse what you did to me. And now this. It's not fair, you can't just come here and disrupt my life like this.'

'You're right. That wasn't my intention. Like I said, I didn't even realize at first that it was your daughter's wedding.'

Philippa stood up abruptly. 'Thank you for your apology, Harry. But I think we've said everything that needs to be said.'

Slowly, Harry rose to his feet. He took a step towards her, his voice low and hoarse. 'Can you honestly tell me you haven't thought about me since?'

'Of course, I've thought about you. You were the first man I loved. My heart was broken . . . but Salvatore put it back together.'

'I'm glad that you found him. You deserved it. But answer me this, and then I'll leave you, I promise. Are you happy?'

Philippa opened her mouth to answer, to insist that of course she was happy, though for some reason the words wouldn't come.

'You're my guest, Harry, now let's leave the past where it is.'

But as they returned to the deck, and blended back into the party, Philippa wondered why she had found it impossible to answer his question.

# Chapter 28

'You're holding a lot of tension,' the masseuse murmured, as she worked ylang-ylang oil into Edie's upper back.

*No shit*, Edie thought irritably, then willed herself to relax, encouraging herself to drift away as the woman worked the oils into her skin to a backdrop of gentle whale song. Face down on the table, with her eyes closed and the masseuse's soft touch on her skin, Edie wished she could stay in this room forever and not have to face reality.

She'd slept badly last night, tossing and turning, despite the extremely comfortable bed in her room at the Villa Amore. She'd been tormented by dreams of Giorgio and Ashley, drifting in and out of sleep as she wrestled with her conscience, wondering whether she should confess everything to Carina. Edie already felt guilty about staying in Carina's home and accepting her family's hospitality, knowing she had information about Giorgio that could shatter Carina's world.

While Edie didn't have any proof that Ashley was involved with Giorgio, Edie had long ago learned to trust her gut – especially where Giorgio was concerned. Having seen the two of them looking very cosy together in Spago, then Ashley turning up in Amalfi the week of Giorgio's wedding . . . something bad was brewing.

It was just one more secret to add to the mix, and Edie was growing sick of keeping secrets.

And now this spa day. Edie had booked it months ago, as a surprise, thinking it would be a lovely treat for her, Carina and Philippa, a couple of days before the wedding when stress levels would be at their highest. The Thalasso Spa at the Hotel San Marco was supposed to be one of the best treatment centres in the country, using water drawn from the depths of the Tyrrhenian Sea. Now the location seemed like the worst choice she could have made, as though they were walking right into the lion's den.

There was a gentle chime of Tingsha bells, signalling the end of the massage.

'Please, take your time. I've left you a cup of cucumber water,' the masseuse murmured, before slipping quietly out of the room.

Edie never wanted to leave, but she knew she couldn't put it off much longer. Carina and Philippa would be finishing their treatments soon, and they'd planned to reconvene in the relaxation room.

As she slid off the bed, wrapping her robe around her and slowly drinking her water, Edie wished she had a coin to flip – *Heads, I tell the truth. Tails, I stay quiet.* But the pockets of her robe were empty and she remained as uncertain as ever as she padded down the candlelit corridor in her complimentary towelling slippers, feeling as though she were going to face her executioner.

\* \* \*

'That was amazing. Thank you so much,' Carina beamed when she saw Edie. She was lying on a heated tiled bed that was perfectly shaped to the contours of her body, as a waterfall trickled gently over an ornamental rock feature behind her. The room was decorated in shades of cream and taupe, the lighting low and subtle, with the ever-present whale song playing quietly in the background. Right now, it was deserted apart from the three women.

'Don't be silly, it was my treat. Where's Philippa?'

'She's having her chakras realigned and an aroma-therapy reiki.'

Edie smiled distractedly as Carina patted the empty bed on the other side of her. 'Come sit next to me.'

Waves of anxiety prickled through Edie as she sat down beside Carina, noticing how naturally beautiful she looked with no make-up, her sun-streaked blonde hair piled up in a top knot. Edie closed her eyes and exhaled slowly.

'Are you OK?' Carina asked in concern. 'You've gone very pale. Here, drink some water.'

Edie wanted to laugh. It would take more than water to make her feel better. She sat up, resting her head in her hands, and took a deep breath.

'Carina, there's something I need to tell you.' Edie hadn't even known what she was going to do until the words came out of her mouth, but there was no going back now.

'What is it?' Carina looked up in alarm; she'd clearly heard something in Edie's tone that implied this was serious. 'Is it to do with Giorgio?'

Edie stared at her best friend, knowing that what she was about to say would shatter her. Slowly, she nodded her head. 'I think . . . I think he's having an affair with Ashley Hall.'

Carina's forehead wrinkled in confusion. 'The model? What are you talking about? He doesn't even know her.'

Edie swallowed. 'He seemed pretty friendly with her when I saw them together in LA.'

Carina gasped. She seemed to deflate before Edie's eyes, almost physically shrinking inside the oversized white dressing gown.

'B-But Giorgio wouldn't do that. He just . . . He . . .'

Edie's heart ached as she watched Carina come to the slow realization of what had happened, understanding that it was exactly the kind of thing Giorgio would do. All those business trips, all those missed flights. Carina had been betrayed, taken for a fool – and not just by Giorgio.

'I need to speak to him.' Carina rose to her feet. 'I need to ask him about . . . He needs to explain himself.'

'Wait,' Edie said. She didn't want to do this, every sinew in her body was screaming at her to stop, but she knew it needed to be out in the open. Carina needed to know everything. 'There's more.'

'More? You mean . . . more women? More affairs?'

Edie nodded almost imperceptibly. 'There was – is – someone called Isabella. I don't know if he's still seeing her. She's Italian. He said she was obsessed with him.'

Carina gave a small cry, choking back a sob. She sat down heavily, as though her legs wouldn't hold her. 'I don't believe you,' she said desperately, clinging onto denial, her final refuge. 'How do you know all of this? And why didn't you tell me?'

'I couldn't,' Edie burst out, her voice breaking. She was close to tears but was determined not to cry; it wasn't fair on Carina. Edie deserved to feel bad, she told herself. She deserved everything that was coming her way. 'I was scared. I was a coward.'

'You were too scared to tell me my fiancé was having affairs with other women? Didn't you think I'd want to know?'

Edie shook her head, staring down at the ground. She found it impossible to meet Carina's accusing eyes. When Edie spoke, her voice was little more than a whisper. 'And there was me.'

The silence that followed felt endless. When Edie finally dared to look up, Carina was staring at her, aghast. 'What do you mean? You? And Giorgio?'

'Let me explain,' Edie begged. 'It's not what you think. It's . . . You remember that first time Giorgio came to LA on business? And you asked me to meet up with him, to show him around?'

'I didn't mean jump into bed with him!'

'Please, it wasn't like that . . .' Edie trailed off, realizing it was like that to Carina, who was looking at her in disgust. She felt disgusting. She couldn't have said why she'd done it. She realized she owed it to Carina to at least give her a proper explanation, but how could she when she didn't understand the reasons herself . . .?

*Dance music was pumping, coloured lights spinning across the dark nightclub. There was a crush of people around the DJ booth, bodies pressed together, everyone having a good time.*

*Edie found her way to the bar, Giorgio beside her. She couldn't remember how many drinks she'd had, and she'd had a pick-me-up of cocaine in the Ladies and was now feeling a million dollars, so she ordered another vodka, lime and soda.*

'Make that two,' Giorgio said smoothly, with a wink at the pretty young server. He looked good, in a black shirt that was unbuttoned to mid-chest, and black chinos with a narrow leather belt.

Edie squinted up at him, bringing him into focus. 'You flirt with everyone,' she said accusingly, her voice a little slurred. 'Is that because you're Italian?'

Giorgio threw back his head and laughed, his teeth gleaming, his skin tanned. It was quieter here by the bar, away from the main dance floor, but Edie still had to lean in close to hear his reply. 'I only flirt with hot women,' he shrugged. 'And that's because they flirt with me first.'

Edie rolled her eyes, shaking her head in disbelief at his arrogance.

'You're flirting with me right now,' Giorgio stated.

'And you're flirting back. So I guess that makes me hot,' Edie grinned, picking up her drink and sucking on the straw.

Distantly, she had the thought that she shouldn't be behaving like this around Carina's boyfriend, but she quickly dismissed it. It was harmless, both of them massaging the other's ego. If anything, Carina would probably be pleased that the two of them were getting along; usually they couldn't stand one another. Edie found Giorgio arrogant and conceited; he acted as though Edie was beneath him, and she got the impression he didn't make an effort with anyone who couldn't further his interests in some way.

Now Giorgio was all alone in California, looking for someone to introduce him to the LA scene, so perhaps Edie was useful to him right now.

'Oh!' Edie exclaimed, as she was pushed from behind and lost her footing, stumbling towards Giorgio. He caught her as she fell forwards, wrapping his arm around her waist to keep her upright.

'Arsehole,' Edie yelled, whipping round to face the guy who'd collided with her, but he was long gone, swallowed up by the crowd.

She took a fortifying sip of her drink – she'd managed not to spill a drop – and noticed that Giorgio's hand was still resting on her waist. He was standing right behind her and Edie was suddenly very aware of his touch, her focus concentrated on that one spot, the feel of his fingers splayed over her hip. As she moved slightly, her sequinned top rose up, his fingers finding her bare skin. Edie realized that she liked it.

It was primal instinct, nothing more, she insisted to herself. She and Nathan had barely seen one another recently, and even when they did, they were too exhausted to have a conversation, let alone go on date nights or have fun in the bedroom. Flirting with Giorgio was making her feel good, so where was the harm?

Experimentally, almost imperceptibly, Edie leaned back against him. She felt Giorgio respond immediately, pressing his muscular body against hers. Edie was surprised to find how strong and powerful he felt; evidently, he kept himself in shape. A bolt of desire shot through her, shocking her in its intensity.

Giorgio took a slug of his drink. He moved with confidence, and he was a good-looking man, dark-haired and chisel-jawed. His style was too clean-cut for Edie's tastes but right now . . .

She gasped as Giorgio's hands ran over the slim curves of her bottom. This was no accident; this was deliberate, blatant. Edie knew she should tell him to go to hell. But she didn't.

Giorgio leaned down, his breath hot against her neck. 'Andiamo,' he murmured, his voice low and his accent delicious. Let's go.

Edie turned to face him, their lips barely inches apart as they looked at one another. He'd taken his hands off her as she moved *and she wanted them back again. She could feel the spots of heat where he'd touched her.*

*'You're Carina's boyfriend,' she murmured. It was a statement of fact, not a reason to stop what they'd started. Edie knew she was playing with fire, but that only made the whole encounter more thrilling.*

*'What Carina doesn't know won't hurt her, right?' Giorgio's eyes flashed wolfishly as desire pulsed through Edie.*

*He took her hand and pulled her towards the exit. She stumbled after him into the street, the night air unexpectedly warm, the neon lights blurring and twinkling. They fell into a cab, Edie almost landing in his lap, which made her giggle hysterically.*

*'The Mondrian,' Giorgio told the driver, adding, 'Take your time.'*

*Then he turned to Edie and it was as though a force had been unleashed, the two of them pulled together in a tangle of limbs and hands and tongues. Edie's head was spinning; she couldn't think about anything except how good it felt to be kissing Giorgio.*

*She felt a brief burst of guilt, mingled with pity, towards Carina. It was obvious that it wasn't the first time Giorgio had done something like this, and there was clearly a whole other side to him that Carina was either unaware of or wilfully blind to. Through the drug-induced, alcoholic haze, uncharitable thoughts flashed across Edie's mind. Carina had led a charmed life, with beauty, wealth and a successful career all handed to her on a plate. She hadn't had to work for anything. It couldn't have been further from Edie's upbringing, where money had been a constant source of worry, and she'd had to fight for every opportunity that came her way, clawing her way up the ladder. Well perhaps Carina's life wasn't quite so perfect after all, Edie thought smugly, as Giorgio pulled Edie closer, his hands sliding tantalizingly beneath her skirt.*

*The taxi pulled up outside the Mondrian hotel and the two of them broke apart, their breathing coming fast as they stared hard at one another. A cocky smirk crossed Giorgio's face. Christ, he was an arrogant bastard, Edie thought. And she wanted him, badly.*

*'You coming?' he asked, raising an eyebrow questioningly, though they both knew what the answer would be.*

*Edie knew that she could stay in the cab, ask the driver to take her home, drink a litre of water and climb into bed. But Nathan was working on a night shoot and she didn't feel like being alone. She was blinded by lust and overcome by recklessness.*

*'Sure,' Edie grinned, swinging her long, toned legs out of the car, and following Giorgio into the hotel.*

At that point Philippa came into the room after her treatment and immediately saw Carina's anguished face.

'What on earth is going on . . . Edie?'

Carina let out a sob, fury, betrayal and sadness fighting across her features. 'You were my best friend. He was my childhood sweetheart. I didn't even think you liked each other.'

'We didn't. We don't,' Edie insisted, tears rolling down her face too. 'It was the biggest mistake of my life, without a doubt.'

'Oh, don't be so melodramatic,' Carina sneered. 'Is that what this is? Another performance? Well you're not convincing anybody, and I'm done listening. I never want to see either of you again.' She jumped to her feet and rushed to the door.

Edie winced, but she wasn't finished yet. She needed Carina to know everything.

'Wait . . . there's something else. A few weeks later, I realized I was pregnant.'

Carina froze. Slowly, she turned around, but Edie didn't dare look at her.

'I knew it wasn't Nathan's. We were always super careful and anyway, we were going through a bad patch back then. We were both working so hard we barely saw each other. Ships in the night.'

This time it was Philippa that broke the silence. 'You were pregnant with Giorgio's baby? My God.'

'I didn't know what to do. Obviously Giorgio and I weren't about to settle down and play happy families. And there was my career to think about. In the end, I didn't have to make a decision.'

Carina and Philippa looked at her quizzically.

'I lost the baby,' Edie said, her voice breaking with sadness. 'I couldn't have been more than eight weeks. I—'

'Did Giorgio know?' Carina asked. Her voice was trembling.

Edie could imagine how hard this was for her to hear. Giorgio had always wanted children – a boy, to carry on the family line – and had been pushing for them to start a family as soon as they were married. Carina wanted to wait a few years, focusing on her career in the family winery in the interim.

'I only told him afterwards. I was trying to decide what to do, whether to contact him. And then it was too late. It didn't matter.'

'What did he say?'

Edie stared at her in confusion. She felt dazed, a fog stealing over her when she tried to think back to that terrible time.

'What did Giorgio say when you told him you'd been pregnant?' Carina repeated, her voice hard as flint.

'He didn't say much . . . I told him when I came to visit you, last spring. But I remember one thing . . .' Edie's voice shook at the memory. 'He threatened me to keep quiet and said that you'd never believe me over him. And he said, *It's convenient that there's no proof.* I hated him after that,' Edie said. A tear rolled down her cheek, but she barely felt it. She was numb, emotionally drained.

She looked up at Carina, wondering if her old friend could ever forgive her. All she saw in Carina's face was loathing, her violet eyes like chips of ice.

'And *I* hate *you*,' Carina shot back. 'You two deserve each other. I never want to see you again.'

Then she pushed past Edie and raced out of the room.

# Chapter 29

'*Sì, capa*. Yes, we're there right now. Everything will go according to plan. You don't need to worry about anything.'

The man hung up the phone and shifted in his seat. He'd been sitting in the Maserati outside the Hotel San Marco for two hours now, along with his colleague. They knew Carina was inside; they'd been keeping tabs on her movements for weeks.

'We're on,' he smiled cruelly.

'If Giorgio wants a bride for his wedding, then he'd better pay up.'

The two men laughed as they scanned the crowd outside the hotel, watching tourists meander in and out, babbles of excited chatter and relaxed holidaymakers enjoying the atmosphere.

'Wait, isn't that her?'

'Looks like it. What the hell is she doing in a dressing gown?'

'I don't know. But this was clearly meant to be – she's been delivered straight to us.'

'*Grazie Dio*, it's true what they say – he works in mysterious ways,' the man smirked as he revved the engine and zeroed in on their prey.

Carina's heart was pounding, the blood roaring in her ears. She couldn't think straight, couldn't even see straight – her vision was blurry and it felt as though she was in shock. Like the aftermath of a bomb that had just exploded. Perhaps she was still in denial; she could hardly believe everything Edie had told her, and she couldn't understand what it meant for her future. All Carina wanted to do was run – to get as far away as possible from everything she'd seen and heard.

She was still wearing the towelling bathrobe and the slippers from the spa, but she didn't care. Her appearance was the last thing on her mind. She fled from the spa, avoiding the main entrance, instead darting through a fire exit propped open at the end of a corridor. Without thinking, she ran through it, finding herself at the back of the hotel, beside the rubbish bins and the staff entrance. There was no one about, and she made her way round the outside of the building towards the front.

She would get a taxi and go back to the Villa Amore. Right now, it would be overrun with friends and relatives here for her and Giorgio's wedding, but perhaps she could sneak into the house, get back to her room without anyone seeing her, and then she could grab her things and slip away to Avellino. All she needed to do was hold it together until then.

Carina squinted in the bright sunshine, realizing she had nothing with her – no bag, no sunglasses, no phone. It didn't matter. She would sort it out later. All she wanted to do was to get home, and she could pay the driver when she arrived at the house. She was well known in Amalfi, and everyone in town knew the Villa Amore. It wouldn't be a problem.

Carina looked up and down the narrow road that snaked past the hotel, the adrenaline urging her to keep going until she found a cab, when a black Maserati screeched towards her. Her thoughts flashed back to that day with Edie in Positano, and instinctively braced as though the car was about to slam into her.

Instead it pulled up beside her, the tinted window rolled down and a man in his mid-thirties, clean-cut and good-looking, wearing a black T-shirt and Ray-Ban sunglasses, smiled up at her. '*Bisogno di un taxi*?'

'*Sì, grazie.*' Carina replied in relief as she opened the back door and slid onto the black leather seat, not registering that taxis in Amalfi were not normally high-end Maseratis driven by men in sharp attire. Instead it was as though someone was looking out for her, sending what she needed in her hour of need. There was a clunk as the doors locked, then the car sped off. Carina's mind was racing as she tried to hold herself together, to stop the tears from falling. In a matter of minutes she would be at Villa Amore and then she could cry, scream, shout – whatever she needed to do. She could think about everything that Edie had told her, decide how she was going to move forward and—

She frowned, realizing something didn't seem right. There were two men in the front – one driving, one in the passenger seat. Of course, it was possible that the driver was giving a lift to his friend at the same as picking up a fare but . . .

The two of them were well dressed; their clothes looked expensive, their sunglasses designer. Carina glanced around. The car was too clean, too fresh. It didn't look as though scores of tourists passed through every day.

A surge of pure panic shot through Carina's veins. She turned to look out of the window and saw they were picking up speed, heading to the coast road going west out of Amalfi, in the opposite direction to the Villa Amore. Then she remembered that she'd never told them her destination. Her stomach lurched, her lungs contracting.

'*Fermi l'auto. Adesso!*' Carina demanded. *Stop the car. Now!*

The driver said nothing, setting his jaw and pressing down on the accelerator. Buildings, trees, mountains were whipping past the window as the vehicle picked up speed, weaving dangerously in and out of traffic, accelerating into blind corners. The road fell away to their left, the glittering sea beyond; it had always been such a beautiful, calming sight for Carina, but now she was terrified.

She let out a scream, banging on the window, and then she remembered – Tom. Where the hell was he? He was supposed to be protecting her.

Carina slumped down in her seat as she recalled how she'd left him waiting in the spa reception at the front of the hotel – and she'd departed in a daze through some side door . . . What had she been thinking? Well, she clearly hadn't been thinking. *Cazzo*. Would Tom have even realized she was gone?

Carina's gut told her the situation was serious. But who were these people, and what did they want with her? She didn't know, and she didn't intend to hang around and find out.

As they slowed a little, seeing traffic up ahead, Carina

unclicked her seatbelt and lunged for the door. Nothing happened and she slammed against it. She remembered hearing the lock click shut as she got in. Whoever these people were, they didn't want to let her go.

Fear washed over Carina, the man in the passenger seat turned around. He was heavier than the driver, his back broad, his upper arms the size of Carina's thighs. Clearly he was the brawn. The look on his face was chilling, as he undid his own seatbelt.

'Oh, Carina. That was a big mistake,' he said in Italian, shaking his head.

Carina's blood ran cold as she realized he knew her name. This was no accident, or case of mistaken identity.

'You're not going anywhere.'

As the vehicle sped west along the Amalfitana, as quick as lightning, the guy nimbly reached over into the back seat, grabbing her forcefully by the back of the head. She tried to scream as he clamped his other hand over her mouth, then everything went black.

In the spa of the Hotel San Marco, the relaxation room was completely silent, except for the soothing sound of whale music. Philippa stared at Edie, who could only look down at the floor, her eyes tracing a vein in the Carrara marble.

'How could you,' Philippa spat. Her expression was one of betrayal. 'You were supposed to be my daughter's best friend.'

'I'm sorry,' Edie apologized. She began to cry again, her whole body trembling.

Philippa was too angry to muster up any sympathy. 'It's a bit too late for tears, don't you think?' She headed for the door.

'Maybe she needs some time alone,' Edie suggested. 'She might—'

Philippa cut her off, her voice like ice. 'How can you possibly imagine that you know what's best for Carina, after everything you've just thrown at her. With friends like you, she certainly doesn't need enemies.'

'I—' Edie began, but Philippa didn't wait to hear the rest. Pulling her robe tightly around her, she marched out of the relaxation room, heading for the spa's reception area.

The first person she saw was Tom, alert and primed, sitting on the edge of one of the impossibly white sofas in front of an enormous mosaic sun. He glanced up as she entered and rose to his feet, sensing immediately that something was wrong.

'Where's Carina?' asked Philippa.

'She isn't here with you?'

'She just left – she ran out. She'd received some rather distressing news. You must have seen her come this way?'

'She hasn't come through here,' Tom insisted, as the two of them hurried up the steps from the basement spa, heading for the hotel's main lobby.

'She's not here,' Philippa said, looking frantically around. Her breath was coming fast and she felt light-headed. She wasn't sure why, but she had a creeping bad feeling about the situation. Carina had been so distressed by Edie's confession; surely she wouldn't do anything silly?

'*Mi scusi,*' Philippa addressed the female receptionist in Italian. 'Have you seen a young woman come through here? Blonde hair, wearing a robe?' She indicated her own, feeling vaguely embarrassed to be dressed inappropriately, with only a bathing costume beneath. 'We were at the spa,' she explained hastily.

'No. I'm sorry,' the young woman replied, shaking her head.

Philippa turned to Tom. The gravity on his face mirrored her own.

'Perhaps she went back to the villa,' he suggested.

'In her robe? I'll check the changing rooms. She might still be there.'

'I'll look outside. Meet back here in five.' Outwardly, he was calm and composed, but Philippa could see he was taking the situation seriously, and for that she was grateful. She'd always thought Salvatore was overreacting by hiring a bodyguard; Carina didn't have any enemies – who could possibly want to hurt her? But she'd gone along with his plan, happy to know that there was someone to keep an eye on her, just in case. Now she wished Salvatore had hired a whole team of security.

Philippa's mind was a whirlwind as she hurried back to the changing rooms, letting out a startled cry as she bumped into Edie.

'What's the matter?' Edie asked.

'Carina's gone missing. If anything happens to her, it'll be your fault.'

Edie's eyes widened in shock. 'I'll help you look.'

'We don't need your sort of help,' Philippa shot back furiously, as she retrieved her bag from her locker, finding her phone and calling Salvatore as she ran back outside to find Tom.

'Any sign of her?' she asked desperately, though she knew straight away what the answer would be. Carina wasn't with him, and he shook his head grimly. 'Please, take me home,' she begged. 'I want to see my husband. I need to speak to him, but he's not picking up his phone.'

Tom hesitated. 'If Carina *has* gone missing, the first thirty minutes are vital. After that, it gets harder to follow the trail. Evidence is covered over, staff change shift, witnesses move on.'

Philippa nodded. 'I understand, but I need to be with Salvatore.'

Tom narrowed his eyes. 'Did something happen in there? You said Carina received distressing news.'

'I'll fill you in on the way,' Philippa replied, as they walked towards the car and Tom grabbed the keys from his pocket. 'Please, just drive.'

# Chapter 30

Carina's limbs ached. She tried to open her eyes, but everything was darkness. Her head felt groggy, her mouth dry. For a moment, she couldn't work out where she was or what was happening. Attempting to move, she realized her hands were bound together, her feet the same.

Then she remembered, a cold sweat crawling over her skin as she recalled the car, the men. Who were they, and what did they want?

She coughed and tried to sit up, shuffling upright as every muscle screamed in pain.

As Carina's eyes adjusted to the gloom, she realized that it wasn't completely dark. A high, narrow, horizontal strip of window let through a crack of light, its positioning suggesting she was in a basement. From the bright blue of the sky, she could tell it was still daytime.

Her robe was dishevelled, and as she tried to pull it over her she was conscious the cord had been lost – or deliberately removed to stop her using it somehow. She only had her striped bikini underneath, and the room was cool, her skin puckering with goosebumps. It was hard to believe that mere hours ago she'd been enjoying a relaxing pampering session as a bride-to-be, and now everything had fallen apart.

What had happened? Why had she run? Carina squinted, trying to recall, as the beginnings of a headache began to thump behind her temples.

Then she remembered, Edie's betrayal hitting her all over again, physically doubling over as though she'd been punched in the stomach. Her fiancé and her best friend. Giorgio had been screwing around. And not just with Edie – with Ashley Hall, the model, of all people. There were likely others too – Edie had mentioned Isabella, and Carina recalled the conversation they'd had at the party two days ago, the odd way Isabella had behaved around her.

She'd been an idiot, Carina thought miserably. No wonder Giorgio never wanted her to accompany him on any business trips, insisting that she stayed home in Italy like a good little wife-to-be, keeping herself pure for her future husband.

Carina shook her head, refusing to feel sorry for herself. That was a distraction from her current situation, and right now she needed to focus on getting away.

She looked around the room, searching for anything that might give her a clue to where she was or how she might escape. There was nothing. The ceilings were high, a crumbling carving over the door indicating that this might once have been a grand villa like so many in the region. She was likely down in what would have been the servants' quarters. Outside it was quiet; she couldn't hear traffic, or the sea, and guessed they were most likely up in the mountains. Carina tried to take in every little detail of her prison, vowing that once she got out of here, whoever had taken her would be arrested and brought to justice.

She tested her bonds experimentally, but the cords were tied tightly. Expertly. Her wrists ached and she tried to move them, and she worried the circulation would be cut off.

Her stomach rumbled. How long had it been since she'd last eaten? She'd had a light breakfast, but they'd been intending to have lunch at the hotel; it was part of Edie's treat. Carina was thirsty too. There was an unpleasant, chemical taste in her mouth, and a sudden image flashed into her mind – the brawnier man lunging from the front seat towards her, covering her mouth with a cloth. That was the last thing she remembered before she passed out. They'd most likely used chloroform, or perhaps some other—

Carina started, every sense alert, a prickle of fear creeping down her spine. She could hear noises outside – a car pulling up, doors slamming, and men talking, though she couldn't make out what they were saying. She strained to listen and the noises grew louder. Now she could hear footsteps, someone walking down a staircase and along the corridor, coming closer.

The sound of the bolt being slid was as loud as a gunshot, and Carina flinched, her heart pounding. It had been terrifying to be left alone and helpless in the darkness, but she knew that what happened next could be worse. She hugged her knees into her chest, looping her arms around them in a protective gesture, like an upright foetal position.

The door swung open and Carina peered into the gloom with frightened eyes. She sensed there was someone there, and the tension and uncertainty were almost unbearable, but she forced herself not to make a noise, not to call out. If the person was trying to intimidate her, she wouldn't give them the satisfaction.

The light was switched on and Carina winced at the unexpected brightness, the bare bulb swinging from the cracked ceiling. The man closed the door and walked towards her. It took a moment for Carina to make out his features as her eyes adjusted, and she felt at even more of a disadvantage, vulnerable and exposed, half-naked on the floor.

The man circled her, and she found herself staring at his shoes – expensive, leather, handmade. He was clearly not some opportunist, or a small-time crook snatching a rich woman to demand a ransom. Carina found herself wondering if this was all part of a practical joke, some pre-wedding prank gone wrong. Perhaps they'd taken the wrong person. She couldn't imagine what they'd want with her.

He came to a stop in front of her. Carina stared upwards, craning her neck as he was standing so close. He was dressed all in black, his clothes well-tailored, and he smelt of expensive cologne. It was neither of the men who'd been in the car, and it was equally clear that this wasn't simply some hired thug.

'You have the wrong person,' she began in Italian. Her voice sounded hoarse, and she choked back a cough. 'Let me go.'

'Carina Russo . . .' the man said, drawing out her name. She remembered how the man in the car had known her name too, and the realization was chilling; this wasn't a case of mistaken identity. They knew exactly who she was. Her eyes blazed as she stared up at him, determined to hide her fear.

'What do you want?'

'We want our money.'

'What money?' Carina wondered briefly if her father had been involved in something, a bad business deal that had got out of control.

'You're getting married very soon, yes?' The man knelt down to her level, his face close to hers, the faint tang of garlic on his breath. He appeared to be in his forties, with a large Roman nose, thick eyebrows and dark, hooded eyes. Carina tried to memorize his features, to share with the police when this was all over. Then she had the horrible thought that if he was letting her see his face, perhaps he didn't expect her to ever be able to identify him.

'You'll make a beautiful bride,' the man continued when Carina didn't reply. His gaze ran over her and she felt horribly self-conscious, her body on display beneath her open robe. 'Now we'll find out how much your fiancé really loves you.'

'Giorgio?' His name came out inadvertently, and Carina realized she'd revealed more than she intended.

The man raised his eyebrows in acknowledgement.

'Giorgio owes you money?' Carina decided to change tack. She would get the man talking, try and find out as much as she could, bring him onside.

'Nothing for you to worry your pretty little head about.' He reached out and stroked her slowly on the cheek, one fingernail running threateningly from her ear to the corner of her mouth. Carina suppressed a shudder.

'Unless, of course, he's too slow to act. Then you might need to worry . . .'

Suddenly it all became horrifyingly clear, as Carina realized who she was dealing with: the Camorra, the Campanian Mafia who ran everything in the region. Her heart sank, a flicker of fear stealing over her. That explained why the man had no qualms about showing his face; the authorities were probably in his pocket, paid handsomely to turn a blind eye.

So Giorgio was involved with the Camorra? He'd borrowed money from them? How could he have been so stupid? And how had he kept it from her? Then Carina remembered that there were a lot of things Giorgio had successfully hidden from her. She barely knew him at all, in fact. Had she been deliberately blind, or was Giorgio exceptionally good at deceiving her?

Carina laughed in disbelief. If her fate rested in Giorgio's hands, she didn't hold out much hope.

'You find this funny?' The man stared at her curiously, as if he couldn't figure her out.

'The wedding's off,' Carina said with certainty. She hadn't thought it all through yet but she saw now there could be no other option. Thank goodness this had all come out now, before they were married. 'We broke up,' she continued. 'So if you're using me to get to Giorgio, he probably won't care.'

The man didn't so much as flinch at the new information, merely stared at her levelly, before making a little shake of his head. He whispered a word under his breath: '*Mannaggia!*' Then he sighed. 'Well then. That makes things pretty bad for you, doesn't it?' He rose to his feet and strode towards the door.

'Wait!' Carina shouted. It sounded ridiculous, but she didn't want the man to leave, and be plunged once again into darkness and solitude and uncertainty. She also had the beginnings of a plan forming in her head. It seemed unlikely that Giorgio would simply pay the money and the Camorra would let her go. If she was going to get out of here, she would have to escape.

'Can I go to the toilet?' Her tone was meek, her head bowed, as she tried to make herself as submissive as possible.

'Sure. I'll get someone to bring in a bucket.'

'Please,' she begged.

He strode back across the room and pulled a knife from his pocket. Carina gasped, but almost before she'd had a chance to grasp what was going on, he sliced through the ties that bound her ankles. The metal glinted dangerously in the overhead light, and Carina realized how sharp it was if it could slice through cord so easily. Her bonds fell away and there was a delicious relief as the blood rushed to her ankles, the red marks around them chafed and sore.

He took hold of the rope that tied her hands together and dragged her to her feet, leading her out of the room. Her robe fell open and she could do nothing to secure it, a rush of cool air finding its way round her body like clammy hands in the dull underground corridor. She did her best to take in her surroundings, to commit it to memory and find anything that might aid her in her escape, but there was nothing. A short way along the passage, he opened a door.

'In there.'

Carina hesitated, then held out her bound wrists. 'Please,' she said again, her voice barely more than a whisper. She hoped he might take pity on her, and didn't care what methods she had to use. Now wasn't the time to show her feisty side.

His eyes lingered on her body, but he did as she asked, slicing through the rope in a single movement. Carina circled her wrists, rubbing them to aid the circulation, then slipped into the toilet before he changed his mind. There was no lock on the door, and she looked around quickly. There was only one small window, high and narrow like the one in her cell. There was no way she could fit through, and she wanted to slam her fists on the wall in frustration.

A sob escaped her, but she quickly pulled herself together. She would think of a new plan. She would get out of here. She had to.

'You almost finished in there?' the man shouted.

'Yes, just coming,' Carina called back. She used the toilet and, with a final glance around, accepted she had no choice but to return to her prison. The man led her back to the room, wordlessly retied her arms and legs with fresh cords, then turned off the light and left.

Carina slumped to the ground, more deflated than she'd been before. Her body felt exhausted, but her mind was working furiously. She was in a dangerous situation, and she knew how quickly it could all go wrong. No one knew where she was; she knew without a shadow of a doubt that Tom was looking for her right now but he might never find her. If she wanted to get out of here alive, the only person she could rely on was herself.

# Chapter 31

'Is Carina here?' Philippa demanded as she marched frantically through the arched stone doorway of the Villa Amore.

'No,' Rafaella replied. 'Is something wrong?'

'It's Carina, she's gone missing.'

Her mother-in-law's hand flew to her face. '*No!*' she cried. 'How can this be – why?'

'She found out something awful about Giorgio, and now we can't find her.'

A dark look passed across Rafaella's face. '*I peccati del padre,*' she whispered, 'You must find her quickly, she might be in danger.'

'Please, Nonna, where's Salvatore?'

'In his study. He—'

But Philippa didn't wait to hear the rest of her response, racing off into the house with Tom at her heels. She was completely blind to the grandeur of the house she'd helped to create, the marble statues and the rare works of art. Today, there was only one thing on her mind.

Salvatore looked up in alarm as Philippa and Tom burst into his office. 'What's happened?'

'We've been trying to call you. Didn't you hear?'

Salvatore picked up his phone to see notifications for a dozen missed calls. 'I've been busy with work,' he explained. His desk was strewn with papers, a dense spreadsheet open on the computer screen in front of him.

'Carina's missing.'

'What?' Salvatore looked from Philippa to Tom in alarm, as though he wanted him to confirm it. 'How . . . I hired you to look out for her,' he raged, getting to his feet.

'I know. I—' Tom looked ashen.

'It wasn't his fault,' Philippa interrupted. 'We were in the spa and—'

'Can I leave you to explain?' Tom cut in. Philippa was taken aback but knew he wouldn't have interrupted unless it was urgent. 'I need to go back to the hotel. The early period after an incident is crucial. I need to speak to witnesses, view the CCTV, see what I can unearth.'

'Go,' Salvatore insisted. As Tom bolted towards the door, Salvatore stopped him. 'Wait! Is it . . . what we thought?'

'That's my suspicion.'

Philippa stared at them in confusion. 'What are you talking about?' A look passed between the two men. Neither of them replied. Both had grave expressions.

'I'll call as soon as I can,' Tom said. 'Keep your phone switched on.' Then he was gone.

Salvatore began to pace the room, running hands through his greying hair. He looked much older suddenly, Philippa realized. The stress of work and Carina's wedding, not to mention the whirlwind of the past few days, making sure the every whim of two hundred guests was catered for, had taken their toll. '*Cazzo*,' he swore under his breath.

'Can you please tell me what the hell is going on?' Philippa demanded. She'd assumed Carina had simply run away after Edie's revelations, devastated and needing some time to herself, but now it seemed the situation was more serious than it appeared.

'No, *you* tell *me*,' Salvatore rounded on her. 'How could you let something happen to Carina? Why weren't you looking after her?' He looked furious, and Philippa was taken aback by his anger. She was worried sick about her only daughter, and Salvatore clearly knew more than he was letting on about what might have happened to Carina, yet he was speaking to his wife as though *she* had done something wrong.

'It was Edie,' Philippa said coldly, her tone blunt. 'She told Carina that she'd slept with Giorgio. She got pregnant by him but lost the baby.'

'*Mannaggia tutto!*' Salvatore looked aghast.

'She told Carina there'd been other women too.' A flicker of acknowledgement, of guilt, crossed Salvatore's face, and Philippa realized that he didn't look wholly surprised.

'You knew, didn't you?' Philippa stared at him in disbelief.

'Not about Edie, but I . . . I had my reasons to suspect that he—'

'What reasons?' Philippa planted her hands on her hips, her eyes blazing. All she wanted to hear was that Carina had been found safely, but instead she seemed to have found herself right at the centre of a tangled web of secrets. 'I think you'd better tell me what's going on, don't you?'

Salvatore's manner seemed to change. He was always in control of every situation, but now he looked overwhelmed and that frightened Philippa. There was never a problem that Salvatore couldn't fix. 'Sit down,' he said quietly.

'I'd rather stand.' She was furious.

'Philippa . . . please, sit.' Salvatore's tone was weary as he closed his eyes and massaged his temples. Philippa perched on the vintage leather armchair, even though the adrenaline pulsing through her made her feel as though she could sprint all the way to Amalfi and carry on along the coast, not stopping until she found her daughter. All this talk felt like they were wasting time, but she needed to hear the whole story.

'Tom hasn't just been here to look after Carina.'

Philippa frowned. 'What do you mean?'

'He's been doing some work for me as well. Surveillance. Investigation. He has a background in intelligence work for the British Army, and he's been looking into Giorgio.'

'Why?' Philippa gasped, though in her heart of hearts she suspected at least some of the reasons. She'd kept her reservations to herself about her future son-in-law, but recently she'd had a terrible feeling that Giorgio was keeping secrets from them all. She hadn't wanted to alarm her daughter, and knew the ultimate decision had to be Carina's, but Philippa had concerns about his behaviour and now it seemed she'd been proved correct. If only she and Salvatore had spoken about this before.

Salvatore checked his phone then walked over to the gold drinks cart that stood in front of the bookcase, pouring them both a neat brandy.

Philippa hesitated then took a deep slug, the alcohol warming and comforting. She braced herself for what she was about to hear.

'I've had my suspicions for a while,' Salvatore began. 'You hear rumours, stories that don't quite add up. Some of the business deals he told us about, the tales he regaled us with over the dinner table, sounded too good to be true.'

Philippa said nothing, sipping her drink as she listened to her husband.

'It turns out that's the case. He's been borrowing money from multiple sources, forging documents as evidence of liquidity, completely unable to make the repayments. He's been lying to his investors, bullshitting everyone, and as he's got in deeper, he's become more desperate. He's got himself into bad company, become involved in activities that aren't legal. Building developments with dirty money – money laundering, essentially.' Salvatore paused, his expression grave as he paced back and forth across the rug in front of Philippa. 'Tom has found evidence that he's in bed with the Camorra.'

'Those criminals!' Philippa was incredulous.

'It looks like he's got himself sucked up into something serious.'

'And now Carina's caught up in it too. My God, Salvatore. The Camorra.'

'We don't know for certain what's happened to her—'

'You know as well as I do what these people are capable of.' Philippa rose to her feet, feeling frantic. She closed her eyes, not wanting to think about what they might be doing to Carina. The possibilities made her physically ill. 'We have to call the police.'

'Look, Philippa, we don't know for certain that the Camorra are involved – Carina could simply be on a beach somewhere. Or perhaps she's gone to find Giorgio and the two of them are having it out. But Tom's on the case. The police aren't the answer at the moment, they might just make things worse.'

Salvatore reached for his phone. Philippa exhaled shakily. She felt as though she might explode with a mixture of worry and anger and frustration. Every second they delayed was a second longer she was separated from Carina.

'Why didn't you tell me – about why you were hiring Tom, your suspicions about Giorgio, everything? Why didn't you tell me?' Philippa's voice was ragged with emotion.

'I know, I know.' Salvatore was rubbing his brow; he looked like a man with the weight of the world on his shoulders. 'I wanted to be sure, the wedding, our families . . . there was so much at stake.'

'Carina is more important than any of that. I've been trying to talk to you for weeks,' Philippa said, sounding anguished. 'I knew something wasn't right, but you brushed me off every time.'

'Did you really?' Salvatore hit back at her. 'How long have you had these doubts? It must be more than a few weeks.'

Philippa bit her lip, momentarily chastened. Then they fell silent for a moment; they both knew that this might never have happened if they'd spoken to one another sooner.

'Look, this anger is futile. I didn't want to worry you unnecessarily . . .' Salvatore tried to justify his actions. 'For all I knew, my hunches could have been completely off. Maybe I was just a paranoid old man who was too protective of his daughter.'

'We've always told each other everything,' Philippa said. How far apart had they drifted over the years without realizing?

Salvatore placed the phone down on the desk. Giorgio wasn't picking up. 'Do we?' he asked, his voice taking on an accusatory tone. 'You didn't tell me that your ex-boyfriend – that arrogant English playboy – is staying in town and planning to attend our daughter's wedding.'

Philippa was shocked at his tone. 'I didn't invite him,' she protested. 'I had no idea he was coming.'

'I understand the two of you were rather cosy together on the yacht yesterday, but you didn't mention that either, did you? Perhaps you're right. Perhaps we have been keeping secrets from one another.'

Philippa felt as though her world was spinning – Carina missing, Giorgio in the pocket of criminals, Salvatore accusing her of being unfaithful. She gripped the back of the armchair, as though it was the only thing keeping her upright. 'You've had Tom spying on me too?' she choked out in disbelief, shaking her head as she looked at him through narrowed eyes. 'Who are you, Salvatore? Not the man that I married.'

'Philippa . . .' Salvatore looked wounded by the barb. He reached for her, but she pulled away, instinctively moving towards the door. 'Come back, we need to talk. Where are you going?'

Philippa spun round, her eyes flashing angrily. She looked proud, determined, beautiful. 'To find my daughter,' she said, before striding out of the door, leaving Salvatore alone and defeated.

# Chapter 32

The car tyres screeched as Tom roared off. He was now more than familiar with the route between the Villa Amore, perched on the edge of the steep mountainside, and the town of Amalfi, a short, winding drive downhill. As he joined the main road, it was clogged with traffic, and he slammed his hand on the steering wheel in frustration.

If anything happened to Carina . . . Perhaps he'd gone soft, taken his eye off the ball. He'd thought it would be fine to wait in the reception area. Now he wished he'd gone right into the spa with Carina and to hell with how it looked.

He would kill Giorgio too, if it turned out he was behind all of this, whether directly or indirectly. What a useless excuse of a man, to put Carina in this position. Giorgio didn't deserve her – surely Carina would finally realize that now?

As the line of cars and buses crawled slowly into town, horns blaring and scooters smugly overtaking, Tom was blind to the stunning view, oblivious to the colourful houses that clung to the mountainside, the wide, blue sweep of the bay and the rugged shoreline dotted with narrow arcs of shingle beach. He could hardly believe it was only a few days since he'd first arrived here with Carina, less than a week since he'd laid eyes on her for the first time since they were teenagers.

If he was being honest, perhaps the real reason he'd been preoccupied was because of his flirtation with Edie and his growing attraction to Carina, his thoughts elsewhere and not on the job in hand. Well that all stopped now. Carina was paying the price for his momentary lapse in concentration, his temporary lapse of professionalism. He needed to throw everything into finding her, and once she was back then . . . Well, he'd cross that bridge later.

Tom reached for his phone and dialled a number. It rang three times before being picked up.

'Nick Fleming.'

'Nick, it's Tom Ryan.'

'Tom, how are you?'

'I've been better. I don't really have time for polite chitchat—'

'You never do. What do you need?' Nick asked good-naturedly.

'Everything you've got on Camorra activities in Amalfi. What they're involved in, who they're involved with. And any properties they own – especially secluded locations where they might take someone.'

'Is that all?' Nick's tone was sarcastic.

'That's all – for now.'

'And the timeframe for this is . . .'

'ASAP. Thanks, Nick, I'll buy you a beer when I'm back.'

284

'You owe me more than a beer.'

'Yep, I know. Hey, if you come through for me on this, I'll buy you a brewery.'

Nick laughed as Tom rang off. The traffic began to move, and moments later Tom swung into the car park of the Hotel San Marco. Tourists milled around outside, enjoying the beautiful weather and incredible location, but Tom was oblivious as he headed for the entrance, noting the location of the CCTV cameras on the front of the building. He approached the doorman, hoping his Italian wouldn't let him down.

'*Scusi, signor*, have you seen my friend?' Tom pulled out his phone, turning it around to show the man a photograph of Carina. 'She was visiting here and left in rather a hurry, about half an hour ago.'

'No, *signor*, I haven't seen her, but I only just started my shift.'

Tom cursed himself for not asking sooner.

'You could try reception,' the young man suggested. 'Oh, wait. Giuseppe!' he called, as another, older man ambled round the corner, smoking a cigarette. He was dressed in shorts and a polo shirt, not the immaculate, formal uniform of the doorman.

'*Sì*?' The man ambled over.

'Giuseppe was on the shift before me,' the doorman explained. 'This guy here's looking for his friend.'

Tom showed him the photo, explaining, 'She'd been to the spa, so she was still in her robe.'

'Oh yeah, I saw her,' the man nodded. 'She got into a car and drove off.'

Alarm surged instantly through Tom. 'A car? Can you tell me more?'

The guy shrugged. He seemed disinterested, like he didn't want to get involved. Tom understood that; you had to make people trust you, to want to give you the information. He needed to calm down.

'She looked a bit . . . dazed,' Giuseppe continued. 'I noticed her because, well, she was a beautiful woman. And she was dressed rather strangely, of course. But you see all sorts working in a hotel. You learn not to bat an eyelid.'

'Thank you,' Tom replied. 'Can you remember anything about the car? The make or the colour? Who was driving?'

'Maserati Quattroporte, black – nice car. It wasn't a licensed taxi, but I thought it could have been a private car service. It had been parked up over the road for a while, so I assumed it was waiting for a pick-up.'

*It had been waiting?* Tom thought back to the car that he'd suspected was tailing them the past few days – also black, also a Maserati. He felt sure it was no coincidence.

'Did she get in voluntarily?' It was possible Carina had called a car to collect her, but from what Philippa had told him, it hadn't been a planned departure.

Giuseppe frowned, 'I think so. She just climbed in.'

'Thank you, Giuseppe. You've been very helpful.'

With no time to lose, Tom ran into the hotel, slowing down as he reached the reception desk. The woman behind the counter was young and attractive, smiling expectantly as he approached.

'*Buongiorno,*' Tom beamed, his eyes twinkling, preparing to be utterly charming. He needed to see that CCTV footage.

Carina was cold. The sliver of sky outside the small, high window was growing darker, and Carina realized it was evening. She'd been alone for hours now, given only a cup of water and a chunk of *pane cafone* – the local 'peasant bread' – which she'd devoured in seconds. Occasionally she heard a low rumble of voices, the occasional shout, cars coming and going.

She needed to think of a way out of here. At first, she'd assumed someone would find her soon: the police, her father, Giorgio, Tom . . . But as the hours passed, she'd grown increasingly despondent.

Perhaps she should shout for the guard – then when he came, she could overpower him somehow and run away . . . Carina almost laughed out loud at her own ridiculousness. The guard was twice the size of her, armed with a knife and probably a gun. She didn't know how many others there were upstairs. Even if she somehow managed to get away from her guard, the doors would be locked – how could she distract someone long enough to find the keys and escape? It was impossible; she wasn't some action hero in a Hollywood blockbuster. It felt surreal that this was even happening to her.

She froze as she heard footsteps on the stairs, the jangle of keys, a man coughing. For a moment, she considered hiding behind the door, taking him by surprise. Perhaps she could use the weight of the door, slam it shut, knock him out . . . Carina realized that she simply wouldn't dare; paralysed by indecision, she remained sitting on the ground in the spot where he'd left her.

The door swung open, the same man as before standing there expectantly.

Carina stared at him, trying to hide her fear with defiance.

'*Allora, cara,*' he began with a cruel smile. 'Your fiancé isn't very cooperative. No one's seen him. He's not answering our phone calls. Any ideas where he might be?'

'No. And he's not my fiancé. He's not anything to do with me, so you might as well let me go.'

'Oh dear. Lovers' tiff?' he snorted. 'I'm not buying it.'

Carina wondered briefly if Giorgio was with Ashley right now. Or with Edie, or Isabella. Did he even know what was happening to her? Did he care? 'Why don't you try one of his other women, you might have more success,' she spat bitterly.

'Oh, has Giorgio been a bad boy? Sounds like we both want to cut his balls off.' The man grinned suddenly but his eyes were cold as a shark's, the expression even more terrifying than his usual poker face. 'Get up,' he snapped suddenly, the smile disappearing as quickly as it had arrived.

'What? Why?'

'Just do as you're told.'

'Get off me,' Carina yelled, as he came over and dragged her upright. He pulled out the knife once again, Carina falling quiet at the sight of the blade, and sliced the bonds around her bare feet, pushing her out of the door.

Despite the terror, Carina felt a sense of exhilaration at being out of the cramped room. Her eyes darted around, trying to find a means of escape, looking for an opportunity to run.

'Don't even think about it,' the man sneered, clamping his hand down hard on her shoulder, his fingertips digging in so that she squirmed away from him.

The lights were off and the building was gloomy, but Carina saw that she was on the basement level, as she'd suspected. Her captor pushed her up a narrow wooden staircase and she almost stumbled, her feet numb from the cold and the ropes. She emerged onto the ground floor of what appeared to be a rundown villa, noticing a large room filled with dusty old furniture, chairs scattered around a table as though they'd been recently vacated.

Through dirty, arched windows she caught a glimpse of the darkening sky, tall pine trees in an overgrown garden. She suspected they were up in the mountains, but she had no idea how far they'd travelled or whether they were near to Amalfi.

The man pushed her towards the main door where a car was waiting outside. It was larger than the one she'd been in before, a black people carrier this time, with two men standing beside it, their arms crossed, their faces blank.

Then the door slid open and a woman climbed out, her red suit a stark contrast to the sea of black around her. Carina gasped as she saw who it was. 'Isabella!' she exclaimed.

'Ciao, Carina,' Isabella said coldly, undisguised hatred written across her face.

Carina screamed as a hood was thrown over her face and she was bundled into the vehicle, her world plunged into darkness once again.

# Chapter 33

Philippa had been driving around for what seemed like hours. The sun was beginning to lose its power and drop lower, pastel colours washing over the sky. It was happening a little earlier each day now, and feeling the end of summer creeping in gave her pause for brief reflection. Had she made the right choices in her life? she asked herself. She'd had experiences beyond her wildest dreams, but perhaps if she'd chosen a different path she wouldn't be where she was right now – her daughter missing, and a question mark hanging over her marriage.

Salvatore had called her repeatedly. Each time Philippa asked the same question, 'Have you found Carina yet?' When the answer was no, she hung up on him. She remembered to call Bianca, the wedding planner, and told her that the dinner they were hosting at the villa would have to be cancelled and the venue moved to a local restaurant. They had no way of knowing what the next forty-eight hours would bring, but the guests still needed to be looked after.

'Don't worry, I'll keep the food and wine flowing and they'll barely notice you aren't there.'

Tom was working on a lead, but Philippa felt impotent. She didn't know what to do with herself, driving around aimlessly in case she happened across Carina. Like Salvatore had suggested, perhaps Carina had taken herself off for some quiet time, to process everything Edie had told her. But Philippa felt in her gut that something was seriously wrong. Perhaps it was a mother's intuition, but this behaviour was out of character for her daughter. She felt sure Carina would have tried to contact her if she could, and wouldn't deliberately put her mother through all this worry.

Philippa had found herself driving up and down the coast road, pulling into the towns en route, occasionally parking up and running into one of Carina's favourite shops or restaurants to see if anyone had seen her. No one had. But she had to do something or else she'd go crazy.

Out of options, Philippa had found herself driving back to the Hotel San Marco where it had all begun. It was hard to believe it was only a matter of hours ago that she, Carina and Edie had been here, enjoying their pampering treatments, only Edie aware of the bombshell she was about to unleash. It felt like days ago now.

Philippa pulled up and killed the engine. Salvatore had refused to call the police. He said they wouldn't take the report seriously at this stage. Carina wasn't officially a missing person yet, but an adult woman who no one had seen for an afternoon. He was also worried about the Camorra being tipped off, explaining to Philippa that they had connections everywhere, even inside the carabinieri. Philippa was left with no choice but to trust him, although she wasn't sure how well that had worked out so far.

Giorgio, too, seemed to have disappeared, despite numerous attempts to find out where he was. It was just as well as Philippa thought she would cheerfully throttle him if she got her hands on him. His stupidity and sheer selfishness had put her daughter in grave danger.

It was only now that Philippa thought back to Rafaella's words when she her told her the news of Carina's disappearance. *I peccati del padre*.

The sins of the father.

What on earth did she mean by that? Was this another secret that the Russos had been keeping to themselves?

She gripped the steering wheel and hung her head in despair, but there was a knock on the car window and Philippa almost jumped out of her skin – it had crossed her mind that she might be a target too. She looked up in terror to see Harry Fanshaw smiling at her.

'Hello,' he said, as she rolled down the window. 'I thought it was you.' His smile fell as he took in her anxious features. 'Pippa, what's the matter – tell me.'

Philippa crumpled at the sight of him, overwhelmed by the sight of a friendly face, suddenly longing to confide in someone. A voice at the back of her mind whispered that it should be Salvatore that she unburdened herself to, but somehow that seemed impossible right now.

'It's Carina,' Philippa fought to keep the sob out of her voice. 'Something's happened to her – she's gone missing. It could be serious, Harry. Giorgio, her fiancé, has been involved in criminal activities, and we think she might have been kidnapped.' It was the first time Philippa had said the words out loud, and it made them seem horribly real as she broke down in tears once again.

'My God,' Harry said. 'But what's being done to find her? Have the police been called? And why are you here on your own? Pippa, tell me everything.'

'I don't want to stay here,' Philippa replied, swiping at her tear-stained face. 'All my relatives and friends are staying at the hotel. I can't face them.'

'No, of course not,' Harry agreed. 'When was the last time you ate something? You need to keep your strength up.'

'I'm not hungry.'

'Come on,' Harry said firmly, taking charge of the situation. 'Give me the car keys. I'll look after you.'

Half an hour later they were sitting outside a bar in Pogerola, a pretty hamlet in the hills above Amalfi. They'd found a quiet spot on the balcony where they wouldn't be disturbed and the views were incredible, the air scented with pine from the nearby forest and swathes of clematis plants hanging from the overhead trellis.

'It's like a nightmare,' Philippa finished. 'A living hell. I feel as though I'm in a bad dream and I can't wake up.' She stared out into the darkening sky, shivering at the thought of Carina being out there alone. She traced the car headlights as they swooped down the mountain, wondering if her daughter was nearby, wondering if she'd be able to sense it if she was.

'They'll find her, it sounds like she needs a bit of time by herself, and Tom knows what he's doing, it will all be OK,' Harry assured her. Philippa had filled him in on everything during the journey. He'd insisted on taking her away to a small trattoria on a quiet backstreet on the edge of the town, ordering food and drink and turning down her request for an espresso – 'You're already wired' – in favour of a brandy, which she drank with shaking hands. She kept checking her phone, but it stubbornly refused to ring.

'I can't believe I've lived here for twenty-something years and never known about this place,' she observed. 'You've been here for a long weekend and are fitting in like a local.'

Despite the remote location, the restaurant was beginning to fill up, clearly a popular dinner spot on a Friday evening.

'I've Ginevra to thank for that,' Harry admitted. 'We ate here the night I arrived.'

'Where is she tonight?' Philippa asked curiously.

'Meeting up with old friends, apparently,' Harry said. 'And I'm surplus to requirements.'

'Oh dear, poor Harry,' Philippa said, with a small smile. 'We were supposed to be hosting a dinner tonight for those in the wedding party. Bianca – the wedding planner – has taken over, but people will be speculating.'

'Everyone will understand. Most weddings have the odd hitch.'

Philippa exhaled shakily, her pale blue eyes wide and luminous. Harry placed his hand over hers and Philippa didn't pull away. It felt reassuring, the gesture comforting in its familiarity, a sense memory ingrained in her skin from over twenty-five years ago. Philippa recognized that she was in a vulnerable place, but she felt reckless, led by her instincts, because reality made no sense. If her world was tilting on its axis, then she was going to go along with it.

'I know I told you before, on the boat,' Harry murmured, 'but the biggest regret of my life was letting you go.'

It sounded like a line, but right now Philippa wanted to hear anything that would distract from the anxious gnawing in her stomach.

'I thought you loved me then,' she whispered, her voice shaking. 'I was young. I believed you, and I was a fool.'

'You weren't. Pippa, believe me, I adored you. I worshipped you, and I never lied about my feelings. I was young and a selfish idiot, too influenced by what my parents thought, too swayed by money, and by who I thought I could be. I didn't realize what was truly important in life, and I've suffered for it ever since. I've never known happiness like I had with you. I've never loved anyone like I loved you.'

The restaurant was busy, every table full and standing room only at the bar. Harry brought his head closer, and Philippa leaned in to hear him. Nostalgia was such a potent force, she realized. Time erased the wrongdoings of the past, painting their shared history with a rosy glow. She found herself reflecting on how different life could have been if she'd forgiven Harry and given him another chance. She had truly loved him, with all the intensity of her first real relationship. Had she been too quick to walk away?

There had been a chasm between herself and Salvatore recently. She was no longer the top of his priority list. Had she ever been? She'd thought he would always adore her – isn't that what they'd said? *Di amarti e onorarti tutti i giorni della mia vita.* To love and honour you every day for the rest of my life. But her husband seemed to have forgotten that promise.

Harry said he'd never stopped loving her. Maybe Salvatore had . . .

'We'd better get you back home. Back to your husband,' Harry said quietly, his sparkling eyes trained on hers. He seemed to be drinking her in, as though he wanted to remember every inch of her face. Philippa couldn't speak, so many unsaid words between them.

She shook her head, finding her voice. 'No. Not yet. Don't leave me, Harry, please. I don't want to be alone tonight.'

# Chapter 34

Tom drove at speed up into the hills above Amalfi, passing the sign for the hamlet of Pogerola. He'd followed the car's navigation system so far, but now he was off grid, working from the directions his contact had given him.

Nick Fleming had called Tom back with a ream of information. Not all of it was good. In fact, what Nick had relayed made Tom more worried than ever for Carina's welfare. Nick had given him a list of properties owned by, or with links to, the Camorra. It was extensive, and Tom hadn't known where to start; they could be hiding her in the basement of a pizzeria in Ravello, whose owner they were extorting for protection monies. They could have driven her inland to a don's palazzo, isolated in the forest where no one could ever find her.

But when the obliging young woman at the Hotel San Marco had let Tom take a peek at the CCTV footage and he'd passed the registration number on to Nick, this place had come up: a deserted villa, not far from Amalfi, high in the hills above town. Intelligence said it was used as a safe house and short-term storage – weapons, money, drugs, people. Anything that needed to be housed before being moved on. The local police were paid off handsomely and knew better than to come nosing around.

Tom turned off the deserted country road onto what was little more than a track. He killed the lights and slowed the car to a crawl. Daylight had almost gone but the moon was bright, and his eyes strained to pick out shapes in the distance. When he thought he could make out a large, sprawling building up ahead, Tom parked the car and quickly climbed out, quietly closing the door.

The adrenaline was flowing, and he tilted his head to one side, listening. It was a clear night with no wind, and he heard nothing. He walked closer, moving quickly and keeping low to the ground, staying in the shadows. The hard metal of his handgun nudged him in the thigh, and he reached into his pocket, curling his fingers around the trigger.

Salvatore had presented him with the weapon the first night he arrived. Tom hadn't asked where he'd got it from – he didn't want to know – but he'd checked it was in working order and loaded it with bullets, keeping it on him at all times. Tom hadn't discharged a weapon since he was in the army. He hoped he wouldn't have to tonight.

He drew closer to the villa, skirting the perimeter. Round the back, a black Maserati Quattroporte was parked up, and Tom's adrenaline spiked. He approached it cautiously, checking the vehicle was deserted before running his phone torch over the registration plate. This was it! This had to be where they'd brought Carina.

Cautiously, Tom moved towards a side door, the blood rushing in his ears, the weapon primed in his hands.

The door was old, but the lock was new; with one swift kick, the wood splintered and Tom prised off the lock, the door swinging open. He stepped inside, his pulse racing as he worked his way through the rooms. Something didn't feel right, and he hoped he wasn't walking into a trap. The place felt deserted; he sensed there was no one inside. He kept on searching, hoping he was wrong. Horrific as it would be to find Carina bound and gagged in a darkened room, that would still be better than not finding her at all, but he had the sinking feeling she wasn't there.

Working his way quickly through each room, he realized that someone – or multiple people – had been here recently. The smell of cigarette smoke hung heavily in the air, the butts stubbed out in an ashtray on a table. Dirty cups lay in the sink, along with a layer of coffee grounds.

As he descended the steps to the basement, he noted the bars on the windows, the coils of rope, the bolts on the outside of the doors. His blood rising in fury, Tom wondered if this was where Carina had been held. He fancied he could smell the lingering scent of her perfume, and he wanted to kill whoever had imprisoned her down here, treating her little better than a dog.

Sweeping his torch over every room, he was about to leave when he saw it. In the corner, something glinting brightly, reflecting the light from his phone. Bending down closer to pick it up, he realized what it was: Carina's engagement ring, *G&C* engraved on the inside.

Tom wanted to howl with rage. He was too late. She'd been here, but now she'd gone. He spun round, torchlight skittering wildly over the room, searching for anything that might tell him where she'd gone, where they'd taken her now, but there was nothing. The trail had gone cold.

Carina sensed that she was being driven downhill. It was horribly disconcerting, not being able to see, but she tried to stay calm. The warmth of her breath made it hot inside the hood, and she could feel the bodies of the men next to her, one on either side. She was tense and alert, listening hard, her other senses working madly to compensate for her lack of sight.

She heard a woman speak, giving commands in a short, sharp tone.

'Isabella,' Carina said gratefully. She hadn't been sure whether she was in the car. 'Please, help me. Tell them it's all a mistake. It's Giorgio, I—' Carina let out a yelp of alarm as she received a sharp blow from one of the guards. She didn't dare to speak again, feeling the tears roll down her face. It didn't make any sense. Isabella had attended her party mere days ago, and now she was complicit in this? What did she want with her? Carina wondered. Why was she being treated like this?

The car pulled to a stop and Carina's stomach churned, wondering where they were now and what was going to happen.

'Get out,' a man said. The hood was pulled from her face, and she blinked as her eyes adjusted. It seemed much darker now than when she'd got in the car, and the moon had risen. She wondered what time it was.

They'd left her feet untied so she could still walk, and as she emerged from the car she felt a jolt of recognition. They were by the sea, parked behind a row of boathouses so they couldn't be seen from the road. She knew this stretch of coastline like the back of her hand; from the sweep of the bay and the buildings beyond, the shape of the mountains and the lights in the distance, she felt almost certain they were just outside Conca dei Marini. If she could just—

'Keep your head down and keep walking.' One of the guards shoved her head roughly, and Carina walked quickly, scared of what might happen if she didn't.

'Where are you taking me?' she asked, hoping to keep him talking, hoping to find out more about her situation. But there was no response.

'My, my, so many questions, Carina.'

It was Isabella's voice. She appeared alongside them and Carina whirled to face her. 'What's happening? What do you want with me?'

'You know something? You're really annoying me now. I don't know how he put up with you all these years.'

Carina narrowed her eyes. Was she referring to Giorgio?

'What do you mean? What's going on, Isabella?'

Isabella threw back her head and laughed, her eyes glinting dangerously. Carina shivered in fear. She knew that Isabella was from a powerful family; it had never been discussed openly in her household, but she understood that Isabella's father, Vito, was a senior figure in the Camorra. The guard had told her that Giorgio owed them money, and Carina had effectively been taken for ransom, but surely Isabella could see that the situation was ludicrous?

'Please,' Carina begged.

'The high and mighty Carina Russo is begging me?' Isabella scoffed. 'Are you stupid or something? I want to get rid of you and make sure you don't come back.'

Carina was having trouble following Isabella's line of thought. The two of them barely knew one another, so why did Isabella hate her so much?

'I don't understand. What are you talking about?'

'*What are you talking about*?' Isabella repeated, her tone mocking, as she screwed up her face and mimicked Carina, in a horrible parody of a crying face. In a swift movement, she stepped closer to Carina, so close that the two women were almost nose to nose. 'When you're gone, then he'll want me,' she hissed. 'He loves me, you know, but *you're* in the way.'

Slowly, the pieces were starting to fall into place for Carina, but it still made little sense. 'Giorgio's in love with you?'

'Yes. He doesn't want you, you frigid little bitch. I know that you don't give him what I can – he told me. The whole time you were in London he was with me behind your back and it was so good. Then you came back and ruined everything. When you're out of the way, he'll want me again. No one will think I had anything to do with your death; Giorgio is up to his neck in bad deals and I'm the only one who can help him. He'll be glad you're gone – you can think about that in your last moments.'

Carina would have laughed if the circumstances hadn't been so dire. What Edie had said was true, then – Giorgio had had an affair with Isabella.

'You're welcome to him,' Carina said with feeling, briefly enjoying the look of confusion that crossed Isabella's face. She'd thought she was in control of everything and it felt good to stop her in her tracks.

'What are you talking about?'

'We broke up. You can have him.'

Isabella shook her head in disbelief. 'No, I don't believe you. You're trying to trick me.'

'I'm really not.' She lifted her hand slowly, her movements slow, her voice calm. 'Look, no ring. He's been screwing my bridesmaid and Ashley Hall, too, so it seems we've both been taken for idiots. Welcome to the club.'

Carina watched the emotions whipping across Isabella's face: confusion, suspicion, and something else: misery and despair. Then her eyes hardened and a cold fury blazed out from them.

'You liar!' she yelled. 'I was only going to scare you, to get you to call the wedding off, but now I want you *dead*. I should have killed you when I had the chance, when I almost ran you over in Positano that time I saw you with your stupid bag of lingerie with that slut of a bridesmaid.'

Carina gasped, 'That was you who nearly ran me over?'

'Yes, and I should have finished the job then. Getting rid of you is the only way Giorgio and I can ever be happy.' Isabella turned to the men who were standing around, watching the spectacle and seemingly enjoying it. 'Kill the bitch!'

Strong arms grabbed her and Carina cried out in pain and fear. 'Please, Isabella,' she said desperately. She was sobbing now as she realized the seriousness of what was happening. Isabella might be crazy, but she meant every word she said. 'You can have him, I'll leave the two of you alone, I'll never speak to him again, I promise.'

She was screaming over her shoulder as the black-clad men dragged her along the jetty, but Isabella remained implacable, her arms crossed over her chest as she watched with barely concealed glee.

As they approached a small boat, Carina panicked. Where could they be taking her? What if they planned to murder her at sea and dump the body where she'd never be found? Or perhaps she was being trafficked, across the sea to who knew where, and she'd be sold and never seen again. The thought was terrifying.

'*Mi aiuti!*' she screamed. 'Help!' But she barely got the words out before a large hand was clamped over her mouth. It smelt of cigarettes and chemicals and she instantly panicked, struggling to breathe, instinctively fighting to get away.

'That was a very stupid thing to do,' hissed a voice in her ear. 'Stop struggling and shut your mouth.'

She felt a hard, solid object pushed into her side, colliding painfully with her ribs – the unmistakable feel of a gun. Carina instantly became still. Her knees almost buckled and she felt as though she couldn't catch her breath, her windpipe closing up. She'd never known fear like it.

'Move,' the guy hissed, shoving her hard.

They drew closer to the shoreline, the familiar smell of engine oil and brine now turning her stomach. Her hands were still bound, and sharp stones on the quayside dug into her bare feet. Her fear was overwhelming, terrified that once she was on the boat she might never see her beloved Italy again. Getting away was imperative but she didn't dare to try, the gun pressing into her lower back, the threat all too real.

The guard pushed her onto the boat and she took a step forward, feeling it rock and sway beneath her. There were three men on board that she hadn't seen before and she eyed them suspiciously. They looked bigger, swarthier, crueller than the others she'd encountered, and her sense of panic was rising as one of them started the engine and they motored away from the shore.

The men looked her up and down, their eyes running hungrily over her figure. She felt horribly vulnerable in just her skimpy bikini, the robe hanging open around her. Instinctively, she moved backwards, finding the edge, the gunwale pressing into her waist. She could hear the waves slapping against the hull, the engine humming as they headed out to sea, the sun now below the horizon as twilight cast its shades of purple and cobalt blue across the sky; the flickering light of the stars, Scorpius and Antares already high above her. The full moonlight shimmered on the water, and the waters were calm as the small boat skimmed over the surface of the bay.

'*Dammi la corda*,' one of the men instructed. *Give me the rope.*

He was overweight and unshaven, a hand-rolled cigarette dangling from his lips. The boat was moving fast, out into the open water, leaving white waves in its wake. Already, they were hundreds of metres from the shore.

'*E la benda*,' he added with a smile that revealed a missing front tooth. *And the blindfold.*

Another man threw him the items and he approached Carina with a swagger, his eyes never leaving her. She felt terrified of what was going to come next. Her only thought was to get away. He bent down in front of her, holding the rope tight between dirty hands.

'Put your legs together,' he instructed. Carina hesitated, knowing that once she was bound again, she had no chance of getting free. 'Now,' he snapped. He reached for her ankle and she reacted instinctively, repulsed by his touch. Raising her knee, it collided with his chin, and she kicked him as hard as she could. His head snapped back and he cried out then fell to the deck, clutching his bleeding nose, swearing profusely. There were shouts of alarm from the other men, but Carina didn't stop to witness any more. In a flash, she hurled herself backwards over the edge of the boat, landing with a splash in the cold, dark water. The men in the boat aimed their guns into the water, shooting indiscriminately into the dark. But Carina was gone.

# Chapter 35

'She's gone,' Tom fumed, as Salvatore picked up the phone.

'Gone?'

'I've found where they held her, but they must have moved her. I'm too late.'

'So where is she now?'

'I don't know.' Tom jogged back to the car, desperate to keep moving. He would drive down the mountain, put together a new plan. 'We need to get the police involved, use their local knowledge.'

Salvatore made a grumbling sound. Tom already knew what he thought of them; that they were corrupt and little better than useless. 'All right,' he acknowledged finally. 'Anything to get my daughter back.'

Tom had reached the car, and he climbed in and started the engine. 'Let me know what the police say. I'll keep looking.'

'Wait,' Salvatore stopped him, sensing that Tom was about to ring off. 'Let's just think about this. What if she managed to get away? I know it's a long shot, but my daughter is smart and highly resourceful.' His voice cracked and Tom could hear how Salvatore was fighting to keep his emotions in check. 'Where would she go, what would she do? Is there anywhere we haven't checked yet? Somewhere she could hide, somewhere she would feel safe?'

His words stirred a memory within Tom, an idea forming at the back of his mind. With startling clarity, he realized there was one place he could think of.

'I'm on it,' he said, revving the accelerator and speeding off.

Carina was shivering, hugging her knees into her chest as she wrapped her arms around them to try and keep warm. Her thick blonde hair was damp and matted, her full lips ringed with blue. She was hungry, scared and alone.

Carina knew it must be early morning as the first shards of daylight were filtering through, the colours around her beginning to come to life. She needed to move, but it was as though she were numb, both physically and emotionally, frozen to the spot by indecision. What if she emerged from her hiding spot and the men found her? Perhaps she should wait until later and there were more people around; she would be safest in a crowd. Or perhaps she should wait until the first tourist boat arrived and ask them for help.

Carina shivered. She'd discarded the robe as soon as she could – it weighed her down in the water – and was wearing only the bikini she'd had in the spa. That seemed like a lifetime ago now; there'd been so many revelations in the past twenty-four hours. Carina found herself wishing she could go back to yesterday morning, to a time when she'd been unaware yet happy. Though, if she was being honest with herself, she hadn't been truly happy. She'd had her suspicions that something wasn't right, she'd suppressed her doubts about Giorgio to keep everyone else happy.

Now it turned out that she hadn't known her fiancé at all. The affairs, the shady business deals . . . Had she been stupid, or just wilfully blind, she wondered. She'd been asking herself the same questions over and over all night, since she'd arrived here, replaying the scene with Edie, the showdown with Isabella. Carina couldn't believe everything that had happened to her recently. It didn't seem real.

Carina flinched then sat bolt upright, listening hard. She could hear a noise, growing louder . . . the low hum of a motorboat. In panic, she scrambled backwards, her back hitting the hard stone of the cave. There was nowhere else to go. She saw flashes of torchlight; they'd be here any second.

Terror flooded through her. She couldn't go back to those men; this time they would surely kill her. Perhaps she could slip into the water? Smoothly and quietly with no splash, dive down under water for as long as she could hold her breath and hope they left quickly.

But Carina couldn't move, she was frozen in terror and exhaustion. She could hear that a boat had entered the cave but all she could see was the brightness of the torch. The light was bouncing all over the walls in the Grotta dello Smeraldo, dancing over stalagmites and stalactites, the strange, twisted shapes eerie in the shadows.

'Carina!' a man's voice shouted.

She shrank back in panic, then realized the voice sounded familiar.

'Carina!' The shout came again.

'Tom?' Carina called out in reply, but her voice was cracked and hoarse. 'Tom!' she tried again, louder this time, scrambling forward to the edge of the ledge.

'Carina!' Tom exclaimed as he spotted her, relief and elation in that one word.

Moments later he was with her, leaping out of the boat and taking her in his arms.

'God, you're freezing,' he said, ripping off his T-shirt and tugging it over her head, wrapping her in a bear hug, pressed against his naked chest.

She was shaking violently but it was from more than merely the cold. Adrenaline and relief flooded through her. She was too shocked to even speak.

'It's OK, you're safe now, I've got you . . .' Tom reassured her, holding her close to keep her warm, stroking her hair to soothe her. Carina clung on like a drowning man to a life raft, terrified that if she let him go something bad would happen to her. As long as Tom was here, she was safe.

'You came for me,' she murmured in disbelief. 'You found me.'

'Of course.' Tom nodded. 'I'd never have stopped looking until I found you.'

'We should go.' Carina looked up at him, her violet eyes wide with fear. 'They might come back.'

'Back? They left you here?'

'No. I escaped. They took me on a boat and—'

'You escaped? From the Camorra? Jesus, how did you manage that?'

'Instinct. I took my chance. It was Isabella – she was the one behind it all.'

312

'Isabella De Luca?' Tom asked grimly, his jaw set.

'Yes. She said she's in love with Giorgio. That if I was dead, then they could be together.' Carina choked up at the memory, before telling him how she had escaped, about the boat and jumping off the side when they tried to tie her legs.

'I kicked as hard as I could, trying to stay low under the water, to get as far away as possible. I knew they were searching for me – I could hear them shouting, saw their searchlights sweeping the water. I even heard gunshots . . .' Carina's voice choked up. 'They were firing into the water, hoping to hit me, the boat circling and circling, looking for me. . .'

'Oh, Carina,' Tom murmured, holding her tightly.

'The tide was with me – the waves pushed me to the shore. I landed up near some rocks. They were sharp and jagged, and I managed to use them to cut through the ropes at my wrist. It took an age, sawing through the tight cords. I was still wearing my towelling robe from the spa – it was so heavy, weighing me down, so I had to leave it. I threw it back into the sea – I was hoping that they might see it and give up, thinking I'd drowned.'

'I've never met anyone like you, you're incredible.' Tom's gaze was intense, holding hers, as though he was terrified she might disappear again if he took his eyes off her.

'I recognized where I was – even though it was dark there was plenty of moonlight,' Carina continued. 'I knew I wasn't far from the grotto so I swam along the coastline. I should have been exhausted, but it was like it was pulling me here. My safe place. My sanctuary.' She looked up at Tom. 'And then you came for me. I prayed you would.'

'I found where they held you. Up in the mountains.'

'You did?'

'I saw the room they'd held you in. I found your engagement ring. I thought I'd lost you. I'd never have forgiven myself if anything had happened to you.'

'Those men were so dangerous. You risked your life for me.'

He was holding her tightly and she never wanted him to let her go. His body was strong and powerful, and she felt secure, wrapped up in the T-shirt that smelled of him, staring up into his handsome, kind face. He was so brave, so fearless, and Carina knew that he would never have let anything happen to her. She believed that he would have tracked her down, wherever they'd taken her. She realized now for the first time that ever since Tom had come into her life, it was he who had overtaken her thoughts and her desires. It was Tom, not Giorgio.

Her hands were stealing over his body, across his powerful shoulder blades, his taut back, finding their way to his face. Her fingertips trailed lightly over his cheeks, holding his face in her hands. They stared at one another for a long moment. Carina parted her lips, sheer desire flooding through her.

Tom backed away. He took hold of her hands, gripping her wrists gently, moving them away from his face.

'We need to go,' he murmured. 'Before they come looking for you. And we need to let everyone know you're safe.'

Carina sensed him withdraw from her, feeling overwhelming frustration. It seemed the moment had passed, and she wondered whether they'd ever get another chance. Perhaps she was simply another job to him, and everything he'd done – rescuing her, finding her, keeping her safe – was all because her father was paying him.

She disentangled herself from him, feeling foolish, and moved towards the boat.

'Carina,' Tom said. Something in his tone stopped her in her tracks and she turned to look at him. There was no mistaking the look of desire in his eyes, and she felt a surge of hope. 'Now's not the right time. We need to let your parents know that you're safe.'

Carina nodded, the ghost of a smile playing on her face, daring to hope that Tom might feel something for her too. She climbed into the boat and Tom followed, starting up the motor and chugging out of the grotto. The sun was rising, and Carina felt calm and protected. Dawn was breaking and it was gearing up to be the most beautiful day, the early morning light washing over the bay and warming her cold and tired bones. She felt light, free as a bird, certain that everything was going to be OK. She might not be marrying Giorgio anymore but, as she glanced across at Tom and he smiled at her, it felt as though she was on the cusp of a new beginning.

# Chapter 36

Church bells were chiming, drifting up from Sant'Andrea cathedral in the town below. She was supposed to be getting married tomorrow, Carina reflected, as she leaned over the balcony of the Villa Amore, taking in the incredible view. But life hadn't turned out that way, and she knew it was for the best.

Carina turned round, looking at Giorgio who had just arrived with his father, wondering if he was thinking the same. He probably hadn't even realized it was supposed to be tomorrow. He'd never paid much attention to their wedding.

Carina had been through the most horrific experience, but she was surprised to discover that she didn't feel angry towards Giorgio. He looked like a broken man, his eyes darting around the terrace, avoiding eye contact with everyone and looking for all the world like a little boy about to be told off for being caught with his fingers in the sweet jar. She knew he'd been incredibly stupid, and it wasn't over yet. The Camorra still wanted their money.

Just because Carina had escaped didn't mean the ordeal was over.

It was why Salvatore had insisted that they all gather here, at the Villa Amore, to find out exactly what was going on and what they could do to solve it. Carina glanced around at the assembled group – these people had been closest in the world to her, but now her relationship with all of them had changed: Salvatore, Philippa, Costa, Giorgio and Tom. Costa looked more defiant than his son. Rafaella, sitting in a comfortable chair beneath the shade of a lemon tree, looked exhausted, but then she hadn't slept for worrying about Carina. Bella the dog was lying at her feet; she'd refused to leave Carina's side since she returned.

Salvatore cleared his throat, and everyone turned to him as he began to speak. 'There are some things we need to discuss, and I think it's best we resolve everything sooner, rather than later. We—'

Salvatore broke off as Paola came running in. 'I'm so sorry, Signor Russo. There is a gentleman and a lady at the door. They would not go away, they insisted on coming in . . .'

She trailed off, as an American voice could be heard bellowing, 'Is he here? I need to speak to him.'

'I'm so sorry, Signor Russo,' Paola apologized, as Sam Quinn came striding out onto the terrace, Ashley Hall hot on his heels. Bella let out a volley of barks, growling suspiciously at the newcomers.

'*Va bene*, Paola,' Salvatore assured her. He rose from his seat and raised himself up to his full height. It was nothing in comparison with Sam's towering stature, but he held himself with undeniable authority, like an immovable cliff in the face of a tsunami. 'Who are you, and what the hell do you think you're doing, invading my home uninvited?'

'I'm looking for Giorgio Bianchi,' Sam explained gruffly. 'And I seem to have found him.'

Carina glanced over at Giorgio and saw he'd gone white. She didn't know who Sam was, but she certainly knew who Ashley was. She stared at her with interest. As far as Carina was concerned, Ashley was welcome to Giorgio – if she still wanted him.

Ashley sensed she was being watched, turned to look at Carina, the two women taking in one another.

'Another one of your unwanted guests, Giorgio?' Salvatore was saying. 'Any more surprises to spring on us? Will my daughter be safe from this one?'

'*Merda*,' Giorgio uttered a curse under his breath.

'What do you want with Giorgio?' Salvatore wondered. When Sam hesitated, he added, 'I don't think there are any secrets left between us, are there? Or do you have more unpleasant news to come?' He was clearly furious with Giorgio, his anger simmering under the surface.

'I want to know when I'm going to receive my ownership papers for the vineyard,' Sam raged. 'I spoke to my attorney and he's received nothing . . . I want to know what the hell's going on.'

'Perhaps, my friend, you could join the queue. I think we all want answers from Giorgio today,' Salvatore commented wryly. 'Paola, please give our new arrivals a drink, and do take a seat, Mr Quinn.'

'You know who I am?'

'Yes, I have been brought up to speed.' Carina looked at Tom, who gave her a slight nod, and guessed he must have filled in some of the blanks for him.

Paola poured a glass of rosolio aperitivo for the new arrivals, who took their seats on the wide terrace around the large marble table.

'What's all this about?' Costa spoke up. 'Giorgio doesn't own a vineyard.'

'He's selling me his family one. Ain't that right, Giorgio?'

Costa looked aghast. 'The Bianchi vineyard? But you can't sell that.'

Giorgio appeared as if caught in a bad dream, his lies confronting him whichever way he turned. 'I'm sorry, Papà. I was desperate. I needed money – you saw what happened to Carina – they were threatening me. I had to save her.'

'Had to save your own hide, more like,' Sam muttered.

'You cannot sell the Bianchi vineyard because it's not yours to sell,' Costa repeated.

'I know, Papà. But, I thought, one day it will be. It's just getting my inheritance early.' Giorgio shrugged sheepishly. Carina recognized that look – she'd been on the receiving end of it too many times as Giorgio tried to manipulate her emotions. She wondered how it had ever worked on her; it was as if her blinkers had fallen off and she could see through him completely.

At that moment Costa reached over to his son and cuffed the back of his head. Giorgio pushed his chair back and exclaimed loudly, '*Smettila*, Papà! Stop it!'

'Your mamma would be turning in her grave, you imbecile!'

Giorgio rubbed the back of his head, looking mutinous.

Costa glanced over at Salvatore. 'Do you want to tell him?'

'Tell me what?'

Salvatore sighed. 'The Bianchi land is held in trust,'

he explained. 'It cannot be sold, or even given away – in short, ownership cannot be changed – without the consent of *both* families.'

Annoyance flashed across Giorgio's face. 'What, Papà? How come I never knew about this?'

'Because I thought it was better that you did not know. Not until you needed to.'

'You should have told me,' Giorgio burst out. 'If I'd known, I—'

'Wouldn't have tried to sell your own father's company out from under him?' Sam finished for him. He stood and placed his Stetson on his head. 'I can see this is family business, and that my expertise won't be needed, so I'll make my excuses and leave now. Ashley and I have some sightseeing to do, as we've come all this way,' he turned, with a nod to Salvatore. 'I appreciate your hospitality, sir.' He cast a glance over at Giorgio. 'We all gotta start somewhere, son, and I like your balls, but you gotta whole lot to learn.' He tipped his Stetson to Salvatore and Philippa, striding leisurely towards the house.

Ashley hesitated, seemingly wanting to say something else.

'The wedding's off,' Carina said coolly. 'He's yours if you want him.'

Ashley raised her eyebrows, looking at Carina. 'Sorry, honey. It looked like it was gonna be a beautiful wedding.' Her gaze turned to Giorgio, but she said nothing, simply smiling and turning on her heel before following her uncle.

'I think there are one or two things you should have told me, too.' Costa's tone was reproachful now rather than angry.

'Papà, I was too ashamed,' Giorgio confessed. 'I made a mess. I kept thinking I could get out of it. I wanted . . . I wanted to make something of my life. I wanted Mamma to be proud of me.'

Giorgio broke down, his body shaking with sobs. Carina knew that previously she would have gone to him, but not this time. She couldn't be that person anymore and her eyes found Tom instead, his calm eyes giving her confidence that she could do this.

She'd spoken briefly on the phone with Giorgio that morning and it was obvious to both of them that the wedding couldn't go ahead, that their relationship was over. She didn't hate him – they'd been in one another's lives for too long. He was troubled, he'd made mistakes, some of which had caused huge damage. It was up to him to find redemption, but Carina wasn't going to be a part of that. A new future lay ahead for her, though she didn't yet know what path it would take.

To everyone's surprise it was Philippa who comforted the sobbing Giorgio, taking him in her arms and letting him cry. Carina understood – Philippa might be furious with him right now, for everything he'd put her daughter through, but she was a mother, and that maternal instinct saw a child who'd lost his own. She'd seen Giorgio grow up, known him since he was little more than a baby, had been there for him when Vittoria died and welcomed him into her home like he was one of their own. The gesture was what Costa needed right now.

As he calmed down, he began to talk. It seemed to be cathartic, and once he'd started, he couldn't stop. He told them how he'd invested in a local property deal, but lost money. Through that, he'd met Gabriel du Lac, a reputable French hotelier, and proposed a deal, but Giorgio hadn't been completely honest with him, and Gabriel pulled out when he discovered Giorgio's lies. Trying to save face, he'd met with investors in the US but quickly realized he was out of his depth. So when some local businessmen had approached him, suggesting a partnership where he used their money for property development, he'd almost bitten their hands off. It had seemed too good to be true – and it was. He'd come to learn that he was dealing with the Camorra, whitewashing their dirty money by siphoning it through legitimate projects such as his. Without realizing it, Giorgio had become an accessory. He'd been so excited by their proposal that he'd said yes straight away, only realizing when it was too late that once he was entangled with them there was no easy way out.

Then they'd asked him to do other favours, transporting counterfeit money and drugs to the US on his 'business trips'. Giorgio had tried to say no, realizing it was getting out of hand, but these weren't people who would take no for an answer. He'd planned to pay them off, hoping to make money from lawful projects like the development in Newport Beach he'd wanted Sam to get involved with, but that had also been a non-starter. All the time, Giorgio was getting in deeper with no way out.

'And then they started threatening me. I thought they were bluffing, trying to scare me – then I heard about what had happened in Positano, when the car almost hit Carina . . .' Giorgio trailed off, finally daring to look at his now ex-fiancée. She saw the guilt and shame written on his face. He'd been a fool, no doubt about that, but she didn't hate him.

'That was Isabella De Luca,' Tom said. 'It seems like it was just a coincidence that she saw Carina in the street and engineered a little guerrilla attack.'

Philippa interjected, 'That woman is insane, but it's also your fault that she targeted Carina.'

'Why didn't you just come to me, Giorgio?' Salvatore looked furious. 'We could have sorted this out. Instead, you made everything ten times worse.'

'How could I?' Giorgio demanded. 'It was a mess. How could I come to you and say your daughter could be in danger and it was all my fault?'

'If you'd been brave enough, you would have. And it looks as though I have to bail you out once again.'

'What do you mean?'

'We may have got Carina back, but the problem hasn't gone away, has it? These guys still want their pound of flesh.'

'I don't know what to do,' Giorgio wailed. 'I don't know how to get out of it. They're relentless.'

Salvatore looked thoughtful. 'I can help.'

Giorgio stared at him in disbelief.

'Look, I've lived in Campania all my life. I run a successful business, and my father before me, God rest his soul. You think I've never dealt with these people? Of course I have. Many years ago, Vito De Luca and I reached an understanding. I still have a few favours I can call in.'

'Nice to see the Russos doing something right for once, eh Salvatore?' Costa said. There was a challenge in his gaze, a change in his tone that told Carina there was more to his comment than there first appeared.

She could see her father's disquiet at Costa's remark.

'Costa, we agreed we wouldn't—'

'Well, I'm tired of bowing to you,' Costa's voice took on a harder edge and he struggled to his feet angrily. He seemed much older, suddenly, than Carina remembered. His face was thin and sallow, his grey hair thinning, but he was defiant. 'I'm tired of doing what the Russos tell us to do. For generations we've taken the fall for you, but it stops now. If you're doing my son a favour, it's a fraction of the amount that we deserve in return for all we've done for you.'

Carina looked at her father in confusion. She expected Salvatore to protest; instead, he let his head and shoulders drop in defeat.

'I thought the wedding would heal our rifts,' he said softly.

'Atoning for past sins?' Costa retorted, his voice mocking.

Carina had never seen her father like this, and it was clear that the balance of power between the two men had shifted.

'The wedding?' Carina frowned. 'To Giorgio? What would it fix?'

'Tell them,' Costa growled. 'Or I will.'

'Tell us what?' demanded Carina.

Philippa looked concerned. 'Yes, what are you both talking about?'

No one paid attention to Rafaella, sitting quietly at a distance, observing the conversation. She'd gone pale, staring at the two men with watchful eyes.

'Go ahead,' Salvatore said.

Costa took a moment, glancing round at the assembled party, ensuring all eyes were on him. Slowly, he sat back down in his chair, his knuckles white as he gripped tightly onto the arms.

'My father, Roberto, and Salvatore's father, Antonio, were great friends. They were born in Campania, and it was their destiny to work these lands, the two families living side by side, the stream feeding both lands. Then the war came.

'Both men were young and loved their country, so they signed up together. One night, when both were off duty, there was a brutal street fight and a soldier lost his life. My father was court-martialled and sent to prison for four years.'

Carina's mouth fell open in shock. She glanced across at Giorgio, who seemed just as stunned as she was. Her gaze found Tom; he caught her look and discreetly moved round to stand beside her, his very presence offering her silent support.

'My grandfather killed a man?' Giorgio gasped. 'A soldier?'

Costa didn't reply, his focus steely as he continued with the tale. 'When Papà came out of jail, everything had changed. The grapes had gone sour and the soil had dried out. Antonio Russo had promised to look after the land for my father, but he deliberately sabotaged the vineyard.' Costa turned to Salvatore accusingly. 'He diverted the course of the stream to benefit the Russos, and left us almost penniless, our reputation in tatters.'

This was too much for Salvatore. He'd sat quietly as he listened to Costa, but now he got to his feet, years of acrimony and anger finally coming to the fore. 'How dare you! My father was an honourable man, he would never—'

'Oh, yes, the Russos are so *honourable*.' Costa's voice was dripping with sarcasm.

'You Bianchis can't manage your own affairs and always blame other people. Even your own son—'

'Stop it! Stop fighting!' Rafaella was on her feet, her breath coming fast, tears rolling down her cheeks. Salvatore moved to settle her, but she shook him off. 'It was all my fault,' she insisted.

'What are you talking about, Mamma? How could it be?'

Everyone turned to her, waiting expectantly, as Rafaella took a deep breath and prepared to tell her own story.

# Chapter 37

'The version of our two families' history that you have all heard is incomplete. It was all a long time ago, and the details . . . well, they get a little misty.' Rafaella clutched her embroidered handkerchief in her hand as she gathered herself, wiping the tears from her brown eyes, still bright and quick despite her advanced years. She took a deep breath. 'Doubtless, parts of the story have been lost over the years, but I know more than most – I was there.'

'But you are a Russo,' Costa cut in. 'Your version will be biased. And there is no one left who can corroborate your story.'

'I was not always a Russo.' Rafaella inclined her head, acknowledging the interruption, not seeming put out by it. She knew there would be questions, curiosity and sadness when she told her tale. She had lived with this story for many years, and the weight of the secret had almost been unbearable. Now, at last, she could share the truth. 'And although I am a Russo now, my first sweetheart was a Bianchi. Roberto – Costa's father.'

There were audible gasps at the revelation.

'I don't understand?' Costa exclaimed.

'But you went on to marry his best friend, my grand-father?' Carina questioned. 'How Nonna? Why?'

Rafaella shook her head and fretted with the hand-kerchief. 'The war came and changed everything, for everybody. You have never known hardship or suffering like Europe did in those days and Italy was changed completely. If Roberto hadn't gone away to fight, maybe we would have married, out of duty and expectation. Perhaps the world has not changed so much,' she said, with a wry glance at Carina and Giorgio. 'But I don't think either of us would have been happy. Roberto was much better suited to your mother, Maria.' Rafaella smiled fondly at Costa.

'But you and Maria were great friends,' Salvatore said. 'Didn't she know about your history with Roberto?'

'I don't believe so, no. It didn't seem important by then. Roberto may have told her, but she never gave any indication that she knew. She was a good woman.'

'So how did you come to marry Antonio?'

Rafaella paused. 'When Roberto went to prison, he asked Antonio to look after three things: his family, his land . . . and me.'

Costa snorted. '*Stronzo!* Sounds like he did a terrible job of all three. This is exactly what I've been saying. He stole my father's sweetheart and poisoned his lands, making his family practically destitute.'

'I'm not proud of what happened,' Rafaella said. 'But I'm not ashamed of it either. Roberto and I . . . It would never have worked. I wrote to him faithfully for two years when he was on active service, but when the war ended and the local men came home . . . Everything had changed. Antonio did look after me, but our feelings were too powerful.' She looked at Philippa, 'A *vortice* . . . a whirlwind. I fell deeply in love, and we were married the following year. You were born a few months before Roberto was released,' Rafaella finished, nodding at Salvatore.

'So, my father came home to find that you had married his best friend and had his baby? His lands had gone bad, and his family were reduced to poverty.' Costa's fury was plain to see.

'But Papà put everything right?' Salvatore leapt in, defending his family, wanting to spare his mother from Costa's relentless questions. 'He gave him the money the family needed, and the land was put in trust. That's the truth, isn't it? It's what Costa and I have always understood.'

Rafaella could sense the desperation in his tone, how badly he needed to know that his father had been an honourable man, and that he hadn't spent his life believing in a lie.

'And surely Roberto couldn't have expected you to wait four years for him?' Carina chimed in. 'You were a young woman, and you were right to move on with your life. He'd committed a terrible crime. If he killed a man, then he deserved everything he got – you shouldn't have had to live with the consequences.'

Carina had intended her words to be comforting, but they had the opposite effect. Rafaella's shoulders dropped and she bowed her head, beginning to sob. She knew she must look a pitiful figure, old and careworn.

'What is it, Mamma?' Salvatore rushed over to her.

'I'm sorry, Nonna.' Carina was mortified. 'I didn't mean to upset you.'

Costa's eyes bore into her, his mouth set in a grim line. He clearly had no sympathy for how difficult Rafaella was finding this. 'There is more to this, I can feel it,' he said, sounding increasingly angry. 'Tell all of us the truth, you owe me that much at least.'

Rafaella looked up at him, eyes ringed with red. 'I'm sorry,' she whispered to him. 'I'm so sorry.'

'For what? Tell me, what happened. Please. I want to know the truth before I die.'

'The truth is hard, and this won't be easy for you to hear, for any of you . . . there are some wounds that time cannot heal . . .'

*Antonio Russo looked up at the imposing walls of the military prison in the town of Santa Maria Capua Vetere.*

*He had travelled to this unpleasant place by bus, a journey which had taken many hours, but he felt compelled to come.*

*His best friend, Roberto Bianchi, was now inside those walls, paying the price for murder. After the two of them had gone their separate ways following the death of the soldier, Antonio had fled to Amalfi, where his family still had an old villa, and lived with his aunt. After some months it felt safe to return to his home in the Avellino valley, but once he was home, the nightmare of the past few months reared its ugly head when he learned that Roberto Bianchi had been arrested for the murder of a fellow soldier, had pleaded guilty and was now serving a sentence inside these terrifying walls.*

*A line of people were waiting outside, comprised primarily of women in headscarves, some of them older with greying hair, others younger, still with traces of prettiness but mostly looking careworn and resigned; some of them had children who gathered about their mother's legs, griping and whingeing in the heat of the midday sun.*

*After a while the gates clanked open and the visitors were led in under the watchful eye of the prison guards, all armed with guns, some of them chewing gum or smoking, most looking bored at this weekly occurrence.*

*Upon entering they were all searched, the younger women loudly complaining as they stood behind a curtain while the male guards rifled through their clothing and belongings. Antonio was dealt with quickly, having nothing about his person other than some cigarettes in his pockets and his fare for the bus journey home.*

*They were taken into a prison yard in which stood a long iron railing behind which was a row of prisoners. There was no privacy afforded any of them, and the visits would have to be held in full view of all the other inmates and their visitors.*

*The women moved quickly to the men they recognized, some embracing through the bars, others handing over cartons of cigarettes. Some argued loudly while others wept quietly into ragged handkerchiefs. Antonio scoured the faces of the men, and wondered for a moment if his friend had decided to stay away, unwilling to see him, and he wouldn't have blamed Roberto; he would have felt the same way if he was in his position . . . but then he saw a glint of teeth and the smile of Roberto Bianchi, who hailed him cheerily, and Antonio quickly made his way towards him.*

*Roberto thrust his hand through the bars, grabbing Antonio's hand. 'Ciao, amico!'*

*Antonio gripped his friend's hand with his own, and despite his vow to rein in his emotions in front of all the other people here, he couldn't help but feel overwhelmed. 'Roberto, I'm so sorry, I didn't know . . .' tears pricked his eyes.*

*'Look, no sadness OK, I'm all right.'*

*'But this place . . . it's awful.'*

# Carol Kirkwood

'Hey, it's not so bad once you get used to it, and I could have been sent somewhere a lot worse. At least this is a military prison, not like that cesspit those poor bastards are sent to in Naples. It's not the Ritz, but . . . I'm getting by.'

'Why didn't you tell them, you know . . . the truth . . . when they arrested you.'

Roberto lowered his voice. 'Tell them what? That in the heat of the moment you killed that poor sucker and not me? Are you crazy? You wouldn't have lasted five minutes in here, and we both know it.'

Antonio lowered his head, knowing Roberto was right. Roberto was always the strong one, had always been like a big brother to him, and now here he was, taking the blame when Antonio should be brave enough to pay the price himself for his drunken mistake.

'Look, I was lucky it was manslaughter, we could both have ended up in front of the firing squad,' Roberto said. 'I'm just going to keep my head down and, before you know it, I'll be back home, and you'll be my best man when I get married.'

Antonio's mouth felt dry.

'You seen my girl, Rafaella? Is she OK?' Roberto asked anxiously, 'She hasn't written for a while.'

Antonio nodded, but his stomach tightened. That was another thing he had come here for today, to tell him that Rafaella wanted to break off their engagement.

'You know, every night I pray to Santa Maria to say thank you that I have a friend who is keeping my girl safe. I know you won't let me down. She's a beautiful girl, many men will want her for a wife.'

Antonio nodded, he knew more than most how beautiful Rafaella was, both inside and out. His thoughts were filled with love for her and it seemed that she felt the same way

334

*about him too. Antonio had come here today to tell his friend the truth: that they had fallen in love. But now he was here, he couldn't bring himself to do it. He'd hoped that Rafaella would have been forgotten after such a long time, but he knew it would break Roberto's heart. Antonio understood it was only the thought of her that was keeping him going.*

*He handed over the packets of cigarettes he had brought along, knowing prisoners used them as currency behind bars. As Roberto questioned him about his parents and the vineyard, Antonio couldn't bear to share the news that catastrophic floods had almost destroyed the valley in the ensuing mudslides. He was helping them to rebuild their business, but it could take years.*

*As the allotted time came to an end, and the visitors said their last tearful goodbyes, Roberto grasped Antonio's hands in his own once again.*

*'Live your life, my friend, you are younger than me, and have growing up to do. This place would have destroyed you, but you have the chance to make something of yourself, no? You can make me proud.'*

*Antonio took one last look at Roberto as he waved goodbye, understanding that today was not the time for the truth. It was too late to change things now; the truth would come in time, and then they would all have to pay the price . . .*

The sun bounced off the sea in the harbour below, the chatter of the sparrows in the oleander bushes filled the silence before Rafaella spoke again.

'It was Antonio,' Rafaella said. The words were little more than a whisper, her voice shaking. 'Antonio shot the soldier. But Roberto went to prison and paid the price for it.'

No one spoke, a stunned silence hanging heavy in the

air. The distant sound of traffic could be heard on the Amalfitana.

Giorgio asked the question everyone was thinking: 'Why . . .?'

'Antonio lied about his age when he signed up to the army. He was only sixteen. He wanted to join up with his friend, Roberto. He wanted to fight for his country and liberate it from the enemy.

'They were off duty the night it happened, and they'd been out drinking. Tensions were running high in the city. You can't imagine what it was like back then. Everyone was on edge, everyone was fearful. The country had split into two factions, and it was impossible to know who was on which side. They ran into a group of Mussolini supporters heading north, there was an argument, weapons were drawn and . . . Antonio fired. He swore to me that it was self-defence, that the others shot first. He lived with the guilt until his dying day.'

Salvatore looked devastated to learn the truth about his father's actions, his usual confidence and ebullience evaporating. 'So why was Roberto the one who went to prison?'

'Antonio asked himself the same question every day. After the incident happened, both men fled. The next thing Antonio heard, Roberto had turned himself into the authorities and confessed to the crime, knowing it would likely be treated as manslaughter as they were men in uniform. Antonio went to visit him in prison, after the war, and Roberto claimed it was because Antonio was like a brother to him. He knew he'd be treated more harshly in the prison system because of his age. Roberto felt that Antonio had his whole life ahead of him, and didn't want it to be tainted. He believed he could cope better with the privations of prison . . . he did it out of a good heart.'

'So *my* father was the honourable one.' Costa looked surprised, and vindicated. 'But after everything that had happened, why did Antonio treat my father so badly? Not content with stealing his sweetheart, he destroyed his land and his livelihood.'

'He didn't, I promise you that,' Rafaella insisted, her voice strong now. 'There was a year when the whole valley was almost washed away, and he did his best to try to repair it for both families. It seems to be a rare phenomenon, but the course of the spring was altered *naturally*. Their relationship never really recovered once Roberto returned to find us married. After a time, Antonio's guilt turned to anger at Roberto; he didn't know how to make things right, and it hardened him.'

Salvatore was shaking his head. 'So many years – *decades* – of resentment and bad feeling. So unnecessary.'

Rafaella didn't respond to her son; she was looking at Costa instead. 'I must take my share of the blame – I should have written to your father and told him the truth right from the very start, that we weren't suited. Can you forgive me?' she asked.

'It was not you that my father felt betrayed by. It was Antonio,' Costa said. 'I knew that my father blamed the Russos for all his misfortune, and I vowed to him that I would get my revenge and make things right. On his deathbed, I made a promise to restore the Bianchi vine-yards to their former glory. And that if I couldn't do it, then my son would.'

'Me?' Giorgio frowned. 'But what—'

He was interrupted by Carina.

'Is that why you wanted Giorgio and I to marry?' Carina asked. It was the first time she'd heard this story, and she found herself wondering how much she'd been a pawn in a game between the two families.

Costa smiled sadly. 'I cannot create love where there is none. I thought you were a love match. Now it seems there are some secrets he kept from me too. But I will not deny that it was . . . useful, and that I encouraged it.'

Philippa was staring at Salvatore. 'How much of this did you know? Is this why you were so adamant that Carina and Giorgio's wedding had to go ahead? Is this why you refused to talk to me when I tried to raise my concerns?'

'No, he didn't know the full truth,' Rafaella insisted.

'I knew there was bad feeling, even if I didn't understand the reasons,' Salvatore told his wife. 'I admit, I hoped this might resolve it.'

Philippa glanced across at her daughter; Carina's expression was one of confusion, clearly unsure how many of her decisions had been her own, and how much she'd been caught up in a family feud.

Carina's gaze slid to Giorgio. No, she knew that she had loved him once. Maybe it was more like a brother, she realized now, but no one had forced either of them into anything. She wondered how he felt and then realized he was staring at his father, an anguished expression on his face.

'What did you mean . . .' he began, in a strangled voice, addressing his father. 'When you said you wanted to know the truth before you die . . .?'

Costa looked away, unable to meet his son's eyes. There was a long pause as Costa exhaled deeply, gathering his thoughts. 'I don't have long left, my son. I'm dying.'

# Chapter 38

Unsurprisingly, Giorgio had been devastated by his father's news. Costa explained he had cancer, that it had progressed, and he couldn't bear the thought of prolonged and invasive treatment. After the death of Vittoria, Costa felt it was his time, and was prepared for it. He had been hoping to live long enough to see Giorgio and Carina marry – partly to know that his son would be looked after, and partly to fulfil the legacy he'd promised his father. But now none of that would be happening.

Carina couldn't let Giorgio leave without talking to him. Yes, he had betrayed her, but they would always be tied together by their families, and Carina still believed that they had loved each other once upon a time.

As the rest of the family absorbed the shock of that day's revelations, Carina saw Giorgio standing a little way apart from everyone else, while Costa and Salvatore had their heads together, talking intently.

She touched Tom on the arm, indicating that she was going to talk to Giorgio, and he understood, stepping back into the house to get them both a drink in order to give them privacy.

Giorgio was staring out into the distance, his mind elsewhere. Though obviously feeling isolated, he turned as she approached.

'Not now, Carina. I know you're angry, but I can't talk anymore today.'

'Listen, I don't want that either. I love Costa. We all do, no matter what has happened between us.'

Giorgio looked choked and nodded.

She touched his shoulder. 'I want you to know that we will always be here for you both.'

'And what about you and me?'

'Maybe one day we can be friends again, I hope so.'

'Me too. Maybe getting married wasn't the right thing, you know. I'm probably not marriage material.'

Carina smiled. 'Maybe not but, Giorgio, there is something I want you to know . . . I haven't always told the truth either.'

He looked confused, and wary. 'What do you mean?'

'Remember when we broke up for a little while when I was in London? I said you weren't spending enough time coming to see me and we argued?'

'Yes, of course.'

'Well, during that time we were apart . . . There was someone else.'

Giorgio's mouth fell open in disbelief, 'Someone else, how?'

'I dated one of the guys at Edie's theatre for a while. It wasn't love, but it was fun, in every sense.' She grinned mischievously. 'I could never have been the good Italian wife you wanted, Giorgio. I can be a naughty girl too.'

Giorgio looked like he was about to explode with anger and then checked himself, took a deep breath and sighed, thrusting his hands into his chinos.

'I deserve that.'

'Yes, but we could never have made a marriage on lies, so this is for the best.'

He nodded with a tight smile and said, 'Have a happy life, Carina.'

It felt right to give him a hug, and he returned it. Carina felt like she had been caught up in a tornado over the last few days, but closing the chapter with Giorgio felt right.

Costa and Giorgio had left soon afterwards, but Philippa hadn't missed the increasingly intense looks passing between Carina and Tom, nor the way they somehow ended up sitting close beside one another as the sun set over the Tyrrhenian Sea.

Everyone was exhausted and had drifted off after dinner, so now the villa was quiet. Salvatore had retired to his study, leaving Philippa alone in their bedroom, but she found to her frustration that she couldn't sleep. Her mind was full of the day's bombshells: that her father-in-law had killed a man, that Costa's father had taken the blame and been sent to prison. That Rafaella had been Roberto's sweetheart before she fell in love with Antonio, and that Costa was a dying man.

It was late, the moon was high in the sky and she felt restless. Philippa slipped out of her bed and into her silk robe, padding into the long hallway and down the ornate stone staircase where she felt herself pulled towards the terrace.

She had lost track of time and it was certainly after midnight; the lights in Amalfi still twinkled down below and the moonlight cast a luminous glow across the sea far into the distance. The air was full of the smell of cypress and citrus, and for a moment Philippa relished the solitude, a moment to centre herself after all that had happened. Carina was safe in her bed, the wedding was halted, a terrible mistake averted, and she and Salvatore . . . where were they now?

She sighed, and threw her head back, letting the breeze ripple across her face and through her hair.

She sensed someone behind her, and opened her eyes. It was Salvatore, looking tired and ruffled, but still handsome and strong. Her husband took his place beside her, his gaze seeming to drink her in.

'Philippa,' Salvatore's voice was low, 'you look as beautiful tonight as the first time I brought you here.'

Philippa took a moment to answer. 'We've both changed, and it happened without me noticing.'

'Do you remember the first time we came here, what I told you then?'

Philippa smiled. 'How could I forget – but that was a lifetime again, I never imagined things could be like this between us. We've got Carina back, thank God, but nothing feels right. I'm scared that we've changed and things will never be the same again.'

Salvatore reached out an arm and wrapped it around the curve of her hip. 'Can you smell the citrus on the air?'

Philippa was puzzled. 'Yes, but what does that have to do with us, with what's happened?'

'You know the story of Hercules, whose heart was broken by the death of his great love Amalfi. He brought her here to be buried so that she would be surrounded by the most beautiful place on earth.'

'Yes, it's a wonderful love story, I remember you telling me about it the first time you brought me here.' She frowned, 'but it's unhappy too, Hercules was left alone.' She regarded her husband solemnly.

'Maybe that is true, but that is not the whole story.'

Philippa turned to him, her eyes now shining with curiosity.

'He wanted her immortal soul to be associated with beauty, but he wanted something else too. Everyone knows about the twelve labours of Hercules, and in one of those he stole the lemon trees from the Garden of the Hesperides.'

'And why did he want the lemon trees?' Philippa asked.

'To bring them here of course, to Amalfi. He wanted this place to be filled with fruits "fragrant and bright as the sun", and that's why Amalfi is full of lemons.'

Salvatore turned to her, his eyes full of love and honesty. 'Every year those lemon trees bear fruit, Philippa, no matter the rain, the soil, or the sun. They are strong, and can bear anything – like us: nothing can separate us.'

'Salvatore . . . I want to believe you, but you've been so distant, pushing me away. You've taken everything on your shoulders and shut me out.' She looked out across the water. 'Do you remember when I first arrived in Italy?'

'How could I forget?' His voice was soft. 'I loved you from the first moment I saw you. I knew that you'd change my life, and that you'd always be a part of it. It wasn't just that you were the most beautiful woman I'd ever seen, standing in that airport like a goddess. I could just sense it, as though the air between us was vibrating. It was *un colpo di fulmine*.'

'A thunderbolt,' Philippa repeated, a smile playing on her lips. 'Or maybe a *vortice* as Rafaella would say.' She reached out and stroked his face with her hands, feeling the familiar dips and contours she knew so well, a thick covering of stubble along his jawline. She could see the softness of his eyes and the truth in them.

'I don't want to lose you, Philippa. I don't want you to be unhappy. I know I always said that anyone who took me on would have to take the vineyard as well, but instead I feel like you are the vine that has grown around me, and now I don't know where you begin and I finish. You are my world.' Salvatore's lips touched hers as they held each other, the distance of the last few months closed.

'If all of this fell away tomorrow – the boat, the house, the wonderful things this life has given us – I wouldn't care. All I need is you and the children,' Philippa told him, her voice catching.

Then Salvatore kissed her again, this time with a sense of urgency, and Philippa felt the passion which she had been missing for so long.

Hours later, shards of light were creeping through the damask curtains as the sun rose outside. Philippa had surrendered to Salvatore's touch, delighting in the feel of him, in the familiar earthy, musky scent of him. He was her soulmate, her true love, and she knew they would never lose each other again.

# Chapter 39

Tom was driving along the Amalfitana, heading west towards the tip of the peninsula. It was a perfect morning, the temperature beginning to heat up, the roof down and the sun on his skin.

Beside him, content to be in the passenger seat for once, Carina felt truly relaxed for the first time in months. She was also exhausted, but that was unsurprising after everything that had happened. She'd barely slept in the past forty-eight hours, and she lounged like a cat on the soft leather seats, basking in the Italian sunshine. She and Tom had both woken early, neither of them able to sleep despite everything that had happened, and Tom had suggested they go for a drive.

Carina sneaked a glance at him, knowing he was a big part of the reason for her current state of happiness. Tom had been through the wringer too – there were bags under his eyes, hidden by his sunglasses, and his hair was a mess, his face unshaven, but Carina found the stubble sexy. Giorgio would never have let himself look so unkempt – but he was her past, Carina reminded herself, and she had to stop comparing the two men. She thought of the beautiful, custom-made wedding dress hanging unworn in her room, but realized she had no regrets. Giorgio was no longer part of her life, but she hoped Tom would be part of her future.

'Thank you,' she said softly. Tom turned to her and grinned, and she felt her heart leap. God, he was handsome. She'd felt attracted to him the instant she'd walked into the room, remembering how he'd blushed as he'd tripped over Bella, but she'd tried to deny it, knowing she was an engaged woman.

'For what?' Tom asked.

'Everything. Looking after me.'

Tom's face darkened momentarily. 'If that was a mission, I would have failed. You got away on your own – you did an incredible job. I don't think you realize how dangerous those people can be.'

Carina shivered. 'Do you think my father can negotiate with them?'

'I don't know. He spoke of a history between them, of being owed a favour, so perhaps he *can* intervene on Giorgio's behalf. Believe it or not, the Camorra have a strong code of honour.'

Carina considered his words as she picked up her phone, which had been retrieved from her locker at the Hotel San Marco. She read the message she'd received:

I'm so sorry about everything. Catching an early flight back to LA but call me if you want to talk. I'll understand if you don't, but I hope we can be friends again. I miss you. E x

Carina frowned as she put the phone back in her bag without replying. While she'd been hiding in the grotto, she'd replayed Edie's revelations a hundred times in her head. She couldn't believe Edie had kept such a huge secret from her. Well, she couldn't believe Edie had slept with Giorgio in the first place – she'd always thought they hated one another. It explained why Edie's acting career was flourishing. But it sounded as though her friend had been through a turbulent time over the last year or two, and she was obviously rather sad and lost after her break-up with Nathan. Carina wanted to be there for Edie, and was glad that the truth had brought her to Tom, but she wasn't ready to forgive her quite yet.

'That was Edie,' Carina said lightly, watching Tom's face for any flicker of a reaction.

'Ah,' was all he said, his tone non-committal. 'Your mother explained everything that happened.'

Carina nodded. She'd been wondering whether he knew, and that answered the question. Now there was one more thing she wanted to know.

'Did anything ever happen between you and Edie?'

Tom looked surprised. 'Jesus, no, it didn't,' he said, hastening to reassure her. 'We may have flirted . . .'

'Edie flirts with everyone,' Carina said, not realizing how it sounded until the words were out of her mouth. 'I just meant—'

'It's OK,' Tom assured her. 'And no, absolutely nothing happened. She's not really my type anyway.'

'What is your type?' Carina couldn't resist asking.

'Blonde. Italian. Always getting in trouble,' Tom grinned, and Carina laughed, unable to keep the smile from her face.

'Can I ask you something else?'

'Of course.'

'Was I . . . just an assignment to you?' Tom took a moment to answer, and Carina continued, 'Coming to find me like you did. Even now – is this all part of the service, or . . .?'

'Or what?'

Carina's cheeks flamed. 'Never mind.'

Tom sighed, as he expertly handled the twists and turns of the narrow, winding road. 'Carina, I . . . I'm not good at talking about my feelings, OK? I'm British, I'm male, I'm ex-Army. All of those things point to one buttoned-up bloke. I find it hard to be as open as I should be. I struggle with allowing myself to open up and fall in love. But when I do, I fall hard, and without reservation. I want you to know that.'

Carina's heart was beating faster at the mention of love. Was Tom suggesting he had feelings for her? Instinctively, she reached across, letting her hand cover his where it was resting on the gearstick. Her fingers slid between his, her pulse racing as she wondered how he would react.

He said nothing, but hit the indicator, pulling into the next rest stop a few metres down the road. It was an observation point, high on the hillside just outside Praiano, and the views over the sapphire-blue sea were spectacular.

Tom hit the brakes and killed the engine. Then he leaned over to Carina and kissed her. The moment took her breath away. She could feel the passion as his lips pressed down on her, the pent-up tension as they pulled one another close. She kissed him hard in return, realizing that this was what she'd wanted since she'd first laid eyes on him. She'd lain awake at night, tortured by the knowledge that he was sleeping in the next room, and she was engaged to another man, and it was impossible for them to be together. But now it was possible.

Carina understood now that she'd been with Giorgio for the wrong reasons. Yes, she'd loved him, but it had never felt like this. With Tom, the future felt limitless. She felt like she was on air. She could simply be herself, unlike with Giorgio and his expectations of her.

Slowly, reluctantly, Tom pulled away. His eyes were shining, and she saw her own desire reflected in them. Carina was tingling, her whole body on fire. She wanted nothing more than for him to kiss her again and again and—

She jumped in shock as she heard cheering and clapping. Glancing around, her cheeks flamed as she noticed that the viewing point they'd stopped at was busy with tourists all watching the morning sun blaze over the Gulf of Salerno. She and Tom had clearly given them much more of a show than they were expecting.

Laughing, Carina leaned in for another kiss, this one slow and lingering. She let her fingertips roam through Tom's hair, tracing his jawline, brushing over his stubble. All she wanted to do was explore every inch of him, but she knew there was no rush. They had all the time in the world.

# Chapter 40

The house was undoubtedly imposing, Salvatore thought grimly, as the security cameras perched high on the building swivelled in his direction and the black metal gates slid aside. He knew he was being watched as he drove along the gravel driveway, pulling up outside the enormous palazzo. Two men in black suits and earpieces observed him from behind dark sunglasses as he got out of the car. They strode forward, and he lifted his arms as they patted him down to check for weapons.

Salvatore found himself wondering whether these two goons had been involved in the kidnap of his daughter – if they'd followed her, taken her, hurt her. He balled up his fists in anger, but knew he had to keep himself calm.

Security check passed, Salvatore was led into the house. As he strode across the spectacular marble floor, he found himself thinking that it was more like a museum than a home. Vito De Luca had certainly gone up in the world from when Salvatore had known him as a boy. But as

Salvatore looked around at the priceless paintings and works of art, the extravagance left a bad taste in his mouth. He knew this was the result of fear, violence and crime. Salvatore might be nowhere near as rich as the De Lucas, but at least he could say his money came from an honest day's labour, not profiting from the misery of others.

'Salvatore!' Vito strode across the domed entrance hall and greeted him warmly. They shook hands, then hugged like brothers. 'Come, let's go to my study, we have much to discuss.'

Even though it was still morning, Vito poured him a large Scotch. Salvatore accepted, understanding that it was his way of being hospitable.

'Firstly, please accept my apologies over everything that happened with your daughter, Carina. Believe me, it was a mistake.'

'But—'

'I regret to say it was all the work of my daughter, Isabella.'

Salvatore frowned in confusion.

'My men believed they were acting under my orders. It's true, Giorgio owes us a considerable amount of money – though I don't want to go too deep into our affairs.'

'I think I have a good understanding. Giorgio has been very forthcoming about his . . . mistakes.'

'Is it a mistake to want to better yourself? To improve your prospects in life?'

Salvatore bit his tongue; Vito hadn't loaned Giorgio the money out of the goodness of his heart, but Salvatore knew he had to tread carefully where Vito was concerned.

'I digress,' Vito continued with a cold smile. 'Isabella got a little carried away – I believe she instructed my men to have your daughter followed and, eventually, to have her taken. Isabella tells me she just wanted to shake your daughter up a bit, she wouldn't have gone through with anything.'

'But why? I know a little of the story from Carina, but—'

'Isabella!' Vito called sharply.

Moments later, Isabella slunk in. Salvatore realized she must have been told to wait nearby; there was no way she could have heard her father from the depths of this enormous house. She'd clearly been crying, and she was dressed casually in sports shorts and a T-shirt, her feet bare. She looked young, Salvatore realized, feeling an unexpected pang of sympathy for her.

'I'm sorry,' she whispered, looking down at the ground. 'I don't know what I was thinking. I was crazy, just a little joke that went wrong.'

'No man is worth losing your self-respect like that,' Vito admonished her.

'The wedding was called off,' Salvatore said. 'He and Carina are no longer together.'

'Don't get any ideas,' Vito said sharply. 'He is not the kind of man I want my daughter to be with. He lies and cheats and displays terrible business judgement.'

'That's what I wanted to talk to you about,' Salvatore began, glancing at Isabella.

Vito seemed to understand what he was trying to say. 'My daughter is going on an extended business trip – aren't you, Bella. I have some business interests in Turkey that need addressing. Let's say they could benefit from her confident approach. Please leave us alone now, Isabella.'

'But—'

One look from her father was enough, and Isabella fled.

'Look,' Salvatore began. 'Giorgio has been stupid, I'd be the first to agree. But for many years he was like a son to me, and I still think of him that way, even if he doesn't deserve it. I discovered last night that his father is dying.'

'You're a good man, Salvatore, and we have always got on well. But the Bianchis are a different matter.'

'Costa doesn't have long to live.'

'That is . . . unfortunate. But it doesn't change the fact that Giorgio owes me money. He asked for it – I didn't force it on him. I'm running a business, not a charity. You run a company, you understand.'

Salvatore swallowed his dislike of the comparison; he was certainly nothing like Vito in the way he ran his business.

'I'm a reasonable man, but I can't simply write this money off.'

Salvatore thought for a moment, drawing himself up to his full height. With men like Vito De Luca, he knew, you could never show weakness. 'How about we come to some sort of arrangement?'

Curiosity flashed across Vito's face, his eyes sharp and wolfish. He took a slug of his drink and cocked his head. 'And what, exactly, are you proposing . . .?'

The sun was reaching its peak, the magical Mediterranean light rendering the view vibrant and fresh. Philippa and Harry walked along the beachfront in Amalfi, their feet crunching on the shingle, waves lapping at their ankles.

Philippa was reminded of doing the same with Salvatore all those years ago. Back then she'd been full of passion and longing; now, with Harry, she felt fondness and affection.

'Thank you for agreeing to meet me,' Harry said softly. He was wearing a cream shirt that accentuated the light tan he'd acquired, and linen trousers rolled up to the knee as he strolled in the shallows.

'Of course,' Philippa nodded. 'Thank you for being so kind and understanding. I haven't been quite myself these past few days.'

'That's understandable,' Harry smiled. 'How is Carina?'

'Shaken, as you'd imagine, but she seems to be coping well.'

'If she has one ounce of your strength and resilience then she'll be fine.'

Philippa didn't react to his comment, continuing to walk in silence. Harry stopped suddenly, resting a hand on her arm, forcing her to stop too. Philippa turned to him, her eyes hidden behind dark sunglasses so that her expression was unreadable.

'Pippa,' he began, and Philippa smiled softly at hearing her name spoken by him.

'I need to know something before I go back to England,' Harry continued. 'I need to know . . . is there a chance for us? Could you and I ever . . .?'

Philippa shook her head.

'Hear me out, these past few days have only reinforced what I've already said – losing you was the biggest mistake of my life, and I'll regret it forever if I don't say anything. My flight leaves this afternoon. Come with me. Come back to England, to Scotland, hell, I'll live wherever you want, and I promise I'll do everything in my power to make you happy.'

Philippa was silent for a few moments, wondering how to say what she needed to say. 'Harry, it's been nice seeing you the past few days, more than I thought it would be, and your kindness has meant a lot . . .'

'Christ, Philippa, you make me sound like some distant relative.'

'But you don't know me at all. You haven't seen me for more than twenty-five years, and my life is in Italy now, with my children. And with Salvatore.'

'But the other night, in Pogerola, you told me—'

'The other night I didn't know what I was doing or saying. My only concern was for my daughter,' Philippa said firmly. She knew now she shouldn't have behaved the way she did – staying out until all hours with Harry, ignoring the messages she'd received from Salvatore asking where she was, confiding in another man about her fears for her marriage. But, despite the emotions swirling in the air, nothing had happened between them. She'd simply needed time and space, and Harry had provided both, making sure she had a driver to take her back to the villa in the late hours. He'd been the perfect gentleman, and she had never wanted anything else from him that night. Philippa had felt glad that she had been able to prove that to herself.

'I'm a changed man. Let me make it up to you. Let me show you. I still love you, Pippa. I always have.'

Philippa caught a brief glimpse of the real man behind the slick exterior at these words. This was his last roll of the dice, his trump card. Harry Fanshaw still expected her to fall at his feet when he declared his feelings for her.

She could see the spoiled young man he'd once been was still there, frustrated at not getting his own way.

'No, you don't, Harry,' she said softly. 'You just don't like to lose.'

Harry laughed wryly, tipping his head. 'You always were far cleverer than me, Pippa. But I understand. You can't win them all.'

'Thank you, Harry,' Philippa replied. Her words were filled with affection.

Harry opened his arms and Philippa reciprocated, the two of them sharing a final embrace, an acknowledgement of all they'd been through together and an understanding that it was likely to be the last time they'd ever see one another.

It didn't feel sad, more like finally closing a chapter. Now, Philippa could look back without rancour on the time they'd spent together all those years ago. Harry had been her first love and her first heartbreak, but he wasn't her man. Salvatore was.

# Epilogue

'Are you sure you're OK doing this?' Philippa asked, as she looked at her daughter. Carina was radiant, positively glowing.

'I think it's a wonderful idea,' Carina smiled. 'Honestly. I don't think I could be happier, despite everything that has happened.'

'Well, it did seem a shame to let all that hard work go to waste. Oh, darling, you look so beautiful. I can't believe we are going to have a wedding after all.'

'You look beautiful, Mamma, like Grace Kelly!'

The two of them looked in the mirror together – Carina in a stunning, strapless blue gown, her long hair half-up with blonde waves tumbling down her back. Philippa's hair was pinned up elegantly, with strands of gypsophila woven through, and she wore a pair of silver kitten heels.

When it became clear that Carina and Giorgio's wedding was cancelled, Philippa had been ready to dispatch Bianca, the wedding planner, to inform all the guests and make their apologies. But then Salvatore had done something unexpected . . .

Tom wrapped his arms around Carina, as they stood on the steps of the Amalfi Cathedral, the Duomo di Sant' Andrea, pulling her closer. She sighed happily and leaned into him, her heart beating against his chest. They'd agreed to take things slowly at first, but the past twenty-four hours had been a whirlwind, and they hadn't left each other's side, neither by day, or by night.

'Are you enjoying your wedding day?' Tom asked, and Carina laughed, feeling as light as air, as if a great weight had been lifted from her shoulders.

'I certainly hadn't imagined it being like this. But I think it's worked out for the best, don't you?' she finished, as she looked up at the church. 'Funny to think that my parents got married here before I was even born.'

'How long have your parents been married now?'

'Over twenty-five years. I doubt that Giorgio and I would have lasted twenty-five hours.'

Tom nuzzled her neck, 'His loss is my gain.'

'I'm feeling like I've won a million dollars,' Carina smiled, returning his embrace, almost oblivious to everyone else around them outside the church.

'Your father has done an amazing job sorting all this mess out,' Tom said, pulling away reluctantly. 'It seems like Giorgio's off the hook.'

'It's more than he deserves, and I hope it's taught him a lesson. I still don't know all the details. I don't think I want to.'

Carina knew that Salvatore had initiated a meeting with Vito de Luca, Isabella's father. By all accounts, it had been an intense meeting involving alcohol, cigars, threats and bluffs. Money had changed hands. But by the end of the night Salvatore had extracted a promise that Giorgio would be free to go; he wouldn't be harassed for the money he owed, and would be released of his commitments to the Camorra. Isabella was apparently in disgrace and had been sent away. Carina shivered at the thought, remembering the hatred in Isabella's eyes that night. . .

'What is Giorgio going to do now?' Tom asked curiously.

'He's going to stay with Costa until the end. He hasn't got long left, it's heart-breaking. Giorgio sees his future in the States beyond that.'

'With that model? Ashley Hall.'

'Who knows.' Carina rolled her eyes, realizing she couldn't care less. 'Her uncle's offered him a job – impressed by his balls, apparently.'

'What about the vineyard? Presumably Giorgio will sell it once he inherits it, like he always planned to.'

'My father and Costa came to an agreement,' Carina began. 'Getting Giorgio out of this mess didn't come cheap for my father, so Costa and my father have made arrangements. The vineyards are going to be consolidated into one. My father will pay for the land, but less than he would have done before he settled with Vito. It means Giorgio's out of this mess, he is free of his obligations to his father and the vineyard but with some capital to start his own business; the operations of Casa di Russo will almost double overnight.' She hesitated. 'So. . . my father's offered me a larger role. I'd be CEO of the company. He wants to take a step back, a non-exec chairman he says, to spend more time with my mother,' she smiled.

'Have you said yes?' Tom asked gently.

'Not yet. I wanted to think about it, about what the future holds . . .' She eyed him shyly. 'What about you? Where do you see yourself next?'

'That's a big question, and I don't have all the answers. . . I *do* know that I'm tired of moving from one place to the next, from one job to the next. It might be nice to stay put in one place for a while.'

'Here in Italy?' Carina grinned, her violet eyes sparkling.

'That could work,' Tom laughed, pulling Carina closer to him, nuzzling her neck. 'I know you'll never leave here,' he murmured. 'It's in your blood.'

'That's true. But I'm keen to expand my horizons . . .'

'We *can* make it work,' Tom grinned, as he pulled Carina in for a kiss, which she returned.

'As much as I'd like to carry on like this all day,' she said, 'I think I'm needed elsewhere right now.'

Tom nodded and pointed with a smile to Salvatore, who had just arrived at the foot of the steps, looking flustered. 'I'd better go and wait inside,' he said, 'good luck!'

'Papa! You're late!' Carina rushed to greet her father, her blue strapless satin dress flowing down the steps after her. 'Here let me help you with your flower, and your shirt, it's all crumpled and there's soil on your collar!'

Carina fussed around her father, tidying up the large pink sprig of bougainvillea in his buttonhole, while he wriggled like a child.

'The weather was just right this morning, I had to make sure the pickers were at work! How do I look?' he asked her anxiously.

'You look handsome and distinguished, and a little like you have just come from the vineyard, just like you always do.'

'Thank you, my darling daughter, are you ready, we mustn't be late?'

'Yes Papa, are you?'

'I've never been readier.'

Salvatore's legs shook a little as he and Carina waited on the pew at the front of the nave in Amalfi's most famous church. He barely noticed the ornate Baroque interiors, or the sumptuous Renaissance frescoes that looked down on the small congregation that gathered near the altar. He only had eyes for one person. His wife, Philippa.

He didn't take his eyes off her as she walked up the aisle, her blonde hair swept up off her face in an elegant chignon; Philippa was dressed in a mid-length, light-grey 1950s-style dress, with three-quarter length sleeves and a delicate set of pearls around her neck which lent a luminosity to her skin. She was escorted up the aisle by their son, Lorenzo, looking dapper in a morning suit.

Following Philippa was her bridesmaid, Flora, looking glorious in a fuchsia-pink gown and an eye-catching black fascinator. The guests in the seats around them were a smaller, select number compared to the extravagant multitude who had been invited to Carina and Giorgio's wedding. Their mothers, Rafaella and Jean, were seated in the front with Carina and Tom, as were some of their staff from the villa and their very closest friends and family, all smiling happily and looking expectant. Some were holding handkerchiefs to their noses and sniffling loudly.

More than anything, after everything that had happened, Salvatore had wanted to show his wife exactly what she meant to him.

Today had seemed to Salvatore like the perfect solution to the many guests that had come from all over the world to Amalfi for a wedding; some had already departed, including Harry Fanshaw and Ginevra he was pleased to learn, but once Salvatore had asked Bianca to rearrange matters, everything had fallen into place quite simply. He had asked Philippa on bended knee to marry him again, and she had said yes, and after the ceremony to renew their wedding vows was over, they were to return to the villa for a wedding breakfast.

Philippa's eyes shone as she joined Salvatore by his side, handing her bouquet of matching bougainvillea to Flora. They turned to each other, as the priest spoke his words of blessing and renewal to them both, binding their hands together.

'Philippa, my darling,' Salvatore said, 'when I asked you to marry me twenty-five years ago, I also gave you a gift of the Villa Amore, but it is you who have given me so much more. Our lives, our family, are more precious to me than I can express. I told you then you had my heart forever, and I meant it. We have had a wonderful life together and there is still so much more to come, promise me that we'll never be parted.'

Philippa's eyes were shining with happy tears. 'When we married, I didn't think I could love you more, but I do. I promise you Salvatore, with all my heart. Now and forever.'

There was a ripple of applause, and smiles and laughter as they left the church. For a moment, Salvatore was overwhelmed, as he stood at the top of the steps, confetti raining down on himself and his beautiful wife. He felt like the luckiest man alive, surrounded by his children, who were his pride, and his wife, who was his joy.

Philippa slipped her arm through his and kissed his cheek. 'It's time to go my darling, she said. 'The Villa Amore is waiting for us.'

# Acknowledgements

My endless thanks to Steve for your patience, love and encouragement throughout this whole process. You are such a tower of strength in my life.

Thanks to the wonderful team at HarperCollins for all your help and guidance — especially Kate Bradley, my editor. Kate, if I were to call you brilliant, that would be the understatement of the year. I love how you 'get' my thought process and understand where I am going with it. You have so much talent.

If it wasn't for the PR department headed up by Liz Dawson, no one would know I am writing books! I would love to have just a smidgen of your enthusiasm, Liz. You are a positive delight to be around.

As I tell everyone, if it wasn't for my publishing agent, Kerr MacRae, none of this would have happened. Kerr, thank you so much for pushing me and believing I could do this . . . even when I doubted myself. I can totally see why you are so successful in the publishing industry.

And once again, Holly Macdonald and Claire Ward have designed a fabulous cover for this book. I had no idea just how much work goes into this. You are stars!

And thank you to HarperCollins for publishing this book – especially Kimberley Young for her unending support.

On a personal level I would also like to thank ALL my family and friends for always being there, and for being so unfalteringly encouraging in everything that I do.

And finally, my grateful thanks to you, my lovely reader. I will never take for granted the time investment involved in reading a book. From the bottom of my heart, I truly hope you enjoyed it.

Until the next time, take good care xxx

Read on for an extract from Carol's new novel

*Once Upon a Time in Venice*

Coming in July 2024

# Prologue

'...*Pie Jesu Domine, Dona eis requiem...*'

The high, sweet voice of the girl rang out across the church of the Holy Trinity, echoing from the ancient altar and drifting up to the heavens. The sound was clear and beautiful, like the voice of an angel but, out in the congregation, Maria Monti found herself distracted, Faure's 'Requiem' little more than background noise to her thoughts. She was worried about her father, Alberto.

Every Sunday, Maria went to church with her parents and siblings, but this week her father had been too ill to attend. They'd left him at home, wracked with coughing and wrapped up in a blanket beside the fireplace.

Maria's brother, Pietro, had been out that morning in the forest surrounding their house, gathering wood to burn; they were down to the last of the oil for the stove and could barely afford any more. Her father worked for one of the tanneries that provided the finest leather to the workshops in nearby Milan, but recently he'd been sick more often than he'd been well, with repeated bouts of bronchitis. The doctor said it was because of the chemicals at the tannery, but Alberto had been unable to find a position elsewhere.

The Monti family grew vegetables and kept chickens, whilst Silvia, Maria's mother, took on cleaning jobs in the big houses on the shores of Lake Como, but with five children to feed it was always a struggle to make ends meet.

When she wasn't skivvying after her untidy siblings, Maria dreamed of escape. She didn't want this to be her future – scratching out a living in a tiny house on the slopes of the mountains outside Milan, spending the rest of her life in the uneventful village of Cannegia. She wanted to be able to buy nice clothes and shoes, to be glamorous like the celebrities she read about in her mother's old copies of *Hello!* that were cast offs from the houses she cleaned for, but it was more than that. Maria wanted to live an extraordinary life and experience incredible things. She wanted her future to be magical, like a fairytale, with palaces and dazzling balls where a handsome prince would sweep her off her feet.

At school, Maria had once read a book about Venice, a floating city built on dozens of islands that had barely changed for centuries. What could be more magical than that? Maria had thought breathlessly, as she pored over pictures of winding canals and pastel-coloured *palazzi*, ornate stone bridges and domed churches and an ancient belltower. Even the names were evocative: *Piazza San Marco, Ponte dei Sospiri, Palazzo Ducale*. Maria could hardly believe that *La Serenissima* was little more than a hundred miles from where she lived her dull existence. It looked like a different world.

She had read about Giacomo Casanova too, a legendary libertine who was born in Venice in the 18th century, when it was the pleasure capital of Europe. Casanova was – amongst other pursuits – a writer, a musician, a spy, and a voracious lover. Maria thought he sounded incredibly exciting. She was fifteen years old and found herself regularly daydreaming about boys, wondering what her future husband would be like. She was excited to have her first kiss, her first boyfriend, her first caress from a lover.

A blush rose in her cheeks at the thought, and she inadvertently glanced across the aisle to see Lorenzo Mancini looking at her. Beneath his gaze her face grew a deeper shade of crimson and she cast her eyes down, feeling heat wash over her body like a warm waterfall. When she glanced up again, Lorenzo was still watching her. Boldly, she held his stare, unconsciously biting her lip.

Lorenzo was classically handsome, with thick, dark hair, a Roman nose and tanned skin. He was twenty-two years old, the same age as her eldest brother, Edoardo, and he was tall and muscular with a broad back and strong arms, his biceps straining against the suit jacket he was wearing. He had deep brown eyes and full lips, and Maria found herself wondering what it would be like to kiss him…

'*Maria! Basta!*' her mother hissed under breath. Guiltily, Maria averted her eyes, her heart racing. She stared down at the worn flagstones beneath her feet, noticing the way her black leather pumps were coming apart at the stitching, and tried to concentrate on the angelic voice singing at the front of the church.

But she was still thinking about Lorenzo.

The congregation spilled out of the Holy Trinity into a beautiful autumnal morning, gathering in pockets to chatter and gossip. It was a small community, and Maria recognised everyone as she stood beside her mother and siblings, twisting her long, dark hair round one finger and wishing she could go home. Silvia Monti loved to natter with her neighbours, or to collar old Padre Bernardi and regale him with tales of her piety. They would be there for hours, Maria groaned inwardly, as her brothers messed around with their friends, her sisters standing beside Silvia knowing they would one day be the matriarch of their own families and hold court like this.

Maria wasn't interested in hearing what the doctor had said about Rosa Greco's bunions, or in the rumours that Giovanna Riccardi was pregnant out of wedlock. She was worried about her father and wanted to get back to him.

Maria adored her *papà*. She was the baby of the family, and Alberto always called her his *piccola bambina*. He never spoke down to her or got angry with her like her mother and siblings did.

Maria's best friend, Elisabetta, once told her that the reason her sisters were so mean to her was because they were jealous that she was cleverer and more beautiful than them, her dark hair glossier, her green eyes brighter, her waist slimmer and her breasts larger. Maria didn't know if that was true, but the boys at school had begun to look at her in a different way and made comments as she passed them. When she walked home one night, Luca Sterpone had shouted out at her asking for a kiss, '*Sei Bellissima... baciami*!', and the others had burst out laughing.

As Maria heard her mother launch into an oft-repeated anecdote about one of the chickens getting loose and flying all the way up to the roof of the house, her mind was made up. She nudged her sister and said, 'Beatrice, tell Mamma I'm going on ahead. I'll see you back at home.'

'But Maria– ' Beatrice began angrily.

Maria didn't stop to listen, skipping out of the gate and making her way through the narrow lanes of the village of Cannegia. She could take the main road which wound slowly up the mountain, but Maria knew it was much quicker to take the steep, rocky path through the woods.

She set off at a brisk pace, enjoying the relative cool of the morning before it grew hotter, her lungs pumping, her breath quickening. She passed into the forest where it was shady and quiet, her feet crunching softly on the fallen leaves. She heard the tapping of a woodpecker in the distance, the noise echoing through the trees, then spotted the white flash of a deer's tail as it turned in fright and hurried silently away.

As the trail wound higher, the route growing more hazardous, Maria's thoughts turned to Lorenzo, daydreaming about his handsome face and perfectly chiselled body. There'd been a definite look of interest in those arrogant, wolfish eyes, smouldering beneath thick brows, as he fixed her with his intense gaze. Lorenzo wasn't like the boys in her class at school; he was tall and strong and muscular. He was a man.

She jumped as she heard a twig snap close behind her, whirling round in alarm. Almost as though she'd summoned him, Lorenzo Mancini was standing there. He smiled when he saw her.

'Lorenzo! You gave me a fright!' Maria's heart was

thumping, and she was both surprised and puzzled to see him.

'I called your name but you didn't hear me. Were you daydreaming?' he teased, and Maria blushed. 'What about?' Lorenzo asked, then laughed as though he knew that she'd been thinking about him.

'Why are you going this way? You don't live up here,' Maria frowned.

'Can't you guess?' His smile grew wider, as Maria's heart skipped a beat.

'You followed me?' she stammered, hardly daring to believe it.

Lorenzo stepped closer. He was over a head taller than her, and she had to tilt her face back to look at him. 'You're so beautiful, Maria,' Lorenzo murmured.

Maria felt as though she were dreaming. Lorenzo Mancini thought *she* was beautiful? *Impossibile!* She didn't even realise he knew her name.

Bashfully, she bowed her head, but Lorenzo reached out and placed one finger under her chin, forcing her gaze upwards. She shivered beneath his touch; the gesture felt so intimate.

'Look at me,' Lorenzo murmured.

Maria did as he commanded, as though she were under his spell. His eyes were dark, the pupils large. There was something intense in his expression, and it frightened her a little.

'Lorenzo,' she breathed, but he took her words away with a kiss, his mouth closing on hers. Maria thought she might faint, her legs threatening to buckle beneath her – she was kissing Lorenzo Mancini!

His mouth was pressed down on hers, but it was harder than she expected, uncomfortable almost. She tried to pull away, but he held her tightly, pushing his tongue inside her mouth. This wasn't loving or tender – it was forceful and rough.

'*Lorenzo, no! Fermare!*' Maria pushed him, feeling confused and a little scared. His body felt so large against hers, as though he could easily physically overpower her. Lorenzo's breathing was coming fast, and there was something animalistic in the way he was looking at her.

A sudden burst of fear surged through Maria. 'I need to go home, Lorenzo. My father's not well. He's waiting for me.' She began to walk away, but Lorenzo ran after her, grabbing her arm so tightly that it hurt. 'Ouch!' Maria exclaimed, trying to shake him free. 'What are you doing?'

'Don't play the innocent with me, Maria Monti. I saw the way you were looking at me in church.'

'What do you mean?' Maria knew exactly what he was referring to. Yes, she'd flirted with him a little, but had she encouraged him? Had she led him on? She knew what the boys at school said about girls like her – that they were a tease.

'I know you want this,' Lorenzo hissed, his face was no longer handsome but twisted with cruelty, his muscular body aggressive and threatening.

Maria's adrenaline spiked. He lunged towards her and she reacted instinctively, both hands on his chest as she pushed him with full force. It was enough to throw him off balance and he stumbled backwards, dislodging loose stones with his heels. The ground seemed to give way beneath him and he tripped, his arms flailing as he vainly tried to stay upright.

With horror, Maria realised that he was teetering on the edge of a ravine, nothing but fresh air between him and the rocky gorge a dozen metres deep.

'Maria!' he yelled, thrusting his hands towards her, his eyes widened in terror, his mouth opening in surprise, as the stones beneath him gave way and he dropped, his body dangling over the side of the gorge as he desperately held on to the craggy stones that jutted out and were all that stopped him from falling.

'Maria, help me!' His eyes beseeched her, but she felt rooted to the spot... she was the only person who could save him now...

Fern
Britton
*Picks*
Exclusively for
**TESCO**

**EXCLUSIVE ADDITIONAL CONTENT**

Includes an author Q&A and details
of how to get involved in *Fern's Picks*

## Dear lovely readers,

You are going to love escaping to the Amalfi coast this summer with Carol Kirkwood's *Secrets of the Villa Amore*! Set in a stunning location and full of glamour and intrigue, you'll fall completely in love with this book.

Carina and Giorgio's families have been linked for generations, and now they are about to get married. On paper, it's the perfect romance, but can Carina really trust her future husband? When the family and guests start arriving at the Villa Amore, and old friends and faces from the past are thrown together, secrets are bound to be revealed. Will the happy couple still be walking down the aisle by the end…?

You'll want to pack your bags and head off to the sunshine yourself when you're done with this gorgeously evocative read. The scandal and romance are waiting…

I hope you enjoy!

*With love*
*Fern x*

# Fern Britton Picks

Exclusively for

**TESCO**

## Look out for more books, coming soon!

For more information on the book club, exclusive Q&As with the authors and reading group questions, visit Fern's website **www.fern-britton.com/ferns-picks**

We'd love you to join in the conversation, so don't forget to share your thoughts using **#FernsPicks**

# A Q&A with
# Carol Kirkwood

*Warning: contains spoilers*

---

**Secrets of the Villa Amore is your third novel. What made you want to write books in addition to your day job as TV's best-loved weather presenter?**

Firstly, I would never call myself 'TV's best-loved weather presenter'! But thank you for the compliment! I was approached by my publishing agent and asked if I would like to write a book. I'll never write about myself as I am quite a private person, so fiction was a challenge I wanted to embrace. Growing up, I had always enjoyed writing at school, and I enjoy making up stories for my nieces and nephews, so I thought there was nothing to lose.

**You've written about Greece, the French Riviera and now Italy. Why do books with glamorous locations have such a strong appeal for you?**

I love anything to do with movies, Hollywood and television – I LOVE glamour! My novels are the kind of books I enjoy reading in my down time and the locations are places I love and have visited myself, so can describe them with conviction. I want to invoke all the senses in my books.

**This novel takes place on the Amalfi coast, is that a place that you have travelled to yourself, too?**

A couple of years ago we visited Amalfi and had the most wonderful time. It is such a beautiful part of the world and the scenery is simply breathtaking, not to mention the evocative scent of lemons – neither of which I will forget in a hurry.

**The book takes place at a big society wedding, did it have anything in common with your own recent experience of tying the knot?**

Although there is an extravagant wedding in *Secrets of the Villa Amore*, I have to say it was nothing like our wedding at the end of last year. Ours was a very small and intimate wedding with no drama!!

**How do you create your characters? Are they ever inspired by people you know or have met?**

I am always people-watching, it's one of my favourite things. If I see someone that particularly interests me, I do create a story around them thinking it may be a good plot or character in a book. I honestly can't help myself! On holiday recently I saw the most elegant lady; she stood out as she looked so chic, her hair was up in a chignon and she was wearing what looked like a Chanel suit. The woman always dined alone with a solitary glass of white wine and a salad. I could not help but wonder what her story was. She will undoubtedly appear in one of my books, as I have already created a story around her!

**There are often a lot of secrets and intrigue for the characters in your books. Where do you find your inspiration?**

I am a great believer in unleashing your imagination – it will take you to all sorts of places. Creating characters (whom you do become attached to) is so exciting, giving them a personality and a life. My editor is brilliant at taming some of my wilder ideas.

I also try to put myself into the mind of my characters and think what I would do in that same situation.

**Secrets of the Villa Amore is perfect holiday reading. Where are you going on holiday this year?**

Back to Amalfi, as I am giving a talk about my books on an organised tour, and we will visit places including Capri, Ravello and Positano. The Amalfi coast is such a beautiful part of the world, the image of it is totally ingrained on my mind. I love it when readers come up to me and say that although they have never visited Amalfi, they could imagine being there with my characters due to the visual imagery provided through my writing. And a lot of readers have said, as a result, that they are planning a holiday themselves to Amalfi. What a fabulous compliment!

**What do you like to do when you are on holiday? Do you read a lot, or do you like active pursuits?**

I like to split my time between relaxing with a good book and a nice glass of cold white wine, and exploring the area I am visiting. When we went to Amalfi a few years ago, we visited Pompeii and Vesuvius – both were brilliant. Capri, Revello and Positano were also gorgeous places to visit.

**What is the best holiday you have ever had?**

My honeymoon in the Maldives with my husband. It was perfect.

**Hotel or Airbnb?**

Both! But some hotels really stick in my mind. When I was a lot younger, I used to read Jackie Collins books. She always mentioned the Polo Lounge in the Beverly Hills Hotel in Los Angeles, so many movie stars have stayed there over the years, and I desperately wanted to go there. Although I only stayed one night (very expensive) it truly lived up to its reputation. The other hotel that is etched on my mind is the Cipriani Hotel in Venice. You travel there by water taxi. It is another glamorous hotel! I have never actually stayed there but have enjoyed a glass of wine, people-watching, as ever! Maybe one day…

**Do people ever recognise you from your TV work when you are on holiday and ask you about the weather?**

Yes, and yes! But I am always flattered by that and delighted to have a chinwag!

**Where will your readers be travelling with you for your next book?**

Venice is the destination for my next book – out in July 2024. It is such a romantic place and I have visited Venice many times over the years. It's the perfect place for hiding all kinds of secrets in a book. I've loved writing about it, and creating a story where the city is a big part of the plot was a dream, it's like going on holiday there all over again. I can't wait for you all to read it, after you've read this one!

# Questions for your Book Club

*Warning: contains spoilers*

- *Secrets of the Villa Amore* begins with a flashback to 1943. How did this inform your reading for the rest of the novel?

- There are a few different narratives running parallel throughout the book. Whose story was your favourite?

- The setting, on the Amalfi coast, is gorgeous. How important do you think the setting is to the story?

- The lives of the Russo and Bianchi families have been intertwined with one another for generations. How does this affect Carina and Giorgio's relationship?

- Philippa's life is shaken up by the arrival of Harry. Were you pleased with how her story was resolved?

- What did you think of Rafaella's revelation at the end of the novel, regarding the families' shared history? How would this affect their lives going forwards?

- Have you read Carol Kirkwood's previous novels? What themes do you see running through them all?

- Would you recommend this book to a friend? How would you describe it to them?

**An exclusive extract from Fern's new novel**

# *The* Good Servant

*March 1932*

Marion Crawford was not able to sleep on the train, or to eat the carefully packed sandwiches her mother had insisted on giving her. Anxiety, and a sudden bout of homesickness, prohibited both.

What on earth was she doing? Leaving Scotland, leaving everything she knew? And all on the whim of the Duchess of York, who had decided that her two girls needed a governess exactly like Miss Crawford.

Marion couldn't quite remember how or when she had agreed to the sudden change. Before she knew it, it was all arranged. The Duchess of York was hardly a woman you said no to.

Once her mother came round to the idea, she was in a state of high excitement and condemnation. 'Why would they want *you?*' she had asked, 'A girl from a good, working class family? What do you know about how these people live?' She had stared at Marion, almost in reverence. 'Working for the royal family . . . They must have seen something in you. My daughter.'

On arrival at King's Cross, Marion took the underground to Paddington. She found the right platform for the Windsor train and, as she had a little time to wait, ordered a cup of tea, a scone and a magazine from the station café.

She tried to imagine what her mother and stepfather were doing right now. They'd have eaten their tea and have the wireless on, tuned to news most likely. Her mother would have her mending basket by her side, telling her husband all about Marion's send off. She imagined her mother rambling on as the fire in the grate hissed and burned.

The train was rather full, but Marion found a seat and settled down to flick through her magazine. Her mind couldn't settle. Through the dusk she watched the alien landscape and houses spool out beside her. Dear God, what was she doing here, so far away from family and home? What was she walking into?

When the conductor walked through the carriage announcing that Windsor would be the next stop, she began to breathe deeply and calmly, as she had been taught to do before her exams. She took from her bag, for the umpteenth time, the letter from her new employers. The instructions were clear: she was to leave the station and look for a uniformed driver with a dark car.

She gazed out of the window as the train began to slow. She took a deep breath, stood up and collected her case and coat. *Come on, Marion. It's only for a few months. You can do this.*

## Available now!

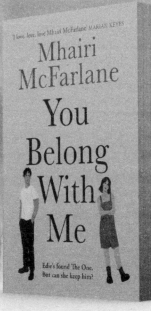

'I love, love, love Mhairi McFarlane' MARIAN KEYES

# Mhairi McFarlane

# You Belong With Me

Edie's found The One.
But can she keep him?

## She found The One. But when everyone wants him, can she keep him?

When there's a ring on her doorbell on Christmas Day, there's only one person Edie Thompson wants it to be. The person who's still in her heart. The person who just might be The One.

She and Elliot Owen called it quits once before – but aren't they too good together not to try? And here he is, offering her everything she dreamed of.

But dating Elliot, an actor, is anything but plain sailing. Being an ocean apart and followed by the press is one thing, but when Edie's friends and Elliot's family are drawn in, things get messy. Then her boss hires a friendly face in the form of Declan Dunne, who's there for her when times are tough, and Edie starts to wonder . . . are she and Elliot a fairytale come true – or a cautionary fable about getting what you wish for?